THE LONELINESS OF ANGELS

A Novel

ALSO BY MYRIAM J.A. CHANCY

Fiction

Spirit of Haiti
The Scorpion's Claw

Non-Fiction

Framing Silence: Revolutionary Novels by Haitian Women
Searching for Safe Spaces: Afro-Caribbean Women Writers in Exile

THE LONELINESS OF ANGELS

MYRIAM J. A. CHANCY

PEEPAL TREE

First published in Great Britain in 2010
Peepal Tree Press Ltd
17 King's Avenue
Leeds LS6 1QS
England

ISBN13: 9781845231224

Supported by
ARTS COUNCIL
ENGLAND

For my parents

"My house says to me, 'Do not leave me, for here dwells your past.' And the road says to me, 'Come and follow me, for I am your future.' And I say to both my house and the road, 'I have no past, nor have I a future. If I stay here, there is a going in my staying; and if I go there is a staying in my going. Only love and death change all things."

— Khalil Gibran

PART ONE:

FALLEN ANGELS

"For our country,
For our forefathers,
United let us march.
United let us march.
Let there be no traitors in our ranks!
Let us be masters of our soil.
United let us march,
United let us march.
For our country,
For our forefathers.
March, march,
United let us march.
For our country,
For our forefathers."

— La Dessalinienne, Haitian National Anthem

RUTH

February 28, 2004, Port-au-Prince Hills, Haiti

Ruth smoothes the plastic covering her memory table as if she is trying to undo wrinkles in time. Below the plastic, the faces of her youth stare up at her along with those of her two brothers, their wives, their children, along with the faces of the young people she has taught for over three decades. All of them had inhabited this house that had been left for her by her parents. She was the only one remaining by the time they passed away, the boys long gone and married with lives and houses of their own.

Her brothers had gone without looking back. They came around for the odd dinner, a family gathering, sometimes alone just to say hello and swap news over strong cups of black coffee. She spent many years in the front room with its see-through lace curtains. These days, visitors are scarce.

Ruth thinks of how she started the memory table ten years ago, when the house had suddenly seemed to loom large all about her, when the rooms crammed with furniture but empty of human voices had suddenly filled her with dread, with the gloom of her life's end in sight and having very little to show for her presence in the dusty bowl of the western half of the island she had refused to leave, even as she watched her students grow up and depart, some never to return.

Her fingers pause on a row of faces – students she had considered full of potential. Among them is her niece, Catherine. Catherine's awkward smile reveals that she had once worn a retainer to straighten a pronounced overbite. She has a dimple like a tear in her right cheek extending itself below the lower sweep of her cheekbone and disappearing into the curvature of her smile. Ruth's gaze pauses fondly on the photo. Catherine has changed since then. Ruth can tell from the timbre of the young woman's voice the odd times she calls. The change makes her smile. The girl has acquired the composure Ruth had wished for her in the moment that she first glimpsed her at the airport, thin and waif-like, clutching the padded handle of a small red valise, her eyes terrified at the chaos and smells inundating her. Catherine had been eleven years old when she had been sent from Canada. The girl's mother, Rose, had been gone three years already. *A waif of a girl*, Ruth thinks to herself.

Ruth moves her fingers down the row, past Catherine, and stops at the photograph of a young man she had introduced to her niece. She had thought then that they might make a good match despite a decade's difference in age, that the one would serve to anchor the other, but she had misread Romulus, headstrong and ambitious, as afraid of his shadow as a mouse. It had been there all along, this fear of his, the self-loathing. Perhaps she had misread Catherine as well, and her adopted son, Lucas, both of whom she had given and lost to the world.

What had she been thinking at the time? She had been so much younger and unaware of all that she had come to understand in recent years. She peers at the photograph of Romulus. It was there, buried in his large brown eyes that seemed to hunger for a world he might never have reason to see, a fleck of fear that gave him a startled expression. Over the years, his eyes had hardened; the edges of his mouth had grown sharp. She hadn't seen him in the flesh for ten years or more. The photos she saw of him in the newspapers showed him sneering with an edge of sarcasm but the eyes never changed. The fleck only seemed to grow larger with time.

Ruth spots the other photographs of Romulus in her collage and sees the shadow of doubt that seems to cloud his every appearance. It is an almost tangible thing that draws her towards the images, an invisible force, something sickly and thick. She closes her eyes against the energy, shakes her head as if to loose a fog thickening in her mind. *You cannot enter*, she thinks, *you cannot enter*. The force pulls away, taking with it its sticky fingers. She should remove his photos but some scrap of loyalty remains lodged within her as if Romulus was her child in need of understanding.

She watches her hand sweep across the plastic. Blue-green veins trace the outline of rivers across the surface of the taut palm-frond brown of the backs of her hands. Rivers, she thinks, all of them rivers crossing her own life, bringing with them the peculiarities of their journeying, some leaving sediment and treasures in their wake while others pulling away something of her own grounding, some corner of her heart.

Her heart is in pieces these days, without true direction and motive. She is waiting. Waiting for Lucas. Waiting for Catherine. Waiting, even, for Romulus. She gazes down at Lucas's photograph at thirteen, the year before Catherine came to live with her. Charismatic already, his brown eyes flash their mischievousness like the startled eyes of a lizard. Lucas had always been her favourite and she considered him a son even though she had not borne him. He came to her at three, left by his father, a former love-interest – if she could even call him that. JP had left him and gone, never to be heard from again, while Ruth became the woman they called *mambo* though she had not been initiated in a *vodou* cult and does not truly know the secrets of that parallel world. She is of Haiti and not of it, following the threads of practices that seem imprinted in her cells that bear no resemblance to the Catholic rites with which she was raised nor the *vodou* of the people whom she supports. They call her *mambo* because they do not know what else to call her. Ruth sighs.

It is almost time to take the photographs from below their plastic frame and store them away, for Catherine, perhaps, for those to come.

It is strange to her, this knowing. Ruth has never understood quite how she knows things before they happen. She knows she is going to see Lucas, Catherine and Romulus soon, though she has seen none of them in the flesh for years. She knows too that she will see them in the opposite order of her preference: Romulus first, then Catherine, Lucas, perhaps never again, and that somewhere in the midst of these reconnections and misconnections, she will lose her life.

Ruth stands to her full height, the tips of her fingers resting against the table, at the bottom of the kaleidoscope of multi-hued faces. There is no way of undoing the future since the past cannot be undone and the present is only a slow pendulum between the two. She can only stand and wait, try to ready herself for the fulfilment of her greatest cause, her grandest sacrifice in the service of fate. It isn't even a question of whether or not she believes in destiny. She has no choice. Everything is written in the stars.

Ruth lifts her hands from the table slowly and then smoothes the front of her pale mauve housedress (it matches the cloth she has wrapped around her head), pulling down on the seams on both sides of her hips. She is seventy-seven years of age and proud of her appearance. The present is all she has, and she knows how to take care of it. Such care makes her believe that there may be something she can do today to make what is to come easier to bear, some small gesture that might tip the scales and save them all.

Her thoughts are growing desperate these days. She feels the anxiety mounting from her chest to her brain, gnawing at her like a small animal desperately seeking a way out of a mesh cage. She has been lucky to live an independent life in a land in which women are forced to stand on their own two feet all too early and yet not often given the reins of their own destinies.

Ruth turns her back on the memory table and faces her front door. She listens to the noises drifting in from the street: the creaking of steel-reinforced wheels below huge loads of cane being pulled and pushed to market in wooden carts, the shocks of the SUVs as they bounce in and out of holes in the road, their drivers leaning on their horns to get mules out of the way. She hears the men with the mules singeing the air with their switches made of string and narrow shoots of bamboo. She imagines the heat of the road creating waves in the atmosphere, the burden of despair hanging halfway between earth and sky.

Somewhere beyond, a woman is singing. It is a song Ruth has heard before. She strains to make out the words. It's the national anthem, so rarely heard these days. The woman's voice is full, high, and light despite the heaviness of humidity in the air. Ruth thinks she is singing about a new day, a new world, as if that world were here already, below the surface, just waiting for them to awaken and peel back the veneer hiding it from view. The voice burrows through the brick separating Ruth's house from the road, through the walls of the house keeping the interior cool, through Ruth's worried mind. It tells her that everything is coming to its inevitable conclusion. Ruth feels relief for the first time in weeks and acknowledges that now is the time of preparation. She must get everything ready, for Romulus, for Catherine, for Lucas, when each of them returns, each in their own way.

In fact, it was for them she had begun the memory table when Lucas had left her hearth in search of something she could not provide.

It is only now that Ruth is beginning to understand that Lucas had left all those years ago in order to flee *her*, to flee what it meant to be associated to her, to flee the responsibility he would need to shoulder, that they all needed to shoulder in order to do something better than only survive.

Lucas had gone in search of the gods, initiating himself in a local *hounfort* and looking for his people where before she had been everything to him: mother, father, a murmur of the gods above. She had not been attentive to Lucas's descent. It is something she will have to answer for up above when she knocks on heaven's doors. She wonders if failing in all she has tried to do will cost her entry.

She turns her back on the noises from the street and faces the memory table again, bending towards the photos of all those she has loved: her parents, Fritz, Max, Yolande, the twins, the children who had traipsed through her garden and past the round table in the foyer which had for so many years stood empty, graced only with a clear glass vase of cut flowers she had grown from her garden. All those lives, Ruth thinks to herself, all those threads of existence passing each other without care for their connectedness. It was too much to consider.

Ruth had done her best through the years to engineer meetings. It had taken her half of her life to discover how to be a crossroads rather than only assist others through their difficult moments. It had only been in the last decade or so that she had understood how to stand in the middle of chaos and be quiet as a stone.

Where had she been when Lucas was on the threshold of his own madness? Dormant, forgetful, fretting about her lilies or crocuses, wondering when the coconut man would come to unburden her trees of their fruit, thinking ahead of the next gathering she would host. There had been a lost moment for which she could no longer account. She had not been fully awake and Lucas had slipped through her fingers like sand until there was not a speck of him left for her to save. Where was he now, her Lucas? Her fingers trailed the table and stopped atop a postcard showing three women dressed in folkloric garb hitched up on their full hips to show off their curving thighs, their ample flesh. They had million dollar smiles. Across their narrow waists, Ruth read: *La cubana: L'Azucar di Havana!* Cuba. He had gone there and returned without a trace. He was somewhere in the anthills of the poor. How could she find him? It was Catherine who would have to find him. And even then, would he return? What was left of him to save?

Ruth withdraws her hand from the memory table and moves quickly past the rounded tabletop and into the hallway. She has a million things to do before the next women's meeting and she must be presentable.

There is no time for guilt, no time for tears.

No time, no time. So much to do.

April 20, 1946, Furcy, Haiti

It is a warm and humid summer day. The wind flows over and between the tops of the mountains; the end of spring hangs in the scent of over-pungent hibiscus. The flat tops of the flamboyant trees are burdened with the bright red of their clustered flowers. There is an itch of rain in the air. The market women secure folded sheets of newspapers behind their chairs. Others prepare oilcloths or discarded sheets of plastic to hang over the tops of the wooden staffs forming the frame of their market stalls.

Young security guards stand, bored, in the threshold of open gates. The wind swirls dust at their feet and leaves traces of sand in the upturned cuffs of their slacks. These men once travelled from the country to the city in search of wealth and easy living. They live with each other, without the women they dreamed of in their country huts sewing proper seams into the extra cloth of their baggy pants. The young men look up at the clouds being pushed slowly across the indigo sky. They sniff the longing of the earth beneath their feet to catch the falling remains of the incoming storm. They commiserate by pulling white and red packs of cigarettes from their shirt pockets. They light up with their red-veined eyes fixed upon the sky leaving swirls of smoke suspended in the thick air as they walk back into the yards that have become the whole of their existence, turning their backs as cars with white-walled tyres barrel down the roads on their way out of the city, towards the country each of them has fled, in search of diversion.

The girls in the car look idly at the backs of the young men as the young men walk slowly from the gates abutting the road and back into rutted yards. Their eyes are drawn to the pools of sweat staining the clothes between the men's shoulders. The girls feel dangerous as they breathe in the hunger of the young men's dreams echoed by the fine dust kicked up by the tyres of their fast cars and twirled in the air by the playful wind.

The girls are nervous. They are not alone. They are being chaperoned by young men so different from those walking in the dusty yards, young men who smell of talc and French cologne, with fingers soft from their lack of labour. The girls spy the rough and calloused hands of the working men. They feel as if they exist in separate worlds even though the working boys are right there, right in front of their eyes.

The girls are dressed in badminton skirts and light cotton shirts. They have brought thin sweaters for sitting in the cool mountain air after the badminton matches are over, for sitting with the young men at the foot of trees eating cold egg sandwiches and chicken drumsticks. Most have their hair held back in ponytails or braided and held together at the tips with ribbons of the palest yellows and blues. They have shaved and creamed their legs so that the bronze of their skins gleams from perspiration in the heat. The girls can feel that they are on the brink of something important. They can see it in the grip of the hands of the young man driving the car, the pearls of sweat on the foreheads of the other boys, the thick scent of fevered masculinity that encircles them from all sides, in the cold glance of one of the security guards beyond the car who looks back at them over his shoulder and stares at them in lonely defiance.

Some of the boys are already working in family businesses but they know them from school. They have all attended Roman Catholic schools leftover from missionary days (were those days over?) run by Jesuit brothers and the nuns of Mary. They are safe with these boys despite the thick cocoon of desire making them heady in the cars whose motors gun as they struggle to climb to higher ground.

There are more boys than girls on the outing. This too makes the girls nervous. It means that some of them will have to entertain each other without the possibility of male attention. Some of them already know that they will not be singled out for courting. Ruth in her horn-rimmed glasses and her ankle-length skirt has reconciled herself to such a fate even though Jean-Pierre, better known as JP, aims jokes in her general direction and includes her in his conversation with Luce who everyone knows has already picked the names of the four children she intends to have with Jean-Pierre, once the two make their engagement official and JP enters his father's law firm in Port-au-Prince. An arrangement has been reached between the two families but it is up to JP to ask for her hand in marriage. Luce has made sure that the other girls have been informed to avoid any confusion. The fact that she allows JP to speak so openly to Ruth is a result of her conviction that her plans cannot, at this point, be derailed. When she looks at Ruth it is with open pity, her wide-set eyes and thin stretch of smile feigning adoration for the smart girl with the awkward grace which she does not feel. All Luce knows is that now is not the time to make JP aware of her limitations: she is not as smart or as ambitious as everyone presumes a girl like Ruth to be. She must seem as open to anyone as he is. She must appear to be the right match.

What Luce doesn't know is that JP is well aware of her limitations. He also knows that he is supposed to marry her because his father's business is failing and Luce's father has the right connections to turn things around for his family.

What Ruth doesn't know but suspects is that JP has already fallen in love with a girl who isn't Luce. Stalling with Luce is the only way he knows of letting the girl know that there is always a choice even when it seems that there isn't any possibility to chart a new course.

The girls in the three cars winding their way up the cord of road traced out in the mountainside giggle as the wheels of the cars bounce in and out of holes. They chatter amiably to relieve the tension of attempting to court in mixed company. They are about fifteen all together, five bodies pressed against each other in three cars, blankets and wicker baskets filled with luncheon piled atop the spare wheels.

Ruth's mind wanders as she sits in the front seat of one of the cars. She is looking forward to getting out of the smog, the bustle of the city, away from the house where her mother keeps a lush garden and where her father scribbles away in one of the rooms on the second floor with its own private porch where he often stands with a faraway look in his eye looking up at the sky as if awaiting further instructions from God himself.

Her parents are both distant people and she often feels lonely in the large house, never mind that her mother often hosts social engagements there, in the garden, out on the lovely terrace made of imported stone. Her father often has his writer friends to the house for cocktails in the airy, sun-lit drawing room on the ground floor. She listens to them go on about political affairs in the country and tries to learn her father's convictions but it always seems to her that he can assume any side of a story and never provide his own point of view. For this reason, he can write what he likes and sticks mostly to rendering translations of others' work. His work has been well received in and out of the island even though it does not sell. He writes poetry in *Kreyol* as if spiting the ancestry to which such a tongue remains foreign. He likes to think of himself as a man of the people even though he spends more time on his porch looking up at the sky than on the ground walking amongst others. He is a man who appreciates tranquillity and he has found it here, in the large house his earnings as a linen-merchant have bought for them. At times, forgetting books and ledgers, the spools of linens left to order for the shop and the other odds and ends they must keep in order to make ends meet, he believes that his current translations are some of the best work he has ever produced. Often, Ruth imagines that words are what he sees in the sky, words and their valances hung as if on an invisible spool of thread, between the stars.

Ruth likes to hear him talk as much as she likes to hear him typing away in his study. She thinks of becoming a writer herself even though when she brings it up, he only smiles at her indulgently, as if she were a small pet able to do a few tricks but nothing more. She swallows her disappointment at those times and thinks to herself that there are other ways to learn, other ways to become who she thinks she ought to be as his daughter even though what she thinks she should be is nothing close to what he sees when he looks at her, the hairs of his blanching moustache hiding the slight curve of his pink lips as he smiles at her suggestions.

Ruth's mother is a better listener but even she doesn't seem to make much sense of her daughter's desire to have a public life. Ruth's mother blooms only in the presence of plants and in social activities that allow her to mask herself beneath the latest fashions and hairdos. She is a woman who revels in the senses, without articulation, without words. The more time she spends in the garden with her mother, the more Ruth realizes that her mother's mind is like a plant, cycling through grief and joy, growth and attrition in a well-ordered pattern in harmony with the world she has created for her family and the natural beauty with which she has surrounded them. After her mother dies, Ruth will plant marigolds in her honour; they are the ultimate symbol of non-materialism.

It was her mother who encouraged Ruth to go on this outing organized by the Catholic schools for the senior class. Ruth tells herself continuously as they make their way up the snakelike road that it is a monumental waste of a perfectly good Saturday she could have spent at the piano of her teacher's house down the road.

Ruth is thinking of the Bach piece she is learning for the end of year concert when JP leans over her right shoulder from the back seat and says something to her. Whatever it is is lost in the sound of the wheels turning up the loose stones of the road.

"*Quoi?*" she asks him, feeling her cheek muscles contort in annoyance. The look on her face is echoed by Luce's expression, an expression that can't be avoided since Luce is sitting next to JP, her thin, long legs clasped at the ankles in mock modesty even though she is wearing the shortest skirt among them.

JP only laughs at them both and leans back in his seat as if he has made the best joke of all.

Annoyed, Ruth asks him again, "What did you say?"

"*Sa pa fè anyen,*" JP replies smugly, certain that she has heard whatever it was that he said.

Ruth can tell by the way Luce is blushing and staring at her that it is something mildly flirtatious. They are laughing at her expense, she feels, and decides to ignore them both as she turns back to the open window and the robust scent of pine in the air. They are almost at the park where they will play the afternoon away as if they don't have a care in the world and, indeed, they don't. They are part of the privileged classes and the part of privilege that never diminishes is the way they can move from place to place as if the crushing poverty all around them is simply a part of life that they can do very little about. Up in the mountains, life appears to be so easy, the people so simple in their ways that they can hardly feel guilty for being able to leave their large houses in the valley for an end of year excursion.

"*Madame,*" JP says to Ruth with mock gallantry as he holds out her hand so that she can press into it as she steadies herself out of the car. He looks up at Luce who has already stepped out along with the others as if to reassure her that he has no true interest in anyone but her, but Luce is beginning to understand that what she has taken as reality may be only an act he is playing. The dream of their marriage begins to evaporate and she wishes that all the girls around them would disappear so that she can make JP come around and see that she is the only one for him.

Ruth leans into JP as she stumbles out of the car.

"*'Tention,*" Luce says laughing wryly. "You could break something and that would be a shame, wouldn't it? We haven't even played yet."

Ruth looks at Luce and senses the girl's sudden hatred. What has she done? She looks into JP's wide smile and it dawns on her that JP is being overly attentive to her needs. Had he helped all of the girls out or just Luce, and then her? She isn't paying enough attention.

"Thank you," she says to JP but looks at Luce so that the girl can see that she has no designs on JP or on anyone else, but Luce just snaps her fingers at JP and turns on her heels as she requests her racket to start the play.

The boys scurry to raise the net and hand out rackets. Ruth thinks this is the stupidest game she has ever witnessed in her life and sits on the sidelines refusing to play. Her long skirt shields her from the sun and from probing eyes. She will take a walk soon, before the play is over, and create a pocket of hunger for the picnic to come.

What Jean-Pierre knows, and Ruth is still hiding from her conscious mind, is the fact that she has a tender spot for him. She might even be in love with him, or the idea of him, were it not for her conviction, and everyone else's conviction, that she is not a girl who should venture too far from home. As far as her father is concerned, Ruth's life should be as his wife's, concerned with the proper order of things in the household, minus the marriage bed. Ruth's mother has not yet let go of the idea of her little girl and thinks of Ruth as a companion who will travel with her into old age.

JP has been watching Ruth from the other side of the net. He is not playing. He has helped put the net up and is cheering on the girls in the short skirts, especially Luce's team at his right. She flashes a toothy smile at him whenever he praises her playing and swishes her racket from side to side to display her pleasure. As Luce does so, JP realizes that Ruth, sitting on the sidelines, is in her own world. She is sitting nearby for the sake of appearances but he can tell that she is soon going to rise and walk away, the way she always does until someone raises the alarm and says, "Where did Ruth go?", and the rest of them shrug their shoulders and make no move to search for her unless it is absolutely necessary.

The group tolerates Ruth because she is the daughter of two prominent citizens, because their mothers want invitations to the house in the hills with the special garden. It would be unthinkable not to include her but the group wishes she would excuse herself more often than she does and not waste their time with her silence and erring away from the activities so meticulously planned to fill the hours between home and school.

JP has a plan. Once Ruth rises, he is going to follow her down the path leading between the fir trees. He is going to follow her and find out what is on her mind. He knows it is certainly more interesting than anything Luce might be thinking as she prances above the balding grass, vying for as much attention as she can from him as well as from the other boys. He knows that he won't be missed. Luce is already half-ignoring him for having given his hand to Ruth as the girls got out of the car. She is flirting madly with a blond American boy whose parents are missionaries.

The blond American is named Tom like all Americans and has a flurry of rust-orange freckles dousing the bridge of his nose. He is a friendly sort and speaks *Kreyol* like a native. He seems to be flirting back with Luce. They are on the same team. Tom touches her waist fleetingly to encourage her. Luce is the first girl who has overlooked his pale skin and made an advance in his direction. Tom understands that JP has other plans and secretly hopes to take Luce to the end of year graduation gala. Tom thinks they are all too young for marriage. *Shouldn't they all enjoy their youth awhile?*, he thinks, smiling at Luce and flirting with her so outrageously the other boys say, "Eh, Kool it!" in mock-American, before returning to counting points.

There is volleying back and forth across the net. It is enough regular motion to put anyone to sleep. Ruth has had enough. She stands up and brushes off the straw grass clinging to the fabric of her skirt and her socks rolled down around her ankles. She does not see JP follow her with his eyes but hears him yell, "Good shot, Luce," at the top of his lungs. She is sure she will not be missed.

They are on the side of a hill in Furcy where the air feels pure even though it isn't any freer of pollutants than down in the smog-filled city. Still, it is quiet here and the soil feels filled with memories of summer outings with her family. Ruth realizes that she is close to no one but she cherishes the memories of a closeness she wishes she could enter more fully at such moments as family gatherings.

Ruth walks away from the group and through the trees hemming them in the clearing where the net has been set up and the picnic baskets piled together beneath the shade of a cluster of pines. She knows they will take no notice of her departure. These are the moments she treasures because they are hers alone, without the imprint of someone else's vision.

As Ruth walks away from the group, hearing them laugh and yell at each other as the game continues without her, she turns her thoughts to what life will be like ten or twenty years from now. She wonders what it would be like to live away from the island, in a more modern world. Could she ever leave it all behind, Maman and Papa, Fritz and Max? Would it be possible to create another world out there?

Ruth walks and the trees seem to part as she approaches the edge of the plateau on which they are perched. The breeze is cool and inviting. She wishes she could sleep under the stars, with nothing between her and the elements. She can see down into the city and across to the mountain ranges that make Haiti one of the most beautiful islands in the Caribbean, even though there are patches of burned soil here and there, interspersed with the dark squares of green cultivated by peasants who still rotate their crops on land they have lived on for generations.

Behind her, Ruth hears the crackle of breaking twigs and branches echoing in the path she has just taken towards the lip of the mountain. Her heart sinks for a moment. Her private moment is to be lost. Ruth turns, expecting to see someone from the group but instead she is forced to look down at two diminutive forms. Two children look up at her, wide-eyed, hesitant, uncertain whether to step forward or back. One is a little girl whose head reaches no higher than Ruth's elbow. She holds the hand of an even smaller boy who rises only to the girl's shoulder. The boy grips the little girl's hand as if she is all the protection he has in the world. The skin over his face and arms is full of raised bumps, some as large as golf balls. *What nature of disease is this*, Ruth wonders and frowns.

Ruth's face softens, her eyebrows raise themselves into arcs of surprise, the sides of her mouth rise into a tentative smile.

The children take their cue from Ruth, their faces echoing her movements.

Ruth finally realizes that she is standing in the children's way.

"*Kote'n pralé?*" she asks them.

The little one points somewhere beyond Ruth's left shoulder as if to say that they are from the next mountain range. This might be so. Ruth has heard of people walking miles to reach relatives, to find work, to go to school. It is still this way even today, even though they are almost halfway across the twentieth century.

The children are dusty and barefoot. The hand the boy holds up, pointing to an indiscernible point behind her, is mottled and discoloured. Ruth wonders at his suffering. What can she do?

But before she has a chance to say anything, there is JP, gesticulating at the children.

"*Allez vous-en,*" he yells, his voice rising as the children stare, immobilized by their fear.

JP is using French in order to intimidate them, to make them feel small.

Ruth pleads with the children with her eyes for them not to go away. *Please don't. Please don't go.*

The two hesitate. Ruth sees almost indiscernible movement in their thin bodies as they waver between staying with her and running away from JP who is fast advancing towards them with a menacing fist in the air.

"*Vous ne m'entendez pas?*" he says. "*Décampez.*"

At the moment that JP reaches her side, Ruth turns away from the children to stop him. Her hands act like levers against his broad chest. She knows in that moment she will never be this close to him again.

"'*Rête!*" she says to him. Stop. What have they done to you?

JP's fist is still up in the air. Ruth hears the children breathing quietly behind her, then the scurrying of their small feet as they go around her and JP to follow the path that leads on to the next mountain. She feels a sudden tug at her heart as she watches their small backs receding.

JP shakes her hands away. "*Sa w'ap fè la-a?*" he says, his eyes flashing. What are you doing here? This is not how he had planned things.

Ruth is silent. She understands JP now more deeply than she would have imagined. He goes after things he cannot have. She is something he wants, an object he will never have. There is no room in his heart for what he perceives as weakness.

27

Ruth walks away from JP.

JP stands there at the edge of the mountain feeling defeated though he is not certain what he has lost.

"I was just protecting you," he says as she walks along the path down which the children have disappeared.

Then, he stands there alone, the wind whispering something indecipherable into his ears, and he gives up. It is as if he has forgotten why he is there and in that moment of forgetting, he remembers Luce in her short skirt. *Ruth's loss*, he thinks, and meanders back towards the badminton set.

Ruth walks along for a while on the dirt road but the children are long gone. She will never see them again. She will never have the opportunity to ask the questions she had wanted to ask them. She will never find out the nature of the boy's skin disease or whether they need help. There are children like them everywhere she realizes and she *can* help. Somehow, she will help them.

By the time Ruth returns to the group, the picnic is almost finished. One of the girls hands Ruth a hard-boiled egg. The rest ignore her. Ruth eats her egg and sees JP and Luce sitting at the base of a large tree trunk. They are lost in confidences. Ruth is certain JP and Luce will get married. She is certain now that this means that she may never marry but she doesn't care. The most important matter on her mind is the thought of the children she cannot save and those she will. A plan hatches in her mind.

There are different ways of bearing young, she realizes, as the yolk separates from the spongy white of the egg in her mouth, different ways of giving and receiving.

March 4, 1969

By the time Ruth meets JP again, they have both grown taller and wider, more violent in their emotions, more narrow of opinion. It is not an easy meeting.

By this time, Ruth's brothers have married. Fritz is about to go North to Canada with his new bride; Max comes and goes and eventually settles in Port-au-Prince. Both of them will have daughters with their first wives. Both will marry again, though

Fritz will do so later in life, at a point when no one believes that he will ever open his heart again. Ruth has gone on with her piano lessons although she will never leave Haiti to chase the dream of becoming a world-class pianist and composer. By this time, she has worked for NGO's and grassroots organizations and, especially, the clandestine women's organizations that rise like lotus flowers from mud, unable to fully display themselves in the wake of the Duvalier regime's relentless brutality. She lives in different worlds, never letting one intersect the other until JP arrives one day, unannounced and unexpected, standing in her garden where the fuchsia is lush and the air heavy with the scent of flowering hibiscus. She is haunted still by the eyes of the two children on a dirt road in Furcy.

Ruth has been walking by the open windows of the sun room at the front of the house, the one where her mother spent countless afternoons entertaining the wives of her husband's friends, women she did not know well enough to count among the circle of her own friends. Only at her mother's funeral will Ruth realize that, like herself, her mother had few friends of her own class. Her mother loved the land, her flowers. Ruth is different from her mother in that she does escape the yard and the hollow nooks of the many-roomed house; she has stepped out from the ideal world of her mother's making, which is only ideal if one is afraid of life, and stepped out into another world she discovered that morning of her senior year in high school.

Despite the memory of JP's raised fist and voice on that day, Ruth has realized that he alone is responsible for the bend in the road that her life took from that day forward, the intense desire she still has to make a difference while remaining anonymous, obscure on the sidelines.

She feels the phantom wavering of the two children she lost that day long ago when she sees JP standing inside the yard, staring at her front door as if deciding whether to advance or to retreat.

Ruth is hidden by the flapping of white curtains. JP's clothes flutter in that same wind. He is wearing an off-white linen suit, the kind that was the fashion for adult men when they were both teenagers and not in love. It is as if he is frozen in time.

Ruth wonders for a moment if JP is a figment of her imagination until he disappears from her sight and she hears the knocking.

When Ruth opens the door, her eyes come to rest on an aged man. JP's face seems elongated, longer than it was in youth, wrinkles spreading out from the corners of his mouth and eyes. His hair is a salt and pepper combination of tight curls shaved close to the hairline. Ruth searches for the young man she used to know beneath the folds of skin and rough patches of beard. Where is the JP she once knew, swaying, cocky? The man standing before her now is unsure of himself, folding and unfolding the edges of a Panama hat banded in black in his hands. She sees now that he is not wearing a new linen suit but loose pants and a loose worker's shirt. They are so faded they almost seem white, a trick of sunlight. He has lost his bravura, his spark. Ruth wonders what she must look like to him but he speaks before she can come to any conclusion.

"You look just the same," he says. "Just the same."

Ruth knows this isn't true but takes the compliment anyway. It is the least she can do after all these years, after not showing up to the wedding all her classmates had been waiting for all through high school, despite JP's betrayals and wandering eye. She had heard news of JP over the years, news of fortunes made and lost. Luce had left him for a man with a green card in Miami. She had never inquired after JP after Luce had departed Haiti. She hadn't seen the point of doing so.

"It's been a long time," she says finally. She is surprised by the warmth in her voice.

"I've thought of you often," JP continues.

"Have you?"

The wind plays with their clothes. Both are nervous even though Ruth tells herself there is no reason to feel this way. There was never anything serious between them.

"Yes, I have. I think…" he hesitates. "I think that I made the wrong choice, back then."

Ruth laughs despite herself showing her large, square white teeth, her full lips stretching widely and creasing the roundness of her cheeks. She laughs with her head thrown back, so unlady-like. JP is entranced by her lack of care. This was always what had made her seem different from the others. He remembers, too late, why he has always thought of her without thinking of her. Ruth was like the startling green moss on a forest bed stretching between trees, covering their roots. She was always there, growing in spite of everything around her, but beautiful in her steadiness, in the brilliance of what she had to offer. He looks away from her teeth, her dimpled smile. Embarrassed at the thoughts he is having, he turns the hat he is holding slowly in his hands by its wide brim, the sweat lodged along the lining of its black band now cold and clammy.

"Can I come in?"

"Why not," Ruth replies nonchalantly as if she is used to visitors appearing out of nowhere on her doorstep, as if she has known all along that JP would materialize some time in a future neither of them could see when they were young and so full of longing for an extraordinary life.

The truth is that Ruth *had* known that JP would come to her one day though she was never certain when that day would be. She had known it clear as day on that afternoon when the children in the mountains had come upon her and departed quickly, leaving the scent of rain behind in their small footsteps.

As her laughter subsides and she lets JP walk through the door and into the round foyer of her home, she realizes that he had never understood that moment in their lives the way she had, that he had thought he had chosen Luce rather than that she had chosen to let him go to her. How she had known that JP would return to her she could not readily explain. Even as she sees him standing there in his seersucker suit, his feet clad in white leather patent shoes resting uncomfortably against the stones of her walkway, she tries to divine what is to come and fails. She knows only that she is to let him into the house and let the spirits guide her as they have always guided her.

"Please," she says, as she takes in the sharp, peppery smell of his cologne, "please come in. Let me take your hat."

JP seems not to hear her gesture of hospitality and walks through the doorjamb as if in a trance. Beads of perspiration trail down from his sideburns towards his protruding jawbones. Mixed in with the scent of his cologne is a whiff of fear. Ruth wonders what he can be afraid of, what powers of persuasion have brought him here. She shrugs off her own questions.

Ruth knows much about men in need and does her best to come to their aid when she can. She is not unlike the market women sitting in their stalls shooing away black flies from their sweaty brows with torn pieces of cardboard, their multicoloured parasols doing little to shield them from the hot rays of sun. Like them, she wheels and deals, barters favours for cash from one to satisfy another, taking her cut from the top as if skimming cream from fresh milk. She knows how to take the sweetness and leave the rest, knows how to make her move before the tide of chance evades her. The men come to her because of her discretion, her loyalty, the way her eyes touch theirs at social gatherings as if she has never seen them before, even though she has disposed of their dirty laundry, the detritus of their unclean lives. Because of this, the men she trades with, usually go-betweens for the market women and some businessmen on their own, tell her secrets. They tell her of killings before they happen, as if they are prophets. They tell her who *not* to do business with, who is unclean, trading with the regime henchmen. They tell her who has what so she can avoid duplicating goods on the market. They tell her who is underselling her and which of the market women keeps some of the profit hidden from her so that she can set her prices in such a way as to still make her margins. They tell her who is organizing and who has disbanded, which of the grassroots leaders is the most trustworthy, who to back, and who to simply tolerate. Unlike the market women, Ruth keeps her profits in a sizable bank account bearing her father's name. She stuffs no soiled bills in the straps of her bra or in an old cardboard box stuffed beneath mattress springs. But the money rotates, going out as fast as it comes in.

Before she can close the door behind them, JP turns towards her. "Wait."

"Yes?" Ruth is quizzical.

JP squints out into the yard. "Just a minute."

Ruth follows his gaze out in the direction of the garden. Her eyes scan the outline of her shrubs, the lilac bushes, the thorny stems of the roses and the coiled trunks of the flamboyants.

Then she sees him, a small, sandy-haired boy flitting about in her yard, chasing an orange-winged butterfly. The boy's skin is too brown to be white and too pale to be brown. His hair is straight and cut cropped across his forehead. His eyes are a hard, dark brown like the pits of peaches.

"Who is that?" she asks JP, even though her mind is already detecting the features of face the boy shares with JP, the long neck, the ears that stick out a little too much, and with Luce, the thin lips, the droopy eyelids that make his eyes seem somewhat bulbous, making her think of tulips in seed.

The boy makes his way to his father, slowly, shyly, unsure on his thin and bony legs.

JP puts an arm out towards the boy, with his hat still in his hand, as if the boy should hold on to it and reel himself in. "This is Lucas," he says as the boy sidles up to him and finds his place in the shadow of JP's arm. "This is my son."

The wind swirls about their feet. JP and the boy stand still at her threshold, Ruth peering out towards them from the foyer almost wishing she had stayed behind the open windows and only looked at the man and not invited him into her home. She knows why he is here. The wind moves about her ankles and she listens to the whispering of the spirits, sees the boy grown and lost, a life of strife and confusion laying itself out before him and she sees herself beside him, trying to ensure his clarity of thought and emotion, guiding him as best she can.

She understands that JP has come to give her the boy even though they have not seen each other in years, even though they might have made such a boy together if things had been different, if – for Ruth – JP had been a different kind of man.

Standing before fate's portal, Ruth can do nothing but step back and gesture them in, assuming a role she had long ago claimed without knowing exactly to whom it might eventually lead.

Ruth leads them to the tables overlooking the garden from the interior courtyard and leaves the boy and father to stare at their shoes in an eerily similar fashion. She feels the desire to flee them both, to refuse her part in the drama about to unfold but she is propelled forward by a force all its own as if she has no control over her limbs. Ruth takes down a package of Rebo from a shelf and mechanically makes the small strong cups of coffee her mother had been known for. She attempts to keep her mind from drifting back towards the boy and to what might come next, knowing already that the journey will be long.

February 28, 2004, Port-au-Prince Hills

Ruth has spent many years in the front room of her house with its gossamer curtains, passers-by peering through at her and her guests from the latticed steel of the front gates which interrupts the otherwise solid mass of the brick walls encircling the property. The only girl in a family of boys, she was the unlikely inheritor of the family business. Her father had been a merchant by trade, buying and reselling sundry goods from detergent to hair clips, to street merchants who either rented stalls from him in the open markets or paid him a cut of their profits. Still others preferred to pay for the goods at a premium and resell them at a still higher price in some of the slightly more up-market squares where the middle-class buyers paid very little attention to the prices tagged on the goods; the prices were still cheaper than retail and that was all that mattered to them. Ruth's father was practical: he sold to whomever would buy, whatever their station or circumstance.

Today, if someone asked the nature of Ruth's father's business, she would have replied export/import. Which could mean any number of things – since everything was being imported from illegal narcotics to Chiclets, even rice, and all their natural resources sold to the highest bidder out of country. They called it "export-led development" which meant that all the global market thought of when they heard the word "Haiti" was the toiling of sweaty, blue-black bodies imprisoned within concrete factory walls. They didn't know that most of the workers in their factories were women, with children, women whose bodies were swollen with gout and bloated from the buildup of unexpended energy due to working in small, cramped spaces.

The global market didn't know, or didn't care, that many of these workers had once been subsistence farmers but that now the land was parched and tired, stripped clean of all that ensured continuing fertility.

Ruth had kept up her father's business, kept up the commerce with the small merchants, most of whom were women, even though those who came for the goods and returned the money were men, often sons or common-law husbands. Even though the women did the work, the men still pocketed the change. She'd expanded her trade in linens and still had a shop near the Port where she sold imported bolts of cloth to the seamstresses who made the coming-out dresses for the upper-class girls by hand and for those who made the children's costumes for carnival.

The money comes in and goes right back out, to wherever it is needed. Beyond what she owes her brothers for their shares in the family business, beyond the wages of her house servants and the needs of the children who have now gone from her, Ruth has spent her adult life investing in Haiti. She doesn't make loans. She gives the money outright, to whomever needs it. She filters it through clandestine operations, grassroots insurgents, through the hands of the men who come to pick up goods and deliver money. In return, they tell her what she needs to know in order to keep the children safe, in order to know to whom to give and keep on giving. Trade has slowed down. It isn't clear who is to be trusted, and who not.

Her fingers stroke the row of faces beneath the plastic on her memory table. Catherine. Rose's remains should have been sent back with the girl, Ruth thinks. Instead, Rose had been buried in a cold ground that she had felt despised her. She would forever be embalmed under ice and snow, her only reprieve the blooming of wildflowers against her headstone in the brief spring season. When the girl had come to Ruth, she brought the long shadow of those northern climes still lodged deep in her bones, despite the heat of the Caribbean sun warming her. It took some time to make her thaw out, that girl. It took everything to make the girl bloom and stay in the spring of her life.

Ruth had made Catherine one of them even though they all suspected that she may have been unrelated by blood. Ruth believed that Catherine's father had been Jérémie – not her brother, Fritz – the one who toted around the gun that made him one of *them,* one of those who spread the terror in those ugly days, even though he would deny it and claim that he was only protecting his own. It was true that they couldn't say for sure that he had ever killed anyone and he did look after Rose when she came home for a few weeks at a time when her mother was still alive. Never let her out of his sight, never laid a harsh hand on her. Rose was calmer when she was around Jérémie, more sure of herself. He had a way of talking to her as if he understood all her secrets. It was a wonder that she had married Fritz at all. But they kept their doubts over Catherine's paternity a secret. Ruth had insisted as much when she took the girl, even as the truth became more and more obvious as Catherine asked questions that could not be answered about whom she resembled most and why. Ruth spoke of Rose rather than of their side of the family. But she deliberately, surreptitiously, taught her her own father's ways, as he had done with her.

Before the girl went to bed at night, Ruth taught her to say: "May Michael be at my right, Gabriel at my left, Uriel in front of me, Raphael behind me, and above my head, the *Shekina* – The Divine Presence." She taught Catherine the prayer when the girl woke up with nightmares about her mother, about Fritz, when she saw women in red dancing wildly against the walls. Ruth's own father had taught her the prayer when she had been a child. For protection, he'd said. The prayer had always comforted her and so she had passed it on to Catherine, explaining, as her father had done, that this was a sacred prayer to the archangels: to Michael, messenger of God; to Gabriel, the strength of God; to Raphael, the healing power of God; to Uriel, the light of God; to Shekina, the feminine presence of God. *In illness or in wellness,* she'd told Catherine, as her father had told her, *in illness or in wellness, these words shall protect you.* For years, she had heard the girl saying the prayer as she knelt by her bedside, hands clasped together. Catherine would then recite the Lord's Prayer, then a Hail Mary, as Rose had taught her, and Ruth would stand, slightly aghast, against the doorframe of the child's bedroom. But what could she have done differently? Did it matter that she was mixing different beliefs, different prayers? The end result would be the same. The girl belonged to all of them and fate could not be avoided.

What had she been thinking, Ruth asks herself now. *What kind of a mixed-up child had she raised?* It was too late to undo the things she had done and Catherine would be well served by the unorthodoxies of her upbringing. This is what made Catherine different from all those who had gone before her: she was a walking contradiction and still survived.

The girl didn't seem to make anything of the prayer. For her, it seemed not at all unusual. Catherine had been pious as a child, as if it might keep the memory of her mother alive. She wasn't so pious any more. Sceptical is what she'd become, almost bitter in fact, far away on the other side of the ocean in Paris where all the troubles – as far as Ruth was concerned – had begun for the Republic after Independence. Toussaint crossing over in a boat christened *Le Héros* as if to mock him, dying in a jail cell of exposure, and his wife, Suzanne, tortured until her body was unhinged like a rag doll's. Her they spared from death, knowing, as most torturers do, that to send a woman back broken was a harsher and more profound punishment for any witness than wiping her out altogether.

Women were symbolic mothers; they passed on culture, life. To kill a man was to cut off a people at the trunk: torture a woman and you poison the root. Ruth had, in the end, she mused, become a kind of honorary man. There was no better proof of this than what was to come, what was only days away from occurring.

No, she hadn't told Catherine about her origins, Fritz's origins. She hadn't revealed the source of the prayer except to say that it was her father, Catherine's grandfather, who had passed it down to them. She didn't tell Catherine what her own mother had finally revealed to her one Easter that was to alter her forever when she had been hardly eleven years of age. Her mother had revealed that her father's father came from far away over the ocean, not from Europe, but from the East where the earth was covered with sand dunes and olives hung from the trees like *quenêpes* here, plentiful and plump, ready for the picking. That was supposed to explain, somehow, why Father didn't go to Church with them on Sunday mornings. As far as Ruth could tell, Father wasn't a religious type at all. But he kept an altar in a dark corner of his office with an effigy on it of Moses holding the two stones etched with the ten commandments. Next to Moses was Papa Legba, god of the crossroads, in the guise of St. Peter. These were his gods and before them he placed bowls of water, a snifter of rum, and the occasional orange. When the Church people came to check on the family's progress with Bible study, Father covered the altar with a white cloth and argued that he was hiding a mess of paper under it, and everyone laughed and pretended to believe him.

It was a strange and difficult time, her tenth going on eleventh year. Still, it was a period before the terrors of the regime. Most people had food enough to eat. There had always been poor people but nothing like the abject conditions she witnessed now when she went down from the hill and into the worst parts of the city to see after her various investments. In that sense, those childhood years had been an almost ideal time. Their lives, however, had been highly regimented by the Americans who had come and changed everything, even the codes by which people knew each other. The Americans with their guns and their thick-soled boots ruined women and killed people in the insurrection. Father had prayed fervently to his gods in those days, his head bent forward so close to the lit candles he had set before his smiling Moses that she was sure that he would set his finely curled hair on fire.

Ruth had watched over her father from a distance, worrying after him as only a daughter can after her father, worried that he might not be all the man he seemed to be. Then came the anti-*vodou* campaigns and the little pamphlets disseminated in Church, denouncing the *vodou* priests, the *hougans*. They were to believe that the *voudouisants* were pawns of Satan, evildoers. When she brought one of the pamphlets home, convinced that she needed to save Papa, her father snatched it from her and burned it on the altar. Of what she'd had the chance to read, she'd seen: "Who is the principal slave of Satan? The principal slave of Satan is the

38

oungan. What names do the *oungans* give to Satan? *The names the oungans give to Satan are the lwa, the angels, the saints, the dead, the twins.* As the piece of paper curled up from the fire, she saw the words: *They are evildoers and liars like Satan.* She grew afraid, then, of what Papa was doing in front of the altar and nightmares came. She started walking in the middle of the night and hearing strange voices. It was then that Father had taught her the prayer of the angels to protect her and she found that the strange voices had their sources and that they were not strange after all. She began to make peace with what was to become of her life, even though she was not quite sure what that might be.

But first there had been that strange Easter when she had learned about Papa's father, her grandfather, about herself.

It had been Lenten season and she had been invited to spend the Friday and Saturday before Easter at a friend's house.

Everyone was feverish with excitement preparing their costumes for Carnival; the *rara* bands were practising the numbers they would play marching down the street with their hollowed-out pipes painted in bright colours and ready to be struck with sticks to make merry in the streets. She'd picked out her outfit already – staid by most standards – a fairy princess. She'd made up the costume from leftover dance materials – a pink and purple skirt made of taffeta that sprung out from her sides, a white leotard that covered her from mid-arm down to beneath the skirt, diaphanous wings made from stockings stretched across a frame made from wire that had been kept in the shed to replace parts of the chicken coop out back, a wand made from a stick on which she'd glued two cut-out paper stars, one for each side of the stick so that it might convince a few people of her powers.

Carnival was a time to let loose before weeks of abstinence from the pleasures of the world during the long Lenten period; it was the spark that made Easter the reward for sacrifice, worth the wait. Mother had explained to her that, in the old days, it was the week that the slaves were allowed to dance without fear of being punished and through the years it had remained a custom among the poorest of the poor, the one week when everyone was made equal and could say and do what they pleased from behind a mask as if they were the Queen and King of Prussia.

That Easter week, she'd been invited down the street and two blocks over to a friend's house. On the porch, they kept a stuffed man like a scarecrow sitting on a chair for everyone to greet. They treated the fake man like a god upon an altar, saluting him as they went by, the women curtsying and the men holding up their hats as they passed by and called their greetings. The housekeeper kept food at his feet and changed the glass of water daily. Ruth imagined that he was simply a larger version of her father's Moses, or perhaps a Legba, though he seemed like an ordinary kind of man in fine pants, a shirt and tie, even a jacket around the stuffed straw that made him look as massive as a field worker. He was bespectacled, which meant that he was a man of knowledge, and in his lap was a ledger. The more she thought about it, the more Ruth thought that the stuffed man bore a vague resemblance to her father bent over the books for the business at his desk, the altar covered with the white cloth at such times, as if numbers were not meant to be seen by the eyes of the gods. He covered the altar out of fear that the gods he worshipped on the island might somehow be the same gods who had banished his father's people into the sea.

The morning after the re-enactment of Christ's crucifixion, Ruth awoke in a house where it seemed that everything had been turned upside down. When everyone came onto the porch, they kicked the straw man rather than saluted him. They drank his water and took away his food so that, knocked about and hungry, drooping in his chair, his sagging form made him seem forlorn and wretched. Ruth felt sorry for him. She followed the rest of the household onto the porch and watched the stuffed man being abused. The boys seemed to have the most fun, but soon the girls were at it too.

"*Judas!*" the children screamed at the straw man. "*Judas.*"

Then they noticed Ruth standing stiff and still by the door, trying to stay hidden and out of sight. The little girl who had invited her pulled her into the light.

"*C'est ton tour,*" the girl said.

The girl had jet-black hair that had been pressed straight with a hot comb. The hair was pinned to the sides of her head and braided into thick plaits. Her skin was the colour of damp bark and her lips an almost ruby red. "Say it," the girl hissed at her. "Say, Judas."

"Judas," Ruth whispered.

"Louder," the boys chimed. "We can't hear you." They laughed at her behind cupped hands.

"Louder," the girl prodded, not to be outdone by her brothers and boy cousins. "Louder. Come on."

"And you have to kick him," one of the boys said. "Hard."

Ruth hesitated. The straw man had lost his spectacles. He was sitting slumped in the chair, unable to run away, unable to speak. He had no mouth in his sock head. His eyes were yellow buttons. He was a sad, sad, hard-working man, just like her father. Why should she abuse him? But, somehow, mechanically, Ruth found herself doing as she was told. She felt her foot come into contact with the soft matter of the straw man's leg and she heard her voice yelling out, squealing, "Judas! Judas!" Then, hot tears of disappointment and shame coursed down her cheeks and as they laughed at her, she sprang from the porch and found her way home, running all the way.

She fell into her mother's arms in the kitchen and told her the story of the straw man and what she had done.

"*Ti fille*," her mother said, stroking her thick hair with the palms of her open hands. "*Pov pitit*. Don't you know you can't kick yourself without it paining you?"

"Who was he, Mama? Why did they do this?"

"Did you never notice before?"

Ruth had shaken her head, no.

"*Jwif*," her mother said. "Like your father's people. In some places in the world, they call him a traitor, which is why they wanted you to call him Judas after the Bible story. But the people you've been hearing in the streets, sounding out metal pipes, they do not call him a Judas, they call him a prophet. Do you know why this is?"

Again, Ruth had shaken her head.

"Because without him, the Christians would not have had their God, and the Jews would have lost a prophet. He had a role to play. He was the only one strong enough to do what had to be done."

"When your father's people were made to leave their place of birth, they had to abandon their gods and their altars and build a new life. Some of them took on new names, new religions, new identities. Some of the people they had to leave behind called them traitors but they had no choice. They had to flee to make a life for themselves and for their children. If your grandfather had not left Syria when he did, your father would not be the man he is today. I would not have met him. You would not be. Everyone has a place in the order of things, Ruth. Do not forget this."

"Does this mean that I'm a 'Jwif'?" Ruth asked.

"Yes," her mother had said, "*Nou tout sé Jwif*. Even those of us who kick ourselves, not knowing any better, and set ourselves on fire as if we might consume the past by repeating its offences."

Ruth had not understood all of her mother's pronouncements in the end. She had fallen asleep in her mother's lap from the exhaustion of the morning's shocking events, from fear of having harmed her father by kicking a straw man who had been made to resemble him and people like him of the merchant class. What did it mean, this word: *Jwif*? It would take her many years to find out and when she was old enough to learn, her father told her very little of his family's past. It took her even longer to realize that what her father had to pass on was very little because very little had survived before him. Her father lived in a world made up of fragments of broken lives. He gathered the bits and pieces of those who had been made to travel far from their mother's bosoms and made it all his own. It was in this way that he kept the memory of his father's faith alive.

"You see this," he had told Ruth, pointing to a diagram in a book that looked like a tree with many circles going off in different directions from its trunk, "this is the secret to life."

Ruth had not understood.

"I know it's hard to know what to believe in. But it's all pretty much the same in the end." They had just burned more of the pamphlets that said that altars to gods other than Catholic ones should be seized and destroyed. They had burned them as Moses looked on, bemused, still holding the tablets made of wood in his hands. "They'll have you believing that my father's people were sorcerers, but look…" he pointed at the many-hued drawing, "they simply wanted to give us a key to how to better balance our higher and baser natures." He sighed and leaned back in his chair. "Ruth, my father's people believed that every human being was made of five elements, all of which were to be revered. Three of those elements correspond to the human body and the last two to aspects of our ability to reason: our will and our pleasure." He smiled at her as if he was hardly seeing her, then focused, took her in, and struggled to make himself understood. "It's like when your mother wants you to read with a light on but you are so engrossed in the story that you don't want to break the pleasure of the reading. Your eyes would do better with a light but you stay with your pleasure. It takes a strong will to do what is right, what will be better for your eyes." He smiled at her again. "In this world, some of the choices you have to make don't have a benefit for yourself. Sometimes you have to choose the thing that will bring you great harm for the greater good." He sighed, leaned forward, closed the book. "They called your mother's people sorcerers and devils too when they rose up and poisoned their masters' wells. That's where we get the word *mackandal*." Ruth nodded. She'd learned this in a history class from a teacher who was ahead of his time, trying to teach them things about Haiti that weren't even in the history books. Her father smiled. "I see. I see." He was slightly amused. His moustache quivered over his lips widening into a smile. "You already know more than I think you do. Then, Ruth, I am not afraid to tell you these things. Your mother's people to this day believe that there are three parts to the soul: the body, the *gwo bon anj*, and the *ti bon anj*." He pointed at his altar, "It's all the same thing. The *gwo bon anj* flies away to some higher place. The *ti bon anj* goes back to the earth along with the body, to be born again in some other time. The *gwo* guides the will and the *ti* the pleasure. The Church people believe that there is the body and the soul and the Holy Spirit. Tell me, Ruth, how is it any different? Remember this Ruth: whatever they're afraid of, they'll call it the devil. Whatever stands in their way, they'll call primitive and backward. So don't worry about what they say. Follow your heart even if what it seems to be telling you makes no sense. *Le coeur, c'est tout!*"

She sat by her father's side as he rambled on as they watched the words on the smouldering pamphlets disappear. Magicians and air. Sorcerers and conjurers.

Her father reopened the magical book with the word *Kabbalah* written on its spine and stabbed at the diagram. "…the tree of life… mysticism, *vodou*," he muttered, "it's all the same." He reached for a cup on his desk that smelled strongly of rum and talked in a low voice to himself. It was then that Ruth learned that when her father retreated to his study, it was not only to work or to pray but it was to lose himself in drink.

Ruth's father had few friends in what they referred to as "polite society", her mother had tried to explain, preferring the company of *vodouisants*, to the pious church goers who came to the house for spontaneous bouts of Bible study. He made large contributions to a Church where he could participate in secret *vodou* activities but he never took Ruth there and seldom her mother.

In the end, Ruth had to tell the girl down the street that she wasn't permitted to play at her house because her father was a "Jwif". The family of the girl took offence, partly because they hadn't known, and partly because they felt that if anyone was doing the dis-inviting, it should have been them.

Once word spread in school that Ruth and her father's people were not what they seemed, she and her brothers were shunned. Max didn't seem to care. He was the oldest and had already formed a world beyond the family's reach, but Fritz, the youngest, could not forgive his father the betrayal, while Ruth, loyal as ever, in effect became her father's only child, which was how she inherited the family business, complete with its wealth – and isolation. Father died early for a man of his generation, at fifty-two years of age, of a diseased liver. Mother followed soon after, dying of a broken heart. Ruth was not so romantic. She took the warning of her father's death and avoided drink; her mother's decline she took as a warning to keep her heart a fortress.

The liver disease skipped a generation. How was she to know that while she was hearing the whispers of the angels, Lucas would be drinking himself to sleep? Forever in search of doing the right, no, the higher thing, she had failed when it came to those closest to her. She had given away her wealth to the least favoured in the city but to her own she had left next to nothing.

She gazes down at Lucas's photograph at fourteen, the year Catherine came to live with them, his green eyes flashing their mischievousness like the startled eyes of a lizard.

Lucas had been a curious child, inquisitive, generous to a fault. Ruth remembers him giving his sweets and toys to Catherine as if they were of no importance to him, with no thought of anything in return. She recognized early that the boy had second sight, that he was driven by what trickled down from above, by what had come before.

Three years earlier, after they had received the news of Rose's car accident, Lucas had stood by the patch of marigolds in the garden and, pointing to them, said, "You'll need to plant more of these."

"Why is that?" she'd asked, perplexed, her mind still on cutting back the bougainvillea bush overrunning the footpath, and on Fritz and the girl and the things it was now too late to do, too late to say.

He'd paused too long before replying, forcing her to look back at him over her shoulder, shears in her hands, the smooth stalks of the plant she was pruning balanced between her fingers.

In that moment, she felt she was seeing Lucas for the first time since he had come to live at the house. The boy was clearly in some kind of trance, swaying from side to side, his arms now limp alongside his narrow body, his eyes fixed on some faraway point. It made his eyes seem as if they were tunnelling inwards rather than looking out, his lips moving as if engaged in intense conversation.

Ruth had looked beyond the boy, over the heads of her sprawl of bushes and flowering plants. There was a soft, lingering wind but there was no one nearby. Who was he talking to?

"Lucas?" she'd asked again.

He looked slowly towards her, the lips no longer moving but parted, and Ruth was certain that the boy was between worlds, seeing and not seeing her. It frightened her for a moment but she caught the fear before it permeated the air between them.

"It's Rose," he'd said, as if reading her mind, "she wants marigolds."

Squinting as she advanced in the sun, Ruth turned towards him. He seemed impossibly small for his eleven years, a shadow against the light flickering in and out of focus like a lit wick. *Don't go there*, she thought. She was thinking of her father, of the things she'd witnessed since his death, trading with the lower classes, seeing the *vodouisants* as they fell in trances. *Wasn't he too young? No*, she thought again, *don't go there*, though she was not sure where "there" was, had no direct experience of the other worlds though she could feel them rippling the air. Her heart lurched in her chest like a caged bird suddenly intent on flight.

It was at that moment that Ruth began to truly love Lucas, at the moment she realized he could so easily be lost.

"She wants marigolds next to your mother's because they are the flower for mothers and, in honour of *Ezili Le Flambo*, she says, for motherless daughters."

Was it her imagination or were the boy's eyes reddening? *Don't go... there...*

But it was too late. Lucas smiled at her as if from a distant plane as if to tell her that she should not be afraid and then he fainted away, his thin body falling, falling into the cushion of bright orange-red flowers poised to receive his weight.

He didn't remember anything he'd said, or the fall, when he came to later, back in his room where she'd had the driver carry him. But he'd gone back out to the garden to plant the marigold seeds a day later, as if fulfilling a promise.

She felt they grew more distant after that – she trying to protect, he hiding his newly awakened gifts. He'd gone on to train at the church/*hounfort* she'd continued to support financially in her father's name, both unaware of the other's involvement until, one day, Lucas announced that he was leaving the house to join *them*, some group in the bush, where still he remained, unrepentant, trying to discover the full extent of his powers.

She had lost sight of him. Yet, she'd come to love him fiercely, in recognition of his higher purpose and of her role in his life. This far exceeded the notion of her adolescent crush on the boy's father or some righteous effort to grasp what she had lost by going her own way, in isolation. The problem was that, even as she manoeuvred her own worlds dextrously, quietly, trying to make as few waves as possible in any direction, she had never managed to teach either

Lucas or Catherine caution. She'd taught them both to fear, and that had made Lucas reckless and Catherine withdrawn.

She knew her gifts were not of the same order as the children's. Her patron saint was St. Peter or Legba, after her father. She opened doors; she did not go through them. She understood the ways of the gods and respected them but she was not one of their emissaries, at least, not like Lucas and Catherine and all the others. She witnessed. She supported. She tried to keep those meant to be doing the *real* work alive.

Ruth realizes now that what she had was uncommon strength, the kind needed to weather regimes and coups, dictators and pundits, shortages and starvation. She had not passed on this gift, nor recognized it as one. Rose. Lucas. Catherine. Romulus. Each had moved through her hands like sand and she could have given them much more: a grasp on life. Lucas was still out there, wandering. He would not come back unless Catherine brought him back. Ruth would have to compel her to go to find him, to bring him back, if she could.

Ruth's heart clenches, its muscles like fingers closing into a fist, making her gasp for breath. It would all be left to Catherine to repair. Though she doesn't know it yet, Catherine is stronger than them all.

Evening, March 6, 2004, Port-au-Prince Hills

The photographs from the memory table on her mind, Ruth walks down the tiled corridor of her empty home. Most of the rooms upstairs have been closed. For years, she has occupied the rooms on the ground floor only. Ruth listens to the soft fall of her black leather slippers against the tiles. There is a breeze coming through the ironwork of the windows. The scent of the flowers drifts in – bougainvillea, irises, flamboyants. Ruth feels her every step grow heavier. Will she have the strength to withstand the pain? They are coming. She smells it in the air. There is no time for heroics.

She walks through the hallway towards a room the size of a closet close to the kitchen, a storage room where Lucas had kept most of his childhood things. After Lucas left, Ruth had the room cleared. She needed a space that could provide focus for her writing work as the house seemed to grow larger with every absence, every departure. She needed to concentrate on what was left for her to do. The walls had been painted a moss green. Ruth had read in an American magazine that a cool green was the colour of choice in hospitals. It soothed patients when their minds played tricks on them, when fear was more powerful than the words of loved ones or nurses – who already had too much to do.

The only furniture that could fit into the closet was a child's desk and a chair. Both were decorated with butterflies painted on a dark blue background. The butterflies were magical and colourful, made for a child's imagination. Ruth had bought the desk for Catherine when Fritz had called from Canada to tell her that he was about to send the child to her, for safekeeping.

She had thought it a strange choice of words. She remembers that day as if it were yesterday.

"*Tout va bien?*" she'd asked, hesitating, straining to take in every nuance of his speech, every sigh and twitch of his cheeks.

Fritz had always been nervous, even as a child, and his twitches revealed his state of mind. She imagined his right cheek jumping up and down as he tried to think of the right words to use with his estranged sister. She had not come to Rose's funeral. He had not forgiven her absence. She had not forgiven herself for what she might have prevented, even though Fritz knew nothing of what she knew, that Rose's death might have been prevented if they had all helped her to shoulder her work among the spirits. At the time of the funeral, they had not spoken in three years.

"What do you need, brother?" she had said to him as she felt his gaze turn inward, searching, searching for the words that would allow him to ask for the unthinkable.

"Catherine," he'd begun, then stopped, then started again, "I want to send her to you."

"She isn't well?"

"She's well. She's well. I need to send her to you for safekeeping."

She had remained silent, then, trying to guess at the situation that had unfolded after Rose's death, since her brother had left the city where he had been living with Rose and his first and only child.

"I'm not well, sister," he'd said then, interrupting the silence. "I'm not well and I don't know who else to ask."

Ruth remembers standing in the foyer where her old rotary dial phone sat in the shadow of the memory-table. It had just been a table then, polished every day by the housekeeper. It had been a dark and still night. There had been a power outage and the only light she could see beyond the house were the lights from the midnight fires and from oil lamps the market woman put outside of their huts and stalls. The darkness made her realize that it was easier for Fritz to ask for what he needed without having to be seen. Even though Fritz was many miles away, he still operated in the old ways, as if he had never left, the codes of his conduct imprinted from birth.

"*Ou là?*" he asked finally, his voice small, distant.

Ruth nodded without saying anything.

She was remembering Fritz as a child. He had always been smaller than the other boys and pudgy, always last to be chosen for teams, often alone, bookish. He had flowered just before meeting elegant Rose, married her, and left the island behind. Losing Rose had turned him back into the brooding child he had been long ago. Ruth wondered if Catherine was like her father. She did not remember her well. Of the three, it was always Rose who had stood out in her mind, eclipsing even the memories she had of Fritz before they grew up and each went their own way. It was Rose she had failed most of all.

"Yes," she'd said. "Of course I'll take her. She'll have Lucas to play with and he can introduce her around. Does she still play the piano?"

"Yes."

"Then we will continue her lessons. When can I expect her?" Her voice had suddenly taken on a firm, businesslike tone. It allowed her brother to retain his dignity.

"In a week," he said.

"Does she know?"

"We haven't talked about it yet."

"Will she come?"

"She must."

Ruth sighed. It was so like Fritz to do as he pleased without talking it over. She was almost surprised that he had called before sending the child to her.

"You should speak to her otherwise she'll feel like you've just given her away."

"I will," he said, but Ruth could sense that he had already disconnected from her and was itching to let her go.

"Really, speak with the child. She needs to know you love her."

She heard the strain in the silence and sighed. "Very well. We will be ready in a week."

"Thank you, sister," Fritz said very formally, as if he were speaking to a well-meaning nun.

"You're very welcome," she said, knowing the child would come to them sullen and broken, convinced that she had been banished to the ends of the earth by a father who no longer loved her and a mother who had disappeared.

The next day she and Lucas had gone out to buy some furniture appropriate for an eleven-year-old girl who had just lost her mother and, now, a father.

As they shopped, Ruth clutched her purse against the pain shooting through her solar plexus. It was as if she was carrying a rock there that was suddenly grating against the sides of her abdomen, trying to exact payment from its lining.

As she walked through the streets and then through the narrow aisles of the stores she and Lucas visited, with Lucas giving his thoughts on the various possibilities of desks like an old crone, she realized that it was guilt suddenly gnawing at her. It had finally resurfaced to hold her accountable to this debt she had to pay, a debt that predated the girl's birth, and thus was payable to the child for whose orphaning she was, in part, if not in whole, responsible.

It would be her last chance to restore unity. The task was daunting.

Ruth thinks back to the first time she had met Rose in 1966. Fritz had insisted that they meet. He had told her some story about ghosts and a history of mental instability in the girl's family. Ruth had only agreed to meet the girl because it was clear that Fritz intended to marry her, crazy or not.

When she had met Rose, Ruth had been struck by her simplicity. Given the stories she'd been told of nocturnal wanderings, of people who presented themselves at the girl's door for a blessing in the hope of being healed of their own demons, she'd expected some touch of flamboyance, some colour, if not in pigmentation, in the manner of her dress. But Rose was simple. There was not much to her. She was thin, so thin that Ruth wondered if she would ever bear Fritz children. She was pale – almost alabaster white. As an old saying went, she was so white she had to have African blood coursing through her veins; their circuitry faintly marbled her skin, making her seem almost ghostly, ephemeral, as if she might disappear at a moment's breath or in a sudden sweep of wind.

Ruth had just inherited Lucas at three years of age and he ran through the garden on his knobby, not-quite-a-little-boy legs and stood just close enough to stare and not close enough to be swatted away for staring for too long.

Ruth remembers as if it were yesterday the way Lucas had cocked his head to the side as if sizing up Rose, his mouth slightly open as if he might begin to ask her questions that only a five year old could ask, like: *Why that colour?* (pointing at skin) *Why your veins?* (still pointing at skin) *Why you eyes so pale?* (looking straight into them) *Why here?* (face emanating jealousy) *Why so sad?* (face falling in empathy) *You don't have to be sad...* (echoing words he'd been told in such a state but never quite believed).

Those days, he began almost every sentence with "why" and Ruth learned from the incessant questioning that there was wisdom in it, in the innocence that chose to believe that there was meaning to everything.

That day, Lucas had held his tongue even though she could see from the way he had held his little body and swayed from one leg to another that he was full up with questions. What held him back, she didn't know, but it had something to do with Rose, something to do with the problem that led Fritz to bring her to his old family home in search of an answer to a question that had not been asked.

They had sat down in the front sitting room, the one with a view onto the garden, the same room she had been walking through when she had spied JP and thought she had seen a ghost.

Fritz explained the trouble: the apparitions in the middle of the night, the woman journalist who had begun to appear after her detention by the Macoutes; he spoke of a great-aunt the family had had locked up in the asylum. He talked until he spent his worry. In the end, Ruth ignored his words. They didn't add up to much more than a man's terror in the face of things he did not want to understand. What could she do about that? Fritz had always been this way. This was nothing new. What was odd was that it would be he who would want to marry someone like Rose, who would bring Rose to Ruth. He had no understanding of his role in the grander scheme, in the process of decay and rebirth that was a part of healing. Ruth knew there could be no healing without pain, no cauterizing of the wound without telltale scarring. Healing involved loss and sacrifice, decimation even, before anything could be built up again. Rose was a part of the dissolution of things; she, Ruth, was a part of the rebuilding. Still, she sympathized with Rose for she recognized that nothing, not even she with her strength and determination, could last forever, especially not when the world laid its woes upon your shoulders. Rose's fragility marked her destiny: she was simply going to leave faster than others, her path unfulfilled; Ruth, on the other hand, was going to have to be pried away from hers, almost against her will, in a flash, once she had completed most of her exchanges.

Had Rose been crazy? Surely not. Ruth had seen that quickly enough even through the woman's sadness, her eyes dry of tears but weeping nonetheless. That Fritz had his doubts was more worrisome than any late evening meetings the young woman was having with terrified souls. She might have done better to tell the girl to run and never come back but then who would have been called the crazy one? Fritz was her brother, after all, and Ruth knew that something was to come of their union, and very shortly. Still, she had failed Rose. She had failed her when the young woman had leaned forward across the low coffee table, Fritz playing outside with the three-year-old Lucas as if in mimicry of what was to come in another place and time. Fritz had played with Lucas, with fear gnawing the pit of his stomach, a deep, gut-wrenching fear that told him that he was in over his head. He was hoping that Ruth might work a miracle, smooth things over as she usually did, making the unpalatable disappear as she often did, as she had always done when it came to the family business so that they never had to ask her for an accounting of things – their part of the family wealth appearing, monthly, like clockwork, with never a penny straying too far from the margin in one direction or another. They knew things could not be as easy as she made it seem but they knew better than to ask questions in uncertain times. If anyone could extract money while all the blood-letting was going on, then their means had to be dubious, complicit in some way with the loss of life.

Ruth kept them ignorant of all this; she knew how to deal with the implausible, the unsavoury, and somehow they overlooked the implications of such facility with terror while she used their contempt of her femaleness as her cover. Her smile, her flowers, the children coming and going in the yard from their piano lessons assuaged doubt and that was enough. They asked her no discomfiting questions.

She liked it this way.

When Ruth met Rose, she recognized an aspect of herself in the young woman: the need for privacy, the intense desire to have some interior secret hidden from view. She could look at Rose and see herself when she was so much younger. Ruth had also seen and felt too much, understood too little though more than she had ever thought possible. When she had met Rose, Ruth felt the young woman was an added burden, too heavy to take on. She rebuffed the girl even when her eyes were pleading for assistance out of the nightmare into which she was descending.

No, Rose had not been mad, though Ruth could also read in her eyes that the girl was comforted by the thought of madness, the escape it offered from the fear, dread, apathy and sheer pain of other human beings.

The girl was a crossroads, it was plain to see. She had the gift. The same gift Ruth had been born with and that her father had taught her to handle by being strong, independent, ready to defend herself and what belonged to her, like a man. This young woman had had no such guidance. She had been born to people who could not see her gift, or could not help her with it.

Ruth could look at Rose and see the girl's famed, notoriously crazed, great-grandmother Elsie as if the woman existed in the mirror of the girl's eyes. She could see that Rose was just one pearl on a string that led all the way back to distant lands, all the way back to Nigeria and to Ireland, to the wandering geography of her father's people, her people. To each generation there was a seer born, and, in turn, each was broken, her gift reviled.

The truth was simple enough. Ruth had been frightened by what she saw before her. She had known Rose's journalist neighbour, Coco, from the clandestine meetings in the back rooms of shops and church basements where she traded. She had known the woman well and read her columns in the newspapers, listened when the woman had made impassioned speeches, her black hair looking like a bush on fire in the orange light of oil lamps. She'd admired her and thought her foolish. The woman had believed in the power of the pen, in the idea that journalists were untouchable and could somehow rebuff the terror emanating from Duvalier's presidential palace. Ruth's informants among the street vendors knew that there was no such safety. Nothing could make you safe. Not money. Not status. Not honour. Hadn't they killed judges as well as football players? Politicians just as well as market women? There was no rhyme or reason to the killings except to keep them all terrified. She had known the woman well. Had seen her wandering in her bathrobe in the dark of night, pink slippers filled with dust. In Rose, Ruth saw herself as well as the crazy aunt that Rose was afraid of becoming. They were all one. This was inescapable.

The girl had leaned across the table and hissed a whisper across to Ruth, "Can you help me?"

Ruth heard the whisper as if it was a sound roiling the wind across the ocean. It was distant and noisy all at the same time. It made her move back in her chair as if to avoid a tidal wave.

She thought for a moment then lurched back towards the girl as if she was about to kiss her but, instead of embracing her, Ruth found a voice just as nightmarish, and from another world, say back to the girl, simply, "No."

She regretted the word as soon as it fell from her lips.

Rose drew herself back into her sitting position and braced

herself over her china espresso cup as if nothing had been said, the grey eyes distant, cold as polished silver.

"That is so," Rose said, looking nowhere in particular, still in that same voice that had pushed Ruth back into the cushions of her antique divan.

Ruth realized then that the girl had known that she would refuse and that some day the debt would have to be repaid. Rose was fragile but she was no fool. She knew already that she carried a girl, another seer, and that she would not live to see the day when the girl would come to know the gifts of her lineage.

They had finished their cups of coffee in utter and glassy silence when Fritz came back into the room on the heels of Lucas who ran through the house as if every room had been built for his pleasure, squealing in delight despite the sombre air of the two women in the sitting room. He seldom had male company and this was all Lucas cared about at that moment.

Fritz gesticulated after the boy as if to apologize for the excitement he had produced.

"Let him run," Ruth smiled indulgently at her brother. "It will make him easier to put to bed tonight."

Fritz smiled and nodded.

"Did she tell you?"

Ruth looked back and forth between them. Fritz was thinking about the child on the way. Rose was thinking about the woman journalist who had died, whose place she would rather take. Ruth was unsure what situation she was being asked about but she knew that Fritz was very much earthbound, despite the fact that he was a musician. Fritz only believed in things that he could touch and hear.

"She's gone, you know," Rose said to Ruth as if to clarify which situation should be addressed.

Fritz was perplexed. "No... didn't you tell her?" He was thinking, miscarriage. "Are you all right? I don't..." He looked back and forth between his sister and his wife. "I don't understand."

"Rose is speaking about her neighbour, Fritz. The journalist."

"That craziness," Fritz responded, dismissively. "You will help her, won't you?"

"There's not much I can do," Ruth said, to both of them.

Rose began to weep, very quietly. She let her head hang down towards her chest until no more tears fell.

"I don't know what to do," Fritz said to his sister.

"There's nothing we can do," Ruth said, speaking of the madness beyond them sweeping up the hill all the way from the Palace, speaking of the child on the way, and their mutual ineptness.

When Fritz had called to tell her that he was sending Catherine to her, Ruth realized it was time to make recompense. It was strange to realize that there was no other choice she could have made back then even though she had the skill to teach Rose how to face her gifts, how to grow strength. She could have taught her but no tutelage would have made up for the brokenness of her past.

Sometimes, there was no use in trying to stay the currents of ancient rivers, Ruth had thought. One only exhausted oneself in vain as well as the person one was trying to save. If she had done anything differently, who was to say that Rose would have survived? This was the way things were meant to be and it was not up to Ruth to question a higher order. Some things were beyond comprehension.

After the memory of Coco had dulled, after Fritz and Rose had left the island for Canada, the vastness of which Ruth could only barely imagine, the stone of guilt furrowed like a feral animal deep into her stomach. She never ate properly again. It was then that she started writing the anonymous letters for the underground papers in Coco's name, and when there was nowhere to publish, she would run off the sheets herself on a portable mimeograph machine with a hand crank. She had bartered a huge amount of refined sugar for it, sugar she would never use and could bet most Haitians could do without, preferring to have their coffee black if a choice had to be made. Then she circulated her writings like flyers by passing them on to the street vendors in small bundles that they carried in their back pockets, beneath their shirts, distributing them amongst the market women as they parcelled out the goods for sale. She signed her pieces, *"Ezili Le Flambo,"* honouring Coco and Rose, both.

Sooner or later, they would catch up with her. She just hadn't thought it would be one of her own who would give her away, one of the men who had trusted her and she him. She didn't think that one of the men who carried the flyers, whose livelihood and protection she had ensured, would turn on her. She didn't think that she would see Romulus heading the group that came to her house that fateful afternoon, even though she realized that they would be coming for her, to collect her wealth and take it for themselves. What they didn't know was that she kept no money in her house, very little jewellery. She had learned long ago that money had to keep circulating if it was to be any use. The land she lived on, the house, it had all been purchased long ago. She had very little need for money even though she made a lot of it. But times had changed and terror had given way to a hardening of the soul in the hearts of younger men who had not witnessed the struggle against the regime that had fallen some twenty years ago.

They were young men who travelled to Miami and New York on American passports. They knew a thing or two about drug trafficking and other kinds of trafficking, the kind that involved other people's flesh, usually women's. They had little conscience between them. They were of a new age. Time held no substance.

Ruth was a relic from the past and all they saw when they looked at her was money. Never mind that her skin was the colour of roasted almonds. Never mind that she had a memory that paired the wanderings of her father's people with the rolls of the drums of her mother's people in their native land where the earth was dark and black like freshly mined coal. Never mind that her father's people had been forced to handle money because in a previous age, their faith and money had been seen as soiling, unclean. Never mind that her mother's people had been treated like cattle, branded and sold. Never mind that both her father's people and her mother's people had been thrown to the wolves by the same zealous mass. And never mind that she had been taught how to love and love and love, learned at both her mother's and father's knees that love meant taking all of your advantages and preserving them so that you had some means to assist others, putting privilege at the service of the less fortunate. If you gave it all away, then what would you have to give?

The young men who were coming to her door didn't see things that way. She was just a bony old woman with lots of money stuffed under her mattress. She was a *foreigner* in their eyes even though her family was as old as the Revolution, as Haitian as any of them. It wasn't worth fighting their delusions.

Ruth sits at the small blue desk and tries to think of the right words to express what she needs to say, with all that history under the bridge, a history that most of her followers know but do not speak of with her since she always insists that their worries are more important than her family troubles and that the next day will bring a brighter sun. It will be her final missive, her final words. They must be carefully chosen. They must be precise.

Fanm vayant, she begins to type on the small manual type-writer. It is the heavy sort with a steel frame and round keys with paper cut-out letters, black on white backgrounds. Her fingers often fall between the narrow gaps between the keys.

She has been writing these editorials longer than the existence of the green room with its blue desk, longer than the closing down of the rooms on the second level of the house. She doesn't tire of writing them although she is tired. Every morning, Ruth's body groans as she wakes with a feeling of surprise at how age has crept up upon her, the children gone, the house emptied of their exuberant energy.

Fanm vayant, she continues, the typewriter keys creating a music in the stillness that feels like a slow march, a dirge. *There is nothing we cannot do.*

She rereads what she has written. Only one sentence. She strikes out the "we" and types "you" above instead since, in a very short while, she will no longer be counted in their number. She will be someone they will remember at the beginning of prayers and rituals, a name to pronounce in order to bring alive the connection between the living and the dead. Fear overtakes her for a moment as she surrenders to the notion that she will soon be a *poto-mitan* – a channel between the dormant and waking worlds, the occupants of neither completely conversant in the ways of the other.

She wants to see them again, her children, as they were before they left her shores, before the waves of destiny pushed them along. Ruth sighs, drops her shoulders. What can she tell the women that they don't already know: women who now stood with their pots and pans in front of the Palais National and chanted for their human rights and the rights of their children? Women who had forsaken the silence of their mothers in favour of a new day. What has she left to say?

Ruth pushes herself away from the desk, the yellowed sheet of paper still in the typewriter with its one sentence etched into its fibres. She needs to think some more about what to say, what to leave behind. It dawns on her that if she hasn't said it yet, perhaps it is too late.

It won't be long now. They are almost upon her, darkening her doorstep with their ignorance and their greed, their belly-aching and their fury. Some of it is justified. Some of it is not. Once they get what they want – not that there is any fortune in her home to find – they won't go back to their people and share it as she was taught to do. She's sure of it.

But it doesn't matter. The world needs everything in order to function. Hate as well as love. Avarice as well as generosity. The problem is that everything has fallen out of balance.

It won't be long. But Ruth is heartened by the fact that she can see that there is more to come beyond her. Catherine will survive her.

Ruth tries not to think of the pain to come. When the cut of the machete will find her, she will think only of the faces on the memory table. Of Lucas and Romulus, of Catherine and Rose, and of Rose's great-grandmother Elsie who died in the state sanatorium prevented from fulfilling the prophecy.

She will think of everyone who has made her, of all the lives that have touched her, of all the hands in the great chain of trade that links them all on the island, from the market women to the dockhands unloading imported goods into the great hangars by the ocean. She can barely imagine how that chain unfurls beyond them to lands she has never seen.

She will think of the recent hurricane floods wiping away the terror from their shores as the waters sweep dust to mud. In the end, she will know that everything, everything she has done or tried to do, even when she has failed miserably, will have been worth the sacrifices of her time, of her father's time, of her mother's time. Remembering, she types her final words:

Early Morning, March 7, 2004, Port-au-Prince, Haiti

"Hinei mah tov omah nayim shevet achim gum yachad."
[Behold how good and pleasant it is when brethren dwell together in unity. – Psalm 133:1]
Fanm Vayant,
There is nothing you cannot do.
There is an order to the universe written in the stars, seen and unseen.
They do not want to admit it down below. Down below, they struggle for certainty, an anchoring to the ground. Were they, our opponents, able to remember their origins, they would be gentle, more compassionate, in recognition of our common and humble beginnings. As it is, the stars can only blink their disbelief while we up above continue with our work, hoping that some of you will awaken to your destinies and open the doors between worlds, so that the healing can begin.
Kembé. Stay strong. *Pa tonbé.* Don't fall.
In solidarity,

Ruth's hand hesitates above the keys of the typewriter. She knows the time has come, that there will be no reprieves after she seals the letter to give the house boy to mail before the rooster's cry, before the dark angels darken her path. She must not give way to ego. She must, to the end, be true to the others and to herself, in her mother's and father's name, in the name of Rose and Catherine, for this country that will forget her passage, soon, too soon, as if she has never walked its dusty ways.
Ruth sighs, accepts her fate, and signs,

Ezili Le Flambo

CATHERINE

Remembering 1977, Montréal/Chicoutimi, Québec, Canada

When my mother died, it was quiet like first snowfall, like everything and everyone was holding in their breath for fear of having the fresh crystals mounding on branches and fences tumble, fall, and ruin the perfection covering all within sight.

It was still, too, and cold. I felt an emptiness I'd never known settle within me. My insides became wide and cavernous. Time became an empty space without much meaning, as if there was no such thing as a before and an after. A before-mother and an after-mother. There was just space, a vast nothingness beyond comprehension, disturbed only by the fact of flesh and bone existence, however much my father denied it. When my mother died, there was just that moment when Fritz sat me down at the kitchen table and I fidgeted, fingering the grooves of its light wood surface as he stumbled for the right words and then, finally, sighed and said flatly, "She's gone."

"What do you mean?" I'd asked, even though I could feel that something had changed in the air, as if there might not be enough of it to keep the two of us alive.

"She's dead. Gone. That's what I mean."

I was nine and I knew what the word "death" meant. Our back yard had a garden corner out of which grew popsicle sticks marking graves for goldfish and gerbils gone "the way of the great beyond", as Fritz called it then. My mother pasted the sticks together, crosses for the shallow graves, and I wrote the names of the deceased pets in coloured marker across the horizontals in block print, looking forward each time to the ceremony at which the three of us would officiate, reciting Joe's or Blondie's litany of attributes as pet and best friend, thanking the departed before lowering the shoebox into the damp earth, covering it up and then spreading flower petals from the rose bushes or multicoloured leaves (depending on the season) across the fresh mound.

As my father spoke, I imagined my mother's grave in the back yard, long and not so very wide to accommodate her tall, svelte frame. I wondered what of hers we would place next to her clasped hands: her rosary? A favourite photograph? What would I say about her as mother, as friend? What could be said at such a moment? It seemed the most unnatural of circumstances.

I glanced up at my father who seemed to have aged within minutes, the lines on his face making his cheeks seem long, sagging. There were deep, dark hollows beneath his eyes and the fine tissue beneath one eye twitched uncontrollably.

"You must be wrong," I whispered.

"*Morte*," he said, switching to our common tongue. "*Elle est morte*," he repeated, as if saying it this way might make it more tangible for me as well as for himself.

Fritz didn't allow me to go to the funeral, to look into the casket, to say a few words at her side, to place rose petals in or over the grave, to choose something to give her comfort as she went down alone into the darkness of a ground that had never seemed home to her, something like the small statue of the Virgin Mary with head inclined over clasped hands I had given her for her birthday only a month before.

Not being a witness to her final moments, it was difficult to believe that she was not about to come drifting into the kitchen, out of breath, cheeks flushed, a brown paper bag filled with groceries burdening her arms.

Even as Fritz tried to explain it to me – the icy road, the busy intersection, the inopportune slipping of her foot on the gas pedal while a drunk driver spun into her car – I was looking over his hunched shoulders, ignoring the patter of words that fell from his mouth like an irritating torrent of rain on a metal roof, instead watching the soft, quiet snow flurries still drifting down to the ground beyond the windows of our kitchen, in case he might be mistaken, in case I might catch a glimpse of her making her way back to us up the driveway.

I spent months after the funeral looking back over my shoulder, in case the touch of the wind's cold fingers might be her, appearing again, belatedly, as if she had forgotten her way in a wooded area not far from the house, as if she might have forgotten the familiar scents of home, the look of our driveway, the number above the door that she had written on the covers of my school notebooks in case I got lost.

In case *I* got lost.

After the funeral, and the ebbing of visitors from our yellow kitchen, I reconsidered the plausibility of a mother being lost and whether there was anything Fritz or I might have done to help her find her way back to us, but it was impossible to imagine. For a time, this kept me from accepting the inevitable. There were stories from the island, after all, of the dead waking again, of *zombies* forced into slave labour far from home waking after years and years of absence, walking home barefoot into the mountains of their youths until they reached home. Here, there were stories of canines and felines walking their paws bare to find their owners, pawing their way cross-country after they had been forgotten or left behind with neighbours.

Even though there had been a funeral, even though she had been buried, I held on to the possibility that my mother might rise up, and return from the frozen ground.

It was a period of looking back rather than looking forward, of pulling in rather than expanding out.

Not wanting to live with the ghost of my mother in the house, my father took a job in Chicoutimi, a small working town far from everything I had grown to know and to love in bustling Montreal.

"You'll thank me when you're older," I remember Fritz saying to me while he packed the car. "You'll thank me when you're driving on that piece of highway and wondering about the exact spot where that lunatic crashed into her."

He spoke to me as if ranting to an invisible audience, as if he'd forgotten how old I was, that certain things shouldn't be said.

Had he been right? Would I have spent my adolescence learning to drive cautiously by following the road where she had died, obsessively wondering where exactly the moment of impact had happened? I don't know. But leaving just didn't feel right, and Chicoutimi had felt wrong from the start.

It's there that everything was slowly stripped away – as if there was anything left of any consequence after mother's death. Even though the hole within me grew larger as we moved away from town, and even though, inwardly, I felt lighter and lighter, the body that trapped me became heavier and heavier, changing in ways for which I was unprepared, ripening from the inside out like a mango left to age under the sun.

It was a blue-collar town without much going on. They were still struggling to diversify after the closing down of the pulp mill in the Thirties. The town hadn't yet recovered from the loss of industry and generations upon generations knew only wood and paper, and were at a loss for some new way to live. It seemed to me that the air still smelled like sodden wood and glue. When we first moved there, I thought I could hear the ghostlike whistle of the factory; I imagined the dead were laid out on its concrete floor, asphyxiated by the vapours, that if you went in, you never came out. But every day I saw the fathers and mothers of my schoolmates return from their jobs and it seemed to me that they were more like *zombies* than I, walking dazed as if under a spell they were afraid to wake from, as if the mundane world in which they existed was everything they could desire.

For six months of the year they trudged through snow. There was a lot of drinking in the town. The pubs were lit up at night with red and blue lights, beckoning workers to stop in for just one more before they headed home. I wondered what it was like to be a girl here, thinking of myself in the abstract as I looked on, as I tried to convince myself that the ripening of my body was happening to somebody else. While other girls grew into their femininity, I was exiled from mine; it had been buried in the grave with my mother.

My father enrolled me in the school where he had been given a post as the music teacher. Tuition was free this way. A conservatory had been established in the town only a few years before to revitalize the economy. It was a private, Catholic, co-ed school built in grey brick, as sombre and dreary as everything else, as grey as the smoke spat out from the factory towers. The school was girded by a low brick wall the students used to sit on, waiting for their parents to pick them up, usually boys trying to act cool by smoking. Smoking was not allowed on school grounds. The boys got away with it by sitting on the low wall with their legs swung over the wall, their sneakered toes on the sidewalk. The sidewalk was public space: it gave them the right. The only girls out there were the loose girls. The ones intent on getting into trouble. And then there was me, trying to understand the meaning of trouble.

There wasn't much to do between letting the hole within me expand, and surviving my father's sullen silence. It was then that the piano became my escape. I'd had a few lessons before, mostly out of the house with a teacher in the neighbourhood who seemed always to be afraid of what my father might think. I assured her he wouldn't care how she taught as long as I didn't come home playing any false notes.

I learned slowly, without, at first, understanding the relationship between note and sound. I was taught to play directly from the Royal Conservatory of Canada notebooks with their pale pastel covers and abbreviated versions of classics from Bach to Rachmaninoff, with a few contemporary, early twentieth-century composers thrown into the mix to give the impression that the Conservatory was hip and up to date. It was that neighbourhood teacher who told me Claude Debussy had once said, "the music is between the notes", as she tried to force me to *emote, emote, emote*, while she shook her hands dramatically above the gleaming black of the piano body, her rows of jewelled bracelets offering their own offbeat syncopation next to the metronome. The more I found the emotional pulse of the pieces I was learning, the more the gap between sound and note widened. I learned to match the position of my fingers on the keyboard with the rounded notes on the staves of the sheet music, memorized the meaning of the Italian notations: *calendo, mezzo forte, pianissimo, allegretto, affretando, comodo*. These words seemed filled with a magic, alchemical power. As they appeared, they would let me know to quiet down the playing or to play moderately loudly or have me shift from very soft playing to a frenetic cadence that would be rounded out by passages at moderate speed, then, a little slower, *a little bit joyful*, as "allegretto" means in the Italian. I wondered about a world where these words had meaning, were used in everyday speech.

In the grey world of Chicoutimi, the notations on my sheet music gave me hope: they told me everything I needed to know about mood and tone, how to colour my playing when I could not reach my own pulse of life. They gave me access to the composer's emotional life when the door to mine had been shut.

The music was all I had left when Fritz continued my lessons by having me play in the school bands, which he directed. I sat to the side of the other instruments and provided the accompaniment, the start-up notes when everyone was fiddling around with their instruments, picking their noses, looking out of the window or knocking the sheets off the worn metal stands their parents had used decades before.

Commitment and talent was rare, but Fritz persevered, pretending that the children cared about what he was saying, pretending that he was teaching at the Conservatory, his real goal. He was creating a world in which to survive and he left me on the outside, looking in. The music was all that linked us.

Playing with every class band meant that I stayed after school every day and he didn't have to pay for a sitter. We ate take-out and rarely used the stove. In this way, we didn't have to remember we weren't hurrying home, me to set the table, Fritz to help my mother with the last-minute preparations. I suppose I looked too much like my mother or not enough like her. It was hard to tell.

We lived like the river rats I saw running along the side of Rivière Saguenay where the logs used to be left floating before being dragged out for mulching at the factory. Wet with fear we ran, *presto, presto,* away from each other, along the narrow strip of shore between the river and dry land, hoping that the despair in our dark eyes could not be seen by those who could make out our scraggly forms as we advanced in the darkness.

We wanted to be invisible and only the music provided a suitable cloak for our desolation. Behind the mellifluous notes of Chopin or Mozart, we could dissemble our grief and appear to be undertaking the journey through it towards wholeness. To the parents of the other students we became known as the music makers, my father and I, even though no sound flowed between us. The fact that we were both brown of skin was overlooked because we could entertain and give voice to the townspeople's emotions, a service they sorely needed. The closest anyone ever came to making a racist remark was to note that I was much lighter than my father, and it was assumed that my mother had been white and we let them think that they were right, that perhaps my mother had left us because the repercussions of a mixed marriage were just too much to handle in those days. Who could blame her, they seemed to say, as they looked at me with pity in their eyes. These weren't easy times. Down in the US there had been bombings and fires over such things. They didn't want any of that kind of trouble. And since neither my father nor I had any desire to explain our existence, or my mother's absence, it made it easier to play at believing that she might still be alive, that she had chosen to leave and might one day reappear.

It was there, in Chicoutimi, with all its quaint and wild nature, that my fascination with classical music took such a tyrannical hold. It took me onto a path that seemed to have no rhyme or reason – except that it held me when there seemed nothing to hold. My solace existed between the sheet music and my fingers, in the reverberation of the taut strings as the felt-covered hammers fell upon them in cacophonous syncopation. Trying to churn some semblance of music out of the barely-in-tune school piano was the peak of my attempts to seem alive while, within, I drifted on the currents of an emotional sea that had no language. When I had the piano all to myself, I worked on Mozart, Bach, and especially Chopin, my own personal holy trinity, until all I could hear was the sound of the drumming keys, my breathing, and the music. The noise of the other kids in school was like a fog beyond the music room, barely real in the world I was fashioning for myself.

"Geez, could you play any *louder*?"

It was Sébastien, a red-headed kid with freckles powdering the bridge of his aquiline nose and the upper reaches of his gaunt cheeks. He was one of the boys who hung out by the grey brick wall, smoking after school. I knew him from one of the upper school choirs my father led, except that in that class, he refused to sing and just sat at the back, watching, until Fritz let them all out for the day.

"It says *fortissimo*," I said, not looking up at Sébastien's string-bean frame as he made his way from the doorway to stand next to the piano.

"You don't always have to do what's written down." I could hear the smirk in his voice without looking up at him.

I shrugged, "That's what it says."

"Scoot over," he said, and pushed himself onto the piano bench.

"Hey…"

"Don't worry. I'm not staying long. Just overheard you clunking about in here and thought I'd give you some pointers."

"What would you know about anything?"

He looked me squarely in the eye. "A whole hell of a lot more than you, *ça c'est sûr*." His eyes were small grey ovals that reminded me of the cottontails of spring. He spoke the low, guttural French of the Québécois. I was uncomfortable; I had never been so close to a boy in my life. He smelled like cigarette smoke and stale beer laced with the homey scent of laundry detergent wafting out from his clothes.

"How long have you been in town, anyway?"

"Long enough," I shrugged diffidently, my shoulder brushing up against his as he inched me down the smooth surface of the wood bench until I stumbled to my feet and stood against the far side of the piano.

"Cheeky," he said as he flexed his fingers and started playing the piece I'd been practising. What he played sounded nothing like what I'd been working on. He played the piano as if he'd been born to it, with his heart and soul. The *fortes* sounded out like pounding drums, the *decrescendos* like wind flurries after fresh snowfall.

I watched from a safe distance. He'd closed his eyes and performed from memory, as if he'd been playing the piece forever. He was practised but honest in his playing. All of his youthful bravado fell away from his shoulders and he became new in front of my eyes, like a swan opening up its wings before flight. I was sorry when he was done. He remained poised over the piano, his fingers sitting lightly above the keys, letting the air around us reverberate with electricity. When he removed his hands from the piano and placed them on his thighs, I could see all the tough-guy pose return. His grey eyes lost their brilliance, the smirk returned. He cocked his head to the side and eyed me.

"How old are you anyway?"

"Too young for you," I ventured, copying a phrase I'd heard in a weekend matinee movie.

"How old is that?"

I ignored him and went about the business of picking up my things. I closed up the kid version of the opening to Beethoven's Fifth Symphony while feeling my ears turn red.

"You play really well," I mumbled.

"I know," he said arrogantly, as he stood as if to walk away from the piano and out of the classroom.

As he made his way to the door, I felt a neediness I hadn't experienced in the two years since my mother's death. I wanted him to stay even though he was several years older, one of the "bad" kids my father had warned me about. Was it him that held me in the trance or the music he'd played? I would never know. At that moment, all that mattered was that he was there and understood the world I lived in, that he lived in it himself.

"I'm thirteen," I lied, adding more than a year to my real age. I was taller than most kids in my class so I thought he might believe me.

Sébastien squinted at me as he kept walking backwards towards the door. "Thought so," he said, then turned around. "Well, kid, I'll see ya around."

At dinner that night, while we ate lukewarm Chinese food, I told my father about Sébastien.

"Not surprising," Fritz said.

"But he doesn't do anything in band practice."

"That's why," my father said. "Feels he's too good for us."

Feels he's too good for *you*, I corrected my father in my mind. "Well, he played for me."

My father's jawline grew taut. "You stay away from that kid, Cathie. He's nothing but trouble."

"You always think you know everything."

"Cat," my father said, as he put down the container of sweet and sour chicken he was eating from with a fork, "I'm your father and I'm telling you what I know. That kid is trouble, *tu comprends?*" His voice was rising. "Just stay away from him."

Fritz stared at me over the table filled with Styrofoam and paper containers. The food smells were nauseating. We'd bought things that didn't go together, pickled pork and beef chow mein, sweet and sour chicken and lemon prawns. For a moment I had a vision of my mother looking down on us wondering how long it would take us to poison ourselves to death. I'd learned in the last two years to let my father have his way or, at least, to let him think he had his way, so that I could retain my freedom. I just looked back into his eyes until he looked away. He always looked away. I always knew he would lose the staring game because he hadn't gotten over what he saw when he looked at me for too long. "Just do as I say," he muttered between bites of sticky chicken. "Do as I say."

"Yes," I said. By then, I had stopped calling my father "Dad" for over a year and he hadn't seemed to notice. I thought of him as a man who used to be my father, who used to be my mother's husband. Now he was just a man who was in charge of me until I could be in charge of myself. In my mind I called him by his formal name, Fritz, as his mother and father would have called him when he was growing up in their house, as I was growing up in his.

Of course, I didn't stay away from Sébastien. The pull I'd felt when he'd left the classroom, combined with my father's prohibition was all I needed to become intoxicated with the desire to see him again and again, as much as possible, until I became a constant fixture at the wall of boys and suspect girls, standing there awkwardly in the middle of winter as we watched our breath freeze in the air, in my knee-length blue-jay coloured parka and cable knit hat with the fuzzy fist of a pom-pom on its crown.

The other boys laughed the first time I showed up.

"Bring your mascot, Seb?" one of them said.

"Shut up," Sébastien replied and went on smoking his cigarette.

Eventually, when I came to the wall, they took to moving away and leaving us alone.

It was an odd pairing. Anyone looking at us would have

thought so. Here I was, an almond-skinned pre-teen girl dressed in blue with a tall boy with bright red hair, who preferred his hands to chap and freeze in the wintry air than to lose an ounce of coolness by wearing gloves, doing something that looked vaguely like courting. When I knew him, Sébastien was fifteen years old.

The time I spent on the wall inhaling second-hand smoke was as silent as the time I spent in company of my father. Somehow, though, it seemed full.

We spoke monosyllabically:

"How you feelin'?"

"Ya know."

"Yeah."

"Yeah."

Anyone overhearing us would have thought we were fools. But between each nonsensical word there was a fullness, like the music we were used to playing for each other. Everything was contained in the in-between.

"I'm not twelve."

"I know."

"I'm only eleven."

"Don't let the rest of the guys on the wall know. I told them you were fifteen."

"Fifteen?"

"Yeah," he shrugged, "small for your age." He gave me a lopsided grin as smoke trailed out of his mouth. "Piano free?"

"I think so."

"Let's go play a thing or two."

We played the piano, sometimes together, sometimes separately, while the other listened, when the teachers were having their meetings after school or cleaning their homerooms.

Sébastien's mother was the dance instructor at the school. She had been a lead dancer with the Royal Winnipeg Ballet long before he was born, long before his father had them move to Chicoutimi in anticipation of the revitalization of the town where he'd grown up. Sébastien was supposed to go to the Conservatory to study the piano after graduating from high school. His mother was petite, graceful, but silent as a pebble. Silent like my father. Sometimes she appeared at the door to the classroom as we played, hovering like a ghost. The first time she did this, I thought it was my mother and I stopped playing.

"Who's there?" I asked.

Sébastien turned around. "Oh, I guess you don't take dance class." I shook my head. "That's my mother."

She stepped into the light, hesitated and said, "Sorry to interrupt but it's time to go home."

"Yeah, *Manman*," Sébastien replied, rolling his eyes at me dramatically. "Gotta go, squirt. I've got chemistry homework to do."

He followed his mother out and I waited for Fritz to appear. He'd relaxed a bit after finding out Sébastien's mother was on the staff. It was a large school after all; he couldn't be expected to know everyone. It was just one more thing on the long list of things we chose not to speak about. But at least I had a friend of my own. Our silences were not so ponderous. Until, that is, the day Sébastien disappeared.

At the time, it seemed that his disappearance happened suddenly but now that I look back, I can see that it was the result of a slow accretion. I could hardly have been expected to see beyond the surface of my own troubles even though I wished, once he was gone, that I had. *Poco a poco*, is the phrase in Italian. Little by little. *Calando.* Quietening. As when snow falls before first light when the city is quiet. *Diminuendo.* Dwindling. Becoming softer. The barely audible murmur of a beating heart as it slows, then stops, never to be heard from again.

He'd held my hands in his, once. It was the closest we ever got to any kind of physical intimacy. He was trying to warm my hands between his own but his were just as cold.

"Squirt," he'd said, "you've got to get a life."

"I've got a life," I'd said defiantly, not wanting him to stop holding my hands. I hadn't been touched like this in over a year. I'd been shoved and pushed around at recess by classmates. I'd been brushed against by the lockers. I'd had teachers touch me lightly on the tip of my shoulders as they glanced at my work. Fritz had nudged my feet once when I'd fallen asleep in front of the television at the house. How I craved touch, something beyond the comforting feel of the smooth piano keys, something animate, that made me come alive. I suppose now that what I had been feeling was the first stirrings of love – a crush, puppy love?

A cigarette dangled from his lips, the ash falling dead on the brittle grey brick, the tip glowing faint then bright red as he sucked on it. I was looking into the grey flint of his eyes as he concentrated on warming my hands and then there was a scream from behind the school, high pitched, girlish. A scream, then a giggle, then the boisterous yells of boys on the rampage. Then the scream, again, this time shrill, without laughter. Sébastien dropped my hands.

"Holy shit," he said, then went running in the direction of the screaming.

I followed.

A parking lot filled the space behind the school. Beyond it there was a park the school was allowed to use for recess. We came running around the edge of the school where the parking lot began and there, against the far wall of the school, a girl Sébastien's age was being pinned to the brick by a pack of five or six boys. Some younger kids looked on from a distance, not knowing what to do.

It was hard to tell from where we were standing what was going on but then one of the boys stepped away. The one who had called me a mascot some months ago. He saw us standing there and walked past us.

"What's going on?" Sébastien asked.

The boy glanced at me then looked away. "You don't want to know." He was still walking when he said to Sébastien over his shoulder, "You should get her out of here."

I took a step forward, then another. *Piano. Piano. Lento. Presto.* At the ready to run forward, backward. I didn't know what would happen next.

The girl was fighting them now. Her screams had become grunts and as the boys' hands flew over her body, her clothes tore, revealing stretches of creamy pink skin. I saw the softness of her belly, then a thigh.

"What are they doing?"

"I should get you out of here."

Then it dawned on me. Of course. They were trying to make her a loose girl. As if it wasn't enough that she'd acquired a reputation from smoking at the wall after school and skipping math to hang out in the girl's john where the upper school girls talked about which teacher they'd most like to make. Fritz came up the most in those discussions. He was branded "most doable" – other phrases were used but I didn't repeat them. When the boys were involved, Sébastien's mother also came up. We didn't discuss it. They were speaking about our *parents* after all. The girl's hands were crossed against her chest. One of the boys held them there and her bright white fingers hung limply against his. They looked like strange, broken bird's wings from a distance.

I thought about Sébastien holding my hands only minutes before.

"Shouldn't you help her?" I asked, knowing without knowing that I should not venture into the fray. I realized that I was just like the girl there in front of us, that what they were doing to her they could just as well be doing to me.

The girl started to laugh suddenly. It was a hysterical, almost maniacal laughter, the kind you hear when people have had too much to drink.

"Get your dad, squirt," Sébastien said, dropping his cigarette.

Just as Sébastien advanced towards the girl, I felt it, the hand going up between her thighs, the fingers jabbing between the folds of her flesh, her giddy laughter and fear, the breaking pull of her heart as she lay there, against the wall, exposed and humiliated, terrified of what might come next. I was too shocked to run for Fritz as he'd told me to do. Too stunned to move.

I saw a million dots of light surrounding her and the boys, each of them outlined in a halo of colours, most of them dark, greenish and blue, muddied colours. Hers was a bright orange and yellow. Whatever she was feeling, I was feeling it too and I started to cry, right there, on the spot. My heart beating very quickly – *affrettando, accelerando*. The girl looked in my direction and her eyes were wild. I felt the grasp of fear bottled at her throat beneath a boy's sweaty, heavy hand. *We would never get away*, her eyes seemed to say. *We would never get away*.

I was screaming and Sébastien was reaching her, the cigarette he hadn't finished smoking against the ground where he had thrown it. The door of the school swung open on its creaking steel hinges and it was my father holding a wooden baseball bat in his hand, the kind that you can't find any more, heavy and harmful. Fritz stared at me as if he had never seen me before.

"What's going on? Why are you screaming? They said a girl…"

I pointed to the boys against the wall, to the girl shivering half-naked between their many hands. Sébastien had just reached them, his hands extended towards her and it was difficult to tell whether he was reaching in to save her or to harm her.

My father ran towards the mêlée and I ran behind. He swung the bat over his head to scare the boys and they dispersed like colts, except for Sébastien who was still intent on reaching the girl and then the bat fell and afterwards it was all a blur, Sébastien slumping down on his knees then falling over sideways. The girl screaming and holding on to herself, her clothes torn, her face turned to the brick of the wall. The bat had fallen against the broadness of Sébastien's shoulders and knocked him out. I felt the burn of the bat against his shoulder blades as if against my own and then everything went black.

When I came to, the world was filled with light. It streamed from people's bodies like neon, transfiguring them from head to toe. It didn't take me long to realize that the colours I saw around them told me something about their states of mind. Yellow for instability and destruction; red for anger and homelessness; blue for higher states of consciousness. The colour didn't match people's social status as you might have thought. A man in the street could just as well be holy as a hospital orderly could be dangerous. Then the fevers started.

I didn't see anyone from school for days. My father would sit by my bed and read the paper. Once, as he read, I thought I saw headlines concerning what had happened. There was a headline that read like this: "High school chemistry genius charged with rape." All this seemed like a dream, however. I woke and fell asleep like a child, my rhythms my own, and thought I'd imagined everything from the headlines to Fritz sitting by the bed, something I never thought it possible for him to do.

Then, finally, some time later, how much later I was not sure,

I woke up free of fever and sat up in bed. There was Fritz. He was reading the paper.

"You're awake," he said, not smiling.

I nodded. "Is it true?" I asked.

"Is what true?"

"Sébastien…" my voice trailed off.

"Yes." He stroked his chin. "Yes, it's true."

I couldn't believe his coldness, "But he didn't commit any rape…" This was a boy I knew, someone we both knew. "He was trying to *help* her. I was there. He has just gotten to her when you came out of the school."

I started to cry even though tears were the last thing I wanted Fritz to see from me. I was tired even though I'd been sleeping for what seemed like weeks. These things seemed impossible. Fritz's eyes lit up with uncertainty and he bent forward in his chair.

"What are you saying?"

"I'm saying that I was there," my voice became high-pitched. I was almost screaming. "I'm saying that you should have talked to me first!" I was spluttering, my nose thick with mucous, my mouth filled with salty spit.

Fritz slumped back into his chair, folded the paper, "You were ill."

He scratched his nose absentmindedly as if trying to recall that day more clearly. I could tell from his startled expression that he had seen everything differently when coming out into the schoolyard waving the bat. By the time he'd come out, Sébastien had reached the girl. Someone who hadn't seen what had been going on might have assumed he'd been there from the start, if they didn't know him like I did, if they were a bad judge of character.

"*Merde*," I said, wiping at my mouth as I uttered a profanity I'd never used before, "bunch of idiots," I said, referring to the adults in the school, and to Fritz, "you hung him out to dry!"

"Watch your language, young lady," Fritz said. "We did no such thing. He was being investigated, along with the others."

"I bet," I said. "I just bet."

"Things have got to change, Catherine," Fritz sighed, ignoring what I'd said. "You're turning into your mother. I don't know what to do with you."

I stared at him. What could he mean? The halo of light around his body was flowing from red to yellow and back again.

"I've decided," he looked at me and paused, then looked away and continued, "I've decided to send you away."

There was nothing I could say. My mind was confused. The lights all around me were very bright. I closed my eyes.

"Far away from here," he continued.

Goddamn you, I thought, *goddamn you*.

By the time I made it back to school, I had lost three weeks. By that time, it had been announced over the PA that, because of the scandal, the high school would close and everyone would be sent to neighbouring schools from grades nine through twelve. Sébastien was already gone and so was the girl from the wall. There was a lot of whispering as people shuffled down the halls. A substitute teacher replaced Sébastien's mother.

When I went out to the wall to find him after school, hoping the headlines were wrong, there was no one there except for the boy who'd called me a mascot that first time. He was just sitting there, thinking, not even smoking a cigarette.

"What do you want?" he asked.

"I'm looking for Sébastien."

"Too late, Mascot."

"What do you mean?"

"Killed himself."

"What?"

"Well, they're saying it was an accident… asphyxiation from a chemistry experiment, but the guy knew what he was doing. He fucking killed himself."

I didn't know what to say. Everything was falling apart, again. Everyone was disappearing.

"Is there going to be a funeral?"

"*Maudit*. Christ. How the hell should I know?"

I left the boy on the wall and went home. There was nothing else to do.

One day, three months after the scandals that had closed down the high school, a small red suitcase sat waiting for me on the other side of the front door. I stepped into the house, home from school, and glanced at the suitcase. I held my breath. Fritz came out of the kitchen and walked slowly towards me. I remember that the lights weren't on, as if he'd been sitting in the dark measuring out the size of his penance until he heard the turning of my key in the lock. He moved towards me until he was towering above me. I was still holding the keys in my hand, apprehensive. By the time he was upon me, I could no longer see the features of his face and when the words came out of his mouth, they were descending from a stranger.

"I'm sending you back to the island," he said.

"What?"

"I'm sending you away."

I threw the keys to the ground and they bounced up from the linoleum and skidded across its smooth surface until they were arrested by the stubby toe of Fritz's boots. "I'm not going!" I screamed.

Fritz stood before me, unmoved. Even though I could not make out his face, I could hear him breathing over me. His breath smelled of onions and peppers and I thought, *How dare he be able to eat at a time like this!* I felt the same disgust for my father that I had felt the day of my mother's funeral when I was left behind to cry alone.

"No discussion," the voice floating above me said dispassionately. "Your Aunt Ruth will be taking you. You remember her, don't you?"

I didn't then, not right away. I shook my head.

Fritz sighed.

"Go through your room and see if there's anything else you might want."

I remember walking around Fritz. I went to my room and cried, sitting on the edge of the bed as if all I knew of life was tears. Then, something within me hardened, and the crying stopped. I felt the hardness accumulate in my centre as if the tears left unshed had gathered themselves up into a large piece of crystal and dropped down into my stomach cavity. The weight steadied me as I ran my fingers over the odds and ends on the top of my desk and bureau. I felt suddenly old, the same way I had felt the night Fritz had told me my mother had died. My body seemed too small for the knowledge now stored within it.

I left everything behind save for a small black and white photograph of my mother in a cinched dress and wide skirt covering her thin legs. A chubby cherub, I am sitting on her knee, my hands reaching out towards the person taking the photograph I imagine must have been my father. It's a memory of another, distant time. I slip the frame into a coat pocket and trudge down the stairs not wanting Fritz to see it. He doesn't say anything as I move past him and take the heavy suitcase with both my hands. What I really want to do is to kick him in the shins but I do my best not to touch him. All I feel is the terrifying force of unspent violence building up in me.

Years later, my husband, Sam, suggests that I must have thought that Fritz would have been unmoved even by a show of violence, that I didn't feel convinced enough of his humanity to even attempt some kind of retaliation. I pondered this for a while and concluded that what I had really been afraid of in that moment was that if I made any show of anger, I would have lost everything that was left to me, that one of us would have broken in the process. I think, looking back, I saw myself and my father as two fragile goblets afraid to be filled with anything so delicate as love again. We did our best not to brush up against anything that might break us, as her disappearance nearly did, even though it meant that we could never bridge the growing gap between us.

Remembering 1980, Port-au-Prince, Haiti

At eleven, I greeted my native land with rage. It answered me with despair. It threw back on me my sorrow, heaped me with disdain and blame. In my mourning, I replied with wide-eyed indifference. I heaped upon her abuse and she responded with calm generosity. I tried to flee from her and she offered me her shadows in which to rest.

I didn't have much to say to Tatie Ruth when I arrived and for quite a time thereafter. She smiled at me across the breakfast table as her cook and maid laid out the table with dishes and plates full of food. It seemed to me that there was too much abundance in my aunt's house and at first I resented her for it. Hers was quite a contrast to the house I had lived in with my father, stripped of my mother's presence, with its white walls and white curtains, the spare furnishings in the small rooms. Tatie Ruth's house was alive with wind and bursting with colour: she kept many of her doors and windows open so that the curtains flapped like the wings of birds insinuating thoughts of freedom and ease in my mind that still, somehow, I could not trust. It took me a time to realize that I believed that sinking into Tatie Ruth's joyful, peaceful space, was to betray my mother's memory and my father's pain, even though on a conscious level, I wanted nothing more than to escape both.

Ruth was insightful even though at that time I thought of her only as a dimwitted, meddling old woman who would not know grief if it hit her square in the nose. I was more like my father than I wanted to admit: I imagined that only I bore the brunt of the full weight of loss, and in my smallness could not imagine that others had known my mother longer and perhaps more deeply than I, and that they mourned her passing with the same unrelenting emptiness. The truth was that Ruth knew the ways of the heart and led me out of myself by setting me in front of her piano early in the morning and after school, pushing me to learn increasingly difficult pieces as I retreated from her and her touch. It was with her that I learned to appreciate Chopin, both for his famed frailty and for his temerity of heart. Each piece seemed to read my emotions and gave me the outlet I needed to express what I could not say in words or express in tears. The piano, Chopin's piano, both effeminate and strong, became my voice box and through it I communicated my loathing and my fear, banging down on the keys with such force that framed photographs Tatie Ruth had set on top of the baby grand would shake and skid as I played. I felt the strings tremor beneath my touch as the small hammers hit them one by one in quick succession. The tremors felt like ropes attached to the valves of my heart, opening and closing them against my will, as if I were a marionette. The music cleansed my soul and readied me for new life at a time when I had no reason to believe that there could be one, when, indeed, I did not want to go on.

On days when I was not at the piano or in school, Tatie Ruth took me into the town in her truck. I sat in the flatbed gripping its smooth but rusting metal sides and all I could do as we careened down the rugged roads was concentrate on my body's centre of gravity as it was thrown from side to side. Tatie Ruth would check on me from time to time, laughing at my furrowed brow, letting the driver know when he should slow down. He looked back at me in the rearview mirror, showed his gums, and went on down the roads as if I were simply a sack of potatoes. These times were fun even though what I saw along the way was distressing, the poor walking without shoes at the sides of the road, babies in sacklike clothing covering their ballooned stomachs. There was always a thickness in the air, even on the brightest days, a weight that hung over everyone that made me feel that I was joined in my mourning. My grief made me feel close to people I did not know and I often stopped to speak to the women in the markets where we shopped, after parking the red truck down the road and walking with our mesh bags to the stalls.

The market women were weary but proud and strong, and they cluck-clucked over me like hens, advising me on how I should wear my hair, criticizing the fact that I was always in blue jeans rather than a polite skirt or dress, asking Tatie what she was doing with me that I looked so ragged. They laughed and I laughed with them, though I did not say much in these exchanges. I looked up to these women and allowed them to mother me in a way that I could not allow Ruth.

They were generous women, all of them, even though they were of a different class and background; many of them had lost children and were doing all they could to subsist and keep the rest of their broods alive. They gave me treats from their trays and packets of tissue paper – for when my tears would come, they said, when Tatie Ruth explained my mother's passing. They gave more than they could afford to give. It was the one day of the week I forgot to think about what I had lost. I was completely taken by these women and their movements of hands and hips. I remember returning to Tatie Ruth's house with cheeks aching from smiling, as if these were muscles whose use I had just regained.

Then, there were the days when I blundered through the hours, with no sense of a future and even less of a present. I could hardly breathe from the effort of trying to sustain the illusion of being able to turn back time.

Between each stolen breath, there was the music filling in the spaces of my longing, giving me weight when I needed to be weighted down, reprieving me from desolation when I'd been lost too long wandering in a featureless desert. The more I saw of the life around me, the more I realized my struggle was just a small fragment of the whole, that my suffering did not exist in isolation, but as part of a greater pool of life.

On the nights I lay in bed crying, unable to sleep, unable to find comfort in my everyday existence, Ruth would quietly enter my room and pray over me until I fell asleep. They were prayers I had never heard before. One day, she taught me one. She said it would keep me safe when I thought I was alone in the world, that it would remind me of a greater purpose to be realized in the years to come that I could hardly begin to imagine.

She taught me to pray to the archangels. First, we prayed to Michael and imagined him materializing on our right side, bringing us messages from God; then we prayed to Gabriel and imagined him on our left, giving us strength to believe in ourselves and to stay on our path; then we prayed to Raphael and imagined his healing hand at our backs, keeping us safe from harm; and then we prayed to the light of Uriel lighting our way before us. When we felt encircled by the web of angelic powers, then we called upon the Shekina – what Ruth called God's feminine power – to let her benevolent light descend from above our heads and protect us with tender love, giving our minds and bodies peace. The prayer always left me feeling quiet and safe, as if somewhere beyond was a force that would connect me to my mother, wherever she was, a force that was not as cruel as I imagined, that would unveil heartbreak as a different reality in the fullness of time. In spite of myself, within weeks of my arrival, Haiti broke my heart and broke me open. There would be no turning back.

When I told Sam about this time in my life, about the prayer, he had laughed out loud.

"Is your Aunt Ruth Jewish?" he'd asked.

"I don't think so," I'd replied, blank-faced.

"That's a Jewish prayer," Sam said, letting his long curling hair cascade across his face as he guffawed with abandon.

"Is it?"

I laughed too.

It hadn't taken long, of course, for Samuel to reveal that he was Jewish when we'd first met.

I had been contemplating the beauty of a Schubert piece in the university cafeteria, poring over a composition from a daily musical journal, my brow furrowed with admiration, my sharpened pencil held tightly between the fingers of my right hand when a bushy-haired man with eyes the colour of cut emeralds loomed over me, grinning. His shadow fell across the score I had laid out across the white formica where I had set up shop. I was not impressed by the interruption, though the green of his eyes startled me, breaking into the stream of notes I was listening to in the quiet of my mind while all around me dishes and utensils clanged. I scowled up into his smiling face. This was the first time I had set eyes on Sam.

"Yes," I asked curtly. "What is it?"

"Are you a musician?"

Was he daft? I opened the hand holding the pencil and gestured at the score in front of me, as if to say, of course, isn't it obvious? He didn't miss a beat.

"Of course. That's what I thought. Piano?" He said the last word as if he already knew me. It was a large school but small in other ways. I was known for ignoring everyone else in public spaces in favour of my music.

"What is it you want?" I asked. I had never been long on charm and didn't feel the need to ingratiate myself to a bushy-haired stranger, however deep the green of his eyes.

Sam took this as his cue to sit down. "Well," he said, "I'm a history student and I've been watching you here every day for a while and I have a question to ask you, if you don't mind."

Of course I minded. The Schubert melody had completely evaporated. "What do you study exactly?" I asked with unmasked annoyance.

"The Jewish Question," he replied without hesitation.

This piqued my interest as the thin man before me, whose chest had yet to fill out, whose joints were still larger than the muscles that would eventually grow to match them, looked – well, to my mind – very, very white.

"What do you mean... what Jewish Question?"

"Well, you know, I'm trying to trace the links between different groups of Jews, people from varying genetic trees, you might say, from North Africa to Palestine, from Russia to Iowa – right here." He laid a proud hand across his chest.

Then, he bent across the music sheets towards me. "I have to apologize before asking you this." He cleared his throat. "I don't want you to think I'm a lunatic or anything but, well, are you Jewish?"

It was the funniest question I had ever been asked and it set me laughing, rocking backwards into my chair, dropping my pencil as I did so. It clattered to the linoleum floor and the tables around us stopped their chatter to stare at me, the olive-skinned girl who never engaged in social conversation, laughing like a hyena at something a raven-haired, green-eyed boy had just said to her.

"No," I said, once I had recovered from the surprise of the question. "At least, I don't think so."

"I thought so. You're not sure, are you?"

I wiped away tears from the corners of my eyes. "Why did you ask me such a question?"

"I have relatives in North Africa who look just like you, and look," he opened a book he had been carrying under his arm, "you look a bit like these women."

It was a book about the Jews of Ethiopia who had been relocated to Israel by the French and when I looked down it was to take in a grainy black and white photograph of the faces of four women who could very well have been mirrors of Tatie Ruth. The same high cheekbones, the lips as long as they were wide, the lower lip protruding outwards like rose petals, the upper lip folded in the middle to leave the impression of a tear below the nostrils. The noses had high bridges – what used to be called Roman noses and then Semitic – the opposite of fine or flat, seemingly incongruous for people of African descent, although (I knew this much) most Ethiopian Jews were not necessarily kin to their Jewish counterparts in other parts of the world, but converts.

I looked up into Sam's emerald eyes, the impish grin sloping to the right of his face, the perfect, narrow teeth, and a look that I could only describe as devoid of any malice, and told him a truth I had never told anyone.

"Could be," I said. "Rumour has it that there is Jewish blood on my father's side... but not from Africa." I pushed back the faces of these forbears across the table towards him as if pushing back the tide of the ocean that must have divided our ancestors long ago. "They came from Syria. There's also some doubt as to whether I'm his natural child. And this," I tapped the high bridge of my nose, "deviated septum," I added, "not natural."

He looked crestfallen. "Really?" He looked down at the book. "I was so sure. I thought for sure she's got to be..." He stroked his stubble, "Well, doesn't matter." He put out a hand for me to shake, "I'm Samuel. It's good to meet you."

I took his hand in mine. I remember still how surprised I was at the softness of his skin, the delicate bone structure beneath, the handshake firm but not strong, the nails clipped and clean.

"Catherine," I said, and then, letting go of his hand, I looked away from him to retrieve my pencil, intent on returning to my notations, to the sheet music before me, to my private, ecstatic world of studying things born long ago.

This initial conversation turned out to be the thread that would hold us together, even when it seemed that the ship had gone down and there was nothing left to hold on to. We both had an insatiable desire to understand our pasts so we could better know ourselves. At the moment of our meeting, however, each of us thought we were doing what we were meant to do, studying and learning, unaware really of how the past was still active within us. We were passive observers but our meeting was to change all that. As death had altered the landscape of my life so long ago, so now the first stirrings of love were to alter the terrain of my future.

Sam set me to asking questions about who I was or thought myself to be: who was Fritz and his family? Why did they silence so many aspects of their lives, my mother chief among them? I liked that he asked these questions even though I seldom had adequate answers; he seemed different even if, in the end, we turned out to be more alike than not. I liked that there were things to talk about other than my music, or my father – all the things I obsessed about in private. Samuel had his own obsessions and he shared them, liberally.

One of them was trying to understand how Sephardic and Ashkenazi Jews were connected. Another was to follow the thread of forbidden mystical practices through the cultural and spiritual beliefs of Jewry. He was fascinated when I told him about the divination practices in *vodou*, certain that there lay a connection there, somehow, between disparate peoples and the lands they were forced to flee to as their own sacred lands were taken over or desecrated in the name of foreign gods.

We shared the dream of escaping the Americas and when the opportunity came for me to study in France six years later, he followed, transferring his Ph. D. studies to one of the branches of the Université de Paris. We settled in the Jewish quarter, *le Marais*, an area that satisfied Sam's historical curiosities and my need to be hemmed in by community. It was in our wanderings of these cobbled streets that we discovered each other more intimately.

Early on he had discovered a poem by Prévert about those streets and it seemed to echo a suffering in Sam I had never really understood, rooted in a faraway time. He recited it so often that we used to walk sometimes and take turns in reciting the lines.

"*On the loveliest rose of the Street of Rose Trees/ Her name was Sarah/ or Rachel/ and her father was a cap maker/ or a furrier/ and he really liked salt herring,*" Sam would recite.

"*…and all we know of her,*" I continued.

"*…is that the king of Sicily loved her,*" Sam would nod. "*When he whistled through his fingers/ the window opened up there where she lived/ but never again will she open the window.*"

"*…the door of a sealed train…*"

"*…shut her in for good/ And the sun tries to forget these things…*"

"*…but it's no use….*"

"Prévert 1946," Sam would say, looking up at the narrow windows of the short stone-hewed buildings in our neighbourhood.

"I know."

"I know you know."

"I'm glad we live here."

"I am too."

"I'm glad you wanted to live in the Troisième."

"I find myself here too."

"I know."

We would stand in the narrow streets and listen to the noise of the cars moving quickly past us, to the sounds of spoons stirring sugar in cups of dense coffee, to the sounds of laughter and sighs, and the occasional pounding of disco beats emanating from the gay bars dotting the area.

Eight years later, I was sad when we began to drift apart, wishing for the simplicity of our walks as I struggled to become more masterful at the piano and the impresario Edouard Le Marin took over my life.

"Do you remember when we met?" Sam asked me once, some years after we'd made the move to France.

"Of course," I'd said, not looking at him, my mind on other things.

"What did you think I did?" he'd asked.

I stopped whatever I was doing long enough to think about it, "What a strange question."

"Really, what did you think?"

I looked over at Sam, the muscles of his face slack, an innocent look in his eye.

Since the beginning, what had made Sam different from all the men I had met since Sébastien, from all the Edouards who would cross my path, and especially from my father, was that Sam knew how to stand in the middle of my storms and how to wait them out. Sam was all about the paths that lead us to the present. He firmly believed that the future would take care of itself.

I looked at him then, intently, all of him, from his open face and bushy head of hair down to his narrow frame, long arms and legs and hands so expressive and full of character that they reminded me of Rodin sculptures.

"I thought," I'd said, "I thought you were a thief, with pretty hands."

"You didn't," Sam replied softly, smiling.

"Yes," I said, allowing him in for a moment before returning to my music, "I did."

It was true. The moment that Sam had walked into my life, those many years ago, I knew he had the capacity to steal my heart.

What was also true was that I was afraid of this quality in Sam, the power he had to create storms within me that would leave me unscathed, breathless for more.

March 10, 2004, Le Marais, Paris, France

How did Noah know he would survive the flood? Why did he trust a God who had already proven so fallible? Hadn't He created each of them in His own image and then sought to rid the earth of a creation that had become too evil to behold? This is what the Bible says, but what did Noah think *then* as he fulfilled the moments of a history yet to be written?

The truth is Noah didn't know he would survive. After the flood, he got drunk, stripped naked and embarrassed his youngest son, Canaan, his grandson really – there are different versions of the story – who sought to protect him from shame. Canaan didn't get much for his trouble. Noah cursed him and all his progeny. Isn't it curious that he cursed his own son in the name of the God of Shem, the God of Japhet? Shem's God. Japhet's God. Had he forsaken God already? Had he cursed Canaan because he no longer believed? This is what I want to know.

The part that gets me is that once firm land had been found, and the belly of the arc emptied, the altar to God made, and the covenant of the rainbow sign accomplished, Noah's only thought was to plant the first vine and make himself some wine so that he could get completely stone drunk. He'd been out navigating the dark seas as all living things died around him, while the whole earth seemed to rot from the inside out, dreaming of that day when he wouldn't have to be responsible for all the remaining things on earth, when he could literally lose his mind.

This must have been the only way Noah could tell that he was still alive: the only way he knew how to bury the sheer terror his God had subjected him to while he built the arc.

He must have thought they were all doomed, especially when he saw the waters rise and waves crash onto what were once the earth's shores, wiping out everything in their wake. There was no guarantee that the boat would be strong enough or that the animals he took on board would survive along with himself and his wife and their children.

What was the name of Noah's wife? That's a detail I can't remember from the story my mother used to read me or the version they taught us in catechism school. No one remembers anyway. It's beside the point. In such stories of heroism, women always are.

Noah must have been good with detail: he built the arc exactly the width and height and depth he was instructed and filled it with all the living things his God wanted to survive. Was he already doubting as he brought hammer to wood? What must he have thought when he heard that big voice booming down at him from the blue heavens? Did his wife and sons think he was losing his mind as he collected his two by fours and set them to work on the largest boat ever built? They must all have been relieved when they smelled the scent of rain in the wind. But how could they account for the voice in their father's head that none of them could hear? How could Noah?

For me, this is the point: Noah got good and drunk when it was all over. He needed to let go of all that exactitude, of the order of things. Getting drunk allowed his mind to overflow and let the visions of annihilation ebb away. That kind of destruction gnaws away a part of your soul and then takes up residence in the hole it's eaten.

I believe Noah got drunk more than once, that he was the world's first alcoholic, giving people like my mother, rest her soul, a God-sanctioned precursor for their addictions. That's what you get for trusting God. Noah's goodness got eaten up while he was trying to save the world. What relief he must have felt when he sent that dove away the third time and she didn't come back. As she disappeared, he might have thought of all the spirits he had witnessed howling as they departed the flooded earth.

When my mother read me the story, I would imagine Noah at the helm of his ship overwhelmed by the stink of the dead, the rotting vegetation. It must have been dark as the rain fell in torrents all those days, and souls crowded the sky as they returned to their maker. He must have felt relief that the ordeal was coming to an end and then felt the weight of a rage he'd been carrying over the unfairness of what he'd been asked to do. He gave up his God to his sons, and then cursed the one who had tried to save him from himself as he sat around naked and drunk, sheltered only by the skin of the first tent he'd been able to pitch on solid ground.

I bet that son was the first wandering Jew in the new world Noah had helped God to birth: cursed by his father and flung out into the world to be a slave to his brothers, all for reminding Noah of his all too human frailty. What kind of vanity allows a father to doom his child? What kind of hardening of the soul could result in such callousness? Did Canaan ever forgive Noah's weakness or did he become weak like a fruit from a diseased tree? I don't remember enough of the story to know. I remember only the fear instilled in Sunday school when they told us that these stories were supposed to prepare us for life. My mother's take was different. She allowed that some of the stories of the Bible were fiction. Any good story had a point for her and you could tell what she preferred you to believe from the way she retold it.

I used to think mother was not quite right. I remember the way she smelled of sweet wine as if she'd been in church all day receiving catechism. It's only since college that I know that she was partly right, that she was like the Talmudic scholars who sit in their long robes and tall hats of learning, reading and rereading the early interpretations, backs bent over the aged reproductions as they sway back and forth still attempting to break the codes of the first scribes.

And what of Job? Job, the eternal believer, the fool who would not renounce a God who let him be tortured and tempted by evil in order to satisfy His ego. Job is another Biblical figure I can't figure out. Sure, I know there was supposed to be more to it than that, that Job was supposed to be an example for all of us too weak to take in the harshness of the world. *See*, they told you in Catholic grade school, *Job sat there and took it all. Why can't you?* If Job could sit up there like a king on a pile of dung, surely you could take a little nap and give everyone else a rest. If you ask me, Job was the original martyr. After all, even Jung had his doubts when he analysed the story and came to the conclusion that it was the account not of Job's testing, but of God's own testing.

God failed, by the way. That's what Jung finally had to conclude: Job's faith was greater than that of the God who created him.

Like Noah, Job had that large voice booming in his ear, but he didn't seem to worry about its source. Unlike Noah, he didn't curse any of his children for his own weaknesses; he even made offerings to God on their behalf in case they had had even the glimmer of an inappropriate thought. What made it possible for Job to sit there smiling on a pile of shit, with scales on his body and suppurating wounds? This I would like to know. I wouldn't be smiling if I'd lost everything, lost it all for a God who didn't even believe in his own rules. And where was that voice today? Why had it gone silent? Or had it?

I worry away at these thoughts because I want to keep the memory of yesterday at bay, my swollen hand the only evidence of the fight between Sam and I, my fingers still moving as if the injury won't keep me from playing my beloved piano again. In just a few moments of grief and jealousy, the career as a soloist I'd worked so hard for has evaporated.

Yesterday's concert had been the first of a series that would have taken me to Prague, Brussels, Buchendorf, London, perhaps even back to America. It had been a beautiful night. I kept my eyes closed as I played:

I hear the syncopation of my short nails dancing their way across the keys, slipping effortlessly between chords, between the black and the ivory, up and down. There is nothing in the world like this. I feel the bones of my slender fingers as they stretch to reach for the trills and sudden movements in Chopin's *Études*, a sequence I had longed to play like this, ever since I was a small child taking lessons from Ruth in the comfortable setting of homes lining the high mountain road. While I trained, down below, Port-au-Prince swelled in the heat and exhaust fumes and impoverished bodies scrambling through hills of refuse like ants in search of crumbs. I had not been aware of the decay below. I knew nothing of it. But even as my fingers follow the now well-travelled pattern of the music's arc, I know that this can't be true, that I am lying to myself. The truth is, I didn't care to know. In the homes in the hills, even in the homes of the politically conscious, of those who tried to alter the course of Haiti's history, children were sheltered from the ugliness of life, sheltered from the hard as iron truth of poverty and fear that courses down from the top of the mountains to the corrugated rooftops of the shantytown huts, emptying their bowels in the makeshift dykes hemming in the *lakous*. I have a worn image in my mind's eye of the poorest of the poor bathing with salvaged slivers of soap, reconciling themselves to the filth floating alongside their waists since some kind of water is better than none.

My eyes stay closed as I make my way through the repertoire. I feel the attention of the audience rising up to embrace me, like a series of undulating waves from a distance some feet below me. But my thoughts are not with them. I am not even with Chopin, though I am well prepared and manage the music well enough. I had read everything I could on Chopin in order to approximate his original performances.

My right ear inches closer and closer to my right hand and I can hear the vibration of the strings inside the belly of the piano as my fingers drum the keys. I marvel at the details of Chopin's composition, the clever counterpoints as delicate as the falling petals of a dying rose.

To me, Chopin's mature work was the product of full bloom, even though he was still young when he died, of consumption or some other frailty. I had reviews of Chopin's recitals from the 1830s. Hector Berlioz had written in *Le Rénovateur* of 1833: "Chopin is the Trilby of pianists... rendering Mazurkas with utmost degree of softness, piano to the extreme, the hammers merely brushing the strings." And in 1836 Charles Hallé had written that "there is nothing to remind one that it is a human being who produces this music. It seems to descend from heaven – so pure, and clear, and spiritual." Of a recital in 1841, Liszt had said of the preludes that they were merely "sketches, beginnings of Études, or, so to speak, ruins, individual eagle pinions, all disorder and wild confusion." He had been misunderstood, scoffed at, his genius lamented. But two hundred years later, pianists still struggle to play his work, to understand the softness behind the forms, the hidden niches of spiritual light between each thrilling movement, each bridging trill. The most ambitious didn't play him at all, claiming that he was too soft, not enough brawn. The most ambitious were young and had not yet learned the force of poetry or of water.

I had learned from watching the older pianists return to Chopin at the end of their careers that there was something unfathomable about his music that was worth taking the time to penetrate, to master even, and I had begun to do this earlier than most, with no fear of being categorized as "soft", since playing Chopin was still seen as slightly emasculating, a womanly pursuit. I wanted only to prove myself as a world-class concert pianist and to play something of worth in the process. I had tried at first to specialize in Mozart and Bach but there was nothing original in this. Why not try what everyone else avoided? Chopin had always stirred something deep within me and I decided that it would be worth flouting convention to specialize in his work. There was a haunting in his music that brushed up against my memories of childhood, of my mother who was no longer, of my father whose presence had eclipsed itself in the mourning that followed his wife's death.

I come to the end of my piece, the *allegros* increasing and moving me through vast waterfalls and dense forests lit with green, leaves slick with rain. Then comes the brusque shift to passages marked *pianissimo*, and my fingers follow obediently as the page-turner at the far left of the bench smoothly turns the final sheet.

I have them in the palm of my hand: I can feel the audience poised for the last note to be struck and the immense silence that follows, enveloping audience, player and instrument in a private bubble for a few long seconds. Then, I stand sharply, turn to face the audience while holding the black edge of the piano with my left hand and bow formally, as the men do, a slight inclination of the waist forward, my forehead horizontal to the floor, and as I rise, the applause fills up the silence.

My first professional solo performance has been a success.

I search the faces in the front rows. I see Edouard first, clapping proudly, like a father. His eyes twinkle with something more and I feel a slight chill go up my spine but I shake it loose by bowing again and when I rise it is Sam's eyes that take me in and I am glad that he has foregone his nightly meeting with the other dissertation fellows to come cheer me on. He comes close to the edge of the stage and holds a single red rose up to me, mouthing the words, *je t'aime*, as he bows slightly towards me so that the crowd might think that we do not know each other, that he is simply a stranger admiring my talent.

I smile at him and take the flower, clasping it over my heart. Other flowers come and fill the front of the stage with their petals and I am glad that I have worn my violet silk dress that makes me look elegant and sophisticated with my mother's long string of pearls strung around my neck and hanging between my small breasts in a loose knot.

Wearing the pearls had been Sam's idea; we had almost fought about it at home before I had left early for the concert hall. Now I am grateful to him. He had been right: it was like having my mother there in some small way.

I bow one last time but squarely towards Sam, though it seems that I might be bowing towards Edouard who is standing right behind him. Edouard reacts as if the bow is for him alone and inclines his head forward just a touch as if accepting my thanks for his mentoring. I smile to myself and thank the audience by placing my hands one on top of each other over my heart and then opening them slightly with the rose stem still cradled between my fingers. Flash bulbs go off and then I turn abruptly away from the noise and walk off the stage, relieved that it is finally over.

The evening had ended badly, over an argument.

I feel as if I'm beginning to sink into quicksand, suffocating in the muck of my life. I'm searching for something to believe in, some remnant of story that might show me the way. I want to believe in something before the ground beneath me falls away. I do. I want to believe in the miracle of the dove returning with that olive branch in her beak and then flying off one last time, never to be seen again. Yes, I do.

I want to believe in the flowering of new things upon the broken land. But, deep down, I don't. As my mother used to say, these are just stories to keep us in line.

I want to believe that Job is a saint to emulate and that if we can survive the ordeals life throws our way, anything can be endured. Now, the older I get, the more it seems that loss is part of the fabric of life. It's the thread that holds everything together, not the thing that tears it apart. My question isn't so much what *I* might survive. I'm not in the line of fire. It's the millions out there living through their nightmares that make me wonder whether God really exists. My hand will heal, eventually, even though the relationship between Sam and I might not. The question isn't how do we survive? It's how do we survive each other?

Sam and I sit in the living room of our flat with only the light from the TV screen washing its tiny waves of simulated colour over us, snatches of conversation wafting up from the cobbled streets. The news flickers on the screen. It's late. I talk about Noah and Job, then fall silent, going over yesterday's piano recital in my mind, replaying every note of the *Études* I had been working on for weeks for the tour that was supposed to follow the Paris debut.

Sam nods when I speak but doesn't answer and I lie here against him, our bodies stiff against each other as if they've never known true intimacy, my injured right hand in its sling going over the notes spasmodically, as I go over the events of the previous night, wondering what could have been done differently – no – better.

We had spent the better part of the day at the hospital. I was trying hard not to blame Sam for what had happened. I rationalized that maybe my playing wasn't really developing that much, that I wasn't the best player out there.

It would have been my first sizable concert tour, the first one that would have had my name up on the marquee as a featured artist along with two others. I was the oldest at thirty-seven, which was late by most standards, a has-been in some eyes. But this was going to be my first big break, courtesy of famous Edouard Le Marin who had been a virtuoso all his life, who somehow thought I was worth taking under his wing at twenty-seven when he had found me playing the piano with a small orchestra in Lisieux. I would not even have come to his attention had I not been replacing the first string pianist who was off sick that particular night. It was probably unusual to see a girl with skin the colour of nutmeg playing Bach in a mid-sized French city with medieval roots. He was impressed even though I hadn't been trying to impress. I hadn't even known he was watching.

You didn't say no to Edouard Le Marin. You said yes and soon. This was what Sam and I had been fighting about.

Minutes after the concert, the two of us had left the theatre through the service door even though I was certain there would not be a crowd up front. After all, I wasn't that well known. But Sam had insisted and we found ourselves in the dark alleyway behind the concert hall, its surface slick with fresh rain. Some of the stagehands were still there. One tipped his cap at me, "*Beau concert, Mademoiselle Cathie,*" he said as I passed. I put out a hand on his arm and thanked him while Sam pulled me in closer against him. I felt the weight of guilt pull down inside me.

I felt Sam's gesture as protective, a belated action against a loss already there between us. Something had changed irrevocably and it had crept up slowly, over time, like silent cancer cells multiplying effortlessly, feeding off toxins only they could detect. I tried to comfort Sam, to communicate that all was not yet lost by snuggling closer towards him, when in the past I would have pushed against him, demanded my liberty, as I always did. It was one of the things he had once said he loved most about me: my recalcitrance against being vulnerable. But instead of confirming that we were going to be all right, I was communicating that we were swimming in uncharted waters, neither of us knowing exactly when the boat had capsized.

Sam gave my arm a tight squeeze. "Where to now, kid?" he asked, forcing lightness into his voice.

"Home," I said.

"Why don't we go out on the town? Celebrate? You deserve it. Come on. Let's have a drink."

"Home," I said again and put a hand up across his chest to grasp his collar in a gesture of mock play. It stopped him.

"Sure," he said. "Whatever you want. Home it is."

We walked along like this, bodies close, arms around each other, walking slowly, as we had done so many times before. Anyone looking at us would have thought us to be just another couple in love. But our coupling was falling apart. I sighed out loud, absentmindedly.

"What are you thinking?" Sam inquired.

I looked up at him, so tall to my five feet and five inches, dark hair fanning across his broad forehead that had only one wrinkle that I could see would grow deeper with age, a vertical fissure running from the middle of his forehead to a spot just above the arch of his nose where it disappeared without a trace.

"Love," I said, smiling wistfully.

"Love?"

"Yes. Of how lovers come here for their honeymoons or to rekindle something they've lost and of how so many of us live here bearing the truth that it's like any other big city, full of stories we can never know, full of love lost and never won, everyday casualties."

"Oh," Sam said, "just that." He smiled at my earnestness as he always did. He liked the way I thought of things on two or three levels at once. "I wasn't thinking about anything."

I laughed at him and shook the lapel I was holding in my hand and swung my free arm around him so that we were even closer than before and seemed even more in love. I felt a sadness sweep over me. "Are we going to be all right?" I asked him then, suddenly, seriously.

He stopped and drew me up against him so that his chin was just above the crown of my head. We were close to the Pont Neuf and the lights of the city shimmered on the water behind us. "I think so, don't you?" he said into my hair, worry tingeing his voice.

I pressed my face into the musky warmth of his chest and didn't answer. Then he continued walking towards our apartment across the bridge and I fell into step, more certain than before that we were about to have to cross our own bridge. I just didn't know when it would come, that perilous journey to parting or finally admitting that we were meant for each other. Neither of us could be certain of anything, of what we had first felt or felt now, or of what we might feel tomorrow. A day could change everything, anything: a day, an hour, a glance down the wrong street or into the wrong face, a phone call that should have been left unanswered.

It was late when he finally dared to ask the question he had been holding back since he had walked in on Edouard and I in my dressing room after the concert. He had been so proud of me, so ready to sweep me up into his arms and take me out for a celebratory drink at his club where our friends, his fellow doctoral students, were waiting for us. But he hadn't told me this, hadn't told me that he had bought a cake at the bakery and had the bartender stick it in the fridge even though it was against the bar rules to keep anything else but bottled *Oranginas*, dry vodka, and olives there. He'd avoided asking me as we walked home through the misty air for fear of losing my body nestled close to his.

We had once made sense together. We had made a world together. But the new baby grand in the living room, shut away behind the glass doors separating the living room from the dining room, stood accusing. He had to ask.

It was late and I didn't want to go through all the questions that I couldn't answer because I didn't really know what was going on between us, between myself and Sam, between Edouard and I. Couldn't this wait until morning, another day? Couldn't he let me savour the victory of the night?

"I'm so tired, Sam," I said in a soft voice, so soft and low that sometimes he couldn't make out what I was saying.

I had seen the question coming for hours, from the moment that he had looked behind him after giving me the rose, looking behind him because of the way my eyes flickered from his to something or to someone just over his shoulder, his own green eyes registering that he was losing me to some force greater than himself, greater than the love he held for me in his heart. I guessed in that moment that the biggest muscle in his body was reduced to the size of a grape, wondering if it would have to become even smaller, drying up to the size of a raisin, emptied of life.

I could see his distress in the way he moved around the room, his chest stiff, almost concave, his shoulders hunched over his solar plexus as if he was afraid that all his best energy would escape, flee from him, as I was fleeing, even though I sat very still on the bed, so very close to him.

So he asked me another question, one he dreaded less. "Where are you these days?"

"What do you mean?" I responded, standing up, looking away from the tight ball of his body as he hunched over his sock drawer and pawed through it as if he would never find what he was looking for. I said this flatly, meaning it as a statement rather than a question. I wanted to stall, to avoid having to move into deeper waters.

"You *know* what I mean," he said, piqued, in a voice as quiet as my own. We were already there, in deep, the water creeping up our necks, the seduction of its darkness licking the bottom of our chins.

I shrugged even though his back was turned, as if he could feel my movements, as the water churned between us. I could feel the pain emanating from his chest. It left me cold, sad.

He didn't say anything.

"I'm right here," I said finally. "I'm right here with you. But I'm exhausted. Can't we do this another night? Can't we just talk about the performance and the lights and the way everyone clapped. Your flower…" my voice faltered. I had forgotten the rose in the dressing room in my haste to smooth things over.

"I got it on the way to the hall," he said. It was a perfect red rose and even though he knew I would get dozens more just like it, I knew he had felt sure that this could make a difference.

"Is there something I've failed to do?" he asked. He turned from the sock drawer to take me in. It was my turn to have my back to him. I was pulling a silk burgundy nightgown over my head. He must have been able to see the wheat-yellow skin of my breasts protruding from the sides, just below my armpits, and the soft curvature of my muscles fanning out from the tight knots of my spine into my shoulders. I had a dancer's back, so he said. I liked to hear him say this. I had always wanted to be a dancer.

"No," I said to the wall. "What more could you be giving me?"

"We could get married," he said, even though he was against marriage, on philosophical grounds, and knew that I felt the same. I knew he was searching for some way to bind us together.

I didn't answer. I let his statement fall to the ground. I was still waiting for the question. I could feel it pushing against me in the thickness of the humid night air. We had opened the windows when we walked in, to change the air as we liked to say, and the mist lifting from the river, as the night grew cold, wafted in on ribbons of smoke. I could smell logs burning somewhere and midnight conversations rising from the street down below. I wished now that we had gone out to celebrate after all.

I could see him thinking of how he should have called the bar where all his friends had waited. He had unanswered messages on his cell phone. They probably all thought that we had gone back to the apartment to celebrate on our own, to make love.

"We could take a trip," he said then, unexpectedly.

The suggestion made me laugh and I turned to face him with a smile. He looked at me as if for the first time. He smiled, boyish, sheepish.

"You hate travelling," I said with mock exasperation, one arm swinging out to him, my long fingers pointing as if to invisible pieces of luggage he would never take the time to pack.

"But *you* like it," he said quietly. "We could go wherever you like."

And we could, just as we had come here so many years ago. Sam would go just about anywhere for me, even to the coldest of places. I suddenly felt cruel. Who was I to be calling the shots?

"I'm tired, Sam."

He nodded as he pulled off his pants. I looked at his bare legs, muscular from bike riding, his muscles lean and long, the curl of his black hairs giving the skin peering through a bluish tinge. I thought of him when he was a boy, hairless and vulnerable, his skinny legs sticking out from his short pants like sticks, never imagining that he would become handsome and sportive, sought after. I had seen the pictures in his mother's house in Iowa, a house that edged sideways towards the right, bending under the weight of time, its breaks beginning to fall out of place, the cement holding it together itself beginning to crack. It was a crowded house. The wallpaper with its crawling green and yellow vines gave you the illusion of standing in some kind of Victorian idea of a forest. The furniture was just as old, beautiful, with wood frames that one could imagine having been cut and carved into shape by artisans rather than by today's robotic machines. But nothing went together, the cloth of the chairs and divans never matched and the tops of the tables were cluttered with gifts Sam's mother had received over the years from her four children who were dispersed all over the world. Each of them was so different and their gifts displayed their uniqueness so that even less on display matched. She had grown a lawyer, a soldier, a historian and a social worker living, respectively, in California, Saudi Arabia, Paris, and the deep South. All of her grandchildren were of different hues and shapes of faces. She told the church ladies that she had her own private UN, and privately wondered how this had come to be. It was on the upright piano on which Sam's mother liked to play old show-tunes that I had seen his childhood picture. He was six. His long face looked up at the photographer who must have been his mother. His thin legs and arms stuck out of his clothes as if he were an animated doll, a Pinocchio. His hair had been lighter then, almost blond. The shorts he was wearing were darker than his bushy head of hair. "I was born blond," he'd said to me then, responding to my unspoken question. I had been thin then, thinner than I am now, as I, too, had been as a child, my thinness captured in a rare photograph I had from childhood months spent in Haiti. In that picture, I stand in a back yard in front of a bougainvillea bush.

Examining the photo of Sam as a child, I had wondered if we were twins though born to different mothers. We had been born in the same year, one day apart, in January, in two parts of the continent where the ground was cold and iced, two parts of the world to which neither of us belonged.

Sam stood in his underwear and folded his dress pants carefully before pulling on his pyjama bottoms. They were a light green with dark navy stripes running down the length of each leg.

I had given them to him on his last birthday. I had bought them because the green of the silk matched his eyes.

"I'm tired too," he said and walked away from me into the bathroom.

I felt relief wash over me as he disappeared behind the door. I heard water running as he brushed his teeth, then I heard liquid hit water, the flush of the toilet. I pulled back the covers from the bed and took off my gold hoop earrings. They were always the last things I took off before I went to sleep, occasionally forgetting to take them off until I figured out why I was having a hard time falling asleep when the metal prongs jabbed beneath my earlobes. I hoped that we could sleep now and start again tomorrow fresh, forgetting the weight between us.

Sam reappeared at the door of the bathroom. I had switched off all of the lights except for the ones on our respective night tables, and the light coming from the bathroom behind him seemed suddenly bright. I took in the outline of his hair and face, guardedly. I was lying in the bed, my long legs stretched across the comforter, the bottom of my breasts resting softly on the lift of my stomach. He looked me over.

"I'd like to know what's going on, Cat," he said, his voice soft, trying to keep the peace.

"What do you mean?" I feigned innocence and started straightening the books on my side of the bed, not wanting him to see the fear that might have shown on my face. What was there to say? Nothing had happened yet between Edouard and I. Nothing was happening. I was not going to let anything happen.

"You know what I mean." Sam ran damp fingers through his thick hair then sighed, exasperated. "I don't want to keep going around in circles."

Then he asked the question I had been waiting for all night, from the moment he entered the dressing room, to his look when we had entered the apartment, and he'd seen the new, black baby grand piano whose lacquer shone even in the dark, illuminated by the light of the blue moon that shone through the balcony windows. It stood there, accusing me.

"What's up between you and Edouard?" He caught his breath, as if wanting to take the words back. It meant now that there was something real between us, something to speak about, a hurdle to leap over or walk around except he didn't want to run away from it or walk around it, ignoring its presence. He wanted to know how high the hurdle, its colour, its width. Tell me, Catherine, he seemed to be pleading with his green eyes flecked with dark spots that made me think of the midday sun glinting off the surface of a dark blue ocean, the ocean of my childhood and summer vacations spent with cousins in Haiti. Where had he been then? Just a shadow in my dark eyes, an unanswered dream.

I looked at him and the space between us suddenly seemed large, unbridgeable. "Nothing," I managed to say, but my voice came out small, the word lost in the chasm that seemed to grow with every second. "Really," I tried again, my voice a little stronger, trying to reach him as he seemed to recede from my vision, back and back until he was just a black spot against the sun, a shadow of a body I once knew but could no longer recognize.

But he had not moved. He was still in the same spot, his hands damp from washing his face and brushing his teeth. His breath sweet with mint paste. I knew he wanted to kiss me, to find out from the tenderness of my tongue that his doubts had no foundation.

"Really, he's just helping me. I'm just being nice. He's done so much for me."

"How nice is nice?"

I shrugged. "Would you say no to a copy of the complete Oxford English Dictionary?"

"Sure," he said. I knew he wasn't lying.

"Well," I continued. "I didn't think I could or *should* say no. He would have felt insulted. He might not have helped."

"I see the way he looks at you." Sam shook his head. "He doesn't just look at you. He devours you. He'll eat you up."

I tried to laugh. "Come on, Sam, you're exaggerating. You're just jealous."

But I knew he was right. I knew that look in Edouard's eyes, had seen it often enough in my life. It was a look that brought me back to a faraway time when women with my tone of skin and high cheekbones were sold to the highest bidder, their breasts exposed and their stomachs groped for their ability to bear young.

It was a look that was meant to reveal to me my beauty but that only revealed the lust of the onlooker – my beauty forgotten, my body scanned only for what pleasures it might provide. It was a look that gave nothing in return, it ravaged.

"You know I'm not the jealous type." He walked towards his side of the bed and sat down with his back to me. I took in his lean back curved over as he held his head in his hands. I wanted to reach out to him, put my hands around the curvature of his back muscles and smooth them out from the top of his shoulders to the small of his back, the way he liked me to do. "Why don't you just tell me the truth?"

"There isn't anything to tell," I said abruptly, my voice rising. I got up and stood by the bed, arms crossed, not wanting to give in even though I knew it would only make him imagine the worst, what hadn't happened, what I wasn't going to let happen.

I felt resentment wash over me. Why couldn't he just let things be? It wasn't really any of his business, except that we were drifting and I was more responsible than he was for the drift.

"Then why do I feel so far from you? Why don't you come here so that I can hold you? You can tell me. I won't get upset. I promise."

I was furious with him for wanting to make peace with me on these terms. Why didn't he fight? Why didn't he become angry and agitated as would most men who were losing their wives? But I wasn't yet his wife, might never be. I walked around the bed to get out of the room, even though it meant moving past him. "There isn't anything to tell. It's all in your mind."

"That piano out there is real. How much did it cost? Thirty grand? Is that how cheap women like you come these days?"

He'd done it, finally, stepped over the line, uttered words I never thought I would hear come out of his mouth. We were within inches from each other. Quickly, he'd reached for me.

"I'm sorry," he said. "I didn't mean that. You know I didn't mean that. I just feel like we're losing each other. I don't want to lose you." He caught my arm as I tried to leave the room.

I struggled against his pull and then felt the tearing before the pain shot up from my wrist to the soft skin on the inside of my arm where my veins pulsed in a trail of blue. The tearing made me think of wrapping paper being torn from gifts.

I thought of my childhood, of standing in the yards with their tall walls and broken bottles, of the sweet-sour smell of jasmine sharp and acrid in the air. White sheets were fluttering in the wind, hanging wide and square on clotheslines. I was hiding behind them when I should have been at the piano studying. My mother, still alive then, spying my short legs at the bottom of the sheets was pretending she could not see me, trying to pull the sheet down low and lower.

Then the pain rose, sharp as a cutting blade, sudden, a tearing that hinted at the impossibility of complete repair. "What are you doing?" I gasped, my body caught between the bedroom and the hallway, not knowing which way to go to stop the pain.

"Sam, you're hurting me."

He hadn't realized yet what had happened. He was still holding me firmly as if holding me there would yield some answer to our troubles, as if he could stop time with a gesture.

I stopped struggling. "Sam," I said, my voice small, "I think you hurt my hand."

"What?" he faltered, opened his hand, looked at my wrist. "What happened?"

The pain was sharper with his hand gone, a dull throbbing from wrist to shoulder, like my funny bone had been twisted out of place. I didn't know what was wrong except this meant the tour would have to be cancelled. I wouldn't be able to give a repeat performance the next day or next week.

"What were you trying to do?" I gasped again, crumpled against the doorjamb, holding the injured hand against my beating heart.

Sam was crouching near me, staring at me, his eyes large. "I'm sorry. I didn't know what I was doing. I was just trying to keep you here, to talk. Oh my god, is it bad?"

The pain made me think of times when I had been afraid of trying things that other kids did all the time, hanging upside down from monkey bars with sheets of ice beneath them, promising a hard fall in the Canadian winter, riding a bike with hands up in the air in the spring, roller-skating in the streets filled with crisp autumn leaves. I was always afraid of injury. I nodded and started to cry.

"I'm so sorry," Sam whispered, sitting down to hold me. I let him and cried into the smooth skin of his freckled shoulder. I cried not only because of the pain but because I couldn't tell him that everything was OK, that he had nothing to fear, that our love was safe. I cried until no more tears came and by then I was too tired to go to the hospital. We would go in the morning.

Sam carried me to the bed and held me while I slept, even though we both knew it meant that the injury would swell and take longer to heal. He hoped it wasn't too bad. What would he do if he had ruined my career because of a momentary impulse to stall the inevitable? He stroked the injured hand.

"Hey," Sam says, stroking my bare arm, bringing me back from yesterday to the present.

"Uhmmm," I croon in an effort not to let Sam distract me from my attempt to reconstruct what had happened between us.

"You need to be watching this."

"Do I?"

He knows how I hate to watch the news. I lie on the couch with him as he watches, counting on him to keep the sound down or even muted, counting on him to distil the horrors of the world in a form I can digest.

"Yes. Come on, Cat. Sit up. You'll regret it if you don't look."

It wasn't his words but the firmness of his voice that made me push off his thigh and prop myself up on an elbow so that I could see the screen.

I look at the screen and immediately wish I had just pretended to look and waited for the usual distillation to be given me in instalments – in bed, in the shower, over breakfast and the morning paper.

I look and what I see is surreal: dead cattle bobbing up and down in what used to be their sparse grazing ground. Little children buried in mud. Mothers wailing beneath their kerchiefed heads. Fathers wading past the rusting tin roofs of their shacks in search of the dead while automobiles lumber past them in the swirling waters that sweep everything in their way.

What I know is that what I will remember most is the bloated corpse of a goat lying on its side as red waters rage past it, the camera zooming in on its inert form, a rigid hoof reaching out of the water as if to its creator, a glassy, unblinking eye magazined with its last glimpse of the living. It is three times its normal size, some farmer's treasure swept out from under him. A farmer who is probably dead by now after the hurricane hit the island I used to call home, where my father, uncles and aunts still live.

"Should we call?" Sam asks gently, even stunned, I think, as I am.

I don't know what to say. It occurs to me that this is something like what Noah had seen, the horrors developing in front of his eyes with no capacity to make a difference, knowing that his bounty (and his curse) was to have been saved and placed out of reach of the sweeping waters.

"I think you should call," Sam says authoritatively, in the voice that had made me look up in the first place.

"Jesus," I say, "why did you make me look?" As if not looking would mean that everyone was safe.

I don't know how to admit to the feeling of powerlessness that has overcome me, as if the she-goat's glassy eye has already stored the fact that I was one of the people that couldn't be counted on as the horror descended upon her futilely upraised hoof; that nothing, not the farmer or his son, stood between the she-goat and the tight fist of the storm.

Sam removes his arm from where he had let it fall as I move to face the television, gently moving my injured arm into my lap.

"Cat," he says. "I'm just trying to help."

I pull my eyes away from the images on the screen in time to see the hurt in his eyes. They look dark as stones in the white of his face tinted blue by the television rays. I pull myself towards him and place my free hand on his cheek. He resists.

"I'm sorry," I whisper against his bristled cheek.

How I had loved that cheek when we had first fallen in love, the way the stubble made the white of his skin seem whiter than it was, recognizable at a distance, especially when he smiled and his straight white teeth gleamed as in a toothpaste ad. "I'm sorry, Sam, really I am." I'm as overwhelmed by my love for him as by the fear of its loss, the two emotions competing as I feel my world shifting further off its axis.

I feel the muscles in his face and neck soften and give a little.

I turn his lips towards mine and kiss him, quickly, just to apologize, and then we turn back towards the television, heads together, as if the tragedy could bind us with common energy.

I hadn't spoken to my father in about three years and hadn't asked about him either, even when I called his brother Max at Christmas and Easter. I'd assumed that if no one told me of an untimely death he was still alive.

Staring at the deluge in Gonaïves, city of revolution, I fear that he could very well be dead and that my call might come too late. I think about all the questions I had never asked him, or was too scared to ask, the fact that I hadn't told him since I was a little girl that I loved him, and hadn't heard him say those words back to me since then either.

I think about calling to find out if he is still alive. For some reason that outcome seems worse and I am too ashamed of thinking this to tell Sam and so I prattle on instead about Noah and Job while Sam stares at me across the kitchen table where we've adjourned after the news, with teacups in our hands, as if a hot drink might make us more courageous.

The phone rings and we both let it go on ringing away, ignoring the possibility that someone might be trying to get in touch from over there, clinging to the comfort of a stabilizing response from outside their impossible inferno.

"It's your call," Sam says finally. He means it's my choice, not that he knows the ringing phone must be for me, and I nod.

"I wonder what Noah felt on his boat, looking out on mass destruction," is all I can say.

Sam stares at me as if he is wondering just who I might be, as if he has never seen me quite clearly before, as if since the day before and our fight over Edouard and the new baby grand in our living room I have gone hazy. Then, he stares up at the ceiling as if tracking a fly against the white paint we'd contemplated changing to a mossy green or cheerful, buttercup yellow only a few weeks ago.

Why I'm so sure someone is dead, I don't know. The sound of the Chopin in my head has gone. It has been replaced by a strange buzzing not unlike the kind I hear after I do a handstand pose in the yoga class I take just down the street at a community space near the

Pompidou Centre, the teacher crooning at us, "*Poussez, Poussez,*" as if we're trees trying to grow new leaves. And maybe we are. Maybe this teacher knows something we don't and is trying to coax new life out of us. Maybe she can tell just by looking at us who is already dead or too far gone to rise again. I never do manage to hold my legs up straight above me in the headstand pose. I'm convinced it's a skill you need to have learned in childhood. Something my father never taught me – among many other things.

"I think he must have been tortured with the souls of the dead and the knowledge that he might have been able to squeeze a few more people onto that boat."

Sam just keeps looking up at the ceiling, his fingers gripping his cup loosely because there is nothing else to hold on to. He's afraid to touch me now, after last night. Besides, he has already told me what he thinks I should do and I can't summon the nerve to do it. The phone keeps ringing until Sam tires of Noah and the rainbow sign, Job and his pile of shit, and moves to answer it.

"It's for you," he says, his voice and face grim.

How do I know someone has died?

I wonder if it is my father. My mother has already been gone for more than twenty years. I'd stopped counting the years when I hit twenty-two and had settled into the normality of her absence by the time I'd met Sam and didn't have anyone to introduce him to. Her absence probably made our courtship easier, though it meant Sam had no points of reference for me as I had for him, with his three siblings and married-for-forty-years-still-together, born-and-raised-in-Iowa, Jewish parents.

"It's not your father," he says, and what I think I hear him say is: "It's your father," as in "Your father has died, don't come unglued."

And so, I don't expect to hear the voice I haven't heard in three years at the other end of the line. I don't expect him to be trying to soothe my pain away as he delivers the news that they are all safe, except for one, and when I hear who is gone, I let out a scream that makes Sam move towards me and hold me against his narrow chest as he did last night, and, again, I cry, cradling him along with my father's voice at the other end of the telephone line.

111

I hear it then, wafting in between my father's voice, Sam's hushing, and my own sobbing. It's the noise I think all the elders heard, from Noah on, down to us today.

It is like the sound of water flowing over stones, rain falling on the ceramic tiles of a roof in the Southwest after a hot summer day, or even like the whisper of a note as a bow slides over the strings of a violin as it is being tuned before a concert. It is the hole between every breath, the suspended sigh, the shape of things before a thought can be articulated. It's a breath away from silence is what it is, enough to drive anyone to the brink of insanity or into unswerving faith for lack of an alternative. I hold my breath and, in that moment, in that very moment of worlds collapsing and of shifting sands, it occurs to me that the sound I'm hearing isn't the voice of God at all. It is the voice of the fallen angels, the ones who never made it back to the Heaven they'd been sent from as ambassadors to a human race that had turned the earth into a sewer where only the odd hot-house rose could bloom or brave lotus rise. They are the ones who whisper to me as I strike the piano keys with the balls of my fingertips and as I fall into and wake from sleep. They, who whispered to Noah and to Job. They, who, just like us, walk upon the crusted ground, lost, forsaken, whispering to whomever can hear and might answer their anguished cries for help, wondering when they might return homewards, wondering if their being cast down to Earth is the price they have to pay for the keeping of paradise.

ROMULUS

Early Afternoon, March 7, 2004, Port-au-Prince Central Prison, Haiti

The moment of awakening reaches Romulus Pierre in the depths of the dank corner of a jail cell, surrounded by the stink of urine, of human and bestial faeces ground into the dirt floors, with only a small square of light streaming in from a brick-size opening up above that allows the prisoners to know when the sun rises and night falls. Some count off the days by etching lines into the pitted walls of the cell; others, without hope of ever being able to wake from the nightmare of their incarceration, let the days run one into another.

For Romulus, awakening comes in the form of muscle tremors, stomach spasms, and hallucinations. The tissues binding his muscle and cartilage hunger for an infusion of narcotics – cocktails of prescribed and illegal drugs – cocaine, heroin, antidepressants, uppers – anything he can get his hands on.

For one hundred and eighty-six days, his hands have had nothing to grasp in the regular schedule he has grown accustomed to – not the comforting smoothness of a small pink pill or the cool plastic cylinder of a needle case.

His hands roam the puckered and uneven walls next to his cot as he tries to grasp the outline of a face floating there, then they cling to his body frame when the convulsions shake him so hard that he feels the bones of his vertebrae lurch back and forth as if ready to leap from his body and leave the flesh behind.

In the span of the first weeks of his incarceration, once it was known who he was and why he was being held, some heady substances did find their way to the cell like the miracle of rain after a long drought. For a few days he was his old self again, bleary-eyed, smiling, stoned, feet on the ground, elbows on his knees, hands cavorting in the air above his thighs as they animate a story he tells of his travels to a prisoner listening at his feet, while others turn away from his suffocating self-importance. They would defecate against the walls in silent protest as Romulus spoke. There wasn't much room for movement. There wasn't any room for heroics.

Romulus did not seem to notice the turned backs. He attended only to the face upturned towards his, as he spoke with authority of things he has seen, even as his tongue became thick and unintelligible, even as he lost track of the events in the tale he was telling and grew silent as the drug took over and left him dumb. He seemed only to notice the punctuated indifference of some of the men in the cell when the drugs leached from his system and left him, insomniac, craving for more. He would have drunk his urine if there had been any privacy in the cell, in case the drugs were still lurking in the warm liquid. For him, these were desperate times.

When the doors of the cells are broken open, he has been sitting there in doubtful company for one hundred and eighty-six days. He has counted each and every one of these days without pencil and paper, without scratches on the wall. Any drug addict worth his salt needs to keep track of things like an eagle-sharp accountant, to count how many pills, how many possible hits, how many highs, and how many hours between, how many days to the next drop, the next payment, the next OD, the next stomach pumping, the next withdrawal, the next averted death. The minutiae of time becomes a science, a honed sequence of small events towards ecstasy, briefly experienced and furiously repeated over and over again in a frenzied pantomime that provides the necessary illusion of having a worthy goal. It functions like an ill-paid but time-consuming occupation; time, therefore, has to be made an ally. Not other people's time, mind you, but the time related to the ups and downs of addict life. Time is a relative invention and a good pal in the world of hallucinations and deprivation. It is all that will remain after the wives are gone, taking their children with them, gone with the friends bearing that look of disgust and despair on their righteous faces. Romulus can do without the lot of them. He thinks this even while imprisoned, surrounded by men he is sure have committed heinous acts against humanity and nature.

On the last of those one hundred and eighty six days, even in the haze of his drug-addled mind, as an empty pocket of time forces him to think about those who once peopled his life, the stadium seats he'd filled with fans, the money he made from records that had gone platinum in the Caribbean and in Europe (he'd never tried to conquer the North American market: it was too vast, too fast, even for his adrenaline-driven life), Romulus has an uncommon realization. He lies there on his cot and grasps that beyond the drugs, beyond the hallucinations and the gripping nature of the loss of time, he has had no life whatsoever for at least twenty years.

It is a sad moment, an empty epiphany that someone of his intelligence should have deciphered earlier had he not been thinking of the next hit, the next score, the little bags of dust floating in his suitcases, many of which had mysteriously gone missing from his last transaction, which was why he found himself penned in between steel bars and an impacted floor of red dirt on his own native ground, a land which, some ten years prior, he had been forbidden by law to re-enter. He had somehow forgotten about this pithy detail when he had agreed to smuggle the suitcase of cocaine past international borders.

When the doors are finally flung open by men in military garb, he is too sad to stand and walk out with the others who jubilantly jump up and down in the mucky excrement of the stall in which they have all been kept, brothers in criminal excess, many for longer than one hundred and eighty six days. Romulus has sat there like a prince amongst his people, the only man with a cot to sleep on while the others slept rolled up in rotting blankets stinking of more than a hundred years of servitude. Romulus thinks that he is unlike the other jailed men. He has had money, position, fame. But, he has come to realize, by the time the doors creak open and the cries of *libéré, nou libéré* go up, that he has thrown away his freedom for little more than year upon year of escape from reality.

Romulus sighs to himself and watches the men throwing themselves into the sunlight, their bodies floating, emblazoned by the light, the darkness they are leaving behind giving them form: dark angels spilling out into a fallen paradise.

Romulus thinks about the faces that have hovered above him throughout his time in the prison. They have been mostly women's faces. They speak to him, he is sure of this, but he is often unsure of what, exactly, they are saying. They seem to be as lost as he is, lost to time, in fantastic worlds of their own making. He sometimes wonders if they are the product of women hallucinating elsewhere in the world. He wonders if being in an altered state can make a person fall into another's dream. He likes this feeling of ambiguity. That and the floating feeling he experiences when taking the drugs makes the trips worth it, like travelling without ever having to board a plane.

At times, the faces seem to prophesy great things that he has yet to do, though he is never sure what those things might be. It is just a feeling they give him, as if there are unexpected heights still to achieve, as if he could undo the train-wreck that he has made of the last twenty years of his life. Other times, there are children in these hallucinations, but none look like the children he has fathered. All of them are white, or white-appearing.

He isn't sure that they should be trusted, those faces. After all, they have come to him in the throes of delusion. One apparition has been especially persistent, a woman with a long, pointy face, a white woman who resembles his first love, with skin so translucent beneath her eyes that he can see the filaments of a blue circuitry of veins. She hovers there, right above his head, whispering crazy pronouncements that Romulus does, in fact, understand, much to his surprise, even though she speaks in a language different from his own.

She speaks to him of rivers below the ground and spirit-dwellers who hide in hollowed trees and vales. She speaks of a landscape unfamiliar to his senses but he follows her there to a country so green it makes his Haiti seem like a heap of bones, a cemetery. She wants him to return to this forgotten place, this place of her first beginnings. He wants her to go away from the space above his eyes, a space gouged by many desperate fingers trying to find a way out. *Go there*, she whispers persistently, ignoring him, in the speech he can't quite place. They are almost mystical, these drug-induced delusions. Why would he ever stop? The only thing that *might* make him stop is the fact that he is afraid of this particular apparition. She makes him question his sanity. The more he sees her, the more he feels that he must be nearing his own pivoting point, walking a line

118

he has crossed many times before with the aid of his many hallucinogens, a line between rationality and destruction, between the real and the fantastic.

He usually prefers the fantastic to anything else life might offer, even the first love of his life with her translucent skin and fine bone structure, her body so narrow that it laboured to produce a first child, who then died in utero, and then contorted itself to produce a pale-as-roses son who survives still. He would be twenty or twenty-one that first son. A full-grown man Romulus didn't even know, born in the years when he was still on the cusp of remaining in the real world. He had not quite been an addict then. But, by the time the boy was three, he had already lost a sense of up and down. They had called him Christian.

She had taken everything, that first love. Her name was – is – Ellen. She had taken the house and the pool and the rights to the royalties from most of his early recordings. The apparition who looked so much like this first wife, who had been there even before he had a first wife, told him to forget such details in her strange tongue that made him think of the word *brogue*. As other faces receded into the wall, hers became more pronounced, coming and going like the fine breath of air that sometimes wafted in from the brick-sized opening up above.

In the end, Romulus did not have the strength to tell her to disappear. He closed his eyes instead and felt her hovering above him, penetrating the soft matter of his mind. He wished she would disappear when the pink pills found their way into his open palms, held out like a supplicant receiving communion after a long period of retreat and contemplation.

After a few weeks, the pills stopped coming. All he was left with was his slackening body, tired muscles, shortening sinews, sluggish blood, rattling bones and rattling teeth, hair falling out, skin flaking.

Romulus did not think that he could bear the periods of withdrawal, his muscles quivering intensely as if in shock.

To distract himself from his own failing form, he watched all the other bodies around him, defecating, peeing, peeling, brown skins turned to odd shades of dullness out of the sun's reach. Smiles turned to grimaces; folds of skin became grotesque as each of them lost weight. They were thrown dirty aluminium bowls filled with a greenish-brown slop once a day, if they were lucky.

He had never seen such shit.

For the first month, he waited for his sister to bring bowls of white rice with dark beans and a stew of chicken falling from the bone. For a time, he traded those meals for his drugs and then, when the pills ran out, he traded the food for his cot and quiet. His frame became lighter and the apparition resembling Ellen haunted his dreams.

L'ap pèdu tèt li, the other men said of him when he would scream at the walls to leave him alone. They laughed at him under the cover of their thin arms and elongated fingers, looking day by day more like the figures of emaciated peasants Romulus had seen captured in the paintings that hung in his Miami houses. He laughed wryly to himself: he had become one of the figures in his own paintings.

She told him to forget about the paintings. He had work to do beyond these prison walls. A land to go to so far away from everything he had known, a history to resurrect. If only he would awaken.

Romulus struggled with her every night. His stomach clenched at the sight of her. His dreams were polluted with her image, the sounds of her foreign tongue. She took him to her land so green it seemed touched by the hand of God. There, the skies hung low above the hills; the clouds embraced their roundness like the suckling child its mother's breast and threw shadows down like blankets of protection. Yet, in places, there were barren mounds without pasture, small crosses by the side of rocky roads weathering heavy rains to commemorate the dead.

Romulus could not understand it but he vowed to her that if he ever got out of this stinking hole of despair, away from the men whose humanity rotted steadily from within, if they hadn't already lost whatever shred of decency they had been born with – if ever he got out, he would go to this land, if she would only leave him alone after that, if she would only relent and let him regain his right mind.

He did not imagine, as he made this promise, that deliverance was already on its way. He had not imagined that he would ever again walk further than five paces forward and two to the right where he urinated against the wall every day, burning a hole of anger into the limestone, washing away someone else's trace of existence with each impotent outpouring, each erasing the other in a dark dance of expiation.

On the one hundredth and eighty-sixth day of Romulus' captivity, deliverance arrived.

On that eighty-sixth day beyond the first hundred, Romulus sits on his pallet and looks out at the sea of legs and arms before him. The stink emanating from the walls and floor is at its worst. He has almost become immune to the shit, the constancy of anxious sweat rising from the serpentine, coiled bodies before him. And then, suddenly, the earth trembles beneath them. The doors are pried open and blinding light streams into the darkness.

Men wearing worn and mismatched army fatigues pull the thronged arms and legs out into the daylight. Romulus has his vision of dark angels in flight. He sits like a rock on the cot while the others precede him. He sees a dark arm hovering in the open space of the door, a space the length of a man, tall and broad, much larger than the brick-sized opening above they have all gotten used to for light. The arm motions in his direction. Romulus does not know if he can move. He closes his eyes and *She* comes to him.

Kanpé. He thinks he hears her tell him to stand up, as if all these days and nights of communication have taught her *his* language.

Kanpé, he hears again but this time it is a man's voice. The dark arm gestures towards him.

Romulus rises and walks towards the light, knowing it could be the death of him. The prison doors have never been opened in all the time he has been there. No one has left. No one has entered. The cell has been filled to capacity with no hope of exit. It is the kind of thing one gets used to in Haiti.

Romulus realizes he is still alive when the heat of the sun hits his skin and the winds play with his tightly curled hair. The dark arm he has seen in the cell is attached to a burly man dressed in army fatigues.

121

Romulus suppresses laughter: the man's head is topped with a red beret recalling scenes from Ramboesque American films.

It surprises him, the gurgling well of happiness in his chest, the desire to feel mirth rather than his stolid apathy. He looks away from the man in the red beret and the fake general turns away from him and begins to exclaim to the company of men that they are all free. All the criminals and innocents, free.

Romulus begins to walk away from the jubilant, stinking men (for they are all men, young and old, well and decrepit, all shades of brown) as they scream their freedom to the blue canopy of sky, as if their deliverers are emissaries from the heavens rather than rogues in borrowed clothing.

Romulus walks away from the group with only one idea pulsing in his mind: to walk all the way through dust and fire, from the hell's edge of the prison walls and into the city's glowing inferno to reach its other side, to reach the roads leading out towards the country of his cursed birth.

March 7, 2004, Streets of Port-au-Prince, Haiti

Romulus pursues his path with driven intent. *Focus*, he thinks, *focus*. He speaks to himself in a colonial tongue, a language he learned in order to get by in the world. Without it in America, *ou banan*: no one with nowhere to go. You might as well be left hung out to dry, as the Americans liked to say, like a sheet of banana leaf.

As soon as he is out of the prison walls, and far enough away so that the men he had been jailed with cannot see him, Romulus begins to run, homewards, not thinking about who might be there to greet him, or if he will be welcome. He does not stop to think about his dishevelled appearance, his sunken cheeks that make his eyes seem as if they are bulging out, froglike.

He has lost many pounds in the prison, pounds he cannot afford to lose from an already slight frame. His shirt is torn in places, missing buttons. Still, he runs. How could his sister turn him away? Blood is blood, as his father had always said, despite his own lack of attention to matters of loyalty. Blood comes back to blood, always, like rivers to their beds.

There is an indescribable stench in the air. Romulus is used to the smells of rotting garbage, has gotten used to the putrid odour of disintegrating human waste. But what he smells in the air now is even more overwhelming than what he has endured in prison. His eyes trail the spumes of smoke rising from behind the crowded buildings on both sides of the road. He is startled, as he looks left and right, to see rubber tyres piled high burning in the middle of what had been open roads.

In one alleyway, a car sits, torched, stripped of its tyres, its windows smashed. Grocery stores that had been off-limits to the poorest of the poor stand looted, usually full shelves empty, products strewn on the floor rendered inedible. He falls into a sea of demonstrators, bodies pushing against him from all sides. As he wades through the crowd, he sees a charred body at the side of the road. The form is carbonized. He cannot tell if it is a man or a woman. What might have been an arm points upwards, a black branch emerging from a charcoal trunk.

A few feet beyond the first corpse, another lies on the ground. Half of the man's face is smashed, stoned to death. An eye stares out at Romulus from its hollowed cavity, blood pooling out from the deep wound staining the broken cement of the road. Romulus winces. *Poor devil*, he thinks.

Romulus' run has slowed to a fast walk as he navigates the debris in the roads as best he can, avoiding the waves of demonstrators emptying from the houses of the *bidonville* and spilling out into the street. His mind reels at the thought of what has been going on outside the jail walls all this time. He has been safer in there than out here, he realizes, and wonders if there is anything to return to, any home left standing, if his sister is still alive.

"Romulus!" He hears his name called. He continues, thinking the voice is in his head. After all, hasn't he gone mad? He keeps on.

"Romeo," the voice calls again, more insistent, distinct. It is a man's voice and Romulus realizes then that the voice is coming from beyond him, from the direction he has just left.

He tries to keep on but as his feet move forward, his head turns back. He walks forward like an ostrich, his feet moving, his long neck peering over his shoulder, his eyes too curious to stay on course.

In the moment of turning his head, Romulus has the sensation of energy slipping away from his being. The feeling is like a small wave washing over him. It leaves a tingling in its wake and a sense of foreboding, of loss. But Romulus cannot fathom what it is that he could be losing, though he knows it has everything to do with this moment of turning around, with the need to hear his name called out more pronounced than his desire for freedom.

"Romeo," the voice says again, using his stage name to good effect. Romulus sees the lips of a square-jawed face mouthing his name. The man's high cheekbones seem to be holding up great folds of skin that embrace his chin in a swath of thickness. The folds stretch and tremble as he speaks. "Romeo, brother-man, where are you going?"

Romulus thinks about his sister's house out in the country cradled by those of neighbours they have known all of their lives who had practically raised them both out of the crib. He looks at the man who towers over him, thick and elongated cords of muscle binding his arms and legs. Romulus recognizes the man from the meeting in Miami that had led him home and then to prison. He remembers that the others had called him Marc or Marco. Romulus had never considered that he would run into him again.

Marc advances towards him, all muscled power. Romulus regrets having stopped. Marc is bad news. Romulus knows he is going to be swept away into something beyond his control and yet he stands still, refuses to turn away. He should keep on walking but he is used to being swept up. It has become a way of life. Romulus tries to think of the fact that Marc knows him only as a first class junky, not as the person he has become in the prison: swept clean, penniless, with only the shirt on his back to show for wealth. He has to maintain the coolness of intent he had had in that meeting in Miami when he had been wearing a designer suit and worn dark glasses to cover up the fact that he had been high even as he had made a deal with people he had never been involved with in his life as a musician, people who were far below him in the food-chain of Haitian life.

Marc's face does nothing to promote trust, with the jagged scar that runs down the length of his left cheek, as if thunder had visited him there and felt his flesh wanting.

Still, Romulus moves towards the man as if he might present salvation. The truth is simply that the fear of returning to a place he can no longer legitimately call home has taken stronger root than the desire to continue running towards the place his youth remembers. He does not realize yet that he is running nonetheless, from one hell to another. Sometimes, one hell was sufficiently different from another to seem like a worthwhile reprieve.

"*Sak pasé?*" Romulus asks, forgetting without truly forgetting, the chaos surrounding them, the burning pyres of car tyres, the crowds emptying into the streets chanting, *libèté, libèté* – a rallying cry not heard for years.

The mantra of the dispossessed had escaped ready definition over the years as the times changed: leaders fleeing and returning while the masses remained prisoners to a land once rich, a land rich still with the echoes of their ancestors' knowledge, their murmurs sounding out in the barren hills, imitating the cries of children at their births. Some of them had no intention of ever leaving. They watched those who left and returned with mirth, sometimes with condescension. Journalists mistook the hard glints in their eyes for murderous envy while their anger festered for expression. Most of them simply wanted their piece of land, their corner of the universe beneath the benighted stars promised to them after the Revolution. They were frustrated by the constant denial. This time, it was for their children that they abandoned shacks and stands, some of the wealthy at long last joining them in solidarity to announce that the future might be different – that the next generations might not have to survive in misery. It was a wonder really, Romulus thinks, that the masses had any energy left at all.

"*Ki bagay sa-a! Yo lagé ko ou nan laru a? Ou pa gen limouzinn ou?*" Marc laughs a wide laugh, baring red-gummed teeth, and sweeps a large hand through the air as if to show an invisible limousine. His head tips backwards, forcing the muscles of his wide neck into half-moon arcs that form an elongated v-shape emanating from the clavicles of his collarbone and ending just below each ear on both sides of his jaw. His laughter ripples out in waves, making passers-by heading out to join the demonstration frown in wonder at this merriment. These are difficult times, after all.

125

Romulus feels only shame rising up from his solar plexus like bitter bile, shame for the loss of his past fortune, shame for the loss of the meaning of his family name. He keeps to himself that he had been heading to his sister's home.

He walks towards Marc and feels, suddenly, for no reason at all, as if he might be letting go of his past forever. It is a feeling not unlike the snap and spin in his head when he flirts on the edge of an OD, a hair's breadth away from the black abyss of non-return.

He should never have turned around.

Romulus had known moments like this before, moments in which the past seemed to recede and the future seemed like a wide, open pit before him in which, without a care, he could fall head first. He had learned that the feeling was deceptive. There was nothing but the present with which to contend. Yet, he knew that what one decided to do could alter one's life so irrevocably that one would want to go back and undo each of those moments as if they were knots on a string. Sometimes, he'd made decisions that altered not only his own life but the lives of those for whom he cared – his wives, his children, his band-mates.

Romulus was an expert at leaving things and people behind as he moved forward. He was like the children in the fable of Hansel and Gretel, leaving houses and cars in his wake as the children had left morsels of bread as they walked through the forest. For Romulus, waiting at the end of the path, in the blistering heat of the witch's oven, was the anger and disappointment he engendered in others and would do everything to avoid. It never occurred to Romulus that others did not see him as an innocent in a hostile world, but as the witch herself, hidden in the woods, waiting to strike. Deep down, as destructive as he was to himself and to others, he sought to be found. It was this yearning that delivered him to Marc, even though Marc's smile was no more convincing than a scorpion's.

"*Ou t'ap pralé?*" Marc asks with false caring.

Romulus feigns ignorance of his motives and smiles sheepishly. Marc wraps a thick, seemingly protective arm around Romulus' diminished frame.

"*E ou menm?*" he asks Marc while he thinks of the last time someone had put an arm around him. His thoughts vaguely drift to Brigitte, his third and last wife, the only one who had looked nothing like the woman who had appeared in his dreams, who persisted her haunting in his hallucinations.

It had been Brigitte who had prompted Romulus' illegal return to Haiti by locking him out of his own house. If it hadn't been for that, Romulus would *never* have agreed to become a carrier. He would *never* have seen Marc standing in the darkness of a room that contained some of the key figures involved in drug trafficking across Haiti's borders. He *never* would have found himself, now, with this fiend's thick arm around his shoulders. It wasn't his fault.

"*Ou pral wè*," Marc says as the two are encircled by a group of young men Romulus has mistakenly assumed to be on their way to the march, heading towards the square in front of the Presidential Palace where the statue of the unknown slave stood blowing his eternal bronze conch shell as if mocking them.

Freedom. Emancipation. These were words that had lost their meaning.

Romulus no longer knows the country well enough any more to identify the group ferrying him along under the protection of Marc's heavy dark arm. He feels suddenly like a child, captive and subservient, afraid of what might happen if he chooses to break away, running, again, towards home or what was left of home. In Miami, he had heard about the paramilitaries dressed from head to toe in futuristic-looking black gear that looked so anachronistic in a Haiti that still appeared almost medieval. As a child he had resented this more than anything. He had wanted to be a part of the modern world he saw advertised in the French press and on the news beamed in from the outside world. He yearned for the pleasures recounted by uncles who floated in and out of the country with unceasing levity, thick gold rings and bracelets shackled to their fingers and arms like spoils of war. These were uncles who fell beyond the circle of his mother's approval. Romulus had to seek them out on his own, surreptitiously. They were dangerous men, men who had links to the government, if one could call it that, men who talked of themselves as existing beyond the laws of any land and seemed successful in doing so. Romulus had wanted to be one of the anointed, not dangerous *per*

127

se, but certainly beyond the law. He had learned that wealth was the key to obtaining this sort of dubious freedom. For him, music had been the way.

They walk against the flow of the crowd, lost in it for long stretches and then, they are suddenly alone, walking up into the hills above the capital where the houses of the rich gleam like white and pink shells rising fresh from the ocean bed. Romulus begins to feel nervous. He knew these homes well once. He had even owned one. There were relatives and friends of his father's who lived there still. What did these men want? He had heard of the *chimères* spreading panic in their wake. He had heard of the kidnappings and ransoms demanded of the wealthy or *diasporas* like himself. Returning *diaspos* were always surprised by such events. They did not realize that what was survival elsewhere constituted wealth here, that for those on the ground they had become part of the elite, however Black they might be.

Romulus wonders again what he has gotten himself into. This is a rare thought for him, one that surely stems from his sobered state. For the first time, Romulus begins to understand the root of his addiction: his fear of being forgotten. He craves recognition of any kind. This is what has brought him within the fold of this unlikely group, men clad in discarded Nike-wear from the factories, brightly coloured short-sleeved shirts and baseball hats advertising Canadian baseball teams. He has been brought amongst them by his fear of refusal at his sister's door. But, as he feels his legs grow leaden as they make their way in convoy to the upper reaches of Lalue, it is a new fear that grips him, the fear of harming, in full consciousness, one of his own.

Romulus wonders if he is imagining the heaviness growing from Marc's encompassing arm dropping into his body like poisonous lead. He wonders when and where the journey will end. Some of the men are speaking in low whispers to each other while they look ahead, determination outlined in their posture and in the straight-ahead doggedness of their heads, eyes fixed on the goal lying before them, in those hills that still sing with green bursts of colour, unlike so many of the bare mountain ranges that ring the city.

They pass tall wall after tall wall, some topped with coils of barbed wire, others with the more colonial lines of jagged, broken bottles: green, amber and clear, cemented to the top of the walls. Romulus recognizes his old house and cringes as they pass it. He does not own it any longer and doesn't know who lives there now. They pass the UNICEF headquarters and its half-mooned entrance filled with a line of high-end jeeps. It is surprising, even to someone of Romulus' background, to note how well-equipped their saviours are. The men point at the jeeps and comment. There is laughter in the ranks for the first time. And then, a few houses later, Marc's arm stops propelling Romulus forward and falls away. It is the moment that Romulus has been waiting for, to breathe again, but his stomach is clenched. They are in front of a house he knows all too well.

Marc smiles upon seeing the light of recognition in Romulus' eyes and the men move forward in unison. Unlike the other houses, the portal to this one has been left unlocked. The men move one by one in an organized single file past the gates and stumble into the yard. There is familiarity in their movement. Romulus feels as if he is experiencing his own, disturbing *déjà vu*.

Romulus feels his hand on the vined gates as he follows Marc and the other men into the yard. His hand has performed this action before, pushed the gate open confidently and ushered himself into another world, a world so unlike the broken and sullen streets that greeted him daily like so much useless ash. He has walked down the flat white slabs shaping a snakelike path to the front door, through the lush flowers of the manicured front garden, his leather school bag bouncing up and down the length of his right thigh. He had come all the way from the private school for boys he attended in the city, brought to the hills in a tap-tap, when such service had been available and reliable, the streets not so far gone as to need American technology to be tackled. Now, there are no black speckled orange lilies craning their necks towards the path, nor the pink leaves of fallen bougainvillea strewn across the stones, making a scratchy, papery noise as the wind lifts them away, nor are there roses in full bloom, their heady perfumes letting him know that more treasures lay ahead behind the heavy oak door of the house.

If Romulus had paused to think about love over the years, in the absence of his mother's arms, and in the silence that enveloped his father's occasional appearances in his life after he had left home at sixteen, he would have remembered his times in this house as defined by such a thing. But since love had so far eluded him, like a glass vase kept out of grasping hands on a high shelf in his grandmother's house, he could not attach the word to the place. He could, though, feel warmth enveloping his chest as he moved forward across the stones that had been reshaped by the many feet that had rubbed away their harshness and left behind telling grooves of movement and hospitality. The owner of the house was as retiring as she was welcoming and only the stones revealed how many guests had quietly and ceaselessly beaten a path to her door. Was this what the men before him were doing? Had done already, in another time? Romulus could only wonder. They seemed so out of place, so ungainly, so unrefined. The owner of the house is nothing if not refined.

If love is not the word that came to mind when Romulus thought about this house and its once lush gardens, it is another word that pronounces itself a close synonym to his mind and in his memory: *music.* It had been here, amongst the sound of the bougainvillea flowers scraping past his feet, the rose bushes and the tall, wild grass, that he had begun to understand the meaning of the word *symphony* and the conjoining of sound and scent to create a language that only the spirit and heart might be able to decipher.

She had been his piano teacher and for a time, in his adolescent years, the years before he had drifted away into the fog of chemically induced visions, his muse. She had been the first woman he had loved without recognizing the feeling as love, and left, never to see her again, as his mother had left him some forty years before, without a trace. It dawned on him fleetingly that he himself was the trace his mother had left behind: the thought gave hollow comfort.

Although it had been the murmur of something akin to love that Romulus had felt then for Tatie Ruth, the owner of this house, Romulus had had no designs on the woman to whom he would dedicate his first songs and empty pop lyrics. He barely took note of the fact that Tatie Ruth had been in her thirties when he had taken lessons from her, still a relatively young woman. He had taken no notice of the curvature of her bare legs shaped by long walks in the mountains when the air was clear and crisp, legs that spindled out from beneath her skirts like the long stems of the most hardy of flowers. She would adjust a thin sweater on her shoulders, push back her reading glasses, and peer over his head at the notations on the weathered sheet music she allowed him to take home so that he could continue to practice, either at the home of the Uncle with a piano, or in the large hall at school where gatherings were held on holidays of the Catholic calendar. In those days, he had no knowledge or interest in the female form, or perhaps Tatie Ruth had simply seemed beyond the reach of his eleven years. He kept all of his energies for the music, as if he was an athlete in strict training, remembering only much later how inebriated and inspired he had been by the pollen of flowers in the garden, by the whiff of Tatie Ruth's thick French perfume.

It is this sensory memory that strikes him as he walks into the foyer, the tiles radiating cold, stunning him into his past, his beginnings, a time that had been so innocent and free of all the madness that followed on its heels.

"*Sak n'ap fè la-a?*" he asks Marc. "*Ou konen Tatie?*" he continues, a childish innocence punctuating his words.

Marc leaves the questions hanging in the air and gestures towards the others to take their positions. He sweeps Romulus back towards the front door.

"*Sak gen la?*" a thin, reedy voice wafts in from the back of the house. Tatie Ruth. Even after all these years, Romulus recognizes her distinctive *Kreyol. Soigné.* Careful and peppered with French intonations. She would be in her late seventies by now, ageing, skin and bones made heavy by the pull of gravity.

Marc signals Romulus to speak. The men are positioned in the darkness of the receding perimeter of the round foyer like foxes circling a chicken coop. He hesitates. Marc gestures more emphatically. This is no rehearsal. What has he gotten himself into?

"*Tatie,*" Romulus begins, "*Romulus ki la, wi.*"

"Romulus!" she exclaims, voice quivering slightly, emotion audibly catching in her throat. He hears her moving hurriedly through the halls of her house to the foyer. "You came back."

131

He sees confusion in her face.

"Are you back at the house?" she asks, referring to his old house up the road, the one he had once lived in with Ellen. He had hardly seen Ruth during the two years he had lived there, trying unsuccessfully to end the drug habit that eventually destroyed the marriage.

Romulus has no answer for her. He becomes suddenly self-conscious of his attire, of the soft layers of dust clinging to his perspiring skin. The heat is suffocating. He feels tired, wan. What can he be doing here? Why this, the gathering place? He has the impulse to tell her to run back, run back, to keep out of sight, but he knows it is too late. He is always too late.

"They let you out?" she says, her voice weak.

"*Wi*," he says finally, because there is nothing else he can say. How did she know? Did everyone know? "Yes. They let me out. I'm out."

She emerges on one of the arcs leading from the foyer to the rest of the house. There are three such arcs. She stands in the hollow of the farthest to his right, the men forming a half-circle in the dark. She is still slightly too far away to see them all gathered there, foxes in the den.

Go back, back, Romulus thinks, hoping she will turn and ask him to follow her to another part of the house, perhaps to the back kitchen for a strong cup of *café*. Then he could tell her about Marc and the men and the need to find shelter in her yard, or elsewhere.

But she stands there like a ghost, waiting for him to speak, and Romulus realizes that she has been waiting for a long while, although he is not so sure that she has been waiting for him in particular. Does she already know what is about to happen? She must have heard about the jails being opened by the rebels.

"I'm sorry," she says, "It's just that…"

"*Je sais*," he responds, feeling the rush of shame travel up the length of his neck.

She has lost nothing of her mystique with her wide robes and flower-imprinted dresses. She is stooped slightly and holds her back with one hand against the pain radiating there to her right hip. Her hair is held back in a tight bun and though they stand some fifteen feet and years apart, he can smell her perfume more strongly than ever, making him wonder at the clarity of his pre-addict memories. They are both like ghosts standing before each other, each remembering the other as they had been in another life, incredulous over the changes that time has wrought. Still, they cannot see each other clearly. The foyer is dimly illuminated by light streaming in from the arcs. There are no windows here. Romulus can make out a table in the centre of the room, a walnut table with a sturdy club-footed stand. A thick plastic sheet seems to cover the surface of the table.

He would think later that this was an odd detail to note at the time – the thick plastic covering nothing like the delicate embroidery that usually graced Tatie Ruth's tabletops, embroidery she taught the young girls who were hired help in the neighbourhood to make, so they would have some kind of a trade. He sees the photographs beneath the plastic, his much younger face staring up at him, as if looking at a stranger. What a failure he must be in her eyes, Romulus thinks, forgetting for the moment the men hidden in the shadows. What a failure.

Then, simultaneously, as if propelled by an invisible shift in gravitational pull, they advance towards each other. Romulus stands closer to the table with its plastic covering. He can see now that the plastic keeps a series of photographs locked in place beneath its weight. Tatie Ruth advances into the circle of awaiting men. He thinks that he sees her smile at them in recognition, a smile quickly dissolving into apprehension.

Their eyes catch and Romulus senses that he is being forgiven his betrayal. Tatie Ruth smiles again quietly, sadly, and then makes a small circular gesture of hand tight against her waist as if to say to them, *Come, come, I have been waiting for you.*

Later, only minutes later, minutes that seem to stretch into an unbearable knowledge of infinity, Romulus falls into a black hole of amnesia, a temporary blackout that will help him to survive the day as he has survived so many others. This time, however, he is sober and he still cannot believe the sight before his eyes: was it she who had fallen, or he? Was it Marc who had used the machete or one of the skinny young men in the troupe too impatient to wait to be led through the house's many halls to a treasure they must have assumed lay beyond? Was it their feet he heard running back up the path, leaving the front door wide open so that light inundated the dark foyer suddenly, like a blast of thunder in a storm, or was it he himself fleeing the scene? Had it been his fourteen-year-old face that he saw looking expectantly up from a jaggedly trimmed black and white photograph beneath a now blood-streaked clear, plastic tablecloth, he standing amidst the bougainvillea in the garden in his Sunday best, sheet music in his hand? Was that his smile as a twenty-four year old, cut from a newspaper and placed next to a picture of a young woman who eerily resembled his visitor in prison, that peaked face hovering above him on the walls? Picture upon picture: brown, yellow, peach complexioned faces – a map of Tatie Ruth's inner world laid out as if she was afraid that she would forget them all, or that the disappearance of the actual people from her hall meant they would never return. There, too, was a photograph of an unsmiling Marc in short pants, exposing knobby knees, skinny fingers poised over piano keys.

In this way, she kept them captive to the echoes of another world that resounded with the sounds of music and laughter, sounds she hardly heard any more, sounds replaced with the ringing of bullets and cries of despair and a silence all the more piercing for its meaning: the absence of love.

Blood speckles the bright faces and white teeth. *Was it hers or his?* There is a wild rush of sound in his ears, making a small whoosh as the liquid particles hit the solid surfaces in random syncopation. He's heard the sound before, usually before hitting the ground after a particularly bad hit. This time, he has to remember his sobered state. It is difficult to mark a difference. He wonders if he has ventured close to death. *His own? Hers?*

The pictures beneath the plastic look up at him, furiously, as if he could have stopped the chaos. It is vertiginous to look down at so many faces and to feel the sensation of falling towards some unknown depth.

As Romulus' body convulses in a cold sweat against the clamminess of the linoleum floor, he hears some of the men walk through the house under Marc's supervision. They seem unable to uncover the treasure they have sought.

He hears them scramble and swear beneath their breaths. *We shouldn't have killed her so fast*, one of them says. He hears them curse him as they step over his body on their way to other parts of the house. Romulus cannot open his eyes. He cannot move. For a moment, he thinks he hears her call out his name. He thinks he can see her in his mind's eye but he cannot move towards her, cannot embrace her. It is too late. All he wants to do is lie there and let life seep out of him. He is a coward too, not wanting to see what has already been done to Ruth. He cannot think ahead to what might happen to him if he is found there, in a house turned upside down with bitterness, a woman's dead body lying not far from him. His body aches; his mind feels on fire. He cannot move. He could be dying. He lets his mind drift away from his body, from the house, from the other men. He thinks about his childhood, of his absent mother and brooding father. He wonders how it could all have been different.

He dares not open his eyes. He does not want to see the sight of blood, his own or another's. He does not want to see the ghost's face mocking him for his cowardice or Ruth's frozen in disbelief at what he has become.

The only thing Romulus can be sure of as he feels his body run cold and slick with sweat, before his head comes in contact with the ground, rendering him unconscious, is that he does not hear their victim scream her surrender or her pain. All he hears as he falls is a throbbing silence in the house and the muted sound of field crickets emanating from somewhere beyond.

March 7, 2004, Port-au-Prince

Romulus wakes and miraculously finds himself walking away from Ruth's body and her deserted house, the other men gone long before him, trailing back down the mountain and into the chaos of the streets below.

There is nothing left it seems, nothing to focus on, except to retrace the steps to where he took a wrong turn at that fork in the road that should have led to his sister's house, to the country of his early childhood.

Romulus walks with slow, deliberate steps, placing one foot in front of the other squarely, carefully, watching the dust lift from the ground, watching the disturbed particles circle his feet and settle on his shoes. Layers of dust: this is all he sees between his sister's house and Ruth's body: layers of things he can't quite comprehend, small particles that make up a whole he cannot quite see. Why did Marc bring him there? Why was he chosen as the decoy? Why would they have wanted to harm Ruth? He doesn't know and doesn't care to try to decipher the mystery on his own.

All around him, there are the remains of lootings. There are smouldering mounds of fire as if cars and other items strewn onto the streets have spontaneously combusted. There are clusters of people on street corners, young men mostly, their shirts hanging in long, torn pieces of cloth across their muscled chests, some bearing the typical country weaponry of worn machetes, swinging them above their heads. They jump up and down in unison and chant. Romulus can't make out what they are saying and doesn't care. He is intent on his feet, walking towards Constance's house until he gets there, burning cars or not. What does he know of looting and despair? He has his own cross to shoulder.

The sun overhead is bright, like a blind sentinel joyous in his position of dogged watchfulness, unseeing of the strife below. It is a curse and a blessing, Romulus thinks, as sweat pours down the dust-encrusted fissures in his middle-aged face. Watching the young men on the road, thinking of the young men in Ruth's house only hours ago, he feels the age of his body, this vessel he has always mistreated and longed to escape. So much time has been lost. *So much time.* He trudges on, wondering how so much dust can reside on an island surrounded with water.

It has been days since the news of the floods and landslides that ravaged areas north of the capital. The capital had hardly felt the touch of the swirling waters, it seems, even though the tide of the waves was high, the fields surrounding the airport swallowed by telltale signs of flooding.

When Constance opens the rust-red, wooden door to her house, the house where she and Romulus were born so many moons ago under skies lit with bright stars, it is to find a bedraggled man in her front yard heaving from a long walk, skin caked with a layer of red dust, the leather of his shoes threatening to come undone at the seams. Still, she feels a sympathy stirring within her, some connection to the man hidden beneath the sweat and the dirt, beyond the heaviness of his dangling arms and worn clothing.

"Who goes there?" she asks, keeping the door still halfway across her body like a shield, in case the man decides to leap across the porch and force his way in. She peers at him across the twenty or so yards that separate them and realizes he is in no shape to do anything to her and moves the door open to stand on the cement stoop. She crosses her arms in front of her chest.

"*C'est moi,*" the man says in a hoarse whisper.

"*Quoi?*" she strains to hear him and cups an ear in the direction of the man's voice. She steps off the stoop and onto the first square tile of the walkway leading to the front door. Grass growing wildly through the cracks between the tiles tickles her ankles and she remembers playing in the yard as a child, the grass stiff like straw poking through their clothes, the rolling of their bodies across the uneven soil, not listening to their mother telling them to stay clean, the dust rising from the ground covering them in its transparent sheen.

"Romy," she gasps. "Romy? How did you get here?" She rushes towards her brother, the distance, the years, the history between them growing smaller and smaller until she is hugging him against her, feeling the boniness of his chest as she clasps him.

Romulus feels his sister's arms around him as if from a vast distance. He remembers hearing her voice at the jail, his laughter echoing down the hall in response. He had been high on something that day. The other prisoners had laughed at him. He doesn't remember her coming after that even though there were packages of clean clothing and carefully packaged meals he either shared or traded for drugs.

He remembers her years ago, backstage at a concert, her face lit with pride, the way he'd brushed past her as if he had better things to do than acknowledge her. He remembers even long before that, when they were children in this yard, waiting for a father who never materialized, waiting to see what life would bring them, rolling in the grass, tickling each other senseless, how it had seemed then that everything was possible, the road of life before them a promise of plenitude neither of them could doubt. The common and uncommon terrains of their lives unfurled in his mind, receding from the present moment image by image until he could no longer feel his own tired body in Constance's embrace, as if he was just floating within the cage of his bone and flesh.

He feels himself falling and, far off, he can feel Constance's frame buckling under his weight, attempting to bring him back to his feet by scooping him up by the armpits.

Kenbé, kenbé, he hears her say into his ears but his ears feel as if they are located at the opposite end of a long tunnel. Hold on. Hold on. The heat of the sun feels unbearable upon his head. Sweat slips down his face in slick streaks.

Kenbé, kenbé, he hears again, but he has let go, falls into Constance, lets her sweep him up onto the porch as his feet stumble and search for a hold upon the ground.

Kenbé. Kenbé.

What is there to hold on to? his mind wonders. *What?*

March 10, 2004, Port-au-Prince

A man of Constance's acquaintance comes to the door late one night as he is tossing and turning, sweating profusely, aching for relief from the gnawing compulsion in the pit of his stomach to get high. Thankfully, Constance has five-star *Barbancourt* rum in the house. He drinks four-ounce shots and falls into a heavy sleep. He hears the door open, hushed tones, haggling over a price and then quiet, the door closing and the shuffling of Constance's feet against the tile floor leading from the entrance to the kitchen where she is going to warm herself some milk before going to sleep. The smell of the scalding milk reminds Romulus of their mother as he drifts off; he recognizes an old habit left over from childhood. In the morning, there are documents left for him at his place at the kitchen table, along with a one-way plane ticket to Miami. Not a word is said about the papers.

Constance goes about her business as if he is just visiting, as if everything is normal, even as the news of lootings and car burnings streams in with the neighbours dropping by for coffee in the late afternoon. The neighbours stare at him as he sits on Constance's sofa with a coffee cup and saucer balanced on his knobby knees. He plays at sipping at the steaming liquid, the heat smudging his nose with dampness. He smiles at their discomfort, at the questions in their eyes, but his smile is empty of any malice, empty of pride. He's been stripped of all that. He is smiling to make them feel more at ease, because he simply has nothing to say.

Constance chatters on with her guests, knowing that he will be leaving in a few days' time and that there is no need for explanations. If she acts as normal as can be, so will everyone else. She is right; the more she behaves as if his sudden appearance is as natural as the sun coming up in the sky in the morning, the more the visitors to the house smile back at him and try to include him in conversation despite his lack of words. His tongue is thick in his mouth, heavy. He's taken to lacing the coffee with rum behind Constance's back.

Finally aboard the Air France plane, his assumed identity firmly fixed on the outside flap of his carry-on bag and printed on his boarding pass, words begin to flit through Romulus' mind at lightning speed. The cottony mass that had lodged itself between his ears while in Constance's home begins to loosen and he hears his thoughts like a deaf man suddenly brought to hearing. The words screech through his mind like the hooves of thundering horses; he cannot grasp them. Soon enough, he realizes that these words make sense. They are his thoughts, about Ruth, about the fires in the streets, the remnants of which they rode past on their way to the airport, of Constance's head bobbing up and down in front of him on the front seat as if she was a doll. He is thinking about her aloofness, the shame he has brought to her house and to their name. He realizes that the identity she has procured for him will allow her a further distancing. She will not have to bear the shame indefinitely; some other man's family, who doesn't yet know that he has been resurrected, will have to bear the burden of his ways. He is thinking of his ex-wives and their children. He is thinking of his songs and that world on stage he used to love so much, do anything for. *A ruined life*, he thinks, *I am sitting on a ruined life. Ashes and shit.* He thinks vaguely of the Bible, of Sodom and Gomorrah, of Job, but the stories are indistinct in his mind.

Guilt is not something Romulus is used to feeling. He recognizes the emotion only from its lack of familiarity. After the anarchy of the days that followed his release from prison, in the wave of absurdity and running blood that bathed Haiti from its most eastern extension to every inch of its shores and jutting mountains, Romulus finds himself sitting, even more incomprehensibly, in the plush, reclining seat of an Air France jet on his way to Miami, his pressed grey suit none the worse for wear after many months of hanging in his older sister's closet.

Romulus' suit is loose and the air around his body reminds him he has shed so much flesh from his always slim body. He sees again the blood pooling out of Ruth's limp body, feels his head throb again from the seizure that had descended upon him, then felled him, leaving him twitching against the cold tile floor, until one of the men he had accompanied took pity and dragged him to the far end of the garden and pushed him into bush-sized weeds, not twenty feet away from the murdered woman.

He isn't sure exactly where he is off to, remembers vaguely telling his sister a dream he had had about a woman who resembled his first wife and a church, rolling green hills, and a request that he follow the woman. He remembers having been delirious, his sister's searching eyes clearly wondering if Romulus had perhaps become as crazy in prison as he had become skinny. He has resisted that notion, resisted the possibility that madness had created his hallucinations. They were dreams. Everyone dreamed, even if they could not remember the design of the images fluttering behind their closed eyelids. Anyone with common sense would want to know the meaning of their dreams, would follow if they could. He had said as much to Constance, she who had always protected him from harm, even against their father who, in his younger days, had regularly been brutal.

He had not told Constance about Ruth, had not told about the men and the machete. He spoke only of his turning head, of falling, of fearing never being able to get up again.

In his first days in the prison, Romulus had seen more than he had wanted of men in despair. He'd seen men babbling to themselves in corners as if they were small children talking to imaginary friends, eating the dirt and shit clinging to the cement as if they had discovered a rare delicacy. The behaviour of such men had the effect of isolating them and Romulus realized that for some it was a way to survive what they thought were worse indignities. He shuddered at the memory of a guard's meaty fingers grasping his sex lasciviously when his body convulsed from want of drugs. He could not remember what had happened to those hands, whether he had responded or not. He remembered only the slow haze that enveloped him afterwards, the deep and sensual pleasure of being lost in the forest of his hallucinations, the feeling of falling into a vast, cottony immensity that carried him away from the present circumstances, from the stink and degeneracy hemming him in.

He had been floundering in just such a heavenly feeling when he heard a familiar voice wafting through the narrow halls of the jail.

"*Li la*," he heard his sister say in a haughty voice. "*Nou konen ké li la-a.*"

The guards protested, "*Madanm, ou fol.*"

Romulus laughed. The guards had no idea who they were dealing with. The worse thing anyone could do was to accuse his sister of being crazy. Romulus laughed again as he heard her flipping out. *Flippin'* as his drug mates in Miami would say. *Flip-pin'*!

"You are going to tell *me* that *I* am crazy," he heard Constance say, "when I hear him laughing like a wild hyena back there."

He could see her wagging a long, manicured finger in the face of the fattest guard.

"Listen here," she said, this time switching from Kreyol to French to distinguish herself from what she considered to be the lowly status of the guards, whatever their power to torture and to arrest whomever they liked. "*Vous ne pouvez pas faire cela. Nous avons les moyens.* You will treat my brother with the dignity he is owed."

This last statement made Romulus laugh so hard he had to hold his stomach with both hands.

"Too late for that, *soeu'*," he interrupted his laughter to yell out towards her.

141

He was seeing dancing girls in his visions. He smiled at them. Didn't Constance know to what depths he had sunk? He watched the dancing girls and held his stomach and became distracted with the lump of his belly button sticking out in the triangle formed by his clasped hands. It was strange the way the body became like a phantom limb under the influence of drugs. Romulus played with the small stump of his belly button. It was comforting. He laughed some more. He wanted to tell Constance to forget about it. He was fine, wasn't he? They might have taken his shoes and his shirt but he was in fine form and this last set of pills had him sailing. What more could he want? The thought stopped him for a second. What. More. Could he want? Well, decent food would be nice. Some cake, some meat.

"Constance," he yelled out, "Constance. Did you bring food, *heinh*? *Clairin*?"

"What are you doing to him back there," he heard her say. "You have him locked up with murderers? Savages? *My* brother? *Vous n'avez pas honte*? I'm sure you go home every night and tell your wives you have the famous singer in here ready to do your bidding. *Ça ne vas pas finir comme ça*," she said. "You will let me see my brother. You will let me give him these clothes and you will treat him correctly until we can get him out of here. Understood?"

Romulus gathered from the jingling of the jailer's keys coming towards him down the hall that Constance had been understood and her terms accepted. *Génial*, he thought, how great to have a sister like this. How wonderful.

Romulus was as high as a kite when Constance appeared at the door of the cell. She glowered at him above the heads of the crouching men.

"*Toi*," she said, calling him up from where he was sitting, "don't you have any pride for yourself?"

He shrugged in her general direction. She reproached him as if he were a small child. He staggered to his feet and moved in slow motion towards her, trying to stifle the laughter still bubbling up in his chest, "What did you think you were doing?"

Then, as he came up close to her and steadied himself by grasping the rusting bars with both hands, feeling the peeling bark of rusted slivers itch against his palms, she hissed at him:

"Why did you come back? Are you crazy, stupid or what?"

He smiled at her. Constance. He felt a drug-induced surge of love for her.

"Con-stance. Con-stance," he stuttered at her. "*Ko-man... ko-man ou ye?*"

She looked at him, embarrassed and saddened. She could see there was no point in having a discussion. His eyes were bloodshot and red-rimmed, his pupils dilated so that she could see ring upon ring moving out from the pinprick middle of his brown eyes. *What a waste*, she thought silently to herself. *What a waste for father and for herself. All their sacrifices for nothing.* She wondered why there was such an investment in the men of their family and almost none in the women. The women were there to support and to assist, and they grew bitter like lemons, bitter and hateful. Constance could feel her own bile rising against the sight of Romulus, shirtless and dirty, his fine dust-blue pants darkened with grime, his unshod feet caked with crusty layers of mud. *Disgusting*, she thought, but to him, for the memory of their common father and long-suffering mother, she said, "Here, take this," and handed him a package of clothes and food. "We will have you moved to a better cell where you will be left alone. Don't worry, we will get you out." But she could see that Romulus wasn't thinking much about getting out. He was seeing something dancing before his eyes of much higher interest.

He was wondering who was the "we" of whom she spoke. Their father had died a few years ago. They were all that was left.

She left him there, standing with the bars in his hands, as she turned her back on him and left the prison.

When she was well beyond the prison walls, and well beyond the sight of the guards whom she had berated and insulted, she retched her stomach to emptiness.

March 13, 2004, Miami, Florida

Three days after descending from his plane into a fog-laden morning, Romulus awakes in a dingy hotel room where the stained carpets give off a strange scent of stale smoke, ground-in dirt and spilled foods, to find that he has slept in his clothes. He cannot remember clearly how he has gotten from the airport to the hotel. He has only a vague picture of being half-carried out of the plane and left, like a sack of dirty laundry, in a chair.

He had sat there, dazed, wondering what to do next, when it occurred to him that he could simply follow the crowds to find his way out of the maze of the airport. This he did though his legs were shaky and his vision seemed to have become less clear since the day he had come out of the cell and the sunlight had fallen hotly across his eyes.

Romulus doggedly kept his group in sight. They brought him out to the luggage carrousels and there he found the battered valise his sister had lent him. It was nothing like the designer luggage his last wife had bought for him. He had come down in the world. But he was on his way up. After that optimistic thought, Romulus could not remember much. His body had floated out of the airport and into a taxi that left him on the kerb in front of a hotel across from the beach, after making him pay fifty American dollars. His body had found the bed in the middle of the room and collapsed and there he was three days later, wondering what had happened to the time.

Romulus panics as he slowly regains his senses. He sits on the edge of the bed, the odour of stale sweat and urine enveloping him as it freed itself from the folds of his crumpled clothing. He feels his slack muscles aching from the travel, from so many months of disuse, lying on the cell cot and staring up at the ceiling, looking away from the mass of despairing bodies to the wall, seeing faces floating there, entrancing him into a world moving to a different rhythm.

Romulus looks around the hotel room. It is stuffed from wall to wall with chintzy furnishings. The wallpaper is a putrid yellow and green with fake vines moving up the walls like snakes. The furnishings clash with red and blue accents. Romulus closes his eyes against the discord. He begins to miss the jail cell. Despite the depravity of the surroundings, he had been somewhat better there than in some other parts of his life. He'd had enough drugs to get through the most difficult times and, mostly, once the others realized that he was being taken care of from the outside and could supply them with some black market substances, they left him alone. (The others wanted freshly cooked food most of all and he let them have his sister's food; it was one of the reasons he'd continued to lose weight despite the constant traffic of packages that made their way to the cell.) He had enjoyed the relative solitude, the absence of criticism from his wives, not having to worry about one of the children finding him in a drugged-out stupor, not having to stay out all night in order to do what he had to do. He had known nothing about his children's pain when his arrest was made public. He was content to let time slip by, to wake and to sleep by the clock of the movements of the men around whom the days rose and abated with the strip of sunlight streaming from the gap above their heads.

The last night he had spent at Constance's, she had patted his hand while it lay on the dining room table as if he were still a boy. She had told him there was almost nothing left in his US bank accounts. She handed him his credit cards and told him she had added a little from what their father had left behind for them both years ago. Constance's eyes welled with tears as she spoke to him. Romulus looked at her eye to eye, but had felt nothing.

Romulus rolls on the bed. What should he do now? He fumbles about in his pockets in search of his wallet. He has numbers there written out on stray pieces of paper. He pulls them out. He has Constance's number and Brigitte's.

Romulus closes his eyes against the past. He needs to focus on the present. What should he do now, locked away in the hotel, afraid to venture out in case someone should spot him and send him back to that inferno of an island he had once called home? He had a green card for the USA but it wasn't in this new 'Robert's' name. His bank accounts had probably been cleaned out by Brigitte. His release from jail had come before his court date and the USA would not normally have let him in, even after all the thousands, no, *millions* of dollars he had poured into their coffers from taxes over the years. *Home of the free, home of the foolish.* Romulus laughs out loud at his thoughts and he keeps on laughing until he finds himself doubled up and crying against the crumpled sheets of the bed. He cries himself to exhaustion. *Brigitte*, he thinks finally, he should call her first. She will know what do to. She always does.

Romulus sits on the edge of the bed and contemplates the phone. It is black with a rotary dial, an old leftover from the days before mobiles, pagers and email. The old familiarity of the curved receiver in the palm of his hand makes him smile against sadness as he had in Constance's living room, keeping company with neighbours that were strangers to him, trying to assist his sister in the keeping up of appearances.

He dials Brigitte's number with a shaky finger and switches the receiver from his right to his left ear. Years of singing by loudspeakers had rendered him almost deaf in the right ear and he hopes he can hear her well enough with the left if the line is a bit fuzzy. He looks up at the smooth ceiling of the room as he lets the phone ring, once, twice, then three, four times. He looks at his watch. What time is it here? He notices then that the small hand on his watch is still. His watch has stopped days ago, in Haiti, or above the ocean, at two o'clock precisely. He isn't quite sure when, whether in the morning or afternoon. Then, he hears a click on the line.

"If you would like to leave a message for Brigitte or Robert, please do so after the tone. Thank you."

Brigitte's voice. Classy. Confident. Smart. She has erased his old message, his voice. Erased him. He hears the long tone and then there is just empty space to fill. He hesitates.

"It's me," he says, then waits. He hesitates again, "Is anyone there?"

He waits. There is just emptiness between him and the phone.

"If you're there, Bri, please pick up the phone. It's Romy. I'm …where am I… I'm in Miami, somewhere… I'm a bit… lost." That was an understatement. He goes to the window and parts the blinds to peer outside. He sees sand and palm trees across the street from the hotel. South Beach. "I'm in one of the hotels down by the water." He looks out again at the dilapidated cars parked across from the hotel. "Definitely South of 7th… I wonder if…"

What can he say to her? They are still legally married and she had done nothing to get him out of the prison. At least, this is what Constance had told him the first night back at her house.

"I don't know why you married her," she'd said. "Anyone could see she was only after you for your money."

He had nodded then, not believing a word she said, even though Constance's was the only face that he thought of after that hellish afternoon at Ruth's, the only face that had sat calmly before him and told him how things were and how they would be.

"Bri," he whimpers into the phone, "...could you... please... answer...?" He is crying now, the slickness of tears surprising his scruffy cheeks. He hears another click on the phone and then an exasperated sigh.

"What do you want?" Brigitte says, crisply, as if he has only been gone a week or two, lost in the bowels of some twenty-four-hour trip.

He ignores her tone of voice. "Bri," he stands at the side of the bed, eyes fixed on a crack in the ceiling. "Bri, I'm so glad to hear your voice. How are you Bri? How is..."

"Like you really care, Romulus," Bri interrupts him.

But he does, he does want to know about Robert, the real one in his life. He's never wanted to know so badly.

Hearing her mispronounce his full name with English inflections, Romulus realizes there will be no way to sweet talk his way around her.

"Listen," he says, trying to cover up the fact that he has been crying. "I need your help."

"What now?"

"I'm ...I don't know... a bit lost. I fell asleep in this hotel room and I'm supposed to be on my way to Boston to check into a... a rehab."

"That's a joke."

"No, really. Constance talked me into it. It's the only way she would pay for everything, seeing as... seeing as I couldn't access our accounts."

There is silence on the other end of the line.

"Bri, are you there?"

"Yeah, I'm still here. What do you want?"

"Can you help me with some cash?"

"I'm not going to meet you, Romy, and I'm not going to let you see Robert in your condition."

He feels her reaching right into his chest to push his buttons. "What condition is that?" he says sarcastically.

"You know what I mean, Romy. I'm not kidding."

He senses that he is about to lose and relents, "I just need some help. You don't know what I've been through."

"I can imagine. I watch TV."

Her voice is neutral and he cannot tell if she is trying to communicate sympathy.

"Look, I'll call the hotel and see if I can wire you something there, OK? Like $500, but that's it."

"That's it?"

"Aren't you going to rehab? What do you need money for?"

"OK. All right. That's fine. That's fine. What about Robert? How's Robert?"

"Like you really care, Romulus," she says again, exasperated. "Look, I can't help you any more. I'm going to wire this money to you but God help you." She pauses. "By the way, your *other* son left three messages for you here. I suggest you call him back."

She hangs up the phone so loudly his right ear hums. He can tell by her tone of voice she means that his eldest, Christian, has called and he wonders what he might have wanted. Christian is not in the habit of calling him. They are not in the habit of having father-son conversations. Brigitte has hung up too soon for him to ask if Christian has given a reason for his calls. Then he realizes that Christian would not have left a clear message anyway. The boy had always been turned in on himself, even more so now that he was becoming full grown, taller even than his father. Bri would not have asked. She loathed his other children with what he felt was unbecoming immaturity and he had done nothing about it.

Romulus sits back down on the edge of the bed, still holding the phone against his left ear. He should have called her *dear* and *sweets*, like he used to, like he had when they first met. That was it, he should have *sweet-talked* her. He should have reined in his despair and put on a surer voice. He should have remembered his old self, the one she'd fallen for, the crooner, the man with charisma who had swept her off her feet only a few years ago when he had been in a dry period, just long enough to record a new "best of" in New York.

Brigitte had sung jazz standards in a dingy bar in SoHo. She was kind on the eyes and sang like he imagined angels might. She was enchanting, singing with her eyes closed as if no one was in the audience, and they sat there before her as if she was a queen, with their breath held and even he had not dared to break the spell as he entered with his brooding entourage. He had sat down quietly and motioned the others to do the same and listened to her rendition of a Nina Simone song. He had been the first to break the silence as the room filled with electric stillness as her last note hung in the air above their heads. She had seduced him with her aloofness and now she had spurned him with it.

Romulus listens to the dead air and then to the buzz of the phone as they are disconnected. He wishes he were the kind of man who would have thought to first leave an apology on the answering machine and then called back. What kind of a man is he? He has three children and he hadn't thought of calling one since he'd gotten out of jail. What is he going to do now? Still holding the phone in one hand, Romulus searches wildly through his pockets for a stray pill. He finds a packet of sleeping pills. He counts them. There are ten in all. He swallows three down with tap water and waits for them to take hold of his senses. He waits until he feels every limb of his body floating on some cottony substance he might call sleep, where there will be nothing to do but surrender.

March 13, 2004, Miami, Florida

True to her word, Brigitte has wired the money by morning. The front desk calls up to tell him that he can pick up his $500, minus the cost of the room. By the time he gets his hands on the money, there is only $300 left and he uses $200 to get himself a few hits to tide him over until his flight, only a couple of days away. He sits on the mounds of sand between the art deco buildings and the ocean and listens to the murmurs of the sea. He watches the tourists drift to and from the hotels, along with the homeless men who call the beach home. In Boston, he will have to present himself to the rehab centre run by a Jesuit order; this is all he knows. *There are Haitians there, both priests and patients. You won't be alone,* Constance had told him, as she stood next to him at her kitchen table where he was seated, both hands on the table before him, locked together as if in prayer. He had nodded contritely. What choice did he have after what he had done?

He'd found her stash of rum after that, the one that had paid for his music lessons and was still apparently being tapped to provide other barters and favours.

Two days later, he's run out of money except for his taxi fare back to the airport, which he had wisely put aside from the first.

He hesitates and then calls Bri again. He waits for the answering machine to start up, listens to her voice, cold and distant. Waits for the tone to sound and for the void of static air in which he will leave his message.

"Bri, it's me." He listens as his voice slurs and tries to control the thickening of his tongue. "I've run out of money. I mean, thanks for the money."

He wishes he could start over, go back to zero, say something else.

"Listen, Bri, I don't want any more money," he says, even though he does, desperately. "I just want Christian's number, I mean, Ellen's number. I don't have my address book." He attempts humour, "I only have the clothes on my back. Um… if you could… call me back at…"

He hears her pick up but what he hears her say is less certain. He has to replay the entire conversation in his mind over and over again to make sure he has heard her correctly.

"You didn't call him back, Rom?"

Her voice is softer than usual.

"No Bri. I was just… you know… taking care of some business. Just getting ready to head up to Boston, like I told you, for rehab."

"You should have called him, Rom."

Something clutches in his chest and he is suddenly frightened. He remembers the sensation from the day Christian had been born and he had seen the tiny member of his child, so fragile, so vulnerable.

"What's happened, Bri? Tell me what's happened."

"He's dead, Rom. Yesterday. We tried to get a hold of you."

"What do you mean *dead*? It hasn't been three days since I called."

"It's been a week, Rom. You probably missed your flight."

"A week? That's not possible. I've been here all the time. Just getting ready, like I was telling you."

"Christian is dead, Rom."

"*Mon Dieu*," he hears himself saying to no one in particular. "*Mon Dieu*. This isn't possible. How?"

"How?" There is a pregnant pause. "He overdosed, Rom. Crystal meth, I think." She pauses. "His system couldn't take it."

Romulus hears an inhuman cry escape his lips as he struggles for breath and clutches at his chest.

"No," he gasps. "Nah, you're lying to get back at me."

"You bitch," he exclaims with his next breath. "You're just trying to get back at me. I told him never to touch any of that crap. He would never have…"

She cuts through his diatribe, "There isn't anything you can say that will change the truth, Romulus."

Her voice is back to being cold, distant. He is caught short by its flint.

"I wasn't gone that long, Bri," he relents, catching the flames of his anger. "What are you trying to do to me?"

"Your son is dead," she repeats even though she knows he doesn't want to hear it.

"Just six months. A year? Not that long…" he babbles. He's trying to grasp time, change things.

"Baby," Brigitte replies, "you've been gone a lot longer than that."

March 20, 2004, Haiti

Romulus thinks he is speaking to Constance from within the frail casing of a dream. He sees her from a distance, plum brown skin lit from within and she seems to be waving to him. She is either waving for him to come towards her or waving him back. He is too far away to tell. Then he hears her voice. It too seems far away. When her words finally reach him, this is what he hears:

"Wake up. Wake up. This isn't a dream. Romulus! Are you there? Are you there?"

Anger tinges the last phrase and he cannot understand why Constance would be so angry. She looks like an angel standing there in the clearing in front of him, her hair a huge Afro framing her almond-shaped face. He has never seen her so beautiful, she who usually irons flat her hair and pins it to the back of her head so that no one can see it. She is ashamed of its waves, its rigid curls. His older sister. He smiles.

"Romulus," comes her voice again. "Romulus. Talk to me. Talk. Into. The. Telephone."

He realizes then that he is holding the receiver, the receiver he cannot remember having put down yesterday. He remembers speaking to another woman. To Brigitte. Yes, to Brigitte. She had had nothing good to say to him. Then he had taken some pills and had, thankfully, a dreamless sleep.

"Cons-tance," he says, pronouncing her name in French. He finds his lips difficult to move as if they are heavy with sand.

"Finally!" Constance exclaims. "It's about time. You called *me*, remember?"

"Yes," he says, but he doesn't remember. He remembers nothing after Brigitte's words and the buzzing of the dead line in his ears. Words about Christian. Dead. Gone. Forever gone.

"Did you hear anything I told you to do?"

"Tell me again, Constance." His voice is contrite, like a child's, the way it was when he was six and she was seventeen, his second mother.

"Get out of the hotel and back into the airport. We'll call the airline from here and you'll be on the next flight out. Just show them your old ticket and your passport and everything will be fine."

"Everything will be fine," he repeats, pausing to think about how Constance uses the familiar "we" when she speaks of things that need to be done, as if there is still some "we" to speak of. Their parents are long dead and Constance's first and only husband had left some time ago and had never come back. Who was this phantom "we" she kept alive for the sake of appearances?

"Yes. There will be a priest meeting you at the flight, a Mr. Tim O'Connor. He's on his way back to his parish in Boston. He'll get you where you're going." She avoids the word rehab. He smirks to himself as the narcotics flow through his veins and make his temples dance. She seems to be listening for a response but he doesn't have anything more to say. "Romulus?"

"Yes?"

"You have to stop sleeping and get back to the airport."

"Yes."

"You need to stop taking the sleeping pills. They're only for the plane."

He smiles again to himself. Constance has no idea of the monster she is dealing with. She doesn't seem to quite understand that her brother is an addict and that anything that can alter his brain matter will find its way into his mouth sooner or later – like a sweet or sparkly object to a child's mouth. But he could try to have a little more discipline, at least to make it to the airport. He could try. There is nothing left for him in Miami. Christian is gone.

"OK," he says.

"OK?" She seems relieved.

"Yes. I'll stop taking them until I'm on the next plane."

"OK. Call me from Boston."

"All right."

They pause, listen to each other breathing as if in want of an echo from another time. She is almost sixty to his forty-four years. Poor Constance. Always having to clean up after other people's shit.

"You can hang up the phone now," she says, knowing she will call back in a half hour to make sure that he has gone out of the room. "Someone from the front desk is coming up to get you."

Romulus finds himself stuttering in front of the flight attendant standing below a sign that reads "Boston". His hands are shaking. His whole body seems to be shaking from the inside out and sweat cascades down his body, down the sides of his face and below his armpits. The attendant seems to be staring him down, questioning whether or not he is fit to enter the plane.

153

"Please," Romulus says. "I… I… miss… ed… my… p-p-p-lane… earlier…" He doesn't know how to explain. He has again lost track of time. This was how he had lost track of Christian. He thinks about Constance. Maybe she has called by now. Maybe her name is in the computer alongside his: Constance, upstanding sister of misfit, druggie brother, Romulus, ex-famous, now down-and-out singer. "I… I… th… thin-k-u… tha-t… u… my siss-t-ur… call-e-d… you for …m… me?" he gasps.

"Ticket, sir," the woman seems to be yelling at him. Her voice is loud, as if she thinks she is speaking to a deaf man. "I'll need your ticket and your passport."

"Ye-s-s-s-s," Romulus manages to say as he fishes out the documents from the inside pocket of his wrinkled jacket. He slept in his suit all night and it shows. His jaw is unshaven and he smells. He should have taken a shower, shaved, changed his underwear and shirt at least, but he had been afraid to still be in the room when Constance called back, afraid that she would give up on him when she is his last hold on any kind of life.

He isn't a short man but he finds himself peering over the desk, standing on the edge of his toes, the leather of his shoes pressing against his oversized big toes, wondering if Constance's name is in the computer but not daring to ask if the call had been registered.

"Ok, sir," the woman says to him loudly, startling even the passengers waiting in line behind him. She has a thick English accent – at least it seems thick to him. "Just take a seat and we'll have this straightened out in a jiffy." He wonders what it would be like to have to make out that accent all day long. There are times when he still can't make out American English.

"First time flying?" someone in the seat next to him asks. Romulus can't place the accent. It doesn't seem to belong to any place he knows.

He makes a sign with his head that it isn't the first time. He doesn't trust his voice, the thick weight of his lips and tongue. His body is still shaking and he is attempting to master himself by holding his hands together as if in prayer.

"First time clean, then?" the man says in a conspiratorial whisper.

Romulus looks sideways at the man. They are about the same

age though the man looks in better shape, his complexion ruddy, his cheeks rounded like ripe crab apples. The man has a becoming smile and straight teeth. One is made of gold. Romulus nods, then looks back at his shaking hands.

"The shaking goes away after a while," the man says then. "That's how it goes."

Romulus has a strange desire to tell the stranger his life story, how it has come to this that he is alone, fleeing his country, unable to return home, and going on to a place he doesn't know at all. He wants to talk about his wives and the one he has never met except in dreams, the face that disappeared from his consciousness the day that Ruth was slain in front of his eyes. He wants to talk about the days before he took drugs, the first day he stepped on a stage with a number one single; then platinum records, playing packed stadiums in Japan, then small holes-in-the-wall in the US. He wants to speak of the rush he felt when the crowd's adulation flowed through him like a gigantic ocean wave. He wants to say his name and have it mean something.

But it is the stranger who speaks first.

"I went through the same thing ten years ago," the man says.

Romulus looks at the man, at the flushed pink skin of his neck. He has a full red beard and liquid-blue eyes of a hue he cannot quite fix. He wonders if the man's skin is flushed because he is embarrassed to admit that he has been an addict of some sort, in some past life he clearly cannot forget.

"It takes time. You backslide and you think you'll never get out of it, but then, if you have the will, you hold on, and you do. You'll see." The man looks Romulus straight in the eyes and Romulus wonders if he wants to hear any more, if getting on a plane is just an excuse for strangers to swap true confessions that they will never reveal to their loved ones. He just nods in response and the man stops talking.

"Sir," the woman from the counter is in front of him now. "Sir?"

Romulus stands with some trouble. His legs feel like noodles beneath him. Should he be going? Shouldn't he try to find out about the funeral? He had called Constance; this he now remembers. But had he told her about Christian? Surely not. She would have found out about the funeral and sent him there instead. Why is he avoiding looking his ex-wife in the face, the woman who reminds him of the ghost of his dreams? He should have asked Constance to call to find out, but that would have meant confronting her denial of his failures, hers. "Yes," he says, his voice grave, unsure of itself.

"Everything has been taken care of. Boarding is in fifteen minutes." She gives him a tight smile as she hands him his ticket and Romulus takes it quietly, without responding. "Did you understand me, sir? You'll be boarding in fifteen minutes."

"He understands," the red-haired man responds in his stead, in an even tone.

The stewardess's fake smile slips. She is surprised that this ruddy man is taking up for this other with the shakes and too-big clothes, this straggler who has probably walked off the streets and wandered into the airport by accident.

"He's with me. Not a problem," the man says and smiles at the stewardess brilliantly.

She nods and leaves them on their own, the stiffness of her back saying that she has washed her hands of the whole affair. The odd couple is on its own as far as she is concerned.

Romulus nods his thanks and lets his knees bend so that he can let his body fall back into the cushioned seat. The ticket shakes between his hands and he tries to concentrate on reducing the vibration running through his body like an electric current.

"Give it time," the red-haired man says and then repeats, "the shaking goes away after a while." He puts out a large hand spotted with orange freckles. Romulus feels the hand move across his chest like a force field. His breathing becomes shallow. He must be anxious. The man leaves his hand hanging in mid air between them. It stays very still at mid-chest, in front of Romulus. "Tim," he says, by way of introduction. "My name is Timothy O'Connor."

Constance had given him this name. Familiarity. Romulus fumbles with the papers in his hands and finds a way to let them rest in his lap while he takes the man's hand in both his own and grasps it. The shaking stops in his body for a long minute and he feels a warmth coming from the man's hand that calms him. He starts to breathe normally again. "Romulus," he says. "My name is Romulus Pierre." He omits his false name, feeling for the first time in a long while that he might be able to detach himself from what his name had come to stand for – the illusory safety of fame, the disgrace of a great fall from the heights.

"A solid name," the man says. "A good name. Pillars of new civilizations." Instead of shaking loose his hand, as Romulus fears he might, the man presses his fingers more deeply into his palms, reassuring Romulus of something he is not yet certain of – the starting point of progress, slow progress, perhaps towards a different life, a new beginning.

When the man removes the warmth of his hand from between his two palms, Romulus senses that the shaking in his body has subsided and he feels suddenly very tired.

"Plenty of time to sleep in the plane," he hears Tim say at his left, as his head begins to incline forwards. "A few hours at least," Tim chuckles and Romulus feels compelled to keep his head up to listen. This is how Tim begins to tell him his story, as if they are brothers who, parted years ago in their youth, have just found each other anew.

Romulus listens as Tim tells him the hard-luck story of an Irish boy who had grown up in the wild and barren flatlands of a place called Connemara. He sees images of dappled grey work-horses standing still in tufts of green grass, their thick manes waving in the wind of approaching storms. He sees the cords of their muscled necks, the thickness of their flanks and legs, the wildness of freedom still stamped in their large black eyes bordered with thick lashes. He smells the smoky, watery, fumes of peat logs burning in steel stoves anchored to the ground by four sturdy legs shaped like claws, and the scent of damp wool as the bodies of young children heat the blankets of the bed in which they sleep, crowded, sometimes six together, lying feet to head, sisters with brothers and cousins, each cocooned in night gowns that made their skins itch. He knows the smell of broth made from fish bones, and the starchy water left over from boiled potatoes that they still ate like their forefathers in the hope that this would make the weakest among them strong. It is a child-hood girded by silent, sullen men: some who disappear in the waters at sea and some who simply walk away and never come

157

back. It makes Romulus think of his own absent father, whose face he cannot remember. It makes him think of his children who probably cannot remember his. But even as he listens, he falls away to sleep.

Tim lets the man sleep without finishing his story, without telling him of the years he spent on the streets, stealing, making trouble for himself and his family. He doesn't tell Romulus about the years he spent in Dublin before returning to the coast, the years he spent in pubs drinking himself into a stupor, of the woman he beat and the child he lost to death without knowing its name. He tells him none of these things, but knows he will tell the story someday, or that the story has already been told, that it lives on in Romulus's trembling hands. They remind Tim of a trout out of water, whipping its tail back and forth in a wild struggle to hold on to the possibility of freedom. For Tim, Romulus is that fish needing to be returned to water.

PART TWO:

SURVIVAL STRATEGIES

"For our forebears,
For our country
Let us toil joyfully.
May the fields be fertile
And our souls take courage.
Let us toil joyfully
For our forebears,
For our country."

— La Dessalinienne, Haitian National Anthem

ROSE

1956, Port-au-Prince, Haiti

Rose feels it in the air, the way a smothering blanket of change is creeping up and rolling over them like dense fog. She laughs when she hears that Président Magloire has gone to New York and wonders what he'll do there. It's the fact that they say his officers were drunk with rum the day he packed up his belongings that makes her laugh. They could all use a good, stiff drink, she thinks, some throat-burning *clairin*. She imagines him there, living in the belly of the beast, walking foot to pavement with the heavy looming of the skyscrapers above his head. Perhaps it's safer there, huddled in the entrails, Rose thinks, but the thought of the bleak harshness of the city makes her doubt the possibility. Still, she wonders what it would be like to flee everything. She's too young to have gone that far into hell or into the plains. Often, she walks from her mother's house down to the port and gazes out at the steel ships moored there, wondering if one day they'll be taking her away to unknown lands. She'd like to get as far away as possible from this stretch of islanded dirt. She'd like to see the old world: Paris and Prague, Luxembourg and Vienna. She doesn't know why she dreams of these places rather than of America. *America's got her goat, that's why.* Rose laughs at herself when she has these thoughts. All she knows is that times were hard when the Americans came to town with their slicked-back hair and yankee-doodle attitudes. Mamie, her mother's mother, spat on the ground whenever there was talk of Americans. *Ameriken sé bèt,* she'd say, leaving Rose to wonder what kind of animal she might mean as they fed the chickens who fought over the grains flowing from their hands to the ground in a dusty golden rainbow.

Rose didn't dare tell *Mamie* that the Americans said such things about them. She'd learned about it in the Haitian history primer she was taking at the university for her baccalaureate. It just wasn't worth contradicting her. *Yes Mamie*, she'd say, *sé konsa vré*. It's like that. She didn't even dare to dream about American men, even though her favourite movie stars were the ones in Hollywood films like Clark Gable and James Stewart. It wasn't worth doing battle with an old goat, as her mother liked to say.

The fog rolls into the New Year like a heavy, wet blanket they can't throw off. They tried with the elections but the skies just grew darker, bleaker. There was no way to change the weather, Rose thought, even though there was no match between the world she saw around her and the world she could feel flirting around the edges of her person like the wind. When she watched her mother defiantly put her cross against a name on the ballot form not the winner's, Rose felt as if she would faint from the thickness enveloping them, the suffocating heat. The sun was unbearably hot and even though she could see that the skies were pale blue, shadows reigned.

They rolled into the New Year with a new president, but no one would say his name or drink to his health as should have been the custom. They called him the "Doc", remembering his days in the bush trailing the white doctors, curing dengue fever. They imagined him brushing through the countryside like a human scythe, and joked that he had saved lives with the plan of cutting them down later.

Rose laughs when she hears it said that over a million people voted for the Doc. She doesn't know if that many people can even read. Her mother hushes her when she laughs, head thrown back, mouth open, showing its red cave behind her flashing white teeth.

Rose laughs because she knows that now begins the carnage, now the madness. Especially hers.

It's the beginning of the end and she has to laugh. She knows all these changes mark a day with which she won't be able to come to terms. She's made to remember *Mamie* prophesying in the family *hounfort*. That girl, she'd say, pointing almost menacingly at Rose, that girl will receive the devil's victims. They'd all stared at Rose and she wished she could have disappeared from view, not understanding her grandmother's words, or wishing not to understand. They were a family who saw the dead in their dreams, but Rose's gift was to be able to see those who dreamed their deaths or survived them. How she is to go about receiving, Rose has no idea. All she knows is that the gift would come during a time of trial and that time has arrived. She can feel it in the air as surely as when the hurricane season descended upon them, as surely as the heaviness of grey clouds, moving quickly across the normally blue skies, conspires to block the sun from view.

Rose can feel it in her bones that the life she has been working diligently to build is going to fall apart. She is studying for her teacher's certificate but every lesson she attends feels like receiving instructions on hopelessness. She isn't ready for the change, the way the ground feels as if it is shifting away from her as she walks the familiar roads to and from school, to market, to the neighbours' houses. She isn't ready. Why her? Why not someone else, older and wiser? *Mamie* never told why, never explained. *Ti fi*, she would say with a shrug of her shoulders aimed her granddaughter's way: *this is just the way.*

January 1958, Port-au-Prince

Bruises, scrapes, smears of pressed dust dusky against the white of her sleeping robe. There isn't any way to hide. Not any more.

The city is on fire.

Rose is standing in the middle of the flames.

Under cover of night, they find her in the kitchen. They come in their bedclothes and make themselves at home. Stare at her. Consuming. Moments she wishes she could crawl out of the envelope of her skin when the intruders leave behind grains of sand to grate between nerve ends and tissue.

The best she can do is run to the harbour when morning comes. Run out of the house letting the small stones that cover the front yard fly loose beneath the soles of her shoes. Run down the cracked pavements while the heat rises from the asphalt and makes the world waver and undulate in front of her eyes. Run until there is no firm ground left to hold her, only the drop of the sea below, dark and deep. She could drown there, down below. She wishes she could keep running and just let her body drop, sink feet to head, her dress billowing around her like a cotton bloom emerging from its pod, the seaweed pawing at her body. The only thing that keeps her from throwing herself into the waves is the memory of her grandmother, and her mother, still bereft, in the house, cleaning rice alongside Virginie, their housekeeper.

Running and sinking.

Every time she thinks she's done it, she wakes in a cold sweat with a feeling of dread clutching at her from her insides, remnants the ghosts have left in their wake.

Rose is afraid of telling anyone what she sees.

Rose's dreams are filled with the noise of spoons and forks leaping to their deaths against the chipped enamel of the kitchen sink where they clatter and bang and wake her from her sleep-walking, waking the entire household with her.

Rose can never remember how she got there.

When they ask her to explain what she's up to, she shrugs her shoulders and scowls. She doesn't answer to anyone but to God. These days, she's beginning to wonder if He exists, if He's disappeared like the others stolen in the night, never to be heard from again.

La cubana, their next-door neighbour, is the one who comes to her the most. No one knows if she's really from Cuba or from somewhere else. She has straight, jet-black hair and a chalky white complexion that recalls the flesh of the coconut. To her face, they call her Coco.

Rose watches the woman from the corners of her eyes as she drifts into the kitchen like the others when night falls. Watches her eat leftover potato pudding with her hands. It's been days since anyone has seen her in person, except for Rose, sitting at her mother's kitchen table in the dark, seeing the ghosts walk by her in search of solace.

Rose knows they aren't really ghosts, or zombies. They sleep-walk in search of rest. Unlike her, they have somewhere to go.

166

It's not that she's never walked in her sleep.

She used to walk the house in the dark, barefoot, inching forward with her splayed toes, trying to remember how the cold ground felt beneath her feet, charting a map of the house around furniture and the corners of walls. Her mother had told her that it would end when she was older and it had, for a time. But since the disappearances started after the elections, or just before – it's hard to keep track – she sleepwalks restlessly, imitating the ponderous fear that catches everyone in the throat when they leave their houses. Some don't even make it that far, don't even make it to the stoop of their houses. One of them had told her, as he ate cold chicken down to the bone, that they'd found him collapsed in a pool of blood pouring out of four bullet holes, still holding a sock in his two hands that he'd been pulling on, sitting on the edge of his bed.

Rose hears the delicate chicken bones grind between his teeth. Is he dead? Must be dead, she thinks, as she listens to the man standing against the kitchen counter dressed in a soccer uniform. She peers down at his feet and sees he has only one sock on. With the bare foot, he scratches the bulging calf muscle above the curled top of the ribbed sock.

Sometimes Rose isn't sure what to believe, but the next morning she reads in the paper that they found the bodies of all the members of a soccer team, killed before a big match, none of them in the same place, as if the killing had been random, unplanned. Except that they were *all* dead. The opposing team won by default. They claimed their victory in silence, wondering who would be next to fall.

Who would be next? No one knew.

They lived daily in an elaborate game of hide and seek. No one knew who was it, who was safe, just that it was necessary to hide away.

They're not always dead, Rose comes to realize. Often, they're only dreaming, sleepwalking like her. They've left their bodies behind and appear to her like mirages. She's meant to be their silent witness. It's all they want. Someone that sees: to be seen.

Rose has no choice in the matter: she sees.

Some of the neighbours saw them take Coco away, the men dressed in lightning blue, saw how they dragged her out of her house in a sheer pink nightgown, the areolas of her breasts like dark eyes beneath the fabric, dragged her out by the hair so that the pebbles of her driveway were marked by scarlet drops. It takes weeks before she returns.

She doesn't have her slippers, is all that her husband can babble. Rose listens to him speak to her mother across the fence. Her mother nods and walks away. What can they do? What can be done? As she watches the two separate, Rose is full of dread. She knows Coco will be next. And she is, standing in the kitchen, eating her way through the leftovers Rose will be blamed for taking in the morning, standing there with the others as they tell their stories, words slipping over each other until she can't make out what they're trying to say. They don't seem to realize that all of this is slowly driving her to the edge. Rose tells this only to the water as she runs to the port and looks down, wanting to plunge.

Once, Rose looks out of a window into the yard and sees Coco's husband sitting on a chair in the middle of the driveway. It's as if he's waiting. It's dark but she can see his eyes are filled with tears, red. He wears the pink slippers, frayed and worn, on his feet, rubs his hands together as if he is a genie who could bring her back with a thought. Rose looks away, ashamed of witnessing something she hasn't been asked to take in: his vulnerability, his nakedness. Feels the grains like sandpaper grating against her nerves. She'd scream if she could. If the night air wasn't already choked with screams. It's her burden. The others dwelling in the house are just bystanders who've heard the car crash but won't inspect the carcass, people too afraid to bear witness in case they recognize a face lying inert against the asphalt, skin pocked with grit from the ground.

Lying in her bed, Rose's body throbs with pain. She doesn't know how to make it stop. She places pillows beneath the places that hurt. She swallows four or five aspirins at a time. She cries softly into the bed sheets that smell of coarse detergent. And once, after seeing Coco in the kitchen, face twisted and wistful, she feels a searing pain in her genitals, as if she's been knifed, flamed there. She presses her hands between her legs but it doesn't go away until she begins to recite Hail Marys. *Hail. Hell. Mary. Mary.* She moans. She twists in the sheets and moans. *Hell.*

She wishes she were dead. Just like the person whose pain she is feeling, with no explanation other than the fact that this is how she is, has always been.

One morning, Coco's husband walks out of his house wearing her slippers on his bare feet as he crosses the sharp stones of their driveway.

He shuts the gates even though they are broken and can't be locked. He places a large metal chain around the two sides of the gates and locks them with a large *cadenas*.

He won't let anyone in, not even Rose.

February 1958, Port-au-Prince

I know the Haitian people because I am the Haitian people. So said the Doc in his palace with his silver-plated guns resting atop a white cloth on his desk.

When Rose lies very still at night, beyond the sound of women cooking late into the night, beyond the sound of radios spitting out the shrill sounds of *konpa*, beyond the sound of roosters crying out at the wrong time and the wind moving in and out of palm fronds, she hears the screams. When she closes her eyes, it is as if the sound is in her ears along with the voices of the screamers telling her their stories. Rose wishes she could sleep with her eyes open.

Rose wakes one morning to see *la cubana*, Coco, returned, sitting in her back yard. *La cubana* is sitting in the sun with her robe open. Beneath it she has on a sheer nightdress. Rose can see the outline of the round of her breasts, the dark of the areolas looking like trapped moths beneath the gauzy fabric. Coco sits there limply, her knees together, while her feet in their worn pink slippers point in different directions, like those of a little girl who has lost all of her friends. Her husband looks up at Rose at her window and places a finger against his lips. Rose wonders if he has lost his mind too, if they have both lost their minds together. He sits at Coco's feet and caresses her hands. In another minute, he is helping her to her feet and they walk slowly back into the house. Coco is wincing in pain and takes small steps down the pebbled driveway.

"*Estropiée*," Rose's mother says when they notice that the gates next door have been opened and that the woman journalist has returned.

Rose's mother holds two fingers in the sign of a V where her legs come together and makes a downward gesture. Rose knows exactly what her mother means, knows it already from Coco's nocturnal visitations in a nightgown, blooming red carnations where her legs "v" with her torso. Rose's mother turns away from her with tears forming in the corners of her eyes.

Rose doesn't want to tell her mother what she knows, that one of the ghosts who rummages through the kitchen at night is the lady journalist. She walks in her yard at night, overturning pebbles, when everyone is asleep and only Rose and Coco's husband can hear her moving in the dark. She floats through the closed gates in search of Rose in the kitchen. Like all the others in pain and turmoil, she's looking for a way out, for a witness, even if the witness doesn't know what she can do for them. Rose has learned that just to sit with them is often enough, to sit and listen, even though what she sees and what they tell her make her want to scream. She feels as if she is ingesting truckloads of waste and that her body will burst from the sheer weight of it all. Worse still is that they don't speak to each other, only to her, one after the other, and all at once like ocean waves that will never end. Only the dawn breaks the spell: daylight and the casting out of shadows.

Coco is the most stubborn. She finds Rose in her room and sits on the edge of her bed. She reaches for Rose under the covers and clutches at her. Rose is afraid. Coco comes with images of violence and bloodshed, her own and those of others. Coco has seen too much. She wants someone to carry on her witnessing. *But I am too young*, Rose tells her. The most Coco ever does to acknowledge her

170

is to give her a tight-lipped smile more frightening to Rose than her disregard. Rose fights with her in the night and in the morning she has long scratches on her arms to show for her nightmares.

Like the others, Coco also comes to the kitchen. Rose doesn't know why ghosts prefer it to other parts of the house. She learned long ago to follow the whispers down the hall and down the stairs to the kitchen, whispers like lisps begging to be deciphered. They gorge themselves on leftovers as if there is no tomorrow and, watching them, she realizes that, for them, there is no such thing. Rose imagines that this is their only recompense for their haunting: the ghosts can eat whatever they want without having to pay the consequences.

After her reappearance, word leaks out that Coco has lost her mind. She is writing articles denouncing the Devil and his Macoutes. *Doesn't she know they don't carry the burlap bags any more? Doesn't she know the walls have ears? What need does she have to write everything down?* These are the things Rose's mother says, clanging through the kitchen, placing breakables out of reach, with Virginie following behind her. Rose's mother prattles on about a great grandmother, Elsie, a woman of Irish stock, who'd told of terrible visions foretelling, Rose's mother thinks, the tortures and terrors going on all about them, happening right now to people like Coco. They'd thought Gran Elsie crazy when, having learned about the *vodou* gods, the *loas*, she'd declared she was an emissary of *Erzulie*, and they would find her wading into the ocean looking for the goddess. Afraid that she would drown herself, she had been committed to the asylum near the port in the capital. Rose's mother wonders out loud if Rose, like this great grandmother and like Coco, is losing her mind. Rose is indignant that her mother should think this, but keeps her journal hidden between the mattress and the bedspring frame in case she might be right, in case Rose *isn't* right.

Sometimes, Rose's mother stares at her, and Rose thinks she must know her secrets.

One morning, as she rounds the last stair, Rose hears the help in the kitchen talking about putting a spell on her to protect her at night. As she walks into the kitchen, Rose's mother signals them to be quiet. They all go on with their daily chores as if everything is normal, even as they hear bullets whizzing through the air, even as Rose's eyes turn from brown to green to grey.

Rose looks out a window and sees the sky filling with ponderous clouds.

1959, Port-au-Prince

Angels are flying at the airport.
 The wind is blowing from the North.
 The dead walk.
 The devils are at the door.
 The hills are filled with light.
 The ancestors must be appeased.
 River water has no source.
 Rose doesn't understand proper speech any more. Everyone speaks in euphemisms.
 White noise is killing her.

Coco is in the kitchen again. She has disappeared from the neighbouring yard. She smiles her cryptic smile at Rose as she moves lightly from the counter where a square dish of *pain patate* has been left out, forgotten after a long meal at which too many dishes have been served. Rose can hear her thinking, *What a waste,* and, *Better eat before the rats climb up the cement stairs.* Rose wishes she wouldn't, that the ghosts would all be kind enough to leave things as they are. It's she who will get accused in the morning while still shaking the dust of sleep from her eyes. They could, at least, be considerate in return for her attention.
 It's a wonder you can eat at all, Rose tells Coco.
 For the first time, Coco addresses Rose directly with a cold stare and keeps on eating chunks of the *pain patate* as if this is the only defiance left to her.
 These days, most people are losing their appetites. It's difficult to consume dead meat, dead anything, when you've seen a corpse rotting in the street on your way home from work. Some people don't even go to work any more.

When things are bad – which is most of the time these days – Rose's mother makes her stay home from school. Those are days when there is shouting in the streets and bullets falling to the ground from their cases. They sound like bees, the bullets, flying through the air, but they sound like something much more lethal when they thud against skin and break through layers of flesh to the softness of inner organs. If she listens closely, Rose can hear them worming through the tender, elastic flesh, the gurgling, the gush of blood, disrupting the flow of vital fluids.

People always seem surprised when they get hit. Rose wonders why. They don't squeal like pigs do when brought to slaughter, even though this is what is happening out there – slaughter, right outside their gates.

People who are shot die with their eyes wide open. Rose wonders if, like her, they die struggling not to go to sleep.

Easter's just passed and they say the Doc has had a heart attack. Funny for a physician that he didn't know how to prevent it. *Too bad he survived*, is all Rose can think, when she hears the news. It would have been nice to have something to celebrate that summer.

July, the Cubans land, then leave again. Rose takes it as a sign that all hope is lost. She doesn't study like she used to. She's lost the belief that history holds the key to things and the illusion that there might be a way to change its future course. In some respects, they've seen all this before and, in others, they have never seen anything like it. Drink helps, Rose discovers, as she begins to frequent the dance halls and bars hidden away in half-lit basements and courtyards at the end of narrow alleys. She's often the only girl there and runs the risk of getting a reputation. After a couple of drinks, though, Rose doesn't care. She stays close to friends, like the housekeeper's son, Jérémie, and hopes for the best. Soon, everyone realizes why she's there and they leave her to drown in drink as she talks to the walls and everything in between.

The alcohol takes away the pain and dulls the stories the ghosts empty into her at night. Sometimes she can get herself to bed and fall into a deep, dull, dreamless sleep and wake the next morning with no memory of anything until she opens her eyes to see the canopy of white mosquito netting stretched over her bed and remembers the war raging beyond the walls of the house. Now she understands why men drink the way they do. Now she knows that what the maids say about their men, that they're just good-for-nothing layabouts drinking their hard-earned money away in any two-bit shack that will have them, isn't the whole truth. They wouldn't drink so much if they weren't in pain.

It's a solution as valid as prayer, Rose thinks, when she sits between her mother and Virginie in the church pew, Virginie's troubled breathing casting a heaviness across the backs of their shoulders as if it wasn't already painfully obvious to them all that they are trapped at every turn, even here, in the house of the Lord.

There's a reason why libations are poured to the gods at the start of any *vodou* ritual. *Even the gods don't object to a good stiff drink now and then*, Rose muses. It does a soul some good.

April 1961, Port-au-Prince

Notre Père qui est dans le Palais…

Is it always the same when a calamity hits? Do people who think about these things always ask the same question: where has God gone?

Here, apparently, God lives in the presidential palace, white against the blue sky.

The Doc has been "elected" again.

If the Doc is God then the Macoutes must be his archangels, like Gabriel, and Lucifer.

What elections? the people say when the results are announced. There's no reprieve, no possibility of a recount or runoff. It is what it is.

December 1963, Port-au-Prince

The poor are getting poorer and the rich richer. Rose has been taking in the news of the thousands killed by the hurricane and more by landslide mud swallowing them whole, as if into the belly of a hungry, voracious, subterranean god. Rose wishes that she'd been dragged into the mud, arms flailing. She's ashamed to think this and doesn't tell anyone her thoughts, just furrows her brow and wishes and wishes that she had been out in the street when the hurricane hit, instead of, as always, safe at home, waiting to hear about the calamities, waiting for the pain to invade her body as her visitors come to regurgitate their stories into her psyche.

Rose can't be drinking all the time and it's when her mind is clear that they come to her, and she must process their pain like a lay shaman, not knowing how to clear herself of the residue, not knowing how to help them process their grief for themselves. She understands that this is her role in the tragedy unfolding before them, but wishes it were different. She's had no training. Mamie died too soon. Left without telling her what to do and how to do it.

Rose doesn't know what she's doing. At times, it's difficult for her to tell the difference between her feelings and those of others. It's as if she's on a roller coaster, such as she's seen in magazines, looping up and down on miniature rails, sending the bodies of their occupants jerkily, wildly, in different directions. So, to be wiped out in a landslide would feel good now, with no good prospects for the future, no chance of study transporting her to a distant land.

Rose and her mother and Virginie live in the house as if in a convent. At night, Rose slips away with Jérémie, but sometimes he doesn't want to take her. He's taken up the *revolver* with the Macoutes and doesn't want her to be associated. It's for their protection that he's done it, he says. Rose doesn't know any more who and what to believe. Ironically, the ghosts who visit have become her only sure measure of reality. Is she losing her mind? But, after the visitations, there is always corroboration. If someone comes to tell her of a rape, a killing, a house burning, it's broadcast through the whispers of the *teledjol* in the days that follow. She knows the truth of what the country is turning into and thinks her listening must be a poor consolation for torture. Why can't they see into the future, these ghosts? Why do they always turn up after the events? It's the anger that drives her to drink. She's not even twenty-two and already she drinks like a sailor. Glides on a sea of drink with her mouth open like a carp trying to swim upstream, against the current.

The Doc has renounced aid from the Americans, but Kennedy was killed just before so they won't be coming to depose him any time soon. The Americans have bigger problems on their hands and are caught up in their grief, unaware that in other places in the world, mourning is like a priest's vestment, something one wears every day, a habit.

But there are murmurs and rumours in the hills that the Dominicans might climb past the border zones and set them free, as Toussaint did at the time of the Revolution, unifying the two sides of the island. It's a wonder that the Dominicans want to help since they've always held their liberation from the Spanish against the Haitians, as if there was some shame in being annexed to a black nation when, in fact, most of them were brown of skin – and not because of Indian blood but because of black blood, slave blood. Rose has to wonder what's in it for them but doesn't know enough about history to figure it out. Maybe, as always, the Dominicans think the western tip of the island is making them look bad.

In any case, if they're trying to get Our Father out of the white, white palace, they can't, they can't. He's like a fox walking sideways across ice, daring the sheet of frozen water to give way. He's like a lion in his den knowing he doesn't have to set foot outdoors: all he needs to do is roar.

It turns out that the Dominican secret militia is occupying the Dominican chancery and President Bosch has to back down. Bosch isn't going to last long on his side of the mountains anyway and everyone knows it. It's a desperate, silent pantomime you wish would end. Such displays always end with the mime pretending to cry, a black tear painted against the white cream of a mask covering stubble and open pores. Only little children like mimes, Rose muses, unlike clowns from whom they run away.

Rose has stopped studying. She doesn't look forward to having children to lead in her classes any more. She doesn't hope for children of her own. She drinks and swims along – watching, escaping – sleeping through the horrors. The more she drinks, the more the ghosts mercifully leave her alone.

There's been an attempted coup too from within the ranks of the

Haitian army; someone who's had enough, or wants more, it's hard to tell. He was trying to work with the Dominicans but once Bosch withdrew the troops advancing to the border, the plan fell apart, and Our Father found the man fomenting the insurrection and had him thrown in prison. He'll be tortured, like all the others. He'll be lucky if he makes it out of Fort Dimanche alive.

Rose hopes he won't come to see her. She wouldn't know what to do with that level of pain and deception. She's become so afraid of witnessing the ghosts, so afraid of the pain they want her to absorb – so that they can go on living in this world – that she prefers the pounding in her head after her drinking sessions. Prefers the twist in her gut as her liver swells and grows toxic. Prefers her bloodshot eyes to clear sight.

She drinks solidly for a week when she hears the news of the foiled coup attempt. She drinks in the hopes of avoiding the apparitions and sleeps like a stone for three days in a row.

February 1965: Fritz

Rose has discovered that drinking like a man has other advantages. For one, you get to be around more men. For two, no one can hold anything you say or do against you when you're sober again. It's like an unwritten rule. Those who drink are free. It's the clear-headed types who are damned. No wonder the poor make vats of *clairin*. This is a country that doesn't need the weed to smoke she's heard about. They don't need that stuff to get high. Here, you can get high on madness and terror, or moonshine close to 99% proof.

When Fritz introduces himself at the bar of a dingy makeshift club that the "elites" have constructed for their children at a villa on the ramparts of Boutillier, up in the white hills beyond the forked corner where the Baptist Church creates a wall of paint with canvases strung in rows between banana trees, Rose says, "What kind of name is that?" and laughs. These days, she feels only two emotions: terror and mirth. Both make her feel strangely alive, a little bit crazy, in a good way.

He stands there in front of her with a blank look on his face holding a paper cup in his hands. Rose wonders if he is drinking moonshine and the laughter streams out of her guilelessly. She takes in the whiteness of his shirt against his dark skin. He is a deep pitch of brown that reminds her always of the colour of wet coffee grounds after brewing, a colour cool to the touch on a summer's day, without having to wear a hat to save the face, as Rose had been taught by her mother to do because of her peachy, freckled complexion.

"I mean," Rose continues, stopping her laughter short as she notices how still he is, and momentarily envies it, "why are Haitians always calling their children crazy-assed names?"

"German," he says, deadpan, looking deep into Rose's eyes. She suddenly has the odd sensation of being like a fish at the bottom of a shallow pond, not wanting to be seen, wanting to hide in the tangle of weeds rising from the mud below.

Could he be serious? Rose peers at him, sobered by his seriousness. He is handsome but nothing about him screams white. His hair is cropped close to his scalp revealing a shapely, rounded head. His ears are delicately creased and don't stick out like the ears of most Haitian men she has known. Rose thinks of Jérémie, suddenly aware that he is somewhere in the crowd, possibly watching. The thought of betrayal flits through her mind, even though Jérémie is like her brother.

"Really," Rose says for lack of anything better to say.

He nods gravely, all the while holding the little cup at chest level, against the dip of the meeting of his breastbones.

"*Vous êtes beau*," Rose hears herself say, knowing that even though she will remember every moment of her drunken actions, everyone else will assume that she would not.

He smiles, quietly, one hand casually hanging from the pocket of his grey, pressed trousers, as Rose has seen fashion models do in glossy magazines from *outre-mer*; the other hand is still at chest level, though now he rocks it back and forth as if it might keep his drink warm.

"So, German, hunh?" Rose fishes for a way to continue the conversation.

"Yes, ma'am," he says, volleying back.

"Related to the Poles in the *bas* country?"

"Those are not my people," he says, smiling still. "Not all White people come from the same chopping block, you know."

"Well, then," Rose says, "maybe you're safe."

"The Poles are good people," he says.

"Are they? I don't know any."

"So why did you think I was related?"

Rose shrugs, "I could be a Pole for all I know."

He looks at her. "You could," he pauses, "but the Poles know how to hold their drink. They stuck their asses out in the wind for us during the Revolution."

Rose ignores the comment about her drinking, "Did they? And what about the Germans?"

"Well, the Germans, excuse my French, let the shit fly."

When they are done laughing, he finishes his drink and asks Rose her name and she tells him.

"Like the flower," he responds.

"Like the verb."

"You're clever."

"Are you really German?"

"No, I was just kidding. I'm Syrian. Well, more accurately, Syrian-Haitian."

"Not possible. You're the wrong shade of light."

Jérémie comes by. Fritz doesn't seem to like the look of him. Jérémie pulls Rose aside.

"Don't you know pretty men are dangerous?" he hisses into her ear, holding her too close for comfort.

She laughs. She hears the sound of ice cubes clinking against each other in her glass like coins in a purse.

"Aren't *you* pretty, Jérémie?" she asks drunkenly.

"I'm warning you."

Rose laughs, "You don't scare me, Jérémie. I've known you too long," and walks back towards Fritz.

But Jérémie does scare her with that gun in the holster hidden by his suit jacket; he has become a different kind of man under the régime, the kind of man who not only straddles a fence but walks both sides of it as well. His breath is stale with cigar smoke and *clairin*.

"But you should," he yells at her back and Rose isn't sure if he is referring to himself or to Fritz or to anything else.

"Madame should know that in Haiti, well, anything is possible," Fritz says, looking past her to Jérémie.

"Mademoiselle," Rose chooses to clarify.

"*Kisa?*" he asks, leaning in.

"Mademoiselle," she says.

Then she inches forward to kiss him, to mark her independence from Jérémie, still looking on.

So starts her courtship under a new red and black flag raised for the nation.

Black for death and red for blood.

He's a musician and he doesn't like to drink. Lethal combination, Fritz says, sipping on *kola*, then kissing her with the sweet, sweet taste.

The thing about Fritz is that he doesn't give Rose time to think. He's like a ready-made storm: there's nothing you can do to stop it. You either have to let yourself be swept up by it or step out of the way.

Rose stands her ground and feels the force that is Fritz sweep all around her, pieces of her flying, molecules rearranging, embracing, destroying. They fight, relentlessly. Two storms fighting each other. She wouldn't call it love. She wouldn't call it hate. It's simply what they are when they come together, trying to make the other bend to her or his own will. Fritz always seems to win but he doesn't realize it's the fight that she's after, anything to make her feel more alive in the emptiness the ghosts have left behind, her nights now empty of their wistful stories.

She drinks with Jérémie and philosophizes with Fritz. Neither knows with which man she dances most or whom she loves. They don't understand that, for her, it isn't about love.

It's about who will be the one to get her off the island fastest.

December 1966, Port-au-Prince

Almost a year has gone by since they met.

Fritz says: It's time to get serious. *Lui ou moi.*

It's not hard to choose. Life abroad. Life next to a gun.

It's hard to choose: dancing until dawn or accepting that she won't be anything more than someone's wife.

She's had another long fever. It seems like she's been lying in bed for ages when the doctor comes to examine her. This time, he has something more to say.

"She's pregnant," he says to Rose's mother, turning his body away from Rose as if she is no longer in the room.

Rose's mother says, "How can that be?" as if it's been a foregone conclusion that she's to die an old maid in her mother's house. How can she be so surprised? Her mother is not so surprised. She knows some part of Rose was broken in the long nights of listening to ghosts with nowhere better to go, that Rose drinks like a man in the company of men. Rose resists the temptation to laugh at her mother's consternation.

Her mother stands at the foot of the bed as the doctor rummages through his bag as if to put order there. She looks at Rose in despair, as if this is the last thing she needs, the last thing she expects from a daughter of hers, her only daughter. She looks at Rose as if Rose has died. *My good girl is gone*, Rose can see her thinking, *and who is this that has taken her place?*

The doctor's face is grim, as if Rose has caught some incurable disease. She would have thought that, in this time, pregnancy is the least awful thing that could have happened to her. They should be happy, or, at least, relieved. The doctor packs away his serpentine stethoscope in his worn case.

"No suitors?" he asks darkly.

Rose's mother gasps as if an immaculate conception might be possible.

"*Docteur*," she says, shocked at the implication that her daughter has been joining the dregs of their capsized nation to rummage through the streets, as if Rose might be some common whore.

He's been the family doctor since before her father died. They were colleagues, along with the Doc in the palace. They knew before anyone else did what would become of the nation. They knew that the Doc was no mild-mannered, bespectacled country doctor. They didn't believe in the myth that he had single-handedly cured dengue fever while working for the US armed forces. *He'd have to have been equipped with wings*, Rose's father had joked years ago. *We went everywhere on our feet. It was a collective effort, a collective triumph*, he would say, stabbing the wood of the dining room table with a long, curving index finger.

"*Ça ne se comprend pas Mathilde*," the doctor says.

"*Mais, quand-même*," Rose's mother responds crisply as if it is obvious that he should not be behaving this way, betraying his friend's memory, whatever the man's daughter might have done, or become. She seems suddenly frail, Rose's mother, like a piece of paper that has been crumpled up, the shape of her life and her very limbs forever distorted. For the first time, Rose sees her mother's age and her fear of being left behind in this crazy island. The fear grips her, ties knots in her stomach. "*Ayez un peu de respect.*"

He huffs and puffs in response, collecting his things, his eyes averted from both women.

"*Il y en a deux*," Rose says before he has a chance to step out of the room.

"*Ah bon*," the doctor responds, turning back to them.

"There are two," she repeats, "two suitors. But one of them is not my lover."

"*Ça ne fait aucun sens*," her mother says, sighing, wringing her thin hands.

"*Non*," Rose says, giggling uncontrollably, turning on her side and lifting the covers to her chin, "it makes no sense at all."

Her giggle turns into a hysterical cackle.

The doctor gives her a sedative.

They marry under a blue sky dry of rains. Rose promises to love, cherish, have faith or was it to be faithful? It's one or the other. She wonders if not knowing absolves her from the commitment.

She doesn't know if she can keep her promises. She's already broken the most important one: not to listen to the voices reaching for her like grasping fingers in the night.

Fritz's sister, Ruth, comes to the wedding. Every time Rose looks at her, she feels a wild desire to be protected by her, and loathing. She doesn't know why this aversion, this hunger, this fear. It is her wedding day and instead of feeling that she is gaining a family

Rose feels herself teetering into an abyss, a vast chasm, a wilderness. She has never felt so alone.

The nightmares come back even though she lives now with Fritz. She knows that it's because she's had to stop drinking. The ghosts come to wake her in the middle of the night to tell her their stories of mutilation and incarceration. She sits and listens to them in Fritz's kitchen and thirsts for a drink, but she can't do it to the baby. She holds on to her stomach as if to shield it, but she knows that everything she hears swoops into her, that the baby will absorb it all. She weeps at the table, not knowing what to tell them. They don't seem to notice her distress and one after the other they take their turn, monotonously telling their stories. It is like hearing a story that never ends, they are so similar. How long can she listen and still remain sane? Outside they hear the bullets sing and the wild songs of those cut down like cane with rusted and pitted machetes. It is revenge without a cause. What is she to do?

Fritz tells Rose that she walks at night and doesn't hear him when he tells her to get back into bed.

She tells him stiffly that he must be joking, pulling her leg.

I've never walked in my sleep in my life, she tells him, lying through her teeth.

Rose tells her mother about the return of the sleepwalking, the long nights weeping in the kitchen.

She says, *Go see Ruth, his sister.*

Rose says, afraid, *Why would I see his sister? She hardly stayed a minute at the wedding.*

Mother says, *Because she's like you*, and leaves it at that.

"Why didn't you tell me your sister walks in her sleep?" Rose asks Fritz, later.

He shrugs as if he's ashamed of the truth.

"You're ashamed?"

He is silent.

"Well," Rose pauses, "if you're ashamed of her, you're going to be ashamed of me."

183

He stays silent.

"*Mon Dieu*," Rose says out loud.

She realizes she didn't know the man she has married but, then again, he doesn't know the woman he's married either.

Rose goes to see Ruth. They sit together in an open alcove of Ruth's sumptuous house in the hills above the city and sip on strong cups of coffee. Ruth is unmarried and gives piano lessons. Rose looks around her and wonders at Ruth's wealth.

Rose tries to talk about herself but the words stay lodged in her throat as if she has swallowed the pit of a prune. She feels Ruth watching her. She feels judged by Ruth's gaze, as if she should already know the answers to the questions that have brought her here. *Why won't you help me?* she asks Ruth. Ruth is like a wall facing her. She prattles on and on about the flowers in her garden, about the students coming for their lessons, asks about the baby on her way. Rose feels as if she could jump out of her skin. She wants to tell Ruth about her walks by the ocean, the wild urge that grips her then to throw herself into the waters and end it all. She has a feeling that Ruth would know what she is talking about. As she thinks this, there is a pause in the conversation. Rose looks up and realizes that she has been thinking to herself and forgotten Ruth entirely.

"What is it you want to tell me?" Ruth asks.

"I have nothing to tell," Rose says. She feels filled with other people's refuse and wishes she could vomit it all up. But when she looks around Ruth's house, all she sees is the order, the newly painted walls, the swept walkways, the freshly scrubbed linoleum floors. It doesn't occur to her until much later that the exactitude of Ruth's surroundings are meant to hide something, that Ruth, too, is afraid of something more powerful than herself disordering her life.

"Are you sure?" Ruth asks again, but she is already looking away as if she wants Rose to leave well alone.

"I'm sure," Rose says, wishing she had never come.

"Well," Ruth says, "it's always good to see you. Let me show you the garden."

That, of course, is Rose's cue to leave her finished cup on the glass-topped coffee table and follow her sister-in-law through the winding path in the gardens to her car. They walk through the gardens and Rose is overwhelmed with the scent of blooming fuchsia, roses, gardenias. Again, she feels like throwing up. She places a hand on her stomach to hold the nausea back but doesn't feel well all the way home. She is sure she will never see Ruth again and bitterly wonders at the woman's feigned joviality. She's probably a *madan sara*, Rose thinks, one of the diabolic women working for Our Father in the Holy Palace. She needs to get off this damn island for ever and ever.

1967, Port-au-Prince

Rose hasn't been faithful. She's miscarried the first baby but there will be another, soon. Fritz has decided that they must leave the country. What kind of man has she married that it takes *this* to make him leave? She's half-ashamed and half-relieved, almost self-righteous in her behaviour.

And the Doc has been excommunicated.

The result is that they are leaving here, forever, and don't have to explain why to anyone.

As their plane climbs into the sky, Rose thinks that maybe she did it on purpose because she knew what he would do.

Now she has her ticket out.

Now no child of hers will have to wake up to the ringing of church bells tolling for the dead.

Snow, snow, and more snow. Mounds and *monticules*, as Rose describes them. Blankets of the stuff as far as the eye can see. Nothing like what Rose had imagined, dreaming about this faraway place in the heat of the island sun. But, unlike in the island, here, everyone thinks of themselves as lucky even if all they have is a pallet in a dingy room. Because they are all expatriated in some way or another, they make friends easily but wearily, and soon, after the baby is born, the house they've rented in a suburb of Montreal feels full of warmth. Rose feels less afraid here, less the need to drink. As a wife and mother, she can be invisible, even to herself.

Still, there are visitations, in the deep velveteen cover of night, but they seem harmless compared to her visitors in the island, these pasty-faced visitors with mundane problems regarding the cost of bread and unfaithful husbands. Occasionally, there is something more serious: a runaway, a beaten wife, and, slowly, without the pressure of knowing that the men in blue are somewhere out there coming after them, at any time of day and night, Rose begins to trust herself with dispensing advice. *You can do better than him*, she tells one. *Leave now*, she tells another. *You're wrong*, she hears herself say once, *it's all in your head*. She does what she can and feels useful. Sometimes, just sitting with them in the kitchen, letting them know she can see them feels like a job well done. She begins to forget the island. Little by little, her memory of the place transforms. She remembers only guava jelly and ripe mangoes, the cooing of birds, long walks in the mountains. The memory of bloodshed and the screams from rapes recede in her mind like the phantom of a nightmare her mind had fabricated out of boredom.

1969, Montréal, Québec

Rose wakes up one morning and can't remember if her mother is dead or alive. For a few wild minutes, she excavates her mind but nothing comes to her except for a memory of watching her mother amongst the ghosts in the kitchen long ago. She reaches for the phone on the bed-stand and dials home. Virginie answers and there is a long quiet between them after Rose says hello that confirms the worst. Virginie sighs. Rose hangs up the phone. Her mother has died. Her mother is dead. The baby cries from the other room. Lately, she has taken to trying to climb out of her crib after Fritz leaves the house for work. Rose lies back against her pillows wishing that this was one of her silly dreams.

Rose feels the umbilical cord tying her to the past unravel and uncoil. Memories she has suppressed rush into the space she has filled with her new life, her daily habits as a wife and mother in a new land. Suddenly, her new life seems unreal. Her real life comes back to her, in pieces and segments, as the loss of her mother overcomes her. Her mother's living presence at home had made it possible for her to move forward without looking back, because she knew someone was back there, looking after things, things she no longer wanted to contemplate.

Her mother's passing has caused a shift within Rose. It's as if a tectonic plate has slipped in her mind and caused the rest of her brain to push and shift, leaving gaps in some areas and closing off apertures in others. She needs to recover everything she's forgotten, every reason she sought to leave the past behind.

Rose feels multiply pregnant, as if there are other things inside, pressing on her, trying to get out. She reads everything she can get her hands on, and as she reads, she holds Catherine in her arms after she suckles, a small bubble of milky spit drawing a bridge between her small pink lips. She props the books between Catherine's small bean-shaped body and her knees, and reads voraciously, as fast as she can, turning the pages with her free hand so fast that the wind of the pages is like music in her ear. When the baby sleeps, she holds a book in one hand and a drink in the other, afraid that the aimless ghosts from her island will find her here as well. She wants to make some sense of the nonsense Fritz says is only in her head, as if he has lost his memory of all that was going on back there, in the wild brush of Haiti, never to be excavated. Rose keeps notes in a notebook she hides in Catherine's room, among the scattered toys.

On the Doc:

> "He was born a few blocks from the National Palace during the military dictatorship of Nord Alexis... When he was one year old General Antoine Simon overthrew Alexis. He was four when a revolution ousted Simon and five when an explosion reduced the old wooden Palais National and President Cincinnatus Leconte along with it into splinters. Duvalier was six when President Tancrede Auguste was poisoned; the funeral was interrupted when two generals began fighting over the succession... One Michel Oreste got the job, but he was overthrown the following year by a man named Zamor, who in turn fell a year later to Davilmar Théodore."

Was it possible to believe that the Doc suffered from posttraumatic stress like those Vietnam vets who were capable of murdering their own children, convinced that they were still fighting a jungle war and that the enemy was upon them even in their own homes?

She reads on.

> Evidently, Théodore wasn't to last long. He was overthrown by Guillaume Sam who in turn was killed inside the walls of the French legion by Haitian gentlemen from the cultured elite who took a machete to his head and split it wide open like a coconut husk. Elite or not, they knew the value of an empty shell.

Rose reads a book by a Black American who is convinced that whatever his "faults", Our Father should be revered for remaining a symbol of what he calls "Black Power" in the New World.

Don't these people know what happened? What's happening still? Rose gets so angry, she forgets Catherine is in her arms and only the feel of her daughter stirring in response to her agitation brings Rose back to their four walls. Funny how infants pick up vibrations in the air, as if their bodies are antennae, she notes, kissing Catherine on her smooth forehead.

Rose makes an altar in her room, a table covered with a red cloth and adorned with candles. In the afternoons, slightly drunk, she dances to Haitian music while Catherine looks on. She places a tablecloth over her creation at night to hide it from Fritz who doesn't approve of *vodou*.

Fritz tells her she asks too many questions. *Why don't you forget about it? Give it a rest?*

She says, *What happened to all your idealism?*

He sighs.

She counters, *And why did we leave if not to remember?*

But she's allowed herself to forget the truth: Fritz had them leave so that he could forget her indiscretions. She had been indiscrete so that they could leave, in order to elude the soon-to-be-dead.

It doesn't take long for the rumours to start after Rose starts talking about the things she's read, about the memories resurfacing that confirm the worst about the country Catherine has never seen.

Rose can't seem to hold two consecutive thoughts together in her mind and can spend a whole morning pondering a page in one of the books she's reading, wondering when it will all end – the killings, the betrayals, the lies. Everything starts to slip away from her and she has no one to talk to, not her mother, not Fritz's sister, who could have helped but refused her so long ago. The smell of the pungent garden comes back to her. She wishes she had an ocean to walk to, to fall into. Here, there's nothing but snow all around, white, mucky snow. Everything has gone cold, inside, outside. There's nothing to live for, nothing to be done. She's as useless as she's always been, failed at her mission to heal wounds not of her making. What she's tried to do has come too late; no late afternoon attempts to rejoin the spirit world can help; no amount of thinking about the past will bring it back.

Rose looks at herself in the mirror and all she can see is her grandmother's disappointment, her mother's disappointment, her daughter's uncomprehending face, Fritz's loathing. She's painted herself into a corner. She's woken up too late.

Their friends start avoiding the house and she's alone most of the time with Catherine. Fritz says she isn't a good mother and she can't deny it, hard as she tries to keep a grip on reality. He takes her to a doctor who prescribes pills she has to take every day. *Happy pills*, she says to Catherine, when the baby points at them on the breakfast table. *Happy pills for Momma*, Rose says, and pops them into her mouth. They don't really make her happy. They make her sluggish. They make her lose her train of thought. Fritz takes the books back to the library, back to the handful of friends who've lent them to her; they thought it would help her to piece together all the fragments of her mind. The doctor tells Fritz it's too late, while Rose sits there, demure, broken like a doll. Like Humpty Dumpty fallen off his wall who can't be put back together again.

All Rose can do is read children's tales to Catherine. She dedicates her moments of lucidity to finding her the best ones with the most colourful pictures and the most instructive stories.

Things that she can hold on to, like the lessons, Rose has decided, she won't be there to give.

1973, Montréal

> "But Minerva, who favours ingenuity, saw Perdix falling, and arrested his fate by changing him into a bird still called after his name, the Partridge. This bird does not build his nest in the trees, nor take lofty flights, but nestles in the hedges and, mindful of his fall, avoids high places."

Rose has bought a children's collection of Greek myths for Catherine. They've been rereading the same story over and over again, the story of Daedalus and Icarus. Catherine is five and she can follow the stories when Rose points to the pictures and sometimes Catherine tells the stories back to her in her broken tongue with dropped articles and dropped verbs. She's always convinced that what she has to say makes sense. She frowns at Rose in her certainty, then laughs.

As she observes her daughter's assurance, Rose feels awe. Perhaps this was how the Almighty felt when he watched his angels sweeping their wings through His kingdom.

Rose tells Catherine her version of the Icarus myth:

"Once there was a man who had a son. He was a very clever man and his son was just a regular boy, not clever like his father, nothing like his father at all. The man's name was Daedalus and he liked to make extraordinary things. (Rose points at the pictures showing Daedalus fabricating gadgets at a work desk; Catherine squeals and looks up at her.) Daedalus was so clever that he was appointed to the biggest court in the land where he made many wondrous things for his King and Queen, even things he should not have made. (She skips over the part about the wooden cow and the Queen and the white bull.) There was a half-man and half-bull beast in this place. They called it a Minotaur and the King wanted it kept out of reach of his children.

190

"So, Daedalus, fearing for his son's life, too, built an intricate labyrinth in which to house the Minotaur. No one but him knew how to get in and out of it and the Minotaur raged inside it, weaving in and out of the alleyways, trying to find his way out. (They trace the path in the picture with their fingers intertwined; Rose notes how Catherine's fingers are smaller versions of her own.) But there's always a way out, you see, Rose continues. (It's no use lying to her.) Theseus, who loved the King's daughter, killed the Minotaur for her. (Rose skips over the gruesome illustration.) Gone to heaven. (She points to the sky and Catherine smiles and points upwards.)

"The king was very upset because Theseus took his daughter away after he killed the Minotaur and he was sure he would never see her again. (Catherine looks at Rose and pulls her lower lip over her top lip.) He had his soldiers place Daedalus and his not-too-clever son in the labyrinth for helping Theseus. But he forgot Daedalus had built the labyrinth and could find his way out. The King was not too worried, however, because he held Daedalus hostage by surrounding the island with all the ships from his kingdom. (*Water*, Catherine says, as they peer at the picture showing the sea and ships.) Daedalus realized the sea was like a wall. The only way to go was up.

"He built two pairs of huge wings for himself and his son, Icarus. (*Ee-carus*, Catherine says.) Yes, Rose confirms, he held the feathers together with wax and thread and soon they were on their way up into the sky and away from the island and the angry king. (Catherine claps her hands.) But before he had put the wings on Icarus's shoulders he had told his not-too-clever-son, 'Don't go too high or the sun will melt the wax and you will fall into the sea; and don't fly too low or the feathers will get wet and heavy with salt and we both know that salt will have you sinking like a stone.' The boy had nodded and agreed but as they flew into the sky, he felt a strange exhilaration. He felt what it was like to taste freedom. It was like the bitter taste of salt on his tongue.

"In his exuberant innocence, Icarus continued to fly up and up into the face of the sun until the wax on his wings dripped away. He fell out of the sky like a stone and into the sea calling back its salt to earth. (*Heaven*, Catherine whispers.) Yes, Rose says, heaven.

Icarus is in heaven. The point is, she continues, you have to learn to fly neither too low nor too high. Icarus was clever in his own way. He was innocent and pure, loved by sea and sky. But you can't live divided between two worlds. It's either here or heaven.

Then Rose tells her about Daedalus travelling on to Sardinia after burying his son. Of how he was made so bitter by his loss that he killed his sister's son who was more clever than Daedalus ever was. Too clever for his own good is what he thought when he saw the boy thread a conical shell by tying a thin string to an ant, as he had done many years before to win the favour of a King."

So don't you be too clever, Rose says to Catherine, hoisting her up into the air.

Catherine laughs; she has no idea what Rose is trying to tell her.

There's nothing wrong with being a grounded bird, Rose says, twirling her daughter above her head.

Catherine screeches her pleasure and spit dribbles out of her mouth. It falls onto Rose's face like a tear, like a remembrance of a purer place where rivers know their beds and blood is contained.

Remember, Catherine, Rose says to her, smiling, even though, inside, what is left of her fragile heart shatters in a thousand directions as if it is made of a thin sheet of glass.

Remember: heaven is a place.

Winter 1977, Montréal

When she was a child, Rose would dream of faraway places where snow fell like the confetti in drum parades from the sky and not from human hands, places where lions and gazelles coexisted as they danced a ritual of life and death and moved with grace across the yellow grass of drought-filled African plains. Sometimes, she would find herself flying in a loose-fitting robe over these foreign cities teeming with life, and imagine that only a few below sensed her presence. She was content to swoop up and down in the night sky, her white robe shimmering in the light of blue moons. She kept a journal of these travels throughout her childhood and early youth. It's been some years since she has perused those zealous, hopeful scribblings of earlier times.

Rose is all grown up now, but she still secretly dreams of her childhood, of horizons filled with mountain ranges on one side and the ocean on the other.

She dreams of waves hitting black sand, burning hot like the paved roads of the island's capital, heat waves rising in horizontal bands above the ground, making everything in the distance seem slightly distorted, disjointed, with bizarre apparitions crossing her line of vision.

Those were days when she would eat ripe mangoes in the back yard, and let the juice of the orange fruit ooze down her arms, streaking her pinkish flesh. Those were the days when she flew out of doors without the wide-brimmed hat the maids were ordered to make her wear to keep her light skin from burning and freckling.

She liked her freckles, the way they drew a constellation of another country across the bridge of her nose and below her eyes on the wide span of her cheekbones.

She escaped them all, dark brown and auburn hair flying out behind her the way she imagined angels' wings stretched from their shoulder blades. Those were the days when she had felt free and hopeful, despite the lack of hope all around her. In those days, she had imagined hope rising like a core of strength up from the centre of the earth into the soles of her feet. She swayed beneath flamboyant trees, eyes closed, arms outstretched for any flurry of wind that might cool her burning skin, and felt the surge of strength through her body, from the tip of her tailbone to the crown of her head.

When it rained, she would hold out her tongue, letting the drops quench her as they glided off the wide span of banana leaves, dribbled down her cheeks, down her long, thin arms, and wet her clothes, soaking her to the bone.

She was wild then in ways she couldn't imagine of her daughter. Catherine, now nine, and a pale, pale shade of olive brown, knew nothing of thin layers of skin peeling off her nose after a sunburn, or of the grave grey of summer skies laden with hurricane storms.

She had followed Fritz to this cold northern place, thinking of her childhood dreams of snow and faraway adventures. It was so far removed from anything she had ever known that she could only wonder if she could survive its starkness, the snowdrifts that piled so high on the house they had to take turns with the shovel to keep the roof from caving in.

She was lonely.

She told no one what she was feeling, not Fritz, not her daughter, though perhaps they could see it in her eyes when she turned away from them in her sadness, unable to speak her truth.

She did not write to Ruth who had once failed her. Not to Coco, the journalist and neighbour who had long ago haunted her dreams and then, one day, disappeared, like so many others, never to be seen again.

All that was left of childhood was the dream of flight: flying far above, anywhere, soaring over lands she had never known, lands she imagined ancestors had once populated, lands divided by hills and valleys, mountain ranges and vast ocean beds, her sleeping-robe like wings keeping her afloat in a world that existed for no one else but her.

She no longer dreams of snow.

Rose is sitting at a four-way intersection on the circuitry of highway just outside the city on her way to nowhere in particular, her right foot on the brake pedal when she should have been advancing.

She hears the horns behind her, urging her forward.

It has been snowing. The streets are paved with ice. It is a dangerous moment. Out of the corner of her left eye, she sees a car swerving into the intersection.

She finds herself holding her breath, suddenly conscious of the relationship between oxygen and life.

Her mind is on her dreams, her eyes on the slick stretch of road ahead, the falling snow a sheet between the windshield and clarity beyond.

It is a split-second decision she believes will leave no trace of memory behind.

She decides, moves her foot slowly from the brake to the gas pedal and presses forward, keeping her eyes not on the road ahead nor on the curtain of falling snowflakes.

They are far prettier than she had imagined as a child, when the word "snow" had meant very little. Snow was a word she had associated with stories of the German Alps and songs about mountain flowers she could not imagine, *edelweiss*, their petals fragile in translucent whites and golds.

She presses the pedal forward, keeping her hands at three and nine o'clock as she had been taught in the driver education classes Fritz had paid for after the baby arrived. She thinks of the baby for a moment, now a little girl with long curly hair like hers when she was young. She smiles and remembers dancing with Catherine in the kitchen one early sunny morning when the weight of loss had momentarily dissipated and she could feel the life around her.

As the windows of the car fog up with the warm breath of her daughter's remembered laughter, she feels the impact. There is a momentary pang of regret. The car she had seen swerving into the intersection has come upon her.

Metal folds to metal and Rose wishes to find herself between mountain and sea once again.

She waits only minutes for her prayer, mercifully, to be answered, before the cars cross the ice-covered ground to stop together in the snow-filled dyke at the feet of massive elms.

She feels the shattering pain as if from a distance, the searing disconnection of her spinal cord as its tautness slackens, coils, disintegrates.

A dull, protective, pulsing throb.

The light of the world flows through the cracked windshield and there is just the snow, the cold, the velvety white dark.

Like rain, on her tongue, in a tropical storm.

CATHERINE

March 11, 2004, Le Marais, Paris and Port-au-Prince, Haiti

After her death, my mother often appeared to me in dreams as a woman wearing a red dress. In the dreams, the woman was always dancing in the dark of a room in which the only light came from votive candles that traced the outline of a large circle in which the woman danced with closed eyes, lifting her skirts up and then down to the rhythm of her bare feet as each foot fell and rose against the wooden floor of the room.

I watched the feet closely, my eyes following the line where the pink-yellow flesh of the soles met the honey-hued skin of the feet, where the candlelight laced each foot. I watched as each foot moved slowly through the air, every movement a caress of some space known only to the dancer, that only she could see behind closed eyelids. I watched the shadows the woman's dancing form threw up against the wall and it seemed to me that there were more women there, as if my mother was dancing with ghosts who had suddenly appeared to keep her company. The women and my mother embraced each other's bodies in ecstatic longing, like long-lost lovers meeting again, shadows moving across walls and ceilings like the flames of a consuming fire spreading from one source of fuel to another, feeding upon whatever lay in its path. I would become lost in the feverish bacchanal of the forms, losing sight of which was the original dancer, some version of my mother whom I would recognize only by her features of face, by the delicate lines beneath the closed lids that betrayed my mother's state of humour at any given time, by the shape of her head and the copper brilliance of her skin, glimpsed only as the candlelight illuminated the dancers in fleeting, flickering movements.

At times, it seemed that a fine powder streamed from beneath the dancing women's feet and into the air and suddenly the

199

honeyed feet would be buried to their ankles in mounds of what looked like sand, the skin still visible turning white like the ash of burnt tobacco. As the feet continued their unstoppable frenzied movement, the sand-like mounds would slip down to the ground and then ripple out, leaving circular designs in the wake of the moving feet, like still water in which stones have been thrown. Later, the dust would rise from the floor into the shape of strange hieroglyphs suspended in the air. They became legible only against the white of the walls, as the candlelight flickered against them, prayers to unseen gods, but I could not read the signs, I recognized them only from drawings my mother had shown me in books about the land she and Fritz had come from, that little sliver of island so far south and beneath us it was hard to imagine its continuing existence.

I swayed in unison with the women to a music only they could hear, fearing to miss any step in a dance that seemed designed to exact vengeance for unforgivable transgressions the women had suffered in the material world. I witnessed the women triumphing over the evils that had assailed them and when the dust rose up in the shapes of adoration my mother called *vèvès*, the women's heads swung back, their mouths opened, and they seemed to be laughing, even though I could hear nothing, only the constant sweeping of feet against the fine grit of the sand-like substance.

It was a sound that would remain with me throughout my life, jolting me out of conversations in places far removed from my childhood memories – while Sam and I, on vacation, walked in Cassis, a small resort town on the Southern coast where the street cleaners still used straw brooms to sweep away the garbage. It was an everyday kind of sound I connected with things falling into disuse; I heard it anywhere it seemed that one set of people had the task of cleaning up after others, where lives were silenced by the stations they occupied. In this way, I found my mother everywhere, even though I had only a fading photograph and her old passport by which to remember her face. I'd always wondered if I looked more like her or like Fritz. Now that I had passed the age at which she had died, when I looked in the mirror, I detected my mother's features in my reflection.

We had been looking into a mirror, Lucas and I, our cheeks so close I could feel the fine hairs of our faces brushing against each other. Our cheeks were soft like the surfaces of the peaches my mother bought at the grocery store.

Rose would hold the peaches in her hands and smile at me. "Feel this," she would say, handing me the fruit, "see how soft it is?"

I would feel the delicate skin with the tips of my fingers and close my eyes.

At home, we would slice the peach into a bowl, pour yogurt over the sections of bright orange flesh, add granola, and eat with our feet up on the narrow balcony on the second floor of our duplex overlooking the neighbouring yards. My mother had seemed happy then.

When Lucas and I had sat on the chair across from the mirror in Ruth's room, I remembered those mornings of peaches with my mother. A pain rose from my chest to my throat as I swallowed the memory back down.

"Keep your eyes open," Lucas said.

"I am," I swallowed, trying to hide what I was feeling.

"I don't think we look anything alike," Lucas continued, squinting first at me, then at himself. "For one thing, your eyes are round and mine are like almonds."

It was true; we didn't look anything alike. I scrutinized Lucas's face. "What about the edge of your nose?"

"No," Lucas said impatiently, "nothing alike."

"What about the clefts?"

Lucas squinted some more. "You really have to look to find yours."

I held up a finger to my chin and felt for the small indentation there that on Lucas split his chin into two small bulbs. He was right, mine could hardly be seen and even less felt.

"Ears?"

"No."

"Lips."

"Ummm… may… be…"

We peered at each other. We had a similar fold on the upper lip. We smiled in the mirror then turned to face each other. I felt

Lucas' breath falling on my face. I had never been so close to another human being aside from my mother, or Sébastien.

Moments like these satisfied a deep yearning I had for closeness, for human touch and warmth. They made me feel safe, the living breath, the human odour.

Lucas's breath had been sweet from candy he had eaten earlier in the day. The sweet breath came closer until I felt soft rose petals brushing up against mine. Flesh against flesh. A kiss or the semblance of a kiss. We were still too young to know what to do. Were we crossing the line of some taboo? Weren't we cousins? I felt a shiver run through me. I laughed and drew away, stood up, wiped my lips.

"Lucas!" I reproached even though I wasn't sure why.

I was fearful, I think, of Ruth finding us there, sitting on the edge of the chair before her boudoir mirror, and looking down at us, disapproving.

Lucas looked up at me, face deadpan, as if the kiss had never happened, "I don't think we look anything alike. I don't think we're even related."

It was a thought that had crossed my mind before. Even the similarity of our lips was no more than what all lips had in common.

Who were we? Where had we come from? These were questions we dared not ask out loud, even though I had long wanted to tell Lucas about the man at the airport from so long ago, the man who had my nose and ears, the high cheekbones that I was always being complimented on by the women who came for the strong cups of coffee *Tatie* served in the late afternoons as the sun disappeared beyond the mountains.

Even though I knew that Lucas was speaking the truth that day, I could not stop laughing in response. I ran away from his words and out into the courtyard where the sun was streaming through the branches of an old almond tree. Lucas stood behind me, watching. We were eleven and fourteen, but he had already realized what it would take me years to understand, that without our mothers, we were truly alone in the world.

As the plane flies over the Atlantic towards my parents' island, I dream of Lucas. What would he do now that the only mother he had known was gone? It had been years since anyone had heard from him. Did he even know what had happened?

I dream of Lucas as he was as a child, wearing his shorts low on his hips, his white, pressed shirts always falling out at the waist, his narrow chest pushed out like a rooster's, a proud little boy with a smile to charm old women out of their wares at market. I had adored Lucas since the moment he had greeted me in Ruth's kitchen with a handful of sweets.

I dream of Lucas running through the dust-clogged streets of our childhood in his leather ankle-shoes, the shoelaces lazily flying about. He was always in a hurry, always a whirlwind. He talked with food still in his mouth, hiding the food with one hand out of politeness, as he had been taught, while gesticulating with the other to animate his wild tales of taming lions and tigers in the *carrefour* by the *marché*, keeping the market women safe as their heaviness quaked beneath the bright pinks and blues of the silk handkerchiefs tied about their heads.

"Lions and tigers?" I'd asked, wide-eyed. "Lions and Tigers! There aren't any such thing in Haiti," I'd exclaimed, indignant.

"Oh, yes there are," Lucas countered. "Haven't you been look-ing at the paintings along the sides of the roads? They're full of tigers and lions and everyone knows artists only paint what's real."

"You lie," I'd said, hesitating. I had watched artists in front of their houses and in the market and it was true that they always seemed to be looking at something, copying nature or the curves of a woman's face, or a grandfather's pursed lips holding on to the thin extension of a pipe.

Lucas grinned widely and pushed out his chest, in victory, like a rooster.

"*Coq*," I laughed. "*Va donc.*"

We liked to tease each other.

Lucas laughed then as he spooned *acassan* into his mouth as he had seen boys on the street do, as if starving. He laughed again and looked up at me. His eyes were deep velvety brown, full of good-natured mischief, conspiratorial.

My cousin, my brother. Had anyone looked at me with such tenderness since?

After a smooth landing in Port-au-Prince, I join the passengers in thanking the pilot by clapping loudly and then follow the arrivants as they brush uneasily against one another, the men perspiring profusely, the women adjusting the folds of dresses that have bunched up around their waists. A young man with a smooth, ebony face takes out a white square kerchief trimmed with blue thread and wipes his brow. He sighs as he places it back in his pantsuit pocket and frets with his passport, checking and re-checking the page on which his visa for re-entry into the United States is affixed. He holds the passport a little too close to his eyes as if he has difficulty seeing. I wonder if he has lost his glasses, then wonder if he is literate. He has one of the new Haitian passports, distinctive with its coat of arms, and peers at the lettering as if he cannot quite make out what it signifies; he has the same look on his face as Sam's four-year-old nephew in Iowa, when the boy tries to read in his grandmother's lap as her fingers underline the words he cannot yet recognize.

The last time I stood in this place with its worn wood-panelled counters and scratched dark floors, I was seventeen, leaving to study in Iowa. The last time I had returned with my mother I had been five or seven. I remember being listless, fatigued after the lengthy journey to the island from wintry Canada. I remember that a man had taken us out of the long queue and held my mother's elbow conspiratorially, whispering to her as we went, as my mother pulled me along. Occasionally, my mother looked back at me, giving me one of the half-smiles I had learned early on meant that my mother was not in full possession of her faculties, but wanted, somehow, to be a dutiful, reassuring mother.

It took me years to realize that the man who had taken us out of the line that day had a face I recognized when I looked at myself in the mirror, once I had lost my baby fat and my face took on its adult proportions; years to acknowledge that the man had looked back at me over my mother's shoulders as much with pity as with startled recognition.

As I wait for the line to advance, I pause and remember my mother's passport, a document I had kept from her private belongings after that other funeral so long ago.

I remember that on our last visit, my mother had been holding

204

me with one hand and our passports in the other. My mother's passport had been Haitian then, black with green pages, the Haitian coat of arms emblazoned with the dictum, "*Liberté, Egalité, Fraternité*", set off in full colour on the front page – just as on the flag my parents were so proud of that they had hung a replica in our living room, just above the sofa, where everyone could see it as soon as they entered the house. In her passport, my mother's photo was set vertically instead of horizontally and details about her were written on the back of the page: *Yeux: bruns; Taille: 5'8"; Date de Naissance: le 8 janvier 1949.*

The line moves ahead a bit and I observe the men in military garb officiously checking passports and papers, sending some out of the line to invisible rooms. Were it still the days of the Duvaliers, I would be worried at the sight of such sorting. Even though things have changed, I feel mildly anxious because all this seems so much the same. A switch in me goes off and I find myself on automatic pilot, observing with detachment, not letting my thoughts stray to things I can't fathom or won't recall. No one is being taken out of the line by a relative or friend the way it was possible back then, when status, money or political ties could get you past customs, whether or not you needed such a favour.

The man who approached my mother and myself that last trip home had worn a fine suit as if he had come directly from his office. I remember his sad, long face, his pointy chin swivelling in my direction, bobbing forward and backward as if it alone, without the head, could assess how I was doing back there, trailing along behind them, trying not to trip on my feet. The lips above the chin revealed long, narrow teeth. I remember a feeling of hesitancy, my stomach clenching, nausea, an uncertainty about the wisdom of following this unknown man who-knew-where as we stepped out of the queue. Some of the people who had been pressed against us while we waited our turn at the immigration officer's desk mumbled and hissed their resentment at seeing us bypass the line altogether.

I advance silently towards the glassed-in counter. I watch as each person hands over his or her papers. My stomach ties itself in knots. I hold my breath and advance towards the customs official. His lips are drawn in a tight line. I hand over my navy blue French passport and he scrutinizes it, flipping through the pages with a thumb as he holds the passport between the index and middle finger of his right hand.

He takes out a customs stamp and without asking me any questions marks a blank visa page and signs it with a flourish. The gesture is ironic, I think, given that his pen is a run-of-the-mill blue plastic *Bic*. He hands me back the passport and smiles. I smile back instinctively, despite the fear still fluttering like a butterfly in my stomach.

"*Bienvenue*," the man says. "Welcome home."

I nod, relieved, and move on with my carry-on baggage, trudging into the crowd before me, feeling the hum in the air. I wonder how many others are here for funerals after the hurricane and mudslides, how many bodies are already buried unnaturally beneath muddy ground.

I stand waiting for my baggage in a space too small to contain us all. There is a dizzying buzz in the air as people search for their bags or chase away baggage handlers, suddenly afraid of theft, while others pay with wads of American dollars for their baggage to be carried out by ragged, hustling men in grey caps lined with red felt, while ignoring the frenzy all about them.

As I wait, I feel the pulsing energy of the shape-shifting going on all around me, like a hand pushing against the small of my back. Apprehensive, I feel the molecules grate and move within my body, rearranging themselves to fit a world I haven't known for years.

March 12, 2004, Port-au-Prince, Haiti

Safely ensconced in Fritz's car, I look into my father's broad smile and hope, despite myself, that he feels better than he looks.

"How is Sam?" Fritz asks as he shifts the jeep's gears and backs out of his parking space after shooing away the beggars with handfuls of coins.

I take in the scene as the red dust swirls around the car. The red makes me think of the island's past, of bloodshed and killings. I sigh.

"He's fine," I say. I feel my father's disapproving eyes on me as he manoeuvres the car out of the makeshift lot and onto the road that leads to the *route nationale*. I am already dreading what will come next: *And do you intend to marry? What exactly are you doing with your life? He may not wait for you forever. Men need their anchors.* I feel my body stiffen in advance against the onslaught of such reproaches. I've heard them all before. He's trying to chip away at me as if I'm a block of ice, as if my falling in line might somehow melt the deep freeze between us.

He glances at me, sees the finger splints on my left hand. "What happened there?"

"Nothing," I say, tucking my arm around my waist, out of sight. It would be so easy to blame Sam, to have my father's opinion of him change in a second, but I know I'm as much to blame. There's no use going into it.

"What more do you know about Tatie?" I ask abruptly, a pre-emptive strike to divert the conversation.

Fritz sighs and hunches his shoulders forward as he speeds up on the stretch of highway leading into the congestion of Port-au-Prince. "The authorities aren't saying much but word on the street is that it was some sort of..." he hesitates, then says it, "*execution.*"

He utters the word as if he can hardly believe it. He sighs again, leans back into his seat, keeping the car steady with one hand on the steering wheel while wiping at his mouth with the other. Then, he gesticulates out the open window as if appealing to hidden gods. "But no one seems to know what has become of the man who led the thugs there, this *Romulus.*" He spits out the familiar name. He turns to me conspiratorially, "We think his family got him out. You know how those people have money." Fritz looks back intently at the broken road before him, shoulders hunched over the wheel making him seem younger than his almost sixty years.

I look at him blankly, take in the deeply etched lines of his face that give him an air of gravity. I think it odd that he should make such a comment about class. Of all of my aunts and uncles, Ruth was the wealthiest. No one could account for all that wealth – her house overlooking the capital surrounded by its sumptuous gardens.

"What about the other men they said were with him? Weren't they just thieves?"

"Catherine," my father said, "it was an orchestrated hit. They all knew her. How…" his fingers stroked the air above the wheel, "we don't know. But they knew her. Somehow."

I look at my father and am perplexed to suddenly recognize a pale resemblance between us: we have the same nose – a rise from the bridge into a point and then a sharp descent as if the bridge cannot sustain its weight. We both have high cheekbones and almond-shaped eyes. It's not something I'm usually able to acknowledge, the possibility that the same blood runs through our veins, that the mystery man who once came to fetch my mother and I at the airport was nothing more than that, a stranger.

"Strange," I say, finally. To myself I think, *Those men must have known something we didn't*.

"She's gone, Catherine," Fritz says, then adds, as if reading my thoughts, "that's all I know." A tremor in his voice gives away the emotion swirling beneath his placid surface. I haven't seen Fritz this agitated since, since, well, since my mother.

My heart lurches suddenly, unexpectedly. I turn towards Fritz, glance at him again. He stares straight ahead, holding the steering wheel tightly.

"I know," I say, "I loved her too."

We fall silent. It isn't clear whether we are thinking of Ruth or of my mother. Perhaps we're thinking about them both. It's the ambiguity that binds us, the invisible cartilage of pain that connects us more closely than shared DNA.

I let my hand grow warm against Fritz's bare arm and then remove it when something tells me that my touch is too much for him to bear. He had always maintained that I had inherited my mother's hands while my mother regarded them as something almost exotic, completely removed from herself, and examined my hands throughout my childhood as if she had never seen anything so perfect, so alien to her, in all her years.

"Max will be putting you up," Fritz says.

"Oh?"

"He has room for you in one of his daughters' rooms."

"And Lucas? You haven't said anything about Lucas."

"What is there to say?"

"Isn't he coming?"

Fritz shrugs his shoulders. We are speeding on the uneven surface of rue Dessalines, heading south of the city into Pétion-Ville. I think for a moment about asking Fritz to drive past the port so that I can glimpse my mother's childhood home, then think better of it. When was the last time we had spoken of my mother? I prefer to keep our shared memories of her at a minimum.

"Isn't he coming to his mother's funeral?" I ask again in a voice tinged with astonishment, even though I had already surmised that Lucas would be missing in action. He hadn't always been this way.

I look out at the worn façades of the buildings lining the road, noting the increased numbers of market stalls filled with multi-coloured goods ranging from the ubiquitous Chiclet packs to cheap plastic ware.

"Since when have there been so many people out in the streets in this area?" I ask, trying to avoid more conversation about Lucas.

"He's not coming."

We pause. I notice that Fritz's breathing is slightly more laboured than usual. He's starting to age. This realization startles me. It's something I don't often think about. My father, I realize with a jolt, even more than Sam, is the sole continuous thread in my life. It's a realization that feels like a curse.

"The people keep coming down from the hills. They have no choice."

"I thought things were getting better."

"You're an optimist."

We both know that this is not true.

Fritz guides the jeep into a short driveway in front of a three-storey house with vines climbing up shiny white walls. A balcony traces the second-floor chambers with a palisade of carved wood. My father honks his horn and the steel gate is opened by a man in his fifties, dressed in plain black pants, a checked brown, yellow and black shirt and worn sandals.

"*Mèsi Dessalines*," my father yells towards the man, waving as he barrels through. Dessalines is about the same age as my father. He waves at us, smiling.

We park. Fritz sits back in his seat. "Catherine, you're here only for a few days. *Kenbé tèt ou*, all right?"

Fritz's words cut to a place deep within me that I didn't know still existed, that I didn't know was still tender and could be wounded. "*Pas de problème, Papa*," I say, calling him father as I never do, as if this pain is the only thing identifying his paternity.

The front door of the house opens to reveal a tall and handsome woman, dark-skinned with her hair cropped fashionably to contour a high forehead, a sculptured head. Then Max, Fritz's brother, appears from behind her, gently moving the woman to the side to grasp Fritz in a sideways hug. Then all three look at me in a way that makes me feel as if I am an alien descended from some faraway planet. Max is the first to acknowledge me, waving at me to get out of the jeep and to come, come. He is Fritz's and Ruth's older brother and it has been years since I've seen him – maybe even as long ago as my arrival in Haiti after my mother's passing. He had been living abroad, for ever it seemed, and then returned after the ousting of the Duvaliers to remake his life. Our lives had seldom intersected, even in the years I had lived with Ruth. Max ran several garages about town and in the provinces. The woman by his side is not the Aunt I had known as a child and vaguely remember, the mother of my older girl-cousins. How things change.

"*Allo, allo*," I wave to Max, feigning good humour, as I advance towards the front door. They all seem so cheerful and, for a moment, I forget that we have gathered for a funeral. There is something joyful about seeing family members I haven't seen for so long and so I utter the ubiquitous Haitian greeting, "*Koman ou yé?*"

The tightness of Max's hug brings me back to the reason for our re-acquaintance. His pain sears through me as if a flame has been set against my skin. It overwhelms me and I pull away from him, gripping his forearms forcefully, trying to smile up at him to reassure him, and myself, that there will be better times, better reasons, to meet. "You've done well, *Tonton*," I say.

"And you," he smiles back, then sees the splint on my wrist. "But what has happened to your hand?" He holds me now at arm's length, to inspect me. He grimaces. "Yolande was so looking forward to hearing you play."

Before I have a chance to say anything, Yolande steps forward and takes me by the shoulders as Max moves aside. She kisses me on both cheeks. "*Bienvenue, ma chère*," she croons in my ear.

Yolande steps back and tries to give me what is meant as a warm look, but her eyes are heavy and watery with pain. I can feel myself teetering on the edge of a precipice, both dreading and desiring the fall, knowing that it cannot be avoided.

"*Merci*," is all I can muster as Yolande shepherds me into the house, the two brothers, talking in low tones, following us, my injured left hand pulsing at my side.

Inside, everyone moves about with utter quiet, as if fearing to disturb each other's grief. Even the cook and housekeeper perform their chores with what appears to be ambulant stillness.

We sit around the dining-room table: Max, Yolande, my two cousins from Max's first marriage, Marie-France and Estelle, and myself. Fritz has not yet returned from his house where he's gone to change. He's picking me up to take us to the wake and funeral at Sacré Cœur, the church in the middle of the square of Pétion-Ville.

I observe my cousins from the corners of my eyes. They, at least, have not changed. The sisters had always been like this, drinking their *cafés au lait* very quietly, as if fearing to disturb the fragile peace, pensive, with nothing much to say to me or to anyone. Lucas had called them simpletons when we were growing up, because they never seemed to want to do anything else but read their books and stare wistfully at the walls of their bedrooms as if they could see pictures of their futures drawn upon the pale yellow taffy paint covering the grey concrete walls. I wonder now what they had dreamed, since they both still lived within those walls, neither married, both childless. I had never known quite what to make of them but, in ways that I feared to recognize, I had grown to resemble them, keeping some part of myself vaulted away.

211

My thoughts turn suddenly to Sam: I have not called him since arriving. I wonder for a moment if he is thinking of me or if he is engrossed in his studies. At that moment, I wish that I could play Yolande's piano and be drawn closer to everything I've loved in my life, from Ruth to Sam, from Paris to Port-au-Prince. The music is the only thing that ties together all of my geographies. My wrist still aches from the fight with Sam and my fingers feel stiff. They pulse with the sensation of needing to rehearse, a need as strong in me as the need others have for their daily hit of morning caffeine. Music is my sole, true companion, having lost Lucas so long ago, and having not yet let Sam in as far as he would like. Edouard, my mentor after Ruth, understands my hunger for the piano and can entertain my desire for hours-long conversations about the pieces I might perform and, of course, can talk at length about his own work. Still, as much as Edouard covets and adores me, he has no interest in my true heart, my hopes and dreams. I've learned to keep these to myself.

I continue to gaze at my cousins. They smile shyly back at me and continue eating their breakfasts as if by rote, methodically. They too had lost a mother. All three of us had lost our mothers and we never talked about that fact. How could that be? I look at the sisters, so smartly dressed in white-accented, black dresses, the curls of their hair pressed out to unnatural smoothness. *They're fine*, I think, almost uncharitably, feeling myself harden. After all, they had only lost their mother to Miami. Mine would never be found again.

"We should be leaving soon," Yolande says. "The showing will be starting around noon."

I help the cook – a young woman about my age, thin and tall with sunken cheeks below her high cheekbones and round, full eyes – to clear the dishes from the table. "Hyacinth," Yolande says to her, "*s'il te plaît, meté tout bagay yo nan frijidè a pou pi ta.*"

"*Wi madamn,*" Hyacinth replies in a too-soft voice, revealing that she is much younger than I had assumed, and uncomfortable with the French language.

I stand up awkwardly, unsure as to whether I should continue to help Hyacinth clear the table and put things away in the fridge as *Tatie* had requested, or if I should retreat to the room one of the cousins had given up for me. They smile at me encouragingly as they, too, begin to clear the table.

"More hands make things go faster," Marie-France says.

I smile her my gratitude. Recognizing that every household has its own etiquette, it comforts me to know what to do and when. At the same time, I feel a sinking feeling of loss that I no longer know members of my own family well enough to be intimately acquainted with their daily habits.

Max has left the table and gone into his study and I'm piqued by the fact that even in this liberal household, in which servants are treated with respect, the line dividing what is and what is not women's work is clear. Men have to be managed, supported, it seems, in all arenas and women *work* whether their work was visible outside of the home, or not. *Tatie* Ruth had been the family exception, the "manless" woman no one dared to criticize, with her own household and servants, a house where men had to earn the privilege of being invited in.

The women move through the kitchen tasks like fish in water, gliding past each other with perfect harmony, each lost in her own thoughts. Hyacinth seems to be calculating the time it will take her to shop for and prepare the meal to follow the burial which will be served at Ruth's house; the sisters ponder how they will overcome their crippling shyness to speak to the mourners, secretly resenting Lucas for his absence. He is the only son, after all. Yolande frets over the brothers, her husband, Fritz, and wonders how they will hold up at their beloved sister's funeral; she frets, too, but about being a very new addition to the family, even though she and Max have been living together at least seven years and have known each other for fifteen.

I feel ill-prepared for the viewing of the body, for the last rites, the rituals of burial. I can't remember the last time I'd spoken to *Tatie* Ruth or sent her a card. Guilt floods me and makes my hands shake. The other sister, Estelle, takes the plates out of my hands.

"Go sit, cousin," she says, not unkindly, and I nod and find my way to the orange living-room chairs, watch the trucks barrel round the elbow of the road in front of the house, wait for my father to reappear.

It wasn't always this way – the kindness of cousins, the care between the related. When I had lived with Tatie Ruth and Lucas for seven years, seven years in which we grew like cane and stronger than seemed possible, our spindly legs and arms grown sinewy from working in Tatie's garden, from the weeding and cultivating, my forearms and fingers strong from practising scales five to six hours a day (two hours in the morning and three at night), Lucas's legs bulging from walking up and down Lalue on his way to school in town with the other sons of the privileged, often walking with Romulus, who seldom had fare for the tap-tap. Sometimes Lucas lent him the money if he didn't want to walk, but most of the time they walked. The two walked quietly, but purposefully, Romulus thinking of his music, Lucas of his plants and their powers to cure or to make ill. Lucas had become fascinated with the *ma'chand fey* – the market women who were probably *mambos* or even *bokos* – selling the products of their garden plots to those who could not afford doctors or who believed in the gods of their forefathers. I travelled with the twins to and from school in a car Tatie Ruth hired for that purpose, so that we would not have to walk and I sat silently with Estelle and Marie-France, ignoring them, thinking them pious as they talked about church services (which they attended daily) and the good-ness of the priest and his plans to re-invigorate the parish. They seemed so distant, even though they sat next to me every morning and late afternoon. I thought then that we had nothing in com-mon, even though we were roughly the same age. Two years had gone by and I knew them no more than I had let them know me. They had reason to keep their distance. Lucas and I were not kind to them. Inwardly – though I never let it show – I was impressed by the way they hid their fear, the terror I assumed they held deep down, over what we had done, how perhaps, in the midnight hours they awoke from nightmares wondering what we might be capable of doing next. We were not kind. We did not ask them to come to the movies or play marbles against the high walls of the house. We did not ask them in for tea, or, if we did, we put salt instead of sugar in their cups. We gave them the smallest cuts of pies and ridiculed their churchgoing while we were dragged kicking and screaming to Sunday services. I did not realize, then, as I do now, that we heaped upon them the pain of our abandonment, for the only difference between us was the fact that the cousins knew where they came from and behaved with certainty about where they belonged and where their lives were meant to go. Though they quarrelled with them, they had parents. We did not.

In our first days, Lucas and I bonded over the mere fact of our abandonment. It opened the door to a deeper knowledge that I resisted more than he, that our aloneness had a purpose.

I wondered often about the man who came to greet my mother and myself on the occasions she fled my father. I tried to ask Ruth about him once. This was just days after Lucas and I had contemplated our faces in the mirror and Lucas had loudly pronounced our absence of kinship. Tatie Ruth was trying on various dresses as she prepared for a night out, and I was sitting on the edge of her bed, going through her box of jewellery. She never spoke of where she went; it was one of her many secrets. I knew that Ruth felt guilty about not sharing everything with me and I used this guilt when I could to get answers to my questions.

As I fingered Ruth's jewellery and came across drop-pearl earrings that resembled a pair my mother had owned, I pondered how to formulate a question that might receive a straightforward answer. I placed the drop-pearl earrings on top of the bedspread and continued digging through the box, disentangling necklace chains, sorting tarnished silver rings from gold ones.

"Do you see my amber earrings there, dear?" Ruth asked once she had settled on a black muslin dress with puffed, see-through sleeves.

I scanned the jewellery for the familiar square pieces of amber framed in gold, "Not yet."

Ruth was sitting on the low bench where Lucas and I had sat not long before and compared our faces. She pulled out a stick of dark red lipstick and applied it liberally to her pursed lips. I tried to remember if my mother had performed the same gestures but could not. I had no memory of a time when my mother had gotten all dressed up to go out with Fritz, or with anyone.

215

"Tatie?"

"Ummm?"

"Who do you think I look like the most, Mother or Fritz?"

Ruth looked at my image in the mirror before her. I recognized her indirect gaze as a trick I had learned from Lucas: that it was often easier to communicate with an image than to look at someone straight on. I caught Ruth's glance and held it as long as was comfortable. Ruth turned her eyes away from mine to apply rouge and powder to her cheeks. She always applied the mascara last, as if it was a crowning touch.

"Why do you want to know?"

I shrugged as my fingers fell on the amber earrings.

"Found them."

"The earrings?"

"Yes."

I went over to Ruth and dangled the earrings over her left shoulder. Ruth took them from me without looking up.

"*Merci,*" she said.

"Ok, but you haven't answered my question."

I returned to the bed and continued to sort the jewellery with quiet deliberation. "Why do you keep everything in such a mess?"

Ruth shrugged her shoulders and laughed. "You sound like your father right now." She sighed, "There are more important things in life than order."

"Like what?"

"Like knowing who you are." Ruth stopped, as if she wished to take back the words she had just uttered. My fingers stilled over the jewellery. Ruth started again, her voice rising in intonation to cover up her mistake, and continued lightly, "Like making your way in the world, being a good person, knowing who you love and why."

"Do you love me?" I asked in an attempt to stir up guilt.

"Of course," Ruth answered. Her hands continued to move about her face in systematic, practised movements. She put the amber earrings on. "Why would you ask me such a question?" Suddenly agitated, she paused for a moment, and then looked at me piercingly as if to divine my thoughts. I'd stopped talking about Mother only a couple of months ago. I could tell Ruth was wondering what had awakened this sudden desire to know more

216

about my parentage. "I want to know if I look more like my mother or like Fritz."

"Why do you call him Fritz, Catherine?" Ruth sighed as she combed through her hair and pulled it up into a chignon. "He's your father."

Chastened, I concentrated more deeply on the sorting of Ruth's jewellery. There were garnets in gold settings and rough-hewn aquamarine stones in finely sculpted silver, brooches with elaborate scenes of wildlife, a string of real pearls, all kinds of rings that made me wonder, at thirteen, if my unmarried aunt had ever been courted.

"What about the man who used to pick us up at the airport?"

Even though I was not looking at her, I could feel Ruth's back tighten, straighten, the hands stop in mid-flight between her face and the surface of the boudoir table filled with her creams and make-up, hair brushes and pins.

"What man?"

"You know," I tried to keep my voice light and even, "the man who would take us through customs when I came home with Mother."

Ruth's hands moved slowly through her hair, smoothing tendrils into place with pins.

"I don't know who you mean."

I frowned at the jewellery, but I was really thinking about whether or not I had ever seen the man elsewhere than at the airport and on the ride home to Ruth's house or to my grand-mother's house. We had gone once to a wooden house painted aquamarine on the outside with light cream-coloured walls inside, where the man had stood too close to my mother and held her around the waist while she cried at something he had whispered in her ear. I was sitting at the aluminium table in the kitchen (it was painted white with matching chairs), while a short woman wearing a rose and white plaid dress covered over with a half-apron cinched behind her fattish waist by two strings – a woman whose name I did not know because we had not been introduced – minced through the room complaining about the lack of ingredients to make the dinner for three the man standing too close to my mother in the living room had requested.

217

"You know," I pushed on, "the thin man who wore the nice suits and picked us up at the airport."

"I really don't know who you mean," Ruth said, shaking her head, but I could tell by the way she was trying to avoid making eye contact even through the mirror that she knew exactly who I was speaking about.

I sifted through the rings and sorted them according to the colour of their stones. I was weighing whether it was worth it right at that moment to try to get more out of Tatie.

"You look like your mother," she said finally, as if to spare her the decision. "You have her shape of face and eyebrows." She looked at me through the mirror, "And her smile – when you smile."

I looked at her reflection in the mirror. It was easy to see the family resemblance between Fritz and Ruth. Why was it so difficult to see myself in them? I tried to smile in order to reassure her.

"That's better," Ruth said. "You smile just like your mother."

I could not remember my mother's smile. In the last years before her death, my mother had hardly smiled, but I kept that fact to myself. I returned the sorted jewellery to the compartments in the black lacquered box and closed the lid quietly on the brilliance of the sparkling stones. I wondered if one day I would have such a box filled with pieces handed down from my mother and from Ruth, given to her by suitors unknown. I wondered if the thin, tall man from the airport had given my mother jewellery. Among her belongings, after the car accident, there had been a chain that Fritz had not recognized. He had given it to me in a plastic bag and I had held up to the light to see it more clearly, before removing it from the bag and placing it around my neck. It was a long daisy chain made of very small purple and white beads. It had no clasp and had to be tied by folding the two long ends of the chain over one another, as if they were pieces of loose string.

"I don't know where this came from," Fritz had said as he gave me the bag. "Did you give it to her?"

Immediately, an image of the thin man in the light-coloured suits had come to my mind from nowhere, and I had not known what to say. I nodded, but Fritz had already turned away from me to rifle through a pile of papers that had accumulated since the day of the accident.

"I won't be in very late," Ruth said, calling me back into the room from my memories. "You can stay up if you like and we'll have mint tea together. Would you like that?"

I knew an olive branch when it was being offered. "Sure," I said.

Ruth smiled at me through the mirror. Her lips were tinged with the plum lipstick she had so carefully applied and her usually yellowed cheeks were suddenly bright with a rose powder.

"You should concentrate on new things, Catherine. It's time to create a new world for yourself." She looked about the room, and cocked her head to the side to listen to the sounds of the house. "That's strange," she said. "Where is Lucas? Lucas?" She called out his name until we heard his footsteps echoing in the back yard. "You two have to look out for one another."

I nodded, but I wondered what Tatie Ruth was trying to hide.

I'd seen the man again a few months ago in the streets of downtown Port-au-Prince. He looked older, his face lined and falling with gravity. I had noticed him right away as I left the cinema with Lucas. We had just seen a film with Roger Moore in which planes crossed the sound barrier and cars sped through mountain roads as if gliding on ice. The technology seemed unimaginable as we came out of the theatre into the choke of diesel streaming from two tap-taps chugging along the broken street, full of office and domestic workers and market-women going home with their straw baskets filled with unsold wares. As the air cleared, I saw the man moving through clouds of dust, as if he was a mirage whose molecules had suddenly gathered and created an image out of thin air for me to see.

"Do you see him?" I'd asked Lucas quickly.

"What? Him who?"

"The man over there."

"Where?" Lucas was staring out into the dust in the opposite direction. "I can't see anything."

I followed the man as he loped across the street in front of us, and had the sudden sensation that if I just reached out my hand,

I could touch him, and just as I had that thought, the man turned his head and stared at me as if I *had* touched him. I reached for Lucas instead and held his forearm.

"What…?"

"There," I said, "across from us. On the other side of the street."

"I don't know who you're…"

The man gave me one of those thin-lipped smiles I remembered from early childhood. His eyes were hard, dark, not giving anything away. But then, he did something strange. He held up a hand and acknowledged us. Then, he turned away, disappearing behind a black jeep that blocked the traffic as the driver picked up two girls dressed in matching green dresses and hair ribbons. Startled, I stepped back towards the theatre doors.

"What's going on?" Lucas asked. "Who were you looking at?"

I felt confused, afraid of admitting to myself what I wanted so much to share with Lucas, who had become my co-conspirator in all things. It was *this* man I felt I resembled, not Fritz, not my mother, even though I did have my mother's smile, her eyebrows. But my most distinct features resembled those of *this* man. We were, as the market women would say, like two drops of water from the same pond. Why would anyone want to deny it?

I shook off the confusion and stepped back out into the light next to the boy who had been introduced to me as my cousin only two years past, but with whom I shared no features, no memories carried by blood.

"I was just joking."

Lucas stared at me the way he stared at most girls, as if they were aliens from another planet. I had suddenly lost my credibility.

"Let's go," I said.

I ran out into the street following a tap-tap belching black diesel fumes into the air.

"Come on," I yelled back at Lucas, "we can make it." Attempting the impossible in order to redeem myself.

I heard Lucas laughing behind me – at me or with me, it didn't matter. All that mattered was that he was following, that I was not alone.

Ruth stood up in front of her boudoir mirror.

"Well, it's time for me to go. Do something fun with Lucas."
We listened for his footsteps in the yard. It sounded as if he was
chasing lizards.

I knew better than to ask Ruth where she was going. I would
only get a vague answer in return. I wanted to tell her about the
sighting in front of the cinema, about the thin man acknowledging Lucas and I, when he had barely spoken to me all those years
ago when he escorted my mother into those rooms reeking of
loneliness in a house I had never seen again after my grandmother's passing.

Ruth was looking down at me. I looked up into eyes that
seemed vaguely like older versions of my own. She stroked my
hair out of my face.

"*Chat*," she said, using a nickname given to me in infancy that
hardly anyone used any more. It signalled that Ruth felt guilt.
"Just let these things go. You'll see, everything will fall into place
in time."

I looked up into her eyes. They were amber, flecked. Sometimes, looking into them, I felt that she could see things that no
one else could. That night, Ruth's eyes spoke of sorrow and loss
and I wondered: Whose sorrow? Whose loss? Hers? Ours?

All I could do was nod and hold back my questions.

As Ruth left, I heard her give instructions in *Kreyol* to the
housekeeper and cook. The two women and a male guard lived
in rooms behind the house, next to the outdoor kitchen. Here, I
was never alone. Here, I was always alone.

Lucas came sauntering in from the yard, "She gone?"
I nodded.

"Come on. We're going to pay the cousins a visit."

I followed Lucas out of the grounds, down the street to the
cousins' house. "What are we doing?"

"Sh…" Lucas hushed me, "you'll see."

We crept below the window of the cousins' room. I saw Lucas
struggle with something in his pocket.

"Knock on the window."

I did as I was told. Estelle came to open the window. She smiled.
Marie-France was behind her shaking sleep from her eyes.

"What are you doing here" Estelle asked.

"Surprise!" Lucas yelled as he threw something into the room.

We all looked as a lizard unfurled its little body in the middle of the room and skittered to a stop, attempting to get its bearings. I was staring as its eyes suddenly grew large, its throat disgorged, its skin turned from yellow to red. Then, suddenly, the lizard exploded, leaving behind only half a body and two little legs burned into the floor. Estelle's robe had received a splatter of lizard blood and her smile had frozen upon her face. "What…" she said.

Marie-France screamed.

The cousins' mother burst into the room followed by a housemaid.

"*Sak pasé la?*"

Lucas turned and ran away. "Come on," he said.

But all I could do was stare, along with Marie-France, at the remains of the lizard while Estelle glanced, horrified, at the red splash on her dress, then at me, in my complicity.

The cousins' mother strode through the room. She pushed Estelle away from the window, "*Enlève ça,*" she said to her daughter. "You," she gestured at the housekeeper, "take care of that," and she pointed down at the lizard whose head was still quivering against the cold of the linoleum. Then, she turned to me, "You should be ashamed of yourself."

"*Sak pasé?*" I heard Max in the hallway of the house as he came towards the room.

I was horrified that he would see me there and I turned away from the window and chased after Lucas.

We returned to Tatie Ruth's house, winded.

"That wasn't very nice," I said to Lucas, once I had caught my breath.

He laughed, "No, it wasn't."

By breakfast time the next morning, Tatie Ruth had heard what had happened and we were sent to join the cousins at mass. At my left, Lucas sat with a smug look on his face, while the cousins sat at my right with rosaries funnelling through their fingers. I felt mortified. The sister-cousins never spoke of the event again and from that day on I went with them to their services, even though I believed no more in their God than I did before. Lucas, on the other hand, stopped going to church completely. Instead of making lizards explode, he snuck off to drink with boys his own age and left me behind at the house.

About a year later, he came to find me one night when Ruth was out and said, "Come, follow me."

I did not know where he was taking me but I followed.

We walked some time in silence, in the dark, until we reached a brick building. There were cars all around it and bicycles propped up against its sides. Inside, people were seated on low, folding chairs or on the ground, and a woman was orating.

"*Loa monté tet li*," a man said towards us.

Lucas nodded and waved me towards an empty chair.

The night unfolded in front of me like a hallucinatory dream. Later, I would hardly remember it all. A woman strutted in front of the crowd like a rooster, sticking her chest out like a man. She drank *Barbancourt* rum and dowsed the people in the front rows. The people sang. Eventually, they moved the chairs out of the way and some people danced, following the woman in a sacred movement for her *loa*. There was an altar where people had placed foods and images. I saw Lucas place two mangoes and a small photograph. I could not make out who was in the photograph. He did not speak to me during the ceremony.

It was all over when a filament of dawn started to show itself on the horizon. The crowd dispersed quietly. Lucas took back his photograph from the altar and asked the woman who had led the ceremony to bless it. Then, he put it back in his wallet.

When we were walking back to Ruth's, I elbowed him.

"Whose picture is that?"

He took out the wallet and handed me the photo.

"My parents," he said.

I looked down and saw a handsome woman and man in elegant clothes.

"Your parents?"

"My parents," he replied.

"I thought…"

"She lied," he said. "She's always lying."

223

"What do you mean?"

"Listen," Lucas said, "we aren't kids any more. We have to see the truth for what it is."

I was confused. Lucas was always first and last to laugh.

I tried to smile.

He looked at me stonily.

"I have to leave here," he said.

"What? Where will you go?"

"I have to serve my gods," he said.

"What are you talking about?" I said. "What gods? You mean what we just saw? The cousins would say that was the work of the devil."

Lucas laughed a dry laugh. "The cousins aren't stupid, Cat. They believe what they want to believe. I believe what I must believe. You will believe what you must."

The trouble, then, was that I didn't believe in much.

"Your god…" Lucas said. "No," he corrected himself, "You will find yours in the sea, or, she will make you find her."

"What are you talking about?" I replied, growing afraid, quickening my step towards Ruth's house.

"You're too young to understand but it will come to you. By and by, it will come to you."

I stopped and stared at Lucas in disgust. "Who are you to be so pious. What's happened to you?"

"I've remembered myself, Cat. The days of playing are over."

I walked on ahead, angry, knowing only that Lucas was telling me that he was about to abandon me, like the others.

Lucas caught up with me.

"Look," he said, "before you came, I knew you. I heard your mother speaking to me in the garden. We planted daffodils for her, for you. Then, you came, and I forgot everything. I wanted to forget everything. I wanted to be a child again. I wanted to be your cousin. But I'm sixteen now. It's time for me to put away childish things."

I kept walking, but my pace was slowing. I listened even though I didn't want to.

"I'm not leaving you. I'm trying to find myself. I have nothing."

"That's not true," I said ruefully, with all the strength of my thirteen going on fourteen years. "You have me and Tatie Ruth and the cousins."

He smiled at me a strange, sad, crooked smile I'll always remember for its broken nakedness. "It's you who has everything. I'm only a visitor."

We walked in silence the rest of the way and parted to go to our respective rooms in the house. We never spoke of that night again, and went on as if nothing had happened, except that we stopped preying upon the cousins. We had both come to understand that our tricks had been only diversions to keep the truth at bay: that we envied their belonging, and their faith. We, separately and together, would have to search long to find our measure of both.

March 12, 2004, Port-au-Prince

Fritz drives us to the cathedral – myself, Max and the sisters. On the way there I can't help but burst into tears. Estelle sits at my right. Max is seated up front and glances back uncomfortably but not unkindly. No one speaks to me. This only makes me cry all the more. Estelle finally places a clammy hand on my right forearm and her touch calms me. Even so, though I try to hold them back, tears seep past the lids of my half-shut eyes like a river thawing after a long frozen winter, overflowing its banks, and I splutter behind the handkerchief Yolande gave me as we walked out of the house. Yolande has a good sense of people, I think, and this thought is mixed up with memories of Ruth as a younger woman teaching me to play the piano for the very first time; of high teas in Ruth's gardens high above the city; of the parties that were thrown and of the secret conversations that went on in the shadows; of Romulus before his rise to fame, his modesty still clinging to the soft contours of his pre-adult face; of Romulus slaying his mentor and letting her lie in a pool of her own blood until she expired; of the muscles of my father's face twitching, because he didn't know how to express grief; of myself, adrift in a life that should otherwise be joyful.

225

The handkerchief cannot contain it all. I gasp for air and try to think of other things, of Sam, of Edouard's piano sitting in my living room; of possible concert dates when my hand has healed; of the day after tomorrow, when I will not feel so bad as at the present moment; of the months and years ahead that will blunt the feeling of loss and almost make it palatable – as time always does.

As we approach the cathedral, I see the neighbouring streets are lined with cars. The more I'm aware of the size of the group assembled to pay their last respects, the more I find it difficult to hold the tears back. It all feels so, so *unearthly*, so impossible. Estelle leads me to the viewing room next to the church where most of the family are already sitting in a wide arc facing the open casket.

Everyone waits for the family to be seated before the procession of last goodbyes takes place. Visitors and less immediate kin queue up at the foot of the long, mahogany casket, view the body, pause to make a prayer or kiss the deceased, and then move on to shake the hands of each member of the family. Depending on the number of people who present themselves, the procession could take several hours. I know the family will then have an opportunity to say their last goodbyes before the casket is closed and moved into the main hall of the cathedral where a final mass will take place before the burial. The wake will follow the burial.

I dread the hours to come; I put the handkerchief to my mouth to stifle an almost hysterical cry and choke instead. One of the ushers hands me a cup of water as I try, vainly, to recover from the coughing. By then, the procession has begun.

The more the flow of people increases, the more it appears that the end of the queue is nowhere in sight, and the less I can control my tears. I weep openly now, seated between Estelle and Marie-France, who remain tight-lipped and courteous throughout the proceedings. Most of the participants pass me by, letting me weep into the handkerchief bunched between my hands, my head down to hide not only the hot tears, but my shame at being unable to withhold my grief unlike the others in the circle. They are so much more used to death, I think to myself, so much more used to seeing life waste away, whether it is in the slaying of chickens in their back yards for the evening meal or mules left to die at the sides of roads, their dried-up flesh outlining the curve of their ribs, the end points pushing against their sides as if somehow the animal had tried to keep breathing. Here, despair hangs in the air like bananas from their trees, overripe, heavy. Every day, one hears of protesters slain in a back street, in some town of the North, or as close as down by the docks. Reports waft in with the odour of freshly brewed coffee in the mornings, of hijackings for ransom and other disappearances. But I have chosen to live a different life, one in which death did not dog my every step, in which I did not have to think about its ubiquity every day, the way I think still of my mother, frozen at thirty-five, in a picture I keep in my purse along with a picture of myself with Tatie Ruth when I'd won first prize for playing a Mozart minuet at an open-air concert. I had been thirteen or fourteen when I'd won that prize and am still proud of it. It marked the beginning of my escape. I had stood before Ruth and Ruth had held me with her arm draped around my neck and shoulders. I feel her arm about me now, like a noose. I was foolish to think there was any way out of this world of unforgiving, unrelenting slayings and massacres.

I feel suddenly claustrophobic, hemmed in. The heat is oppressive as more bodies enter the space and sit behind the circle of the family. I want to scream out, cry with full force. Instead, all I do is continue to splutter into my handkerchief. Fortunately, Max offered me a larger square as I entered the hall, just in case, his eyes looking away rapidly, despite the gesture, as if my display of sorrow might be contagious.

Now, at least, I am no longer the sole weeper. Estelle and Marie-France have pulled out their own handkerchiefs and dab the half-moons beneath their eyes.

The room has filled to capacity. I dread the singing of the traditional *Ave Maria* and yearn for the soothing strains of a Chopin *ballade*, the quiet rhythms of a music made for escape. I cling to the memory of the notes like an addict, measuring time, giving in to the notion of death and birth, to the pain caused by openings and closings, with closings looming more distinctly over the rest. Edouard always insists that it is impermanence that human beings cannot fathom, the lesson it takes a lifetime to master, if at all. Sam believes in the idea that all things coexist at given times for a reason and then change. Time, for him, is simply a mechanism for exalting the presence of simultaneous existence. And what do I believe in? I no longer know.

The photograph of myself as a child with Ruth seems to take on a life of its own in my purse. It's like a heavy stone waiting to be released. I had shown it to the cousins after breakfast as we waited for Fritz to arrive. I had not known how to speak, adequately, of its importance. They were kind, the cousins, having forgotten, or at least, forgiven, my childhood disdain for their difference.

"How young she looks," Estelle had said, peering at the picture. "Always ravishing."

"Yes," Marie-France concurred, "and how happy *you* looked."

They gave me the affirmation needed, a confirmation that I, beyond them all, had lost a precious relationship. Why had I needed that sense of exclusivity, of a special bond to Ruth that no one else could have? I refused to think of the connections Tatie Ruth might have forged with each of the others and they with her. My pain sits within me like bile, moving slowly, poisonously through arteries that feel grated and bruised. The bile, grainy as salt, moves from the lining of my stomach where it sat through meals, to the outer layer of my heart, trying with all its might to push into and through the soft valves. Or, maybe it is the other way around. Perhaps the pain has already made its way in and is a ball of despair trying to fight its way out of the heart, the pain being too much to bear. I have burdened my heart with unresolved losses. Besides the pain of Ruth's and my mother's passing, my exile from Haiti could barely be examined. Slowly, I'm becoming aware that, like the sisters, I'm an observer, not an actor, satisfied to live on the banks of life, watching the waters swirl.

As the crowd behind me rises to move towards the interior of the cathedral, leaving the family to say our last goodbyes before the closing of the casket, I feel the bile within me rise up from the area of my heart where it has lingered, and force itself into my gullet, lodging between the sticky folds of my vocal chords.

The sister-cousins stand up on either side of me, leaving the scent of flowers in their wake, the fabric of their loose blouses brushing against my bare arms and urging me to stand with them.

I do so with trepidation, my legs feeling heavy, waterlogged. A rising tide of a hysteria grows mightily in my chest and I panic that the stone of bile in my throat will force me to vomit.

I teeter on the edge of what feels like the portal to certain loss of sanity, loss of self. Who am I without Ruth? Without these cousins and aunts I hardly know any more? Who am I when I'm separated from this place where I learned to survive my orphaning, to create myself anew? Time has swept everything from my grasp. My feet cannot anchor me. I am certain that moving in any direction will send me reeling head first into depths I cannot fathom.

I move forward, behind Estelle, and find myself reaching out to grasp my cousin's left elbow, but have to steady myself between chairs. Then, losing a sense of time, of the sequence of events that ties moments to other moments, I find myself between Max and Fritz, the cousins gone ahead to the service in the church. Our three bodies loom over Tatie Ruth's face: it is thickened by stilled blood and the absence of breath.

My body feels rigid. My arms are lead by my sides, my right hand holding a thin piece of a paper I cannot remember having taken out of my purse. The heaviness gives me the sensation of limbs without end, that stretch to the hot centre of the earth. Is that where Ruth has gone, to the underground city of *Vilokan* where *vodouisants* believe the dead reside? Why can't the dead return from that far place? Or is Ruth still with us, hovering in the corners of rooms, watching with her still and quiet eyes?

I sense Max and Fritz at the head of the casket, hear their whispers. Fritz mumbles about forgiveness, wanting Ruth to forgive him for not listening to her in the last days of her life, for not coming around more often to help her. Max says goodbye, quietly, telling Ruth how much he will miss her, how much he and the girls and Yolande will miss her. Then it is my turn and I feel the rough cloth of the men's suit jackets brush past me, my father's tweed jacket scratching my bare left arm as he passes me and moves to stand by the foot of the casket with Max.

I clutch at the photograph, bring it up to my face, but I can no longer see the image. My vision clouds over. I feel so heavy in my body, so fogged up. Everyone is waiting for me.

"Ti fi, pa blie'm."

How can I forget? Hasn't Ruth inscribed her memory in the palms of my hands?

I stare desolately at my hands as if seeing them for the first time.

"*Pa blie'm!*"

The voice is more insistent this time, almost threatening.

I look past my hands to glance at Ruth's still face. Can she really be dead? Perhaps some mistake has been made, her pulse slowed down by that puffer-fish dust they said the *bokors* used to zombify.

"*M'di, pa blie'm!*"

It would not surprise me if the closed eyes were to flutter open, and Ruth's face break into a mischievous smile.

But the face does not move, the eyes stay low in their sockets, made deeper by a layer of wrinkled, darkened brown skin. How tired had Ruth been at the time of her death? How exhausted? How despairing? What was known about Ruth's life anyway for this death to have taken place, this murder? What did her brothers know of those admitted within her walls? They only cared about what they received from her, revelling in her light, not thinking to ask about the other, darker aspects of her life, not digging after the rumours that rose like a stench from the earth. They told themselves that they left her alone out of respect, but it was really a selfish act, an effort to keep a version of Ruth that meant they did not have to offer more than they were able, because they knew that they could not match what Ruth brought them.

They left her alone out of shame, to avoid culpability. I look at Fritz and Max, their two heads leaning towards each other like mirrored reflections. I turn back towards Ruth's body and decide that it is time to give her a parting kiss, to let go. The picture still clutched in my hand, I will my body to move forward.

I've never kissed a corpse before. I've never kissed *Ruth* like this before. I concentrate on moving forward but all I can think is *ohmygod, ohmygod. This is not Ruth.* My body feels like a stiff, unbendable board, my brain detached from my limbs, my waist immoveable. Then, suddenly, without a sense of my having any power over it, my body jackknifes. *What is it to be among the dead?* The question reverberates in my mind as I find myself falling into darkness, my head plunging ahead, my lips trying in vain to make contact with the cold, powdered, ashen, nutmeg skin. It's as if *she* is pulling me in, into the cold and the dark. I feel my mother there, all blue and pink light, confusing. The feel of her is like a seduction and I'm falling headfirst into it, whatever *it* is, wherever they've gone, some place where I can be free of pain and love – sweet pain, bitter love. I can let all of it go into this darkness, this nothingness.

I reach out towards Ruth but the photograph in my hand is gone. Where has it gone? I panic suddenly, free-falling, falling into the tunnel of darkness.

A hand grasps me, hard. A hand unsure of whether or not to love me. Fritz pulls me up, steadying me.

I wake from the trance of falling at the same time as my lips make contact with the cold of Ruth's right cheek. My right hand lets go of the slip of paper still in my hand. Letting go. Of Ruth. Of Fritz. Of whatever had gone on before our separation. I can't go on like this, buried in this anger. I feel like an orphan even with Fritz holding on to my wrist. What is he afraid of? I've never felt so tired. I will never see Ruth again. We will never see each other again. *Remember me.* What right have the dead to speak to the living?

The bilious stone rises from my throat and leaps up into my mouth, making me cry out in pain. I'm aware of sounding like a wounded animal, oh, so wounded. Tired. Broken. But I can't stop myself. I can't stop. What is there left to live for? Fritz's hand grips me harder. Why can't he cry? Why can't he let me cry? He pulls me away from the casket and then pushes me towards the sister-cousins. Why couldn't he hold me for just a moment? He had left me alone after my mother's death. Why couldn't he feel my pain?

Women's hands, arms, get hold of me. I cry against the softness.

There are songs. Someone sings the dreaded *Ave Maria* in an operatic voice. But I can't sing. How can music suddenly have become so excruciating? Why can't there just be crying? Emptiness. A body has been emptied, returned to earth and sea. Why can't we honour its return to nothing and everything with silence and tears? Why is everyone so heartless?

My thoughts, ungracious, selfish, pound through my mind as if competing with the choir. The women next to me hold me up

231

against their own staffs of grief, hold me up while the music drowns out the grating, disembodied heavings of my weeping.

March 13, 2004, Outskirts of Pétion-Ville

Once the coffin has been eased slowly into its cement cubicle, the family breaks apart, fanning out from beneath the tent in small groups. Marie-France comes to find me in my corner even though I'm not ready to leave this sanctified ground. I watch as the gravediggers lower the casket, yelling at each other as it swings between knotted cords. I hold my breath as the box tilts and turns as, between intervening hands and warning shouts, it is lowered and then slid into a cement block below ground that will be impossible to loot. Maybe they've already stripped the corpse, between the closing of the casket and its transportation to the burial ground. Maybe, these days, looting is more discrete.

Estelle and Marie-France each lace an arm around one of my elbows and lead me towards Fritz's waiting car. The sister-cousins are grim. Uncharacteristically, they attempt to lighten the mood with small talk.

"It may rain this afternoon."

"Will it?"

"It may."

"But it was such a lovely morning."

"…and a lovely ceremony."

"Yes, yes it was…"

They go on like this for quite some time, each responding to the other's nonsense, as if everyone in the car is participating in the conversation. They seem unaware of the blanket of silence surrounding them. I turn my head away towards the window and try to hide my tears. I've embarrassed my father enough today, but the tears keep coming. The cousins don't seem to mind, though they redouble their attempts to keep the conversation on its feet until they too fall silent.

We've reached *Tatie* Ruth's house well behind most of the others as we can see from the cars lining the street and the entrance.

"*Il ne faut pas avoir peur de la mort*," Marie France whispers, before she enters Ruth's garden.

"*Elle est surement mieux ou elle est*," says Estelle. "At least, she's better off than the rest." With a desultory wave of her right hand, Estelle gestures to indicate the masses beyond, the unfortunate hordes crawling like ants through the narrow alleyways of the shantytowns.

Yes, I nod, unable to speak, unable to give shape to my personal torment; maybe this is so, maybe Ruth is the most fortunate among us now that she has gone to the other side. *Le paradis, Vilokan* – or whatever it is that awaits us after death. But what a sordid death it had been! Why didn't anyone have answers? Why couldn't anyone answer my questions as to what had happened to Ruth in her own house, this house, in which we were now all standing and making small talk?

As I walk into the house, I hear the whispers:

"*On ne si attendait pas.*"

"*Qui pouvait si attendre?*"

"*Elle faisait partie de l'insurrection. Je l'ai d'une source fiable.*"

"*...ce n'était pas... les chimères?*" a voice interjects in a hush.

Insurrection. Chimeras. Code-words for the rebels. They all think that Ruth was involved somehow. There are whispers and rumours. Why are they all speculating? Doesn't anyone know the truth? Why doesn't someone speak of what they know? Beyond me, the murmurs join the redolence of the plants, equally offensive in the thickness of their innuendo. I have a wild desire to uproot them, to strike back at their mocking beauty and bold scents.

The voices swirl around me like river water flowing to some unseen sink hole. I hear the grating of the stones beneath the feet of this well-heeled crowd, the dogs whimpering at the back of the house where they've been tethered for the day, and the clinking of ice cubes against glass as people move from one flower to another, as if this were a garden party rather than a funeral. A drink would help just now – a nice rum and coke on the rocks. Two or three might keep me from screaming, prevent me from denouncing those hypocrites who have shown up to Ruth's funeral, who failed to protect her from harm and probably benefited from her generosity at some time or other in the past.

233

I fume but know that I'm as angry with myself for not knowing, for my absence from Ruth's life these last years, as I've focused on Sam, my career, on anything that would rid me of the memory of this ground, of Fritz and my mother. A drink is certainly in order.

With this thought, I spin on my heels and leave the sister-cousins in search of the open bar.

It's in the foyer, against the right wall, only a foot or two away from where I was told that Ruth's body had been found. I close my eyes. Yolande had clearly not been in charge of setting up the wake; she would have been more thoughtful. I take a deep breath and can sense the bodies that, only a few days before, had moved through the room, panther-like, closing in on her. I can't imagine Romulus there. In many ways, the man he had become was unreal to me; I can only conjure up the young boy and then the young man I had known – talented and bashful, incapable, I had thought, of extreme emotions. But when I think of Ruth in that moment, I'm surprised that I feel only quiet resignation instead of the terror I imagined would have accompanied her final breaths. To the bar, I think, finally passing the area Max had described as her slaying ground.

The way to the bar also led past the table covered with plastic, beneath which lay photographs of her family and friends. Mourners looked for their faces beneath the worn and scratched plastic as if to measure their importance in Ruth's life and, if they could not find themselves, hid their disappointment by trying to make out the faces of others they might know. Some of the faces were those of children who had long since grown up, some with children of their own, whose little faces had been placed next to those of their parents. The heat and humidity had turned all the photographs yellow and bleached them, so that it was difficult to say which of the children were actually children in the present or past. Only the clothing gave away when the photographs had been taken.

I, too, glance furtively at the photos. I'm surprised to find myself in the middle of the collage, in a picture my mother would certainly have sent, a year or so before her death, of me smiling a gap-toothed smile. I must have been six or seven years old and missing a front tooth. My hair had been braided and tied in two loops behind and above both my ears with two wide, white ribbons. The picture was washed out but still revealed the honey-coloured tone of my skin and the pale brown of my eyes.

Next to me there is a picture of my mother in her twenties, with her long hair looped around the crown of her head, looking like a matinee idol. I smile, feeling wistful. Above us there's a photograph of Fritz when he was still in short pants, going to elementary school in the country. He sits on a low wall in front of his father's house with a smug look on his face. Even though the photograph is in black and white, I think I can make out the tangles in his dark brown hair. When had Fritz lost his playfulness? I couldn't remember when I'd last heard him laugh or when he had last made me feel as if the world was a warm and playful place. He'd only ever made me feel as if I could never attain my dreams, that the world was cold and unforgiving. Had he been this way before Mother's death? It's hard to remember.

When I reach the bar it's surrounded by Haitian men garbed in well-fitted, tailored suits.

"*Ba'm mwen yon rumcola,*" I say in my worn *Kreyol*.

The server looks at me with a raised eyebrow, then looks somewhere behind my right shoulder. I become impatient, testy, imperious, and rap the wooden surface of the serving counter with my knuckles. I haven't forgotten that in this country women of a certain class and age are not supposed to drink openly. I just don't care. My left hand is twitching at my side, questioning my behaviour.

"*Mwen pa vle tend leve soley, non, tandem?*" I don't have time to wait for the sun to rise, you hear me, I say.

The man's eyes flicker. It's the look of someone who is trapped but knows he's worth more than what he seems in this moment of confrontation, in his ill-fitting, starched white shirt overlaid with a doublet with missing buttons, the cuffs of the clean shirt worn to shreds, the stray threads cut back to the level of the fabric to hide its wear. He pours the drink while looking at me with contempt, then pushes the glass towards me with the tips of his fingers, the nails ragged.

I don't even mutter a thank you. I know I'm being disgraceful, disgracing Ruth and my family, but I just don't care. Passages from the Bible drift through my mind and I think of Noah getting drunk on dry shore, losing his composure. Why can't I do the same? I stay at the bar and swallow my drink down with two long draws. I set the glass down on the counter. "*Enco'*," I say. I can sense the men around the bar holding their breath, but there's nothing they can say to me. I'm in Ruth's house, a house where no man held court. They aren't my kin so they watch to see what my father or uncle will say.

When I ask for the third drink, the barman's eyes flicker again to a spot above my right shoulder.

"What are you looking at?" I ask and turn around. It's Fritz standing there, watching me, and being watched by the men around the bar. A scowl frames his eyes.

I shrug and turn back to the bartender, "Give me the drink."

The man holds the rum bottle suspended above the glass and watches Fritz above my shoulder. I close my eyes. I know Fritz is nodding behind me, giving the barman permission to serve me when the liquid hits the ice. I bring it up to my lips and this time I feel the buzz of the drinks as they begin to take their effect. *Thank goodness*, I think, *thank God*. Noah's revelation wasn't much deeper than this. There are moments when you want to lose yourself. Moments when you don't want to remember your responsibilities or contracts. The truth is that I don't really know what mine are; I'm not wholly committed to Sam and playing the piano isn't my vocation, it's my addiction. I can't play now, so why not drink. I have a vague recollection of Mother drinking when she was sad, of watching her with my head on my arms, falling asleep as she sang quietly to herself while Fritz prepared his lessons in another room with his door closed, as if he couldn't bear our presence.

Then, there he is, Fritz, right upon me, as he had been earlier as I bent down to kiss Ruth's cold, ashen lips.

I shrug him off as I demand a fourth drink.

"Catherine," he says, "stop…. Our guests…"

I twirl around to face him. "You mean *your* guests. I don't know these people."

"But they know *you*. They know us." He leans in to say, grasping my elbow again, "Keep your voice down, Cathie."

I feel the rush of the last drink hit my temples. Suddenly dizzy,

I am not sure if it is the drink or the touch of Fritz's hand upon me creating the effect. One is as incensing as the other. I want to claw his hand away.

"Who do you think you are?" I say. "Who the hell do you think you are. You *men*," I continue, "why do you always need to *grab* us to get our attention! Goddamn it." I hold up the injured hand. "You asked me about this yesterday. Well, get ready, Pops: Sam did this. Your precious Sam did this. Do you want to get rid of the other arm now too? Make me completely useless so I'll never play again?"

Fritz's grey eyes grow dark as watermelon seeds. He's looking at me with disgust and contempt. The feelings are mutual.

"Cat got your tongue, Father," I say. "Why aren't you *hissing* at me? You damn lizard. Let go of me."

"Cathie," Fritz says, his hand back on my elbow, as if he's afraid that if he isn't touching me I'll somehow disappear.

"Just leave me alone, Pops," I say. "What can you do now?"

"I just want to be here for you," he says. "Shouldn't we be here for each other? For Ruth's sake?"

"Oh my God. Oh my goodness," I say. I feel myself torn between the desire to simply retreat and the desire to rip into Fritz with all my years of unexpressed frustration. Laughter cascades out of me until tears leak from the corners of my eyes. There is an eerie quiet all around us. I'm aware that others are watching but I can't stop myself. And then I utter words I've never used before, vulgar words, words no daughter should say to her father.

"*Va te faire foutre, Fritz*," I say. "Where the hell were you when my mother died? You didn't seem to feel any need to be *present* then, did you? Save me the good-daddy act. You're just full of it."

Fritz's hold on my elbow tightens. He pulls me into his chest. "Get hold of yourself Catherine. You know I did the best I could." I see him make a sign to the others, pantomiming my drinking to indicate what is wrong with me, like I'm some kind of crazy woman. Like your mother, I hear him think, crazy like your mother. Except that he isn't saying those words now; he said them once, long ago, when he got rid of me by sending me back to the island. I push away from him.

What did Canaan say to his father when he was banished, kept from God? I don't remember. I'm sure he didn't tell Noah to fuck himself right after trying to cover up his father's nudity. But at least Noah had vulnerabilities. Fritz is cold as ice. Well-named, I think, a Germanic name for a man of the tropics who would never let an emotion get the better of him.

"So what if I've been drinking!" I finally say. "It doesn't make you *right*. It doesn't make anything you did *right*."

Then a surge of despair overtakes me, displacing the mirth of only a minute ago with suffocating weight.

"God," I say, "Oh my God. What's going to happen to me?" I begin to weep again, uncontrollably, and clutch at the fabric of my dress draped across my chest. I wipe away at my tears and look out at the onlookers, their faces and bodies a smudge of black and brown before me. "Sam? Ruth? Where is everyone?"

"*Chérie*," I hear a voice say close to my ear as arms softly enfold me from behind, "*Chérie, vin ak mwen.*"

I let the arms lead me away from the onlookers, and away from my father's bitter glance.

"*Calme toi*," the voice says. It's an old voice, ageless. A woman's voice. It feels like a voice I've heard before but cannot place.

I try to breathe but calm will not come. My heart is beating fast. I'm perspiring. I have an intense desire to break glass, to punch someone or something, to scream so loudly and deeply that doves will come screeching out of the trees. To pull my hair out by the roots. To rend my black mourning dress at the cleavage in the manner of a biblical revelation. Yet I know that no gesture, no act of destruction, no utterance, no scream of anguish, will restore what has been lost. It's the futility that makes me rage on, not stopping to listen to the voice at my side, whispering into my ear.

"I don't want to," I say as I turn to face the woman to find it is Marie-France. "I don't want to be calm ever again."

"There's a time for rage and a time for quiet. This is a time for quiet. Silence."

"No," I say, like a child refusing to obey. No, I don't ever want to be quiet again. I want to sit at the piano keys while my fingers make it sing the songs and anguish of my heart. "You don't understand," I say to Marie-France as she guides me away from the staring eyes of the crowd. "You don't understand how it feels to be invisible."

"I understand more than you think," Marie-France whispers. "But this isn't the way to be seen."

I let her take me into the garden. My head is buzzing. Everywhere I look, I see emptiness. I see myself as a child running through Ruth's garden but no Ruth. I see myself playing hopscotch with Lucas but no Lucas. I see myself playing with the maid's children but no mother, no father. It feels that everything that matters has gone and that somehow I am still there, left behind, like a leftover sum in some complex mathematical equation.

She has me sit on a concrete ledge in the courtyard at the back of the house. This is just as well for the ground is spinning beneath me. I hear the tethered dogs panting somewhere beyond us both.

"It's all going to be all right," Marie-France says. Then, a pause, and she continues. "You're not alone. Estelle and I are here for you," she sighs. "I... we promised Ruth, and your mother, that we would be here when they passed, and that we would lead you to Lucas."

I hold my head in my hands. This is too much for me. Have the twins been drinking too? One crazy woman talking to another?

"What the hell are you talking about?" I ask her, indignant. If Edouard and Sam could see me now. But I just don't care for airs and graces any more. I just want someone to tell me the truth of why my mothers have gone. I feel only bitterness as I look at my cousin and see a halo of black hair surrounding a face of a creamy white complexion, the nose wide, the eyes large and round, dark as obsidian. Even in my less than sober state, I can see the eyes are intelligent, sorrowfully so. I look away, not wanting to take in whatever those eyes may know. "You're about twenty years too late," I say quietly.

"I know it feels that way to you."

These words inflame my anger. "I'm sorry, but you don't know me and you don't know what I feel." I stand up and walk back towards the house. "I need to get out of here."

"As you wish," Marie-France says. "We'll be here when you get back and then we can talk about Lucas."

How dare she be so presumptuous, I think to myself. I haven't even stepped off the property and she's already telling me what to expect.

"What the hell do you know about Lucas?" I spit back at her.

Where had the cousins been when my mother had lost her life on a slippery road? Where were they when Fritz dumped me here and walked away? When Lucas left us and never sent word of his whereabouts? When a band of ruffians walked into Ruth's house and splayed her like a goat? How dare these people *return* as if they have all the answers. Damn their arrogance!

I stumble wildly towards the parked cars.

"You," I say, pointing to one of the drivers.

The man nods at me. "*Madanm?*"

"*Wap pralé.*"

"*Wi, madanm,*" he says.

"I want you to take me down to the port. *M'ap pralé we kay manman mwen.*"

"*Wi madanm.*"

"We'll come back," I say. "We'll come back."

"*Wi madanm,*" the man says, knowing he has no choice.

I see him look over at Max who nods. I can't seem to make a move without a man at my side. This awareness does nothing for my mood.

March 13, 2004, Port-au-Prince Port

We careen down Lalue in a rumble of dust and flying pebbles and suddenly we are upon the wide roads leading to the presidential palace and old promenades next to the port, now desolate.

"Down this way," I say to the driver, pointing. My head is beginning to clear. "This way, this way," I repeat impatiently as he hesitates and the car stalls.

And finally, there it is, the house we were brought to the last time my mother and I came to Haiti together, the pale yellow façade coming into view like a faded memory.

"This is it," I whisper, and the driver begins to park the car in front of a row of market women selling their wares.

"*Kote ou vlé'm kanpé?*" the driver asks, peering over the frame of his imitation aviator sunglasses. Where do you want me to wait?

"*Ici*," I reply, gesturing towards the overcrowded curb where a woman squats in front of a pile of woven baskets. The woman has an unfinished basket in her hand and is smoothing straw between her lips, watching the car as it approaches her. She makes it clear that she does not plan to move.

"*Madanm*," the driver says to her, his head cocked out the driver's window, an arm firmly hugging the carcass of the car.

"I'll get out here," I say as I open the passenger door. "There's no need to park if you can't. I won't be long."

"*Bien, bien*," the driver says as soon as I've slammed the door shut behind me. He parks the car in the middle of the road and begins to chat with the women on the sidewalk. The women are old enough to be his mother but he flirts good-naturedly with them and they cluck back reprimands like mother hens.

I navigate through the thick sea of merchants in front of these clapboard houses that haunt me still when I come across their likeness in places like New Orleans and the south of France. I do not know why they loom so large in my memory. Ruth had seldom brought me here and I'd never seen the man who'd brought my mother and I again since spotting him that day with Lucas.

As I look at my mother's house, I feel an insistent pulling at the hem of my skirt. I look down and there is a child offering me a handful of grimy, cut sugarcane stalks. One greenish stalk looks as if it has already been chewed on along its edges. I wave the child away: *M' pap bezwin sa-a*. I don't need that. But the child, whose hair is a wild tangle atop her head, her body covered only by a torn and faded orange T-shirt that barely covers her naked form beneath it, insists. I give up and fish out a soiled *gourde* note. The Haitian dollar isn't worth much but it is better than nothing.

"*Tiens*," I say to the girl, holding the note above her head.

The girl's eyes shift slowly from my face to the money above her. Just as slowly, and holding on tightly still to her sugar cane pieces, she lets go of my hem and reaches up for the money. I carefully fold her fingers over the bill. *Prend-garde*, I think, looking into the little girl's averted eyes. Whatever alcohol buzz was left has gone. The little girl goes off to the next person on the sidewalk, to the *madanm sara* weaving her baskets. The woman offers the girl some corn then passes her on to the next woman on the sidewalk. I recognize the ritual of their exchange. The little girl belongs to the whole street and to no one. *Heartbreaking*, I think.

"My mother's house," I say to no one in particular.

It's difficult to walk while looking up. The once open sidewalks that sprawled below the two- and three-storey wooden buildings, whose once brilliant bright colours have faded to pastel hues, are clogged with street vendors selling everything from sticks of bread to tinware for makeshift kitchens. Some women are hard at work creating the crafts they are simultaneously trying to sell, cooing "*Vini-la, vini-la,*" to the passers-by as their fingers deftly continue to do their work. Most of the pedestrians are *habitués* who walk the same street day in, day out. There are no tourists here. *It's hope they're weaving*, I think, foolishly romanticizing the women. *And even if it's only that*, I continue my line of thought, the alcohol clearly not wholly out of my system, *they have more than the rest of us in the civilized world*.

I stop in front of a more formal *quincaillerie* announcing its household wares in *Kreyol* words followed by a series of exclamation points in thick black letters. The words fill floor to ceiling windows that have been blocked with off-white butcher paper so it isn't at all clear if the goods which the misspelled words on the windows proclaim actually exist. The windows are barred with steel grates. I assume a legitimate business given the worry for theft. I wonder how anyone survives here.

I look up at the windows of the building perched above. The original colours are faded to a muted pink and green. I wonder what it would have looked like new but I know there are no surviving photographs. Nothing survives. Nothing survives but me, I think. And Lucas. There was Fritz, of course, but he was like a vacuum. Then there was Marie-France claiming that she had been told to take me to Lucas. Why hadn't Lucas come on his own? Even now, I would have followed him anywhere.

I wish Sam was here, next to me, and I think of him absentmindedly searching for things in the apartment without me there to bring some order to his chaos, but I push past this thought like a swimmer springing back into a lap pool, braced by

242

the cold of the water, pulled back to reality as feet touch the bottom. I look down at my feet, as if realizing for the first time that I do have feet to stand on, that the concrete below is solid, unbroken, at least in this precise spot. Then, my eyes catch the long pieces of wood nailed down to the door leading upstairs. There is no way in to the building. The nails are rusted, bent. There are too many of them to pull against. Even this door is refusing me entry. I feel defeat. Frustration floods over me once more.

I turn back towards the car.

The weaver stops for a moment, her hands in mid-movement, the end of a piece of straw being moistened between her lips.

I'm suddenly afraid of her for no apparent reason. The woman's eyes seem to see right through me. What does she see?

Simultaneously, the driver makes his way to me. "Ready to go?"

"*Li pap-pralé*," the weaver woman cackles. She's not ready at all.

I stop before her.

She looks right through me, smiling. What does she know? What am I not ready for? An itch seems to crawl through my nervous system, as if I'm being poisoned.

"*Li peu tèt li*," the woman continues.

Afraid of myself?

She nods. "*Ou pa peu loas yo? Ou peu manman'w maren ou?*"

The gods? My mother? Godmother? What is she speaking of?

"No," I turn to her defiantly. "I'm not afraid."

"Ah," the woman says in *Kreyol*, "the beginning of all fear is its denial."

What can be said in response to such a pronouncement? The itch crawls through me, serpentine, as invasive as the alcohol I've imbibed. What is happening to me?

"Are you ready?" the driver says again.

"Yes," I say, as the weaver woman behind me rocks her head back and forth. No, no, she's not ready. What is it that I'm to be ready for? There's nothing left, I think, as I walk away from the ruin of my mother's house, the house she left to marry my father before moving to Canada where the winters held her in a melancholic spell.

243

I turn back to the disapproving woman and choose a small basket from the heap at her feet. It is blond with a purple strip around the circumference, dividing the top half from the bottom. "This is for my mother," I say.

"*Li la*," the woman says as she takes the soiled Haitian currency from my hands. "*Li la menm jan ke ou la ou menm.*"

She's here as clearly as I am?

A chill goes through me and I know that the woman is right, that my mother is here, walking with me, watching me, breathing in me. I am not ready for this, for whatever is coming.

"Ready?" the driver asks again, looking sheepish. He is impatient, anxious to return me to my father.

I nod and walk with him back to the car. He encourages me forward by keeping a hand hovering over the small of my back, without making physical contact.

When we reach the car, he hastens to open the door for me.

"*Mèci*," I say.

As the driver eases into his seat, I try to catch his eye but he looks away from me. "What is your name?" I suddenly think of asking.

His eyes look up, startled, and catch mine in the rearview mirror, "Dieudonné."

Given to God. I nod. Of course, I think, of course. Given to God.

Was he sent to me *by* God? Is he my rainbow sign? I don't even know if I believe in God or gods. The strange tightening in my head creeps back like a long shadow on a hot summer day. I don't want to go back there, to Ruth's house. The sea, I think, only the sea will do.

"Can you drive along the port?" I ask the driver.

He nods as if my request makes perfect sense, even though it will take us in the opposite direction from the hills we'd descended earlier.

"It's nearby," I say apologetically.

"*Wi*," he says. "*Je sais*," accepting the half-lie.

I look away from the driver and watch the pastel-coloured buildings move past us in a blur, remnants of the past falling hopelessly into crumbled heaps. I do not want him to see the doubt in my eyes.

We head in the direction of the port, turning left on Avenue Harry S. Truman. I wonder if Truman ever set foot on Haitian soil. Even though my mother had been interested in history, this is something I don't know. In the last years of her life, she spoke only of Greek myths, tragedies all, and biblical stories that seemed just as tragic and impossible.

The salt of the sea air calls me out of the car, out into its thickness. "Stop here," I say in *Kreyol*.

Before the driver has even stopped the car, I am opening the door, stepping out onto the pavement.

"*Madanm*," Dieudonné calls after me. A shudder goes through me and I close my eyes to shake it off at the same time as the pungency of the sea hits. I freeze and look out over the water. In the distance there are ships docked, tankers. I have no idea what they could be carrying into these waters. I shield my eyes from the sun and peer at them. They are too far away for me to read the lettering on their rusting bodies. I walk carefully out onto the jetty.

"Careful *manm'zelle*," Dieudonné yells after me, his tone suddenly familiar. It was like this all the time here, wasn't it? All men became brothers or fathers or lovers, thinking of women as charges they had to protect from harm – or subject to harm.

But I'm not feeling very careful. I want to throw myself into the waves crashing against the wooden poles below. I walk towards the waves, venturing further and further away from the car. I can imagine Dieudonné's perplexed face watching me, can still feel the phantom presence of his hand at my lower back, moving me forward.

I reach a square platform at the end of the jetty. Two men are sitting there, talking. It isn't clear what they are doing. Alarms go off in the pit of my stomach. One has a bottle of *clairin* in his hand. The other has a makeshift fishing rod. They ignore me but my body leans into the defensive. I try to talk myself out of these alarms; my fears have to do only with class and this is a prejudice I have to overcome. But it makes no sense to say hello to them. I'm too far from the car. I fold my arms across my body protectively. My desire to throw myself into the ocean recedes. I waver as I walk a little beyond the men, closer to the entrancing deep of the ocean. *What is happening to me?*

The men laugh as I pass. The bottle falls and clatters against the concrete. I try to hide my startle and stand still again. I close my eyes and pray that they will ignore me, pray for invisibility.

And then I feel something, a churning from the deep, rising from below, a dull throb as if some entity is trying to come up through the concrete and into my body. I open my eyes and look out to sea. Whatever it is is coming from out there. I'm not sure whether or not I should be frightened. The bottle comes to rest by my foot. I push it back towards the men.

I peer out across the dark blue vastness and feel the power beneath the waves. I feel the surge again, rising up through my feet all the way to the top of my head, the way I feel the musical notes of a symphony. The crown of my skull tingles oddly. I press my right hand to the top of my head and try to hold down the pulsing there, as if somehow this gesture will ensure my hold on reality.

The men laugh again.

I want to throw myself into the ocean.

"*Madanm!*" the driver calls out to me, alarmed, the sound of his voice muted by the offshore winds.

As if in love with death, I step forward. Something jars me, stills me, some movement from below.

All I can see at first are the beams of an older jetty that has fallen apart. Only the cross beams are left. The waves move them to and fro slowly, like the legs of giants, against the currents. The buzzing at my head intensifies. I let my hand fall limply at my side, suddenly feeling fatigued.

More laughter from the men.

Shielding my eyes from the sun, I look out towards the beams. It is then that I see her, the woman holding on to one of the beams.

She is wearing a faded blue dress. Its skirt floats around her next to the beam, its folds echoing the waves that push past the woman's body towards the shore. She is very still. My first impulse is to strip out of my clothes and to jump into the sea to save the woman. But I realize that the woman is not drowning, not thrashing around for assistance, not seeking anything from the shore. She is looking landwards – towards me and the two men on the concrete slab – without looking at anything in particular. Her face is expressionless. She seems young, thin, her head covered with twisted locks that rise up from her scalp in all directions. Had something happened to her? With these men? Had they harmed her in some way and that was why she was in the water? Healing? But the men don't seem to be paying her any attention and she doesn't look frightened. I pause. *Menses?* But why to the water? An abortion slipping out? Or had the woman just felt the same urge as I had, the need to be submerged? I want to follow suit but all I can do is take in the woman's hard glance, her body holding on quietly to the beam, even though it is clear that something, somewhere, has fallen apart, something that can never be righted again. Or maybe it's the way other way around. Maybe the whole world is waiting to be submerged beneath saltwater, waiting to be wiped out and to rise again to surface. This makes sense, somehow.

The first two movements of Chopin's *Études, Opus 10*, run through my mind, the fingering quick, *allegro, allegro* and then *non troppo allegro*, fingers having to slow down each *crescendo* punctuated by the ponderous, heavy anchoring notes played by the left hand, as the right creates a smooth ebb and flow. The music runs through me like a wash of rain, like a soundtrack to my fear, forcing me back towards the car.

A greater power still whispers at my back, but I resist the urge to walk into the water, to swim out to the woman by the beam, to embrace her. I know that it is a desire born of nothing. I have nothing to give, nothing to offer.

Back at the car, I find Dieudonné napping in the back seat.

"Give me the keys. I'm driving." This is the only way I can think of regaining some measure of control.

Dieudonné startles. He recovers quickly, however. I can tell from the look in his eye what he thinks of people like me, that he has learned long ago that the bourgeois are of fickle humour. That they can kiss you one day and spit on you the next. He hurries out of the car and hands me the keys.

He holds on tightly to the frame of the open window as I lurch the jeep back onto the broken road heading north towards Ruth's house. I hunch over the leather of the wheel.

"Hold on," I grimace through clenched teeth. "This is going to be a bumpy ride."

That it is, all the way up the winding road of the hill and into the congested streets of the capital where labourers are still using wooden wheelbarrows to clear away the *fatras* lining the side of the road. The men are lean, serpentine muscles winding the length of their lank bodies. As we speed up, they become a blur, bodies jumping out of the way of the jeep, swearing at us and waving what seem like exaggeratedly elongated hands. In my mind, I'm in the *Études'* second movement, No. 2 in A Minor, *crescendo fortissimo*, both hands attacking the keys simultaneously. Then suddenly the *pianissimi* as everything quietens, as when the waves recede, taking their ounce of sand with each sweep. It's always the audience that's surprised. Out of softness comes hardness and the softest movement is suddenly followed by a volley and crash of notes, punctuated by anchoring chords while the right hand continues up and down the scales, the left trying to interrupt, to control, but there is no such possibility. The music continues, seemingly out of control and all you can do is hold on to your breath as the notes move faster, faster, and then, as suddenly as they poured out, end.

My mind is still on the woman in the water and the deep dark swirling beneath her suspended body and my desire to join her there, as if all my life was leading only to that moment of submersion. Was the woman wading down below on the sea bed, or was she standing on sharp rocks unseen from the shore, juts cutting the soles of her feet as she danced on their surface, trying to keep her balance, her arms keeping track of the moving water by holding on to the jetty mast? Was she happy or sad? Had she been harmed, her body separated from a mind too overwrought to know what else to do? Had she walked into the sea, as I had wanted to, with the desire to be enveloped by its vastness, to become truly insignificant in the eye of the storms gathering all around her, in the grind of the poverty of the colliding worlds daily surrounding her? Whatever she had intended, I will remember this woman always. Why I feel this I don't know, but *she* is my rainbow sign after the floods, the unreturning dove sent to let me know that some new day is coming.

The only person I want to talk to is Sam. He'd listen to me. It's a sign. I know it's a sign: something that will explain the disappearances of my mother and Ruth, even of Lucas. It has something to do with what Noah and Job knew, that "something" that impelled them to face disaster patiently. I have the suspicion that the shore might be dotted with similar women holding on to staffs, floating in the water like a congregation of seers. At the same time, I know I don't have that kind of faith and that it must be the alcohol still churning in my veins. What is the secret for cultivating perfect faith?

I'm driving recklessly away from the port, *fortissimo, fortissimo,* in search of the women, past the statue of the unknown slave holding up his conch towards the placid blue sky. How long will he have to stand there, prostrated to the heavens? How long will it be until we are all truly free?

A memory drifts back from when I was about eleven or twelve, in those first years of trying to understand my parents' country without them. I had been crying in the kitchen. What had I been crying over? I furrow my brow but, dangerously, my concentration is aimed inwards, towards memory, rather than towards the cluttered road in front of me. I remember the dancing women cast by my mother's candle flames. *Ezili Le Flambo.* The goddess of anger and retribution, the patroness of abandoned single mothers. But I had not been abandoned. My mother had died on a road, alone, while her husband taught music and her daughter slept.

Out of the periphery of my vision I catch sight of people leaping onto the sidewalks, pulling others to safety by their shirt sleeves. I realise it's me they are avoiding, and begin gesturing to pedestrians to get themselves out of the way, quick, moving one hand erratically outside my window and using the other to manoeuvre the jeep through the bodies and potholes, and pressing the *klaxon*.

Why is all this is happening now?

"*Madanm* Catherine! Stop!"

Dieudonné's shout penetrates the dense matter of my pensiveness and I slam on the brakes as his left hand comes down, hard, on my right. But the warning has come too late.

Out of a thick throng of people who have just descended from an over-full tap-tap in front of the parliament buildings, a low-riding grey Pinto had emerged, its driver also intent on getting somewhere quickly. The Pinto is to our left and I see it too late.

I quickly calculate the speed of the oncoming car and my own lack of speed. I should shift to the gas pedal but it's as if time has stilled and I'm unsure of what to do now we are at rest.

"Move, *Madamn*, move."

I feel irritation towards Dieudonné. First he tells me to stop and now he tells me to move. Which is it? I feel rebellious. Despite the impending danger, my mind is still on the woman in the water, the women dancing with my mother in the candle flames. Did these women experience the same dilemma? Go. Stop. Go? Remaining still seems like the only solution to some problem.

I sense the grey Pinto as it grows big upon us. It's going to hit us full on, on my side of the car. I will take the full impact of the crash. Would I survive the blow? I resign myself and let my breath escape my body. I think about my mother's death. I hadn't seen the body afterwards. Had it been too disfigured to be seen? I imagine my mother's bones splintering, and wonder about passing from this material world to some vast unknown I've kept myself from pondering. Then I think about survival – plaster covering my body, going home to Sam in a wheelchair. Would he still have me in such a state? How would I survive? What would I do? What was there to do? I need the warmth of a mother's embrace.

"Move, Cathie, move!"

This time the voice is softer and my foot seems to slip as if by magic from the brake to the gas pedal and the jeep jerks forward just as the Pinto slams into the tail of our four by four, sending it twirling around in the crossroads just beyond the parliament square.

As we spin above the broken asphalt, I feel my own mind and body rise with lightness and it seems to me that despite the dust and glass flying in the air I can see everything around me with stunning clarity. There is the smell of decaying food accumulating in piles in the middle of the road. There is a thin, frail woman in a side street squatting, defecating, while the rest of her body is covered, her hair carefully wrapped. There are birds flying out of the flat canopy of a flamboyant whose red fruit appears to be on fire. The white of the parliament buildings is, in fact, yellow, decaying, and there are women striking pots and pans for their rights below the windows that are said to house the president's office. In front of the parliament's official doors, merchants have strung up multicoloured paintings that illumine the lives of the peasant and make the land seem greener than it is. The cloth these workers wear to do their trade is jubilant in its brilliance. There are scrawny dogs with their tongues hanging out crisscrossing the roads, lurking in the shadows, waiting for their turn to scrounge through heaps of scraps after human hands have made their selection. The air is dry and added to the scent of garbage is the sweet scent of burning wood and coal.

Suddenly, as the car continues to spin, the scene before my eyes changes from the heat and squalor of Haiti to the vast coldness of the winters I had known as a child.

I see snowsuits, toboggans, snowball fights and forts built to invoke Inuit igloos. I remember how we had been told in school never to build into the side of snowdrifts lest we be suffocated in them and I remember that the warning had come after one of the boys in class had disappeared. His name was Adam. He'd died inside the walls of a snowdrift while trying to make a secret passageway from his parents' front door to the street. They found him twelve hours after he had begun to burrow into the snowdrift, blue from head to toe inside a purple parka, his eyes still open as if waiting to see what was on the other end of his wormhole.

But the snow in my mind's eye before me is blueishly unfamiliar. The vehicle keeps spinning. I am watching myself in another body. *Mother's*, I think. *Will it ever stop?* Resignation washes over me from this other body that has temporarily become mine and I see another car plough into the rust red Chevrolet in which my mother died. As the jeep twists and turns, I see the face of a man, a white man with a grizzly five o'clock shadow covering his cheeks, his face contorted in a mask of horrified terror. I see the knuckles of his hands gone white with fear. I see my mother's hands losing their grip on the steering wheel. *Resignation.* Her foot on the brake pedal, not moving. *Resignation. Not moving.* I feel myself in my mother's body, jerking, and then a searing pain as bone after bone breaks, and a series of small fireworks detonate all at once in my brain, simultaneously fierce and wondrous as the pain becomes overwhelming and then yields to nothingness. I feel my mother's body and mind acquiescing. *Regret.* I want to fight for my mother's life as I look out through her eyes onto the whiteness beyond the two cars gliding on black ice, but the remembering body is not fighting. It has no will. Its mind is fogged up. Its limbs are limp. And now there is nothing but pain rushing through. I want to urge my mother to do something, anything, to just *move now*, and as I become filled with perplexed rage, I remember the hands moving away from the steering wheel and the foot from the brake pedal, the man's face behind the windshield of the oncoming car wishing that he were anywhere but *there*, and I realize, in this moment suspended between nowhere and everywhere, time collapsing onto itself as the blue of the Haitian sky comes back into view, and the stink of the refuse beyond the jeep barrels through the shell of the twisting care, that my mother's death had not been an accident. It had never been an accident. The man involved in the accident hadn't been drunk as Fritz had said. It had been my mother. I realize with shock, disgust and dismay that my mother had chosen her exit, and I remember, horrified, our dance in the kitchen before she had got into the car. Whatever I had meant to her, it had not been enough to keep her there with us in the yellow house on the outskirts of Montreal, on that cold winter night.

The jeep comes to a sudden, jolting stop. Dieudonné whistles between his teeth beside me.

We sit there in silence for a full five minutes while beyond us a crowd assembles. Those closest to the car touch its metal frame gingerly, then make the sign of the cross as if at an altar. Once they have touched the car after bringing two fingers to their lips, they step back and others take their place. The ritual goes on for some time until an army officer pushes his way through the crowd and peers at us inside the car.

"*Koman ou ye?*" he asks as if this crash is nothing unusual.

I stare at him. The four by four is a wreck. The rear window has shattered, the pieces thrown forward into the car, shards of glass littering the back seat. The rear of the vehicle has compressed like an accordion and, at the point of impact, just a foot directly behind my seat, the car has bent, leaving an ugly gash and depression that extends almost to the driver's seat. Had my foot not slipped from brake to pedal at the moment that I heard a voice, not Dieudonné's, but a voice from somewhere beyond, urging me to move, one of us could be dead.

"Let's get you out," the officer says, waving two other officers to the car.

The men heave open the doors of the vehicle and assist us out.

"*Hôpital?*" the officer asks.

"*Ça va,*" I say, regaining use of speech. "*Nous devons remonter,*" I say, pointing to the hills above and behind us.

The officer takes in my dark clothing with one look and knows where I belong. "*Madanm Ruth,*" he says automatically.

"Yes," I nod.

"We will take you back," he says very formally, concerned, aware of who I am.

I sit in the back of the officer's car. Dieudonné sits silently in the front seat. The lesser officers have been left behind to clear up the mess. I'm alone in the back of the car. I cannot understand this unravelling, what is happening to me. The woman in the sea, the urge to sink into the water, the accident, then my mother's memory coming back to me like a forgotten language.

A wave of despair overtakes me and I cannot tell if it is my mother's or mine. The men in front are talking in low whispers. I curl up in the back seat as the car moves up and back into the hills in a surprisingly smooth ride. My face against the sticky leather of the seat, I let gush the tears I've been holding back since leaving the church.

The grief pulls me down to such depths of sorrow that, when we reach the house, Dieudonné has to lift me out of the car and carry me past the remaining, stunned mourners. He follows the speechless sister-cousins guiding us to Ruth's room where they will all leave me to find comfort in the folds of a dreamless sleep.

March 14, 2004 Port-au-Prince

Why didn't Noah just jump into the swirling waters when he saw the world being wiped out? Why didn't he join the dying in their finite pain rather than survive to feel endless grief and torment? Did he feel so beholden to God or did he lose his faith in that moment of yielding to his own mortality, safeguarding himself for dry land? It's a wonder that he survived. But perhaps this is part of the myth. Perhaps Noah didn't survive unharmed. Maybe by the time he'd let the grapes ripen on the vine to make his wine, he'd already become something other than himself, a godless man who could curse and banish his beloved son. But perhaps he had to become something other than himself so that his son could fulfil the prophecy of the chosen people, the chosen land, by being torn from his father's side.

I wake in Ruth's bed, prepared to believe that everything – the singing of the *Ave Maria*, the funeral, my weeping – that everything has been a dream. The air in the room is light and rays of sun stream in along with gusts of wind, making the sheer white window drapes flutter like butterfly wings. I shut my eyes against the light, trying to keep the weight of reality from filling me up.

I hear talk coming from the kitchen and move to get up. My whole body aches and then I remember the accident, and being taken over by my mother's memory. How was it possible that I could feel everything she had felt in her last moments and why had her suicide been revealed to me now? Why had they all lied to me, Fritz most of all?

I hear his voice coming from the kitchen on the back of wafts of coffee and I feel resentment, a feeling close to hatred. In a moment I'm not proud of, I almost wish that Fritz were dead instead of Rose or Ruth; a moment when I wish I'd jumped in the sea yesterday and wouldn't have to endure hearing him talk this morning as if it were just any old morning. The feeling propels me out of bed.

They watch me curiously as I enter the kitchen, the sister-cousins, Fritz, Max, Yolande, the woman with the white-white complexion, and the kitchen help. I realize I'm standing there with hair uncombed, in my slip, but I don't care. It's taken me twenty years to wake up from a nightmare as harrowing as the great flood to its survivors. I look around the room and realize that this is what we are, even though the deluge that I had seen on my television screen in Paris had stayed clear of Port-au-Prince. This is what we are: survivors of a flood that has wiped the more deserving from the face of the earth. It's we who are left behind to clean up the debris or look away. It's up to us to stay the course or abandon our gods for something as flimsy as the arrogance of our continued survival.

"Why didn't you tell me?" I ask Fritz, who has his back to me.

He turns around, "What are you talking about, Cathie?"

"You know what I'm taking about." I look around the room and then I realize that they've all known, all along. "Why didn't anyone tell me?"

They look away from me in what seems the discomfort of guilt.

"How could it have helped you?" Fritz says, frowning, holding a cup of coffee in his hands.

"We should have told her," says Marie-France. She looks around the room. "Someone should have told her."

Estelle nods.

Max excuses himself, soon to be followed by Yolande. He puts a hand on my shoulder as he passes, as if to say he's sorry for whatever he may or may not have done.

Was this how the survivors felt when they exited the ark, knowing that their leader had both saved and failed them, that the world would never be the same? I remember them now, the visitors who came to her kitchen table telling her harrowing stories. Though she told me to go to my room, I'd creep back to listen at the doorway. I remember them crying in their hands and my mother attempting to alleviate their pain, and the look of defeat on her face when they left. I realize for the first time my father's sacrifice and my mother's pain, her inability to cope with having to love us as well as the sufferers who came to her. Fritz had known she'd given up and he'd spared me the truth in order to save me for other possibilities, while all the time afraid that I would turn out the same way as her, able to see and feel the pain of others, or, like Ruth, committed to a life of service that would lead to the same end as those she was trying to save. But something made me different. I'd had the love of my parents, of Ruth. I'd grown up protected from the horrors of the regime. The difference, too, was that Sam had found me and saved me from

255

disappearing into the music; Sam saw me as no one else did, in a way that Fritz had not allowed himself to look at either my mother or his sister. I had a witness and this made me safe. Could I be seen whole as both a healer and a sufferer? Sam allowed me both. Could I allow myself the treasure of his love? Could I forgive Fritz for his inability to be such a witness, even as he imagined he could save me by attempting to hide my history, an attempt that only delivered me more fully to my destiny?

I swallow hard and look at the faces in front of me: Fritz, Max, Estelle and Marie-France.

"I don't understand anything," I say, feeling suddenly dizzy, speaking to no one in particular.

My father reaches for me as he had done at yesterday's viewing and pulls me into a chair.

"What could I tell her?" he says to Max. "What was there to say? Her mother went mad hearing them. Ruth was killed for listening to them."

"No," Estelle interjects, "Ruth was not killed for that."

Fritz stares at her, "What do you know about it?"

"That was not what killed Ruth."

"What killed Ruth?" I ask.

Everyone is quiet. The cook brushes past the table towards the stove, then disappears down the stairwell leading to the back yard holding a crock between two towels.

"It wasn't them, is all she's saying," Marie-France intones.

"Who are you taking about?" I persist, confused.

"The sirens," Estelle replies. "They're talking about the sirens. *Métrès Dlo*. Like the woman you saw yesterday in the water, one among millions waiting for you to pay attention to her."

"What do you know about that?" I ask, suddenly afraid. It had been one thing to see the woman in the water. It was another to have it confirmed that she had been real and not a vision, not a misunderstanding of sight. A chill runs through me and I hold myself tightly against the cold.

"She's going to know sooner or later," Estelle says. "And then there's Lucas. We haven't told her about Lucas."

They all nod gravely and I feel as if I am losing my mind. Why hadn't I thrown myself into the waters yesterday? Why hadn't I let the forces drawing me forward pull me under?

"You could," Estelle says, as if hearing me, "but then you'd only be passing it on."

"Passing what on?"

"What your mother and Ruth have passed on to you."

I gaze at Estelle and see her surrounded by a blue-white light. Marie-France has it too, while Fritz is laced in red and orange as if he doesn't know quite what he's doing there.

"For the love of God," I say, "would one of you just speak plainly. What about Lucas?"

"It's all a mess, isn't it?" Marie-France says to no one in particular.

"She could still do it," Estelle replies.

"No!" Fritz says, slamming down his cup on the table making all of us women startle. "This has got to stop."

The women look at him with pity in their eyes, as if he's a small child who is taking too long to learn how to walk, struggling against gravity. They ignore him.

Estelle addresses me, "There's a reason Lucas didn't make it here for the funeral."

"What is it?"

"You have to see him in person to understand."

"Does it have to do with Ruth's killing?"

"Not exactly," she says; "it has something in common with your mother's death."

"You mean her suicide," I say bitterly, as tears flood out of me. "How could she have done that, left me behind? How could you not have told me?"

Fritz sighs, then yells at the women, "Do you want her to lose her mind as well? I can't stand here and watch this." He leaves the room.

How did Noah have it in him to curse his son, abandon him to his fate? Was it an act of courage or of supreme egoism? Was it love or was it hate that drove him to the point of wanting to save face rather than embrace the one who loved him more than God himself?

"There is no choice, Catherine," Estelle says.

"There's always *some* choice," Marie-France says as she toys with the hem of her impeccably stitched skirt.

"There's always some choice," her twin says, looking up at the ceiling as they hear the cook coming up the steel stairs with the empty crock in her hands.

"What choice have I got?" I ask the women, knowing they aren't going to offer me anything I don't already know.

"You have to go see Lucas for yourself," Estelle says, "then you'll understand everything."

"Everything?"

"As much as is possible to understand," she says.

"Yes," Marie-France confirms; "I will take you to him. To-morrow."

I'm out of my depth. I hear echoes of Chopin's *Études* in my mind, the relentless trills and span of movement, the intensity of its harmonious discord. It's as if the music has prepared me for this moment in which nothing I'm being told makes sense, but must be followed. I know I've got to trust these women even though it feels as if my mothers have failed me, even though it feels as if I should never trust anyone again. My injured hand still aches in my lap as I listen to the women make plans for me to go with Marie-France to meet Lucas, and I sit there knowing I will never use these hands to play in public again, that they're some-how reserved for some other use I haven't understood until now, until I heeded the call of the sirens.

I watch my father lost in his own thoughts in the next room, looking out of the picture window onto the busy street below, fretting to himself. I think of my mother's biblical stories and Greek myths, of her telling me about Icarus and the partridge, of how I should stay close to the ground and not fly too high. I know now that she was wrong, that they were both wrong: that it was they who were afraid to fly, to surrender, as I'm being asked to do now.

Watching Fritz, I think again of Noah and Canaan and realize that all this time I've been trying to make sense of Noah when it was Canaan who held the key to that story. He had accepted his father's humiliation, his nakedness, and his fragility, had held it in his hands as his father cursed him in the name of his brother's god, as his father forsook his faith for fear. Canaan had accepted his fate, held the curse like some rare treasure as his father slipped from between his palms and abandoned him so that he, Canaan, could be free to lead the people his father had saved into the promised land.

March 16, 2004, Pétion-Ville, Haiti

"*Quien te ha trajera aquí?*" the *houngan* quietly mutters in a Spanish clearly not his own.

"*Ki moun ki mennen'w isit la?*" he asks again, every word slurred, looking up at me with bloodshot eyes.

I watch him and cannot respond. I am translating both words and eyes. I know these eyes. Slowly. *Who... brought...*

"*Qui?*" more insistently, this time, stabbing the carpet beneath him with a knobby forefinger.

Those eyes. The body, no, I do not recognize. But, those eyes... Lucas...

"Lucas?" I peer into the bloated face, the folds of skin almost closing the red of the eyes shut.

He interrupts, taps the ground impatiently with a long forefinger, the nail of which protrudes like a hook.

"There is no Lucas here," he says. "Answer me!"

"*Je... oh,*" I am thinking in French, then in Kreyol, then in Spanish. The languages, the words, are suddenly confused in my mind. Lucas had been here, in Haiti, all this time. Why had they not looked for him? Had they looked for him? Why was he in such a state? So agitated and unwelcoming? I look to Marie-France for help. She is sitting to my right, a little behind me but close by. I can feel the warmth of her breath on the nape of my neck.

"He wants to know who brought you here," she whispers over my shoulder.

Wasn't it you? I want to say but know that this would be to miss the point.

I watch the veins in the *houngan*'s neck bulge and imagine that the spider's web of red lines I see in the whites of his eyes is an extension of those lifelines. Why is he so agitated?

I think of the things that have brought me to this place, to this grown man I had once known as a child, revered even, a man who now sits bloated, corpulent, stinking of alcohol and stale cigars. I think of all the knowledge that has come to me recently that I could hardly make sense of, wanting to find some reason that would make sense of all the lives lost, Ruth's and Rose's deaths. Lucas's question makes me wonder how much I can reveal of myself to him, or to anyone. In Haiti, we had been raised in a world in which to reveal one's self was dangerous. All we had were our stories, what we passed from mouth to mouth in person and over telephone wires, seeking the morsels of truth lodged in the pauses of breath as minds wandered and stories took on lives of their own.

It wasn't easy to speak about what one knew since much of it came secondhand, information that would never stand up in a court of law. It would be dismissed with one word: hearsay. But here, hearsay was all we had, along with gossip and innuendo, which amounted to much the same thing. Between each nuanced variation in a story lay worlds of truth. I had been raised to sieve through sounds to seek the nugget of gold that would ensure our safe passage through a minefield of lies and deception. How else could the Duvalier years have been survived? Those who came through unscathed were like spawning salmon, letting themselves be carried by the currents of a wild stream, knowing just when to give a quick flick of their tails to change course or head in a different direction to avoid being caught in the fishermen's net. Sometimes the nets were invisible. Sometimes the water was not so clear.

Something tells me that the *houngan*'s question is designed to upset my balance rather than to restore it. This is not Lucas speaking to me, not my Lucas. It is some distortion of Lucas sitting there in front of me, some version I have never known.

Now you understand, I hear Ruth's voice. Yes, there it is. Ruth, speaking to me. *Nothing is as it seems.* Rose's voice. Yet, the *houngan*'s question is one I do not want to escape. I've had enough of escape routes and survival strategies. It is clear that he will not go on until I answer.

Who *had* brought me there? Had it been Ruth? Estelle? Marie-France? Even Rose? I'd had a feeling for days, ever since I'd seen the woman floating in the sea and felt a presence calling from the ocean floor, of a presentiment, of something to come, something so large that it would change me from the inside out.

Anger blazes from the *curandero*'s red-rimmed eyes. I feel unsure of myself. Do I really want to know? Whatever is causing the man's agitation is more powerful than either of us, more powerful than what had brought me there – doubt, and fear. I have the itching urge to stand up and walk out through the curtains garishly embroidered with sequins of all colours. I squint until the sequins blur into a murky wash.

"It was me," I say, finally, to both Marie-France and to the man who is Lucas and no longer Lucas. "I brought myself here."

Marie-France translates. I hear the *curandero* sigh in relief. I refocus on his face and chest. His muscles have relaxed. He no longer looks angry. The divining stones echo hollowly against the woven rug beneath him, like dominos slapped against a wooden table by the old men wrinkling day after day beneath the afternoon sun, seemingly with no cares in the world.

I keep my eyes closed against the sight of Lucas's decaying body. Distractedly, I hear the stones, tied together by coarse string, and captive to the diviner, hit fleshy fingers, the floor, the long wooden handle into which the strings are woven.

I sit on the edge of the low stool in front of the mat, wavering between matter and air, between the man at my feet and the gods above he thinks he serves. I am entranced by his low mutters as he recites the incantations I intuitively want to believe in but do not know. I listen to the drone, the slapping of the stones, and focus on what it is I am here to find out, what drove me here to find Lucas.

The man, who was once Lucas but is no longer him, begins to make his pronouncements.

"Beware of cars," he says. "You could be involved in an accident."

More slapping of tiles.

"Snow," he says, "I see lots and lots of snow."

The tiles sing out.

261

"A woman, running, blood on her gown," he continues, his voice faraway, until he has retold me my mother's nightmares.

Marie-France sits behind me stiffly, recognizing some of the stories as her own, and I begin to weep quietly when I realize that Lucas can only see into the past because he is lost in time, lost in the space between faith and belief, between surrender and divination.

"What about her work?" Marie-France says finally.

"The work is always going to be fine," the *curandero* says, looking over my shoulder at Marie-France as if seeing her for the first time. "It was always fine."

"And you," he says, his eyes focusing back on me, "you, my sister, need to get married."

There is a pause. I wipe away the tears from my cheeks.

"Is there something you need to say to me, sister?"

I look into Lucas's face, suddenly aware of what has gone wrong: with no one to teach him, he has absorbed every ill he was meant to cure, every sorrow he was meant to heal. I remember telling him about my mother's dances, about the altar for *Ezili Le Flambo*, about Chicoutimi. He was my confessor. Unlike her, he lives on, between worlds; like her, he has lost his mind. He has remained to warn me.

"I am sorry, Lucas," I say, "I'm sorry I didn't come to you sooner." I hold my face in my fingers, wiping away at the remnant of salty tears. "I just… I just did not understand. I left you to yourself as others left me." I look at my hands and spread the fingers a foot from my face. I watch Lucas through the gaps between my fingers, ten strong and wiry. All the time, everything was right there in front of me. How selfish I've been pursuing some other life with these hands. "I take back my burden."

Lucas smiles and I recognize his smile from somewhere below the folds of skin that mask his face.

I smile back at him hesitantly, hoping that he sees me as the sister he once knew.

"Thank you, sister," he says, "thank you for your blessing." He takes my hands in his and brings them to his face. His face is hot and oily beneath the dry coolness of my palms. His pain shoots through me but I am grounded enough to receive it, grounded

262

enough to let it flow down into the earth where it will become something else, a healing something.

"Sister," Lucas says, in a voice sounding more like his own, "you don't know your power. You feel it. But you don't believe it. Believe it. This is all I have to say to you."

I know that these words are true even though my conscious mind wants to refuse them.

"Your power will carve its way through stone. Surround yourself with believers and all will be fine. You will not suffer your mother's fate."

I study Lucas then, all thirty-nine of his years, his paunch stretching the fabric of his red T-shirt, the swell of his hips in the faded blue jeans, the long nails in need of cleaning, the curled hair atop his head like peppercorns upon a roast, the brown of his scalp gleaming from sweat and oils.

Then he lets me go and the glimpse of Lucas I once knew disappears.

I bring my hands back into my lap. Behind me, Marie-France sighs, as if a weight has been lifted from her.

The *houngan* holds out a hand to receive the five dollars I'd agreed to pay for the reading when we arrived at the pale blue door of his house. I'd wanted to believe that the gods would speak to me through him, I who had not been initiated in the world of the *orishas* or the *loas* of my own country.

As if sensing the movement of my eyes over his body, Lucas takes the hand still holding the divining tablets and passes it over his head. The other hand remains still, waiting. His red eyes glaze over and look right through me.

"Was that all he wanted to tell me?" I ask Marie-France. I keep my eyes on Lucas.

She says nothing, nods; I guess but do not need to look at her to hear the answer. Our time is done. I reach into a pocket of my satchel for the promised five American dollars. I hand the faded bill over and Lucas takes the money from me with the very tips of his fingers, as if fearing to be soiled.

"Shall I pray for you? For five more dollars I can place a prayer for you on the altar, over there." He points to a shabby altar in the corner with effigies of St. Peter and Mary, Mother of God, encircled by melted candles and small basins of water. "I can add a candle for you. Place your prayer beneath it."

"Let's go," Marie-France says and stands.

"No," I say, "I don't need anything more."

"Go to the water, sister," Lucas says, his eyes gleaming like stones at the bottom of a river.

"We must go," Marie-France says.

"But…"

"I shall go for you," Marie-France says and she goes to the altar and puts a finger in the water and crosses herself. As I see her touch the water, a strange itching inches over me. Marie-France returns and pushes me out through the curtains.

"Sister," Lucas says after us. "Know your power."

"It was good to see you," I say over my shoulder, even though the itching is getting worse and the phrase is trite. It's as if I believe I will see Lucas again while knowing I won't.

We walk briskly down the street as if a devil is chasing us but there's only a stray dog trying to keep up with us, hoping for a bone to be thrown his way. Marie-France turns around and throws rocks at the dog until he skitters away, yelping.

"*Merde!*" she yells, "*Merde!*"

Tears are streaming down her cheeks.

"You've seen him, our Lucas! Are you satisfied?"

I am shocked by her anger. "I didn't *ask* to come here. You brought me here."

"Of course you asked. Of course you asked. You don't even know what you ask for. You asked, in front of the water, when the goddess came to see you after the rising of the waters."

I flash back to the scene of the woman holding on to the pier in the Port near my mother's birthplace.

"I don't know. I…"

"Of course you did. You asked and then I was *made* to bring you here."

"No one forced you."

"*Dieu merci! Dieu merci!* And you are the one we're supposed to follow! You who don't understand a thing."

Marie-France tries to take a deep breath, but it's as if her lungs have lost any capacity to hold oxygen. She gasps.

The itching suddenly stops and I see two lines of light surround Marie-France, one white and blue, the other dark red and black, two lines fighting each other. I, to my surprise, know what to do. I place my hand on Marie-France's solar plexus and I tell her to breathe, just breathe, and to think of the breath going through her and through her, in circles from the top of her head down to her spine.

"You're going to be all right," I tell her, and as I say those words, I feel the palms of my hands pulsate as they used to when I played the piano. I see Marie-France as she was as a child, sullen and complex, withdrawn but generous. I remember her as Lucas and I had never seen her at that time.

It comes upon me then, as I feel the heat of my palms, that I understand why the composers of old believed in the mystics and why some were mystics themselves. I understand for the very first time that my hands have held the secret all along. I have just been playing the wrong instrument.

Marie-France's breath returns to her and then I am holding her, hushing her, as she cries against my shoulder. Marie-France is a middle-aged woman now, but I hold her as her mother may have held her when she was young, as my mother had held me when I was a baby.

"There is our Lucas," she says between sobs. "There is our Lucas."

"Yes," I say, because there are no two ways about it. "Our Lucas has gone."

Later, much later, she will explain to me how Ruth had allowed Lucas to go away to Havana when it seemed as if she might lose him to drink because his visions were so strong she was afraid of what they could mean. She told me how Lucas had seemed to find his way, through Santeria, how he loved everything that reminded him of Haiti and what Haiti could have been had our history been different. The more he saw the contrast, the more his anger swelled and he returned to drinking. He could find no one to save him through love. Ruth had been too old to reach him in any way that seemed to matter. He was young and alone. Embittered, Lucas had turned to the secret societies of men, the *Abakua*, who convinced him that it was the women in his life who had poisoned his purpose, like *Sika*, robbing him of the word of God as Synogoga had robbed Ecclesia of her third eye by becoming impregnated by a serpent. He vowed never to touch a woman again and it was with this bitterness in his heart that he had returned to Haiti. Broken, crazed, muddled, untrusting of the very women who had surrounded him and brought him up.

At first, he had been very powerful and his reputation grew and grew. People came to him from far and wide to be cured of their illnesses but Lucas took everything in, as he always had, feeding his despair on the ills others had no answers for, until he was bypassed by the events of others' pasts that his own mind could not decipher. At times, there were flashes of insight. Mostly, there was hogwash. Over time, his body putrified.

"Is there no way out for him?" I ask Marie-France as she finishes the story, as I realize she and Estelle were the women my mother saw in her dreams.

"We must go on without him."

I nod, even though her answer means that the Lucas I knew will never be with us again.

"We are glad you returned," she says to me.

"Even though it has caused you pain?"

"Yes," she says, "because of it."

"Because of it?"

"Yes," Marie-France continues, "because now we know that it is not our pain alone." She smiles to me, the smile of women the world over who have lost men and children, who are wise enough to know that there are more men and more children to take their place, to be taken care of, even though the ones who have gone can never truly be replaced.

I know that one day I will be able to forgive my father and thank him for giving me over to Ruth, now that I have only just begun to awaken to the strength of my hands as I felt their heat go through Marie-France's body and cast out whatever spell Lucas had put in that water meant for me. This is a beginning, not an end.

Eventually, I will go back to Paris and our Rue des Rosiers to find Sam and start again, knowing that the two of us will never have to say with Jacques Prévert:

But never again will she open the window
the door of a sealed train
shut her in for good
And the sun tries to forget those things
but it's no use.
There is hope because we are.

For now, Marie-France and I ferry our way to Ruth's house in the dark of night, the cicadas whistling and the frogs singing, mourning two departed souls instead of one.

"Never forget," Marie-France says to me as we make our way through the dark. "Never forget what you have seen and what you have done," she continues. "It is the seed for all beginning."

PART THREE:

ILLUSIONS

"For our country
And for our forefathers,
Let us train our sons.
Free, strong, and prosperous,
We shall always be as brothers.
Let us train our sons
For our country
And for our forefathers."

— La Dessalinienne, Haitian National Anthem

ROMULUS

May 23, 2004, the streets, small-town USA

Down in the streets, they call him John. He thinks he inherited the name the day he showed up in the hospital. He'd twisted to his right to peer at the tag they had attached to his wrist hanging limply over the side of the gurney. They'd labelled him a "John Doe", and he didn't see any point in correcting them all, so John it was and has remained. No last name, just John. No more Robert. No more Romulus. It's a name he hasn't gotten used to, a mask he's designed to wear until he can figure out what his real face was once like, until he can find his real place in the continuum of time.

Down in the streets, time doesn't really seem to exist. It's a function of other people's priorities, not theirs. They show up when the doors are opened at the soup kitchen and at the shelter, *if* the doors are unlocked because sometimes they aren't. There are days when they wait in line, as if the opening of the doors is like the parting of the Red Sea, some miracle they've heard about and have come to witness. But sometimes, it doesn't happen, and still they remain, believers. They stand there waiting for longer than any normal person would, and then, when it's clear that the doors aren't to open, they shuffle away, peering out of the corners of their eyes into the darkness, wondering if there might be a welcome space at the bottom of a tree or a street bench to spend the night, some place where they won't have to fight someone else in the bunch for the chance to claim some shut-eye.

He goes his own way, as if he doesn't care, as if he isn't one of them, until he's clear of their stench, their troubles, until he's far from anyone who might call out this name that isn't his name, John, and confirm him in this life he would never have imagined for himself in a hundred years of yesterdays.

273

He's found a small town for himself. A liveable space. What might once have been called a one-horse town. He ended up here by following a group of other men who'd decided they preferred their chances in the streets to the regimented living of the rehab centre in Boston where they'd been summarily dumped by friends, family, or by case workers for the state. He'd gotten to Boston by plane, courtesy of Constance, but he left it by foot with nothing more than a knapsack on his back and a dry mouth for company. He's followed the men this time, rather than being dragged, though they are men not unlike the ones who'd pulled him into the fray as they made their way up the Haitian hills to Ruth's house in search of some secret treasure they never found. He'd left Boston without proper papers and despite the promises of the priests that they would assist what they called his "mainstreaming" into the regular world, not because he had given up, but because rehab seemed to be the best place to learn more about how to stay a junkie or become an alcoholic. He was desperate to come clean before someone else lay dead at his feet because of his lack of a clear mind.

He had not gotten to Christian's funeral. He had been too ashamed to call Brigitte back to find out where it was being held. His son had needed him and he had failed. The woman who had pulled Romulus out of his childhood apathy had lain in a pool of her own blood after looking into his eyes, and all he had done, once he had come to and taken stock of his senses, was descend into the smouldering refuse of the city below and follow his feet home to Constance's red door, devoid of any feeling, devoid of regret, guilt, even of fear. Now that they were both gone, he felt all of these emotions and more and, for the first time in his life, he wanted to feel them to the core of his being. And so he had followed the other men who'd escaped the rehab for the streets, few of them escaping for reasons like his, most of them leaving because they wanted an unobstructed path to their drug of choice. He wanted to find some way of being free, some way of feeling again without the sensation of being submerged and unable to float to the surface of whatever wave might knock him down to his knees.

They drifted west and south of Boston into Puritan New

England where it was possible to subsist on much less. These men taught him that the small towns were often liberal enclaves where you might not get chased off a bench in the middle of the night, where someone who had seen you sitting on a concrete stoop outside a restaurant might actually come back to you with some warm food wrapped in cellophane. These were the kinds of places where the town-folk were not overrun with misery. They could deal with a few panhandlers. Still, he figured out within a few hours that small New England towns were as segregated as Southern ones and that panhandling on their main streets, and his dark brown skin made him stand out in a crowd. Not only was he dark of skin, but he was tall, often drunk and, initially, unable to make sense of the swirl of emotions that shook him like storm winds would shake a tree by its roots. This did not make for easy living.

This night, like most nights, he is heading to a stoop close to the only major intersection in town. When the lights all turn to red, a bell sounds, like the trill of an artificial bird, and pedestrians head into the intersection from every direction, even walking diagonally from one corner to the other. He's never seen anything like it and he enjoys witnessing the organized confusion. The people crossing enjoy it as well and that is always good for him, sitting there, with his cup outstretched before him, smiling his gap-toothed grin if halfway sober, his chin tucked in if not, revealing nothing of his features except for a growing bald patch at the crown of his head.

He hasn't even reached the stoop when it begins to rain.

"Goddamn it," one of the other men hounding the corner says to no one in particular. "How're we going to make change tonight?"

It's a statement more than a real question. No one stops on rainy nights. The passers-by are all bent on getting home or ducking into the restaurant of their choice. The men on the street (because they are mostly men) watch the pedestrians hurry past them, some seemingly embarrassed by their lack of grace as the rain slicks down their hair and runs into the creases of their thick necks; the women giggle, with upturned collars shielding their faces to protect their make-up. The men feel sure that they can detect coins lining the pockets moving smoothly by, as if they have x-ray vision like comic-book heroes. Lost coins mock them with their musical jingle-jangle. They watch the pockets glide past, swallowing the spit of their despair and chant towards the preoccupied faces of privilege, "Money, please. Got any change?" It's a process designed to humiliate, but this is all they have left – those whose health or moral compass keeps them from stealing, or worse, to make it through the days.

He nods towards the voice.

"Hey, John, whatcha romancin' tonight?" and the man pulls at an imaginary organ in front of his unzipped pants. Then he suddenly forgets his taunting and his face grows slack, concerned, "Hey, man, you got any change?"

He can now recognize the voice as Henry's – Henry from the male-only showers in the shelter down in Springfield, who jumps up and down like a child while the shower water falls down on his pink-brown skin marked with razor cuts that are so old and so deep they look as if they were inflicted in a distant childhood Henry will spend the rest of his days trying to flee. He hasn't succeeded yet.

"No, man," he answers Henry. "Nothin' tonight."

He feels the bile of guilt rise up from his gullet. It's a constant presence, a very physical aftertaste. He has some coins rolling around in his jeans pockets but figures he'll need them as much as any man on the street, especially tonight. He thrusts his fists into his pockets and hunches his shoulders so that they touch the base of his ears.

"It's the goddamn rain," he says to Henry as if that explains everything. He looks away from Henry's disappointed, pudgy face, away from the creased, unshaven cheeks.

"Yeah, John," Henry laughs and his laugh is highpitched like a woman's as he throws back his head, his scraggly brown hair catching across his throat and ears, lacing his face like fingers. "Yeah. It's the goddamn rain."

He walks on, smiling to himself at Henry's childlike nature, while Henry turns to another man on the street and punches him in the arm. The two men struggle with each other, wrestling under the rain like Jacob with his angel as startled pedestrians part to let them stumble by. Henry is a large, robust man who in another time had probably been a construction worker. He wrestles a diminutive man he has seen before but whose name he does not know. The two men leave the distinct odour of day-long drinking in their wake. The scent reminds him that this is the first day in a long while that he has had nothing to drink. The reprieve might only last for this day but he is enjoying the feeling of clarity that has crept into him without it, the way he can feel everything that is wrong in his body but still walk on without stumbling. It's the only way he knows how to mourn his dead.

He steps off the sidewalk into the traffic. Drivers in small towns stop for pedestrians. He regards this as a small but amusing miracle. Gone is the bedlam of Port-au-Prince, the crowding bodies, the jeeps flying above pot-holes, weaving past bodies and wares. Gone is the stench of refuse piled up in the streets, the meaty smell of charred bodies and the sharp bittersweet odour of burning tyres. He waves a hand at the driver who is probably cursing the big black man crossing the street wherever he feels like it. He chuckles to himself. These are the small acts of vindictiveness he has remaining and he isn't letting them go. If he isn't going to make any money standing out in the rain, he might as well find a dry spot to think about his next move, whatever that might be.

What he does not see as he makes a beeline for the concrete benches in front of the city law buildings is Henry and the smaller man careening towards him across the street as cars slam on their brakes and pedestrians leap aside. Henry is puffing and grunting. He walks without hearing the sounds around him.

"Watch out," a pedestrian yells out towards him but it is too late. The struggling men fall onto the ground only feet behind him and roll into his legs, knocking him down like a pin at a bowling alley. They roll atop him as if he is grass rather than flesh.

"*Sak gen la-a?*" he says, his *Kreyol* slipping out unmonitored, trying to lift himself up by poking out his elbows against the weight of the men. "Get off, will ya?"

But the men seem deaf and dumb, as grunting and heaving against each other, they crush John onto the wet ground, grinding his face into the mud as they loll back and forth.

"Henry!" he yells. "Hen-ry!"

But the men keep on tussling, impervious to his plight

277

beneath them as he kicks and punches in a wild effort to free himself.

"Henry!"

The men stop, their arms entwined in each other's. They look about as if hearing an angry ghost.

"Down here," he gasps. "Will you get off of me?"

Henry looks down at him, startled, and lets go of the smaller man who rolls off into the wet grass like a spring fallen from a tightly wound mechanism.

"Geez, Louise. Didn't see you there, John."

Henry leaps to his feet as best he can, grabbing him by an elbow and pulling him to his feet in one smooth motion.

He is surprised at Henry's ability to move with such oiled synchronicity despite the drink. He himself stumbles as he stands, his elbow still in Henry's beefy grip.

"Why don't you come and have a drink with us?" Henry waves towards the smaller man still lying in a puddle of mud as the rain continues to pour over them.

"Drink?" he says, disentangling himself from Henry's hold on his arm. He feels the bruises rising on various parts of his body, behind his knees where he was knocked off his feet. There isn't any point in brushing off the pellets of mud on his jeans or the grass smeared across his back.

"Yeah. We have a stash over there." Henry points into the darkness behind the concrete benches.

"Nah," he responds. "I'm…"

"What? Come on. How can you pass up a free drink?"

The smaller man on the ground stirs at last and rolls onto his back. He sends puffs of breath into the cold air. "C'mon, John. Have a drink with us."

He peers at the diminutive man and wonders how he knows his name. Henry leans into his body and grabs both his elbows impulsively. "C'mon, John. A drink with the guys."

The stink of stale drink is potent. He wavers. What could it hurt? But then he remembers why he isn't drinking today, why he wants to stop drinking every day if he can. He moves brusquely out of Henry's grasp and turns away. "I'll see you later," he says.

"C'mon," the men protest, their words piling into each other in the same way they had careened across the street. "What can it hurt?"

"Later," he yells back over his shoulder and waves them away. How can he explain to these men that he has entered a period of penance? That nothing will drive him to drink again. He'd made the decision yesterday, under a chalkboard sky lit up with white white stars. He'd seen a shooting star and made a simple wish: that he could turn back time, take back the last twenty years and replay them, sober. As the star fell off into the distance, he had the epiphany that if he had been sober and clean the last twenty years of his life, he would have stayed with his first wife. Christian would be alive – maybe – though he would not have had his two other children by the second and third wives. He could not regret them. Yet, sober, he might never have had the courage to leave the island or to step onto those wide open stages singing out to stadiums. He might have done very little. He concluded that the world was as it was but that he could perhaps avoid future errors. He could be there for the other children. He could return to Robert his rightful name. He could begin to make amends.

The town is so small he wonders where he can go to find his quiet piece of ground. Some place dry seems out of the question at this point, as the cords of rain continue to fall on his head.

The only thing on his mind is rest, some kind of hollow resting place. He doesn't feel like finding his way back to Springfield in the pitch dark, only to find himself sardined in the shelter with men falling apart at the seams, in various stages of mental disintegration. He has no strength to battle their nightmares or their hacking coughs telling of disease coursing through their bodies at a rate no one has measured. Compared to the rest of them, he isn't in bad shape. But he doesn't want to be in a cell ever again, of any kind. Even though in the eyes of the town-folk he seems to have hit bottom, this is actually the way up for him, one step above the hell he's already survived.

Head down, he heads towards the private school on the hill. If he walks far enough, he will find a quiet, grassy spot at the base of some trees close to the water on the other side of the school. He has his mind set on peace and quiet even as the rain falls more heavily all around him giving no hope for dry comfort.

The rain turns the concrete beneath his feet into tar-black slickness. He pulls the hood from the grey sweatshirt he is wearing beneath his jacket up onto his head. This will make him pass for a student when his feet bring him up to the rise of the hill. The dry warmth of the hood is comforting against his wet, shaved scalp.

He isn't halfway up the hill when he hears the sound of footsteps behind him, steps that seem to be matching his own. He stops and the steps stop. He advances and they move towards him. He turns around to find Henry following him, minus the diminutive man from earlier. Startled, he tries to stay calm.

"Whatcha doin' Henry?"

Henry just smiles at him, a toothy grin of yellowed teeth.

"Henry?" He feels his body incline towards the man. Why does he feel responsible for him? He is suddenly aware of Henry's size despite his childlike mental state. "Henry?"

The smile never wavers. This is what he will remember later. Henry headbutts him with the full force of his muscled body and he falls back onto the concrete, his head slipping back and hitting the hardness beneath. And all the while Henry smiles like a child.

Henry the child roughs him up until he can't move, until his head hurts so much it feels better to just lie there in the rain with the cement for a pillow.

Henry the child empties his pockets of their puny collection of coins, finds the crumpled dollar in the inner pocket of his jacket and leaves him there to bleed into the rainwater pooling at the side of the road. Poetic justice, he thinks, his mind on Haiti, knowing nonetheless that the next time he sees Henry, Henry will have forgotten the incident, as he has forgotten most of his life. He's seen Henry do things like this before but never to him, never to him. *What has changed?* He doesn't know and the throbbing in his head keeps him from focusing too much on the question: *What has changed?* Everything. From moment to moment, by small increments, the balance of the world changes, but no one walking by and over him, as if he's some kind of excrement waiting to be picked up by the road-cleaning crew in the dead of night, has any idea.

He was christened Romulus Pierre. Romulus for a destiny of leadership, to be an Emperor like King Christophe in northern Haiti. Pierre for the rock, the cornerstone of the Catholic faith. He might become a Catholic priest was the thought behind the second name. It was an addition, as if some entity had whispered in his mother's ear that he was meant for a spiritual life. Romulus Pierre hasn't lived up to either of these names, although for a time it seemed as if he might have made something of himself, as if he might be destined for great and worldly things. He used to fly on private jet planes, drink the best wines of France, dance all night, eat at the best restaurants in cities whose names he could not remember, after being there for a night or two of work. These days, being anonymous, being John, feels about right, the way of unfulfilled destiny.

It was only a few weeks ago that he had been in prison far from here, with the world beyond the four walls of the jail an unholy mess of chaos and despair. His head against the pavement, the rain pelting down on him, he thinks of those long months and can't help but feel that being out here, even without roof or shelter, is a world of improvement on what he has survived. No one looking at him on the streets could imagine the lives he has already moved through, what he has gained and lost. Despite appearances to the contrary, at the moment being on the street is in his column of gain. He wishes only that he could connect the last months with his present condition. It isn't easy to do, not clear at all. His mind gets caught up in the things he can't change, the things he regrets. The thread in all of it is his weakness, his failure to acknowledge that if he'd put his mind to it, he might have transformed weakness into strength a long time ago.

He thinks about his days in the Haitian prison: the constant thirst of the early days.

"Could I have some water?" he remembered asking more than once.

The guards didn't seem to hear him.

"Water?" he asked again as they shut the door of the cell against his back.

A man with a gash in his forehead pointed to a pail next to one of the dingy walls and Romulus went to it but found that the water was dirty.

"I can't drink this," he said to no one in particular and went back to the barred door. "Officer," he called to one of the jailers. "Please. Water."

The man ignored him and went on talking on a black phone, the kind with the rotary dial, as he sat behind an old school desk that had been placed there to give him an air of importance. Romulus was sure that his keeper could neither read nor write, and probably didn't speak a word of French.

"*Compè*," he tried again. Brother. This time the man looked up. "*Compè, ban mwen d'lo. M'prié ou.*" Water. Please.

The man smiled and Romulus, before his legs gave way under him, saw yellow teeth coming towards him in the darkness.

When he came to, he was lying on the only cot in the cell. His neck and upper chest were damp. They had thrown water on his face to revive him. It was doing the job. "Water," he said again, and a hand handed him a dirty goblet. This time he drank from it without saying a word about how dirty the water was. He drank it and then fell into a heavy sleep.

For the first time in a very long while, along with the hallucinations of the woman with a pointy face, came dreams. He saw a child coming out from the womb, head first with a tuft of hair covering his crown. The baby came out slick with blood, excrement, and a filmy white-green substance. Its face was shrivelled like an old man's but still Romulus recognized in it Christian's features, his firstborn. The baby already had the tiny cleft in his chin that would become more pronounced with age, a shock of black curls that would get longer and heavier, spiralling out from the soft centre of his cranium.

Romulus had been shocked at how small Christian was, how fragile, his small fists scratching out into the air, his cry highpitched and plaintive like a kitten's. Romulus had only ever kept dogs, mastiffs that had to be chained to fences in order to be controlled. There had been something unsettling about seeing the baby emerge from his wife's torn and bleeding vulva, hearing her grunting with pain as the baby cried from the sudden intake and outtake of breath, its sudden expulsion from the safety of a warm, dark, liquid cocoon, into the cold air of the delivery room, the rubbery, gloved fingers of the doctors and nurses who handled Christian to clear his passages from the build up of mucous, who counted his fingers and toes to make sure that everything was there, who wiped him down and handed him back to his mother.

Romulus had felt shame for all of it. The natural order of things had been lost to him in that moment. He felt only shame at seeing his wife on her back, convulsing like an animal, shame at seeing the small protruding flesh of his son's penis, shrivelled, less than a quarter of the length of his small finger. He didn't know quite what he had expected. He would have preferred Christian to be more robust, wider in his chest, virile looking from the moment of his emergence. It was not love he had felt at first sight.

Where had he been standing? At the end of the bed, then somewhere near the door, hovering, about to take flight. He was beginning to be good at that – hovering, then disappearing.

Romulus had looked across the blinding white light of the overhead lamps to his wife and child together in the bed. The bloody sheets had been removed or covered over. Christian held a small fist up into the air as if he rued the day of his birth. Ellen looked briefly up at Romulus with sad eyes, as if he were a ghost appearing from beyond the grave, already gone and grieved for.

He was holding a green surgical mask in his right hand. Green booties covered his leather boots, the ones he liked to wear to auditions, that made him feel taller than his five feet eight inches. His clothes were covered by a matching green robe. The nurses hadn't had time to close the strings at the back. He felt himself receding from the scene even as he stood there taking them both in, wondering if he belonged there at all, or if he would be better off in some back room somewhere, sniffing his way into oblivion.

He'd only had one thought in his head when he left the hospital, promising Ellen that he would be back when they'd all had time to sleep. He'd actually said to her, "when we've all had some time to think." He'd already half made up his mind, and walked out with the plan to give away his dogs to the pound. He never bought another dog. That was as close as he would allow himself to get to love.

His next memory of Christian was when he was five, two years after they had spent some time in Haiti, living off money he'd made from his first record. But Ellen hadn't been able to adapt to the Haitian way of doing things. She didn't like spending her afternoons visiting or being a hostess to other men's wives who wanted to see the inside of her house. Most of all, she didn't like being kept out of her own kitchen, having to pay a woman she couldn't communicate with to make meals for her family. They'd sold the house, come back to Miami and found a nice house on the water. Christian at five had knobby knees, just like Romulus at that age, thin legs that carried him miraculously across green lawns and up and down the lengths of baseball diamonds. Romulus saw his son falling from his bicycle, crying for his mother.

Christian had always been his mother's son, but the day, some five years later, when he fell from the monkey-bars and broke an arm, he allowed Romulus who was home from the recording studio to carry him out to the car. They drove to the emergency room in strangled silence, the boy whimpering in the passenger seat, tears rolling down his narrow cheeks, Romulus staring straight ahead, not seeing exactly where he was going, a lump in his throat keeping him from saying the words he should have said, "Everything is going to be all right, son." The boy (for this was how Romulus thought of him) had been ten then. They did not communicate very well. Romulus remembered that Christian had smiled at him when his cast had set. He had been sitting on the edge of a roll-a-bed waiting for Romulus to come back to retrieve him. Romulus remembered how the smile had startled him. His heart jumped for a second and he imagined that this was what was meant by love but he couldn't be sure. Even then he could not say the words. He wasn't even sure if he had smiled back at the boy, remembered only his relief that the tears had gone and that he could bring him back to Ellen more or less in one piece and have everything be calm for once in the house where no one seemed to have more than a few words to say to each other.

They'd had a large house by then with too many rooms for the three of them. The rooms always seemed to have one or more visitor, someone from the band or a family member down on their luck. Romulus didn't keep track. He paid the bills with the money that streamed in from record deals and concert appearances; the cheques seemed to be getting smaller and smaller but, as far as he could tell, things were fine.

The boy grew to be skinny like a scarecrow. In his pre-teens, he spent most of his time shut up in his room. By that time, Romulus was no longer living with them in the big house. He'd given it up in the divorce. He remembered only that his son had not stepped out of his room to say goodbye when he left. Not a word. That had hurt him. He still thought about what he could have done to end things differently. But when he thought of his skinny son, he still felt only the shame of his birth, saw only the tiny fist raised up in the air, the skin thin and translucent like the membrane surrounding an egg yolk. His pale-as-roses son with the cry of a kitten and the small penis seemed more like an accident than something he could believe in.

Romulus had pictured himself leaving the house he had shared with his first son and first wife. It had rained that day. He had been soaked to the bone. He had worn the same boots he had worn the day of Christian's birth. They were no longer waterproof. He had felt his feet grow damp and then cold. He had tried to see if Christian was at his window, but he could see nothing through the fog misting up the car windows. He waved in case Christian was watching. He waved and his arm felt as small and limp as Christian had seemed that first night he had seen him emerging from between a woman's legs covered with the shit of life.

How was he to know that sons were meant to believe in their fathers' strength, as much as fathers were meant to have faith in their sons growing up to fill their shoes? Romulus had grown up with a silent father and an absent mother. Neither had given him much of an example to follow. When his son was born, he had been struck by the fact that he was inept at the job. He saw himself looking at his son's vulnerability but seeing only his own. Perhaps, he was still seeking a father, and when he saw his son, his shame came from the knowledge that he'd always wished he'd had a father to show him the way.

When he awoke after these dreams, whether in prison or in rehab, whoever was in the bed or cot next to him would ask, "Who's Christian?"

"No one," Romulus would reply, surprised that he'd spoken his son's name in his sleep. "No one," he repeated, even though the man would have already gone about his business, the empty space being quickly filled by another squatting man with a hungry gaze.

He'd thought about how he might put a bit of money aside and take Christian on a trip somewhere, just the two of them. He fantasized about showing Christian where he had played to sold-out stadiums: Brazil, Japan, New York. He wanted to show his son who he once had been and might be still. But he had known then that before any of that could happen, he had to get clean. For some reason, getting clean seemed to involve taking a side trip into getting-in-deeper. It was the only way he could make some money, fast. The rest would come in time. Getting clean would happen later.

He hadn't counted on getting clean in prison, in Haiti. What a welcome. No marching bands. No appearances on the local television shows or radio. No, for him there was shaking on a soiled cot while others looked on, laughing at him, feeling better about the arc of their own lives at the sight of him there, among them, screaming in the darkness and seeing faces on the walls in the half-light between dawn and dusk.

He'd had more than one period of withdrawal in the half year he spent in jail, the flow of narcotics irregular. Dreams seemed to replace drugs. He was hooked on visions from the past. He remembered his piano lessons with fierce intensity, the lushness of Ruth's garden and the snapping turtles she kept in the back yard for resale at market. He remembered a boy who had come out of nowhere to live with Ruth when he himself was already in long pants and ready to seek his own adventures. The boy, Lucas, doted on the smaller turtles, making them his pets even though he knew they were being grown for slaughter. He'd tried to warn the boy, but Lucas had only smiled at him, as if he knew something that Romulus could only guess at, and then ignored him. And then there'd been Catherine, arriving only a couple of years before he left Haiti to seek his fortunes in New York and

Miami. Catherine who, at eleven, already had a glow of future grace about her, who resembled in a faint, faint way the woman whose pointed face floated through his dreams.

He'd heard about the death of Catherine's mother, wondered what it was like to have the luxury of remembrance, his own mother having faded from his consciousness long ago, and watched her grow out of grief into budding adolescence as she played Ruth's piano, as he never had, with uncommon elegance. He would listen to her playing as he approached the house, close his eyes at the doorway between the gardens and the house, distracted by Lucas who at fifteen was still tending the turtles, but allowing Catherine's notes to cut through everything. If he'd had *that* talent, he'd thought, he could have had anything under the sun. But Catherine hadn't seemed to realize the power she possessed. He could hear it in the way she wrenched emotion from every note, the way each sound coursed through him in a way that nothing else could. The music, this was what they'd had in common. That, and Ruth. But then he had left and never seen her again, gone on to his life, to his women, the children, the drugs, fallen into the vast chasm between reality and delusion.

Walking into Ruth's yard in the company of Marc, now weeks ago, he'd remembered Catherine as she had been then, almost expecting her to walk out of the house towards him. The memory of the music he'd heard her play, music Ruth had helped him discover for himself, had peeled back a layer of fossilized emotion. But then his head had spun as Marc's thick hand had pushed him ahead, forward, into the trap they'd laid for Ruth, and he'd felt the apprehension of what was to come crawling over him like a mutiny of ants. There'd been no way out. No way out.

However much he played the events of his life over and over again in his mind, sitting in the smelly prison cell with the moving bodies squirming in their discomfort all around him, Romulus could not see how anything might have come out differently. Should he have waited for Catherine to grow up, waited before leaving the island? Should he have married her instead of Ellen? Surely not, for then there would have been no Christian.

The rain continues to come down hard. There was no Christian.

Christian was dead. Christian, who would-not-have-been had he made a different choice at a pivotal moment in his young life, was not. The arrogance of youth had kept him from choosing Catherine. And now, the arrogance of regret had him believing that he could have lived a different life. All was as it was and yet he knew it could have been something else, somehow, had he been a stronger man. It could all have been the same, but different, had he somehow known how to follow these women in these lives, from the woman who traversed his dreams and hallucinations with her whispers of some faraway land that could have been the Haiti he never knew, lush and green and bursting with fruit; to Catherine with the haunting of her classical music displaced from faraway Europe into the Haitian hills and the phantomlike features of her growing-to-adulthood face; to Ellen with her wistful smile birthing their son as she recognized that Romulus was already slipping from their lives, slipping and sliding into a life unbecoming even for a man made weak by his father's neglect and the unrelenting despair of his birthplace – though his circumstances had been privileged.

The world is upside down with change, he thinks, as the rain washes over his face. He is so tired he wishes he could sink into the sidewalk and grow a grave beneath the surface. This could be his final resting place, he thinks, as the evening crowds thin, and he curls up on the sidewalk still thinking of the priest who had taken him to rehab, the priest who had encouraged him to get dry, to pull his life together, who had listened to his story about the woman who had spoken to him about rolling green hills ever since he could remember. Tim had listened and had not judged him, did not think any of the stories strange. Tim had promised to take him to Ireland when he went next, but Romulus had not taken him seriously. He hid himself away and drank, but Tim knew. Tim was no fool. When he was drunk, Tim walked away from him and talked to someone else in the centre, ignored him, which only made Romulus feel worse, though he felt he deserved to be ignored. He hadn't told Tim about Ruth or about Christian. He'd told him only that he had gotten into some trouble back on the island and had assumed another man's identity whom he vaguely resembled. Tim had nodded when shown the papers but hadn't reported him. *I'll take you to Ireland with me*, he'd said, *next month or month after next. I can take you as part of your treatment and bring you back.* But Romulus didn't believe in strange coincidences that allowed your life to work out. He believed in paying for his crimes. The worst thing he could imagine was going dry and so he told Tim the night before he left the rehab centre with the men that he would be going. Tim had just nodded gravely and shook his hand, turned and walked away as if there was nothing left for him to do. Romulus had cried himself to sleep that night as if he had been abandoned by his father.

It's then he hears the small voice, a girl's voice, asking him how he is, even as he remains slumped on the sodden ground, his pockets emptied, pellets of rain falling all around him.

"Are you all right?" the voice says again.

He thinks he's dreaming and keeps his eyes closed. At his worst moments, his mind always wanders to the women in his life, to the women he has loved and who eventually left him. His girl-child. The women who used to come to his concerts yelling out a version of his god-given name.

"Are you alright?" the voice says again, and this time he feels a hand prodding him at the elbow, pulling at him. He pulls his elbow in, refusing the voice, the hand, the gestures of compassion.

"He doesn't seem well," another voice says. Another girl, another voice from the past.

Something breaks in his chest, a filament of the web that has been holding him together ever since he returned here to find that there was nothing left to come back to: no home, no woman, no holy child, only the habits of his mind, habits he'd picked up on the street as a teenager, survival habits. He finds himself weeping, the warmth of his tears mildly comforting in the cold of the rain.

"Let's get him up." A teenage boy's voice, quietly authoritative the way they often are even when their owners aren't sure who they are or who they might become. Romulus thinks of Christian, wonders whether Christian's voice had begun to take on this assertiveness. Then he remembers why he is here in the northeast rather than at his son's side, and the tears fall more plentifully.

The three young people pull him to his feet, prop him up between their young bodies. One puts a clean but torn garbage bag around his body. "For protection," she says, ignoring the fact that his clothes are already soaked through.

"Let's take him to the boathouse," the boy says.

"It's locked," one of the girls says.

"It's always locked," the older one says.

"I've got a key," the boy says.

"You've got a key?" the first girl says, incredulous.

"That's right," he says.

"Right on," the other girl says.

The four of them stumble up the hill and make their way towards the river at the back of the school. There's a boathouse there. Romulus remembers lying on the other side of the bank on another day, sitting under leafy trees, watching the kids paddle around in the pond. He doesn't remember ever being so young.

The boathouse is dingy, dusty. The large windows facing the pond are dirty but let in moonlight. Boats dance like corks on the water in the half-darkness.

"Where are we going to put him?"

The boy hesitates, then Romulus feels the certainty in the boy's grip before he speaks. "There," he says, "against the wall."

They move towards the side of the boathouse like some strange sea animal with too many legs for dry land and then they collapse into a heap against it. The young people disentangle themselves from his arms and legs quickly, almost reverently, and this makes him cry all the more. His weeping is silently dignified, as if his tears are simply a mirror of the rain showers outside. The young people look up to the ceiling as the falling water dances on the corrugated roof making a sound like music.

"It will let up soon," the boy says.

"Here," one of the girl says, and hands him a wet bag. It smells like food. His stomach growls. He remembers his hunger at the scent of the food.

"Thank you," he says finally.

"Yeah, sure," the boy says, embarrassed. "Just try to get out of here as soon as it's light, OK?"

He nods. He knows all about making quick exits. "No worries," he says. "No worries." He looks away from the fresh faces of the three, watching as they hesitate and then finally move away from him back out into the darkness of the wet night.

One of the girls stops at the front of the boathouse after the others have gone. She pauses and stares at him as if she has a message for him but can't quite decipher the meaning of the words she's about to say.

"I'll see you around," she finally says, not saying what is on her mind.

"Yeah," he mumbles, suddenly exhausted, the bag of cold food still pressed in his hand. "Sure." He tries to smile, even though he speaks to her back as she turns to follow her friends.

He hears the wooden door clang shut and the space is enveloped in darkness. He is sitting on a dry piece of ground. The river water in the middle of the boathouse gently rocks back and forth. That and the sound of the falling rain above lull him to sleep almost immediately. He sleeps sitting up with the dull throb in his head fading into his dreams.

Down in the streets, by the time Romulus can recognize how lucky he has been throughout his life, he finds he has already fallen so far that he has emerged, whole, on the other side of remorse, covered with the same film of blood, mucous and shit that had covered his firstborn on the day of his emergence into the fine, fine world.

May 24, 2004

"What's your name?" a voice asks him.

It's morning, again. The boats in the water next to him are butting against the wood of the uneven floor of the boathouse. Romulus rubs his eyes, loosening the crusts that the tears from the previous night have created on his lashes. The blue of early morning light floods the interior of the boathouse. The windows in front of him seem cleaner because of the light, as if they have been cleansed by virtue of the dawn.

291

"What do they call you?" the voice asks again.

Romulus sits up and twists his torso in the direction of the voice, wincing as he does so, his body stiff and sore from the tussle with Henry. He remembers it all, for once, since he hasn't been drinking. He peers up at the girl standing there. Her body posture bespeaks fear and curiosity. One of her hands lingers on the door behind her while her opposite foot seems to reach out towards him like an offering. Light encircles her and she seems to shimmer there, balanced in the threshold between his life and whatever lies beyond. He hears panting then realizes she has a white-haired dog on a leash at her feet. It's a small dog, a terrier, the kind of dog he would never own. Romulus isn't sure what is being offered and if he should be entertaining it.

"John," he finally says to her, not wanting to be familiar with this strange, waif-like girl who would do better to leave strange men like him be.

"You don't look like a John," she says then, suspiciously.

Her tone makes him laugh. The white-haired dog barks. She smiles.

The smile startles him. It unveils her youth, her innocence, and reminds him of his own corruption. He looks away from her and back towards the dingy windows. His clothes are stiff, still heavy from the night rains. What does she want with him?

"And yours?" he asks her, still facing the windows, listening to the lapping of the water against the wooden floor beneath him. He becomes suddenly aware of how tenuous everything is around him, the beams holding the boathouse erect over them, his aching bones, this girl in her posture of anxiety.

"My what?" she responds, as if she has suddenly lost track of why they are there, of how they had been acquainted in the rain the night before, that she is a skinny white girl in a boathouse alone with a coloured man.

"Your name," he stretches back to look at her again.

She looks forlorn, her rose-pink skin glowing in the early morning light. *Whiter than white*, he thinks, a phrase he'd heard from African Americans down in Miami. *So white she's gotta be black*. He peers at her again. She is holding the same posture, the same uncertainty locked in her muscles. She seems to be weighing whether or not to be afraid even though her face reveals the curiosity that keeps her firmly rooted there, frail and strong all at once like a water lily growing out of mud despite itself.

"Oh, that," the girl seems slightly embarrassed then, as if she has forgotten her well-bred manners.

This surprises him since there is no reason for her to stand on ceremony with him. He is just a homeless guy to her, a hobo, scum even. He looks away from her then, not wanting her to see the self-loathing spreading across his face, a loathing that spreads from his innermost self to whatever thoughts he is forming about her. If he were a different kind of man, she could very well be in danger. What if someone happened by and caught them there, talking to each other, and did not think that it was all that innocent? The light on the other side of the windows brightens.

"Sun's almost all the way up," he says, not to her in particular. The water around the boats slaps against the wood as if in response. The ground he is sitting on is not stable at all.

"You remind me of my father," she says, almost in a whisper.

The words startle him and his blood runs cold. An image of Christian in a casket floats through his mind. He shivers in his stiff clothes. What he would do for a warm fire. He doesn't look in her direction. "You wouldn't want me as a father."

The dog whimpers.

"Yea, well, my father was a drunk like you."

This stops him. He holds his breath then says, "I'm more than a drunk," thinking of his panoply of drugs over the years.

"So was he," she responds, defence laid like bricks between each word.

He relents, looks at her, still at the door, lit up like some angelic figure.

"I'm sure he was," he says.

"He was a teacher."

"What did he teach?"

"High school English."

He nods at her, imagines her a little girl, some other man's daughter.

"For a minute, yesterday," she continues, "I thought you were him."

Whiter than white, he thinks again. Like some of the children he'd had, pale like Christian. Like Catherine. There's nothing to say to that.

"Don't worry," she says, "I realized you weren't him right away. I'm not going to come after you for child support."

This makes him laugh, even though it isn't a laughing matter. Laughing not to cry. Then, he stands up and walks towards her on shaky legs. The dog, agitated at his movements, barks and lunges towards him at the end of his short leash. The girl yanks him back.

"Stop, Ryan," she says. "He's OK."

"How do you know?" he asks.

"Like I said," she responds, moving away from the door and fully into the light, "you remind me of my father."

He squints at her, takes in the fine features of her face, the long face that reminds him of the woman from his dreams, the grey eyes so much the same. The only difference is her hair, blond and straight, framing the high cheekbones, the narrow, thin lips. "You didn't tell me your name."

"You didn't tell me yours."

He measures her with his eyes then decides to tell the truth. "Romulus," he says.

She nods, smiles slightly, "Siobhan."

He hears her name like the flapping of butterfly wings, imperceptible but capable of creating storms on the other side of the world. The sound moves something deep within him, makes his heart lurch the way it did when he heard Brigitte tell him that his son was dead, the pain making him come alive like nothing else had in years, no, decades.

"Siobhan," he whispers. Green hills like nothing he's ever known. "Irish?" he asks.

"Yes," she says, then smiles, "Black Irish."

He laughs at her joke, then says seriously, "I'm sure he misses you."

"He better," she says ruefully, and he wonders if Christian had thought of him in this way, with desperate, wistful, hopeless longing.

"I'm sure your father thinks about you all the time," he says, trying to be comforting despite the ridiculousness of the situation, the stink of his body like an impenetrable sheet of glass between them.

"Sure," she says doubtfully, "when he can remember his name."

"When he can remember his name," he echoes, nods, acknowledging the effects of addiction. "Yeah, sure, when he can remember he has a name."

"I'm glad we met you last night," she says.

He doesn't know what to say. The girl doesn't know anything about him, who he is, who he's been. What can he say to this? He is taking in the light streaming all around her. The light is bright, orange-hued, caramel-like. The sky beyond is a cottony blue. If this had been any other day in his life, he would have thought it was a beautiful sunrise, but since his life was as it was, he thought only that it would be a good day for others, like her.

"It makes me feel like he might come back," she continues.

"But he might not," he says, thinking of the man whose name he borrowed to leave Haiti behind, thinking of the men in the Springfield shelter trying against hope to scrub away the dirt of their lives, thinking of Christian overdosing in some skanky alleyway.

"Times change," she adds, in a voice older than her years. "Anyway, I just came here to make sure that you were… well, still alive or whatever… and Colin, my boyfriend, thought you might like these."

He hears paper crinkling as she extends another brown bag towards him. He advances into the light. He looms over her. He passes a hand over his shaved head to make himself seem smaller and gives her a sideways glance.

"I don't bite," he says, piqued by her body language.

The girl steps back, and then forward towards him. "I know," she says even though her voice betrays uncertainty. "It's just breakfast food." She shrugs as she hands him the bag as if to counter whatever disappointing response he might give.

He takes the bag from her. "Breakfast food? I didn't even eat what you left me last night." He gestures to the spot where he had slept through the night while rain pelted the corrugated roof of the boathouse.

The girl is looking at the soiled bag with the leftovers they had left with him the night before. She shrugs again. "We figured you might be hungry." She pauses and stares at him. "I've got to go," she continues. "We just wanted to make sure you'd be OK from here on out."

"Yeah, OK, I got it. You all are concerned about my getting you in trouble, is that it?"

She stares at him again, hard. There is a coolness in her grey eyes that makes him feel ashamed of himself. She is so young, trying so hard.

"No," she says, that strength again in her voice. "We – I – just wanted to see how you were. Do for you what I *can't* do for my father." She turns away from him then, back towards the light at the door. "You have any kids?" She peers at him and her eyelashes are translucent. He thinks of each of his children when they were small, fine eyelashes framing their large eyes. It was all they had in common, those eyelashes, those big eyes.

"Three," he says. "One just died. Two, I guess."

"No," she says, "you'll always have three. What was his name?"

"Chris-tian. Christian," he stumbles on the name, a ball of shame rising up his gullet.

"OK," she says, "Christian. I'll remember that."

Then she is gone with the white terrier bouncing on its short legs at her heels. He feels loss and pride for this girl some other man has left behind, a girl who has departed with his son's name on her lips, as if to keep his son alive in spite of him.

He watches her disappear, hears her muffled footsteps through the tall grass beyond the door and then peers into the brown bag she brought him. There are two raisin-studded rolls sitting there and he eats them while watching the sun rise. For a moment, he feels as if he is inhabiting someone else's life, someone else's body, as if he might be *normal* or as close to normal as he could become these days.

As he munches on the rolls, he pretends that Siobhan is his daughter and that he is a doting father visiting the college from far away. He imagines that he might meet her and her friends later to take a walk along the riverbank. A murmur of voices floats down towards him from the top of the hill and he laughs at himself. It is time to resume his act as an invisible man, to blend into the foliage, make tracks along the soft earth close to the river, disappear.

By the time the kids from the college reach the boathouse, he is long gone, a solitary figure they can hardly make out edging his way into the forest beyond the school grounds like a ghost returning to its grave.

August 12, 2004

The plane is descending quickly and Romulus looks around the plane at the faces of the others who are also making their way to Dublin, some to go home, some to discover a new country. Most have smiles on their faces and Romulus feels as if they are all meant to be on the plane together, like strange angelic creatures suddenly sent out to do some good down below. He looks over at Father Tim who is rearranging his rucksack full of books, papers and pens. He had been working on something during the flight; Romulus didn't know what. He wonders if Father Tim is going to say mass after their arrival in Ireland and is preparing a sermon. He isn't sure what day of the week it is, whether there's a Sunday around the corner, but the world is full of Sundays, days set apart for contemplation by other names in every culture.

He looks around and has the strange sensation that they are bodies floating in space, their body tissues suddenly light and filled with possibility. The feeling gives him a little high and he wonders if happiness feels something like this, if all it takes is a disciplined suspension of disbelief to turn the corner and start a new life.

Father Tim looks over at him as he finishes straightening out his things and pushes back the bag under the seat in front of him with his feet.

"I'm glad you came back, Romulus," he says, using his proper name even though it isn't the name on his papers. "I'm glad you came clean."

Romulus nods. It's been a long journey. He isn't even sure why or how he's come to trust the Irish priest. A couple of days after the meeting with Siobhan, he'd left the one-horse town and made his way back to Springfield, had a shower and picked up some half-decent clothes from the pile in the basement, a clean pair of loose, worn blue jeans and an off-grey sweatshirt with red accents with the letters "U. of Mass" emblazoned on the front. He'd hitchhiked all the way back to the rehab in Boston and found Father Tim in the rectory next door, praying.

If Tim was surprised to see Romulus Pierre, he didn't show it. All he cared was that Romulus was back in the fold, was avoiding the others who had drugs smuggled in, avoiding the paper cups filled with amber liquid that stank of the life the man needed to put behind him.

Weeks went by and Romulus remembered, remembered, and allowed the pain of the past to flow over him in acknowledgement that re-encountering it would be the only way to heal the future he didn't know yet, the future that might look something like the carefree innocence of Siobhan, if he could remember, if he could get to know his other children, and make amends to Christian by emerging out of this mess a new kind of man. He was forced to remember the strange turns his life had taken.

Slowly, imperceptibly, Romulus began to recollect, and own, snippets of his past life – an early childhood that had been more joyful than embittered, a sister and mother who had played with him when he was still small, a father who had smiled at his antics behind the sheets of newspaper that hid him from view at the breakfast and dinner table.

The house they had lived in before his mother had left had been filled with imposing furniture made of *acajou*, the dark wood that had become scarce over the years and golden in price. It had had five rooms and two shared bathrooms; one of the extra rooms served as a study for his father, while another was set up to receive guests, usually a family member from his father's side down on his or her luck and in need of a place to re-group. The house had a courtyard out the back where a small building housed the kitchen and the help's quarters. In those days, the house was considered modest, its household staunchly middle- class. These days it would have been termed luxurious.

He had a pet dog there, a small black pup that had wandered out of nowhere into their yard. No one had the heart to turn her away and she grew alongside him, a faithful companion.

In those days, he'd never noticed his father's aloofness. His mother had been enough for him, filling his days with activities or letting him do as he wanted when Constance was away at school. With the dog, Ni, named after one of the cooks, Ninette, who gave the pup scraps from the table after she'd cleared the remains of meals away, he spent many of his days out of doors, exploring the dirt roads that led from their house away from the city and towards the countryside where the neighbours kept horses and work dogs.

On the weekends, his boy cousins, who registered in his mind as interesting only because they were older and stronger, would take him out to watering holes deep in the bush, in secret places he could not see from the house, even if he stood on the elevated porch overhanging the courtyard and pushed himself up against the balustrade on the tips of his small brown toes. Romulus was the youngest of the group. They called him *crapaud* – ugly as a toad, and slippery as one as well.

The cousins were often accompanied by friends from school who were spending their weekends at the country homes of relatives. The cousins usually left him alone but some of the friends tried to exercise their newfound masculinity by pushing him around, though Romulus, smaller and more agile, usually found a way to slip out of reach and into the water. He became a good swimmer on those weekend escapades, even better than his cousins who feigned dislike for him in front of their friends, saying that they were only letting him tag along because of their aunt. This was especially after she'd become so ill that she lay most days in bed without walking out to the front sitting room to drink *café crème* with the boys before sending them on their way with luncheon pails the cook had prepared for their journey to the ponds. Secretly, they were pleased that Romulus was clever enough to get away and they took pleasure in his swimming abilities that outstripped even their own. He was a good-natured boy after all. Why would they want to harm him?

Romulus had pushed back memories of this time into the deep corners of his mind. As his body purged itself of intoxicants in rehab, his memory had begun to resurface. It was as if he was still that small child, struggling against the older and stronger boys, his body slipping out of their grasp and plunging into the murky pond water, then letting go of his breath so that his body would sink down like a stone. In rehab, these recollections returned, sharp with detail.

Even though he'd only been five or six, fanning his arms out on both sides of him in the watery darkness, he'd felt less afraid of what might lurk beneath the pond's surface than he had been of his cousin's friends. He'd wait until their screams receded above him before bringing himself back up. Sometimes, he would sink as far down as the floor of the pond and sit there for a few seconds in a pose he would learn years later was the lotus position in yoga or Buddhism. He had allowed a girlfriend to drag him to a meditation workshop and found himself laughing so uncontrollably in the familiar pose that he had to be escorted out of the studio; the girl who'd taken him had never forgiven him the outburst. He'd thought it a moment of absurdity to discover in himself what the guru had called "Buddha" nature. At that time, he'd been on the verge of his first drug-induced breakdown.

In rehab, Romulus wondered if there had ever truly been a time when life was only a series of sun-filled, tranquil days following one another like the stringed pearls his mother wore to Sunday mass and on her birthday; or when the weeks flowed into each other like the relentless outpouring of underground streams making their way to rivers, to be joined there by rains falling from the heavens, from the four corners of the earth.

It had been a weekend like all the others. He followed his older cousins with an old towel slung over his right shoulder. It brushed the crevices of his back annoyingly, but in order to keep up with the older boys he did not stop to scratch it. They hardly glanced his way, measuring his progress only by the sound of his small feet falling on the grass behind their own footfall, and the wheezing thrust of his breath as he did his best to keep up.

That particular weekend, one of the cousins' friends had brought a new toy to the pond for them to play with. Romulus remembered the way the light fell on the blade, blinding him temporarily as the older boy held the hunting knife up above his head as if he were a Haitian Zorro. The boys took turns holding the knife, holding it up towards the sun to see the blade gleam, then thrusting it towards the other boys' bellies as they yelled out "'tention" and rounded their backs to keep out of reach. This was not the kind of play Romulus was used to. He was afraid of knives. He had seen what they could do to chickens – one day happily scratching at grain in the courtyard and the next stripped bare of their plumage lying belly up on a bed of stewed tomatoes. Knives were bad news as far as he was concerned. He made his usual exit into the pond as the boys laughed at him for not wanting to touch the blade.

At the bottom of the pond, his eyes open, his arms loosely moving at his sides against the weight of the water, the water flowing past his neck and through the thick curls of his hair, he watched the long, hair-like algae moving up from dirt, dancing along with his hands as if they had been waiting for his descent all along. Fish skirted past him and he felt their small, lithe bodies flicker against his skin. They reminded him of falling leaves in the fall, surprising him when they landed on him, reminders of the cycle of life and death all around him. With his eyes open under the surface of the murky water, the muted voices of the older boys swimming above him between the clouds and the roots of trees, he wondered if it might be possible to hold his breath forever and stay there with the underwater life. There were emptied shells beneath his feet and his hands stirred particles of disintegrating matter suspended in the water. It struck him that it might be something to come back in the next life as a fish or a mollusc with his own home on his back.

Romulus lay back on his cot and stumbled on the part of the memory that had forced him to lock the rest away, even the face of his mother on a day before illness had struck her down, when her hazel eyes shone brightly in the sunlight and he had walked hand in hand with her to and from the market to buy plantain or avocados for the midday meal.

He was still underwater and waiting for the vibrations of the voices above to diminish to let his body slowly float to the surface. He looked up and saw no shadows breaking the surface. Usually, when he stayed underwater for so long, the cousins would cluster around the edge of the pond and yell for him to come up, assuring him that the older, tougher boys were gone. On that particular day, everyone seemed to have gone. Romulus had felt a mixture of relief and dread – relief at the thought that they were all gone and that he might resurface to the forest and her magic, and dread that he would have to walk all alone through the trees as darkness fell.

He had unfolded his thin legs and pushed against the ground. The silty basin gave beneath his effort like a spongy spring. He felt the sand particles crowding between his toes. It was a familiar feeling. It calmed him as he raised his arms above his head and they felt even longer than they really were, as he pushed up. He felt the coolness of the air first as his hands reached out of the pond. His eyes were closed. He'd felt tempted to remain in the water, remain there in the warmth, in a hermetic world that seemed so much safer than the world of his boy cousins and their loutish friends. But he bobbed up to the surface, his head following his outstretched hands, the pond water streaming down his head and neck in droplets. He brought his arms down across his chest and shivered and looked around. The boys seemed to have gone. He began to swim towards the shore, wondering how he would get home and looked around for Ninou, who also appeared to have abandoned him.

He called out for her. There was an eerie silence as he climbed out of the water onto the sandy shore. He wiped the water from his eyes and looked about for his clothes. They were still there, slung over the lower branch of an old oak tree. As he advanced towards them, gingerly stepping across the protruding roots of the tree and uneven stones that kept him a little off balance, he heard stifled laughter. He looked behind him. There was no one. He turned back towards the clothes and the laughter came again. He hurried towards the clothes, tripping over a root as he did so and falling on his knees. He did not stop to notice the deep cut that had split open his right knee across the knee joint. He had a vague feeling of pain that was superseded by the acuteness of his fear and he felt a hot dampness oozing from the wound down his leg without registering that it came from his own body.

He dressed hurriedly, struggling with his clothes as they clung to the dampness of his body. He heard branches breaking beneath the weight of walking feet behind him but dared not look back.

Then he heard Ninou yelping behind the tree where he had left his clothes. He ventured behind the tree and found Ninou in a pool of blood. He stumbled towards her and held her head as she gazed up at him, trying to lick him. His small hands ran over the body looking for the source of the bleeding. He felt for lumps and cuts as he had always done from the day she'd been given to him. He wasn't sure what he was looking for until his right hand slipped from fur into flesh. He removed his hand and brought it up to his face. His hand was covered in red from the tips of his fingers to the base of his palms. He dropped his hands against Ninou's body who had inched her way into his lap. She licked the blood from his hand and whimpered.

Romulus sat there and cried, not knowing what to do.

The sound of breaking branches continued, and then, from behind him, came the voice that had sent him into the pond in the first place. The voice was laughing.

"Romeo! *Sé nom ou, pa vré*? How do you like that?"

Romulus didn't turn around.

"Turn around when I'm speaking to you."

Romulus just sat and continued crying until he could no longer see straight, until his thin body was curled over the dog's and shaking from hiccups. Where were the cousins?

"Do as he says, Romeo," he finally heard one of the cousins say.

He looked up and wiped at his eyes. The boys surrounded him. They were all there. The cousins' faces were grim. It was hard to tell whether they had been pushed into this by the older boys or if they too had wanted to harm him. Ninou was no longer whimpering. Her small frame was no longer lifting and deflating as she struggled to breathe. Romulus knew enough about the difference between life and death to know that she was gone. He stood up, his two hands clenched in small fists at his side. He was ready to turn around and fight, to do whatever it took to avenge Ninou, his only true friend.

He turned, ready to fight, to find a boy two feet taller than he was holding a knife in front of his chest as if he was ready to let Romulus fall onto the blade and call the movement an accident. Romulus froze. What were the cousins doing? He looked around the circle of boys. They were all just standing there, watching him

303

and the boy with the long blade as if they were at a movie show, as if they were absolutely helpless. It was then that Romulus realized that blood was not necessarily thicker than water. Fear was thicker than anything. Fear and self-preservation. The two in combination could lead to all sorts of betrayals.

Romulus turned back towards the boy with the blade. The boy sneered at him. Romulus took a step back. The boy advanced, grimacing, the soft, boyish lines of his face twisting themselves into a maniacal mask of ill intent. The evil that bloomed across the boy's young face was startling enough for Romulus, who had never seen anything like it, to step back in sheer surprise. Evil was something that he assumed only existed in adults, on movie-screens, and in the streets after night fell and he was safe indoors. It had never occurred to him that evil was a seed that could be set to bloom in the most innocent of grounds, in a boy who seemed so much like himself that he would have done anything to emulate him, to be accepted by him. At that moment, Romulus realized that the cousins would just stand and watch him fall on the knife blade, just as they had probably stood around as he had sunk like a stone to the bottom of the pond, and watched the boy slice open Ninou's stomach so that she could not walk without losing her intestines, could not find him to warn him with her highpitched barks about the impending danger.

The fear of the boys in the circle and his own aloneness fell on Romulus like a dark shadow that he was afraid would simply swallow him up. He felt his neck drop back and a scream loose from his throat even though at the same time he felt nothing at all. It was in that moment of looking up that he had seen her for the first time, the woman of the pale face who, so many years later, he had come to call Elsie, for reasons that were beyond him. He had seen a face hovering in the clouds, a woman's face, pale like the cloud matter from which she had emerged, her skin milky, her eyes soft and limpid. She smiled at him the way he imagined angels smiled from the images he had seen in the illustrated children's Bibles they read from in Sunday school, books that contained no images of brown-skinned people. Wherever she came from, Elsie seemed out of this world, safe, an envoy sent to him just for that moment. Romulus found himself praying to the face since, in the next moment, he might very well find himself huddled up between the legs of a tree, bleeding to death as Ninou had, never to see his mother's face again. In that moment, Romulus even missed his silent and aloof father. But Elsie was there, looking over him, watching out for him.

The sound rising from his throat was grating, loud, a howl like an old dog's when it has no routine and no master, just reflex left over from habit. His body felt leaden. He felt the weight of his arms as they hung from their shoulder sockets. He felt the scissoring of his shoulder blades and the weight of his rib-cage, weights so heavy he thought he might collapse there and then. The older boy continued staring him down, grimacing crazily with the knife outstretched in front of him, the blade suspended between them and held tautly there by the boy's tightened muscles. Romulus could see the boy's muscles straining, coiled and ready to lunge at him and plunge the knife into his flesh. Ninou's blood was still on the blade, not yet fully dried.

Romulus closed his eyes as he felt the muscled body moving towards him and readied himself for the knife thrust, the blade pushing past the surface flesh of his body, splicing him open like an animal. It was then that he heard someone say, *Water doesn't run upstream.* It was a woman's voice, soft, careful. And even though he understood the words, they weren't in any language he had ever heard. Was it the woman from the clouds speaking to him? His mind decided then that it must have been his mother speaking from her sick-bed, reaching out to him as if their souls were crossing each other's in a space made for people reaching out of bodies from fear, on the threshold between safety and insecurity, life and certain death. Was this how his mother felt as she sank more deeply into illness day by day? Her body growing heavy and her eyes turned to the heavens in search of respite? Was this where she receded to on the days when he spoke to her by the side of her bed, while she lay, her head held up by her pillow covered over with her favourite blue slip, her lips moving but no sound seeming to come out of her mouth – this place where spirits crossed and spoke to each other without moving their lips?

At the moment when the blade should have pushed through skin, he felt only the boy's shoulder push his body aside while the other boys followed him out of the forest, leaving Romulus behind, fallen on the ground, dazed, wondering what the standoff had really been about, his dog still at his feet, her fur matted with her own coagulated blood.

Romulus almost wished that the gaps in his memory would not return. He knew their recovery would lead to more unsavoury recollections, to actions he may have committed under the influence of his intoxications and nights out on the town. He had vague memories of being verbally abusive to his wives and had blocked out whatever he may have said or done to his children. He wondered what Christian remembered and the thought that Christian might think of him as he did that young boy with the knife by the pond, as some sort of incarnate evil, made him curl up into a ball against the tired covering of his mattress, and place one of his large hands in front of his face to hide the tears that slowly meandered across his weathered cheeks.

In detox, Romulus came to remember that his relationship to time in prison had shifted as the days passed, had become more fluid, less frantic. He had not then been able to see an end to his ordeal and so the gradually accumulating days gave him a sense of the movement of time even as he had stayed still in the cell, moving only to get to the urinal or the water bucket – difficult as it was to tell the difference between the two. The prisoners distinguished them by smell.

In detox, Romulus got through the days of sweats and shakes, remembering nights when he had crawled into a corner of the cell and furrowed in excrement like an animal. He had folded into corners in a foetal position, his hands gripping the bricks for dear life. He had wanted to howl with the pain he felt in his twisting intestines but he found a way to silence in the darkness, surrounded by the raspy breathing of the other prisoners. It hadn't take him long to realize that the men surrounding him had had far harsher lives. Some were criminals. Some were not. They were locked in a shared fate. They were brothers despite themselves. There was no room for softness of character; no room for tears.

Water doesn't flow upstream.

Romulus found himself wading into the cool water of a river pond. Mist from falling water sprayed his face and he opened his eyes to see the foam of a waterfall hitting the surface of the pond in which he was standing. The water soothed him and he watched himself in the dream as if he was a ghost or an angel looking down from the beyond at his bare and muscular shoulders, as he tipped his face back, closed his eyes, and waited for the mist to settle on the surface of his skin again, relieving him of the heat that had been burning him up from the inside for days on end. His shoulder blades relaxed and his long arms dipped down into the water where he opened up his hands, letting the fingers go loose, splaying them open, trying to hold the coolness. He recognized the pond from his childhood and the recognition brought him into the body he was watching, feeling from within his younger self the relief of the cool water, of the long shadows cast by the overhanging, full-lipped branches of the nearby banana trees.

Water doesn't flow upstream.

He heard the voice again and thought of the waterfall. A true statement. The river pond was evidence of it. The water falling over the outcrop of rock a testament. He relaxed more profoundly, the muscles in his back letting go of the tightness stored from curling up in the dank corner of the cell all of those many nights. He could have stood there forever but something from beneath the surface of the water suddenly swirled through and around his legs, forcing him to open his eyes and to bend forward, peering into the water, using his hands to part the surface to see beneath. It was a snake. He couldn't tell if it was poisonous or not. But, before he could move anywhere, the pool filled with snakes. They were even falling with the waterfall, turning its cascade into a dark brew.

Romulus panicked. He looked into the surrounding forest and wondered what lay beyond the trees. He tried to move forward, to push through the thickening pond water, to ignore the piling bodies of the slick sinewy snakes. He wondered if he should try to swim through them. It was the panic that drew him down into the swirling currents where the snakes seemed to be waiting to drag him down by twining around his limbs.

Water doesn't flow upstream, the voice said again. It was clear to Romulus as he watched himself drowning, felt the snake bodies wet and fluid against the skin of his arms and legs, closing around his neck, that he hadn't understood the words' meaning and that it was now too late to do anything about it.

He woke from the dream with a vague but deep feeling of loss, and a notion that his mother had been a witness to his shameful fall from grace, wherever she was.

Romulus had turned over and sat up on the cot he had been assigned in rehab, wondering when the days would stop piling one on top of the other, realizing again that this was the first time in twenty years that he had truly been clean.

"What made you change your mind?" Tim asks.

"A dream," Romulus says, thinking of Elsie's face in the prison cell, of Christian's little boy face, of Siobhan, the virtual stranger who had cared enough to find him a dry place to sleep, who had brought him some food as one of his children might have done. He smiles at Father Tim. "A dream of green, rolling hills and air heavy with salt."

Father Tim smiles at Romulus with paternal pride, even though he is at least ten years his junior, "Ah my lad," he says in a mock Irish accent since he now spoke like an American, "here's where you'll be coming home."

August 13, 2004, Ireland

> *The currachs are sailing way out on the blue*
> *Laden with herring of silvery hue*

He navigates the streets with care, like a boat with a delimited area in which to flow with the currents. Father Tim is his rudder, clasping him by the elbow to stir him towards and away from things, paving the way with his ruddy cheeks and wide smile, his glittering square teeth when in the rural areas men and women stare at them for too long, stare at this stranger in their midst with a skin that reminds them of imported copper pans from the north of France. Like them, he's exotic, and disturbing in an age when some Irish feel overrun by migrants, with Africans making their way across Europe in search of a better life, while the Irish feel as if they are just beginning to enjoy their new prosperity. Theirs is the last stop before falling into the ocean.

Romulus finds a flourishing country, the streets are wide and paved, smooth beneath the wheels of the rented Fiat they pick-up at the airport, and drive all the way across the wide girth of the island from Dublin to Galway where they will rest a night before moving on to Father Tim's county, Connemara, and from there down to Dingle where he will be assisting with Father Tim's youth programme by exchanging folk songs from their two countries. He has prepared *Ayiti Chérie* for the occasion, even though he thinks it lacks relevance in these days when Ayiti is falling to pieces, no longer dear; he's prepared Belafonte's *Yellow Bird* and Haiti's official anthem, *La Dessalinienne*, which he thinks his fellow countrymen should really be listening to, a call to arms, to patriotism. They know all about that here, fighting for your country, fighting for your land. Father Tim had given him the sheet music to *Connemara Cradle Song* and so he has learned that and a few other things that he thought might come in handy if the young men at the programme should stare at him with their flecked grey and green eyes and wonder what a man like him has crossed the ocean for.

Father Tim talks as they drive and Romulus peers out at the land's ruggedness. It is early in the morning and the fog jockeys low over the undulating terrain as if upon the backs of horses. Father Tim talks about his family, his mother and father they are about to stay with, who run a bed and breakfast business out of their home, of the six siblings with whom he was raised, four of them priests like him, the two girls married with small children. Father Tim speaks with his hands flying from the steering wheel with such rhythm that Romulus worries at times that neither hand is steering them but, somehow, they stay on course, guided by the grey of the road beneath them, the coarse ground on both sides of the road seeming to move swiftly, swiftly past.

Christian has been dead for five months now and for the past couple of months Romulus has been clean and sober. He thinks about his son daily. As they drive from one side of Tim's land to the other, he imagines describing what he sees to his departed son: the wild grass, the ancient ruins sitting in the middle of fields encircled with low fences, cows grazing all about, the signage for places written in a language he cannot decipher the further they head west, white letters on green, the gauntness of working men they meet at roadside cafes, their raven-black hair, the flinty eyes, some dark, some light, the way they pour cream into their coffee as if it is the most natural thing in the world.

"English influence," Tim says when he sees Romulus staring.

Romulus shrugs, smiles. "Like *café au lait*," he says then, "French influence."

They laugh at this, together. Their laughter contains the knowledge of island people who have had to struggle for their harsh piece of earth, for the one, withstanding the hiss of the slave master's whip, for the other, the door shut in the face of hunger by the master of the house. A hard-won brotherhood forged across the years of want and hope, though now memory for one, and continuing reality for the other – everything they had once thought only someone just like them could understand, meaning someone from home, from their island.

As they head back onto the road, Romulus realizes that Father Tim is speaking as he is, like a torrent without end, because he has known the loneliness of insularity, of a place hemmed in by ocean water. The sweetness of salt in the air becomes bitter on the tongue when it is the only water given to purge thirst. He too has known the solitude of a fisherman out to sea with only his vessel for company.

The more Romulus realizes the beauty of their uncommon alliance, the more his resolve grows to turn away from the easy lure of losing himself in another drink, another quick fix. The sensations wafting over his body, penetrating his pores, attain an almost electric purity. Each wave of feeling, each flurry of awakening, he sends on to Christian, wherever he is, with the poignant realization that Christian had probably known more about life and living than he would ever have been able to impart himself. And what had Christian done in the end? For want of guidance, followed in his father's footsteps. He'd never heard that Christian was doing drugs, or was in trouble, heard nothing from the other children, from Brigitte, from Ellen. It must have been something recent, all of a sudden, improvised to get his attention when his back was turned. The boy – his son – must have heard that he had been let out of prison, as they all had, innocent and guilty alike, let loose to face a burned and looted world, the capital lying in ruins at their dirty feet. He must have guessed that Constance would put him on a plane, destination Miami. His son had reached out and he hadn't heard the call.

Here, Romulus hears everything, the constant flow of Father Tim's words, the scream of the cormorants that make him think of banshees, the wild spirit women of Tim's nighttime stories, the sharp whistle of the wind bearing low like a burglar as it creeps and swoops over the ground. He hears every sprout of grass breaking through loam, hears the ghostly memories of the impatient hooving of moist ground by workhorses, the murmur of men as they amble out of the pubs warbling sea shanties to make their mothers blush. He hears all these echoes of the past and the redolent remembrances of childhood and young adulthood surge up from his once dormant memory, from glad moments to the most pained, and he can withstand it. He can actually withstand the cacophony of regret, despair, even *love* – that word he would never utter and thought he'd never felt. And the magic of it is that the heart muscles can take the pain, the hurt, the disappointment of everyday life, and still beat, beat, beat.

His heart breaks open as they make their way past pastures filled with bleating sheep standing like sentinels in the wilderness, their heavy coats pelted with rain. They stand there in the middle of the road and Father Tim has to swing around them, laughing as their small red car makes its way past. And the sheep stand, sheepishly (now he understands the word), as if this is the way it should be, as if they are meditating and in search of grander gods than the men who sweat milk and Guinness and brand them with their names so each flock can be told apart. They are looking beyond all of this, these sheep: they know something that isn't readily apparent to the eye.

Silver the herring and silver the sea
And soon they'll be silver for my love and me

Of love, Romulus knows very little more than the sum of the emotions he has allowed himself to feel in the culmination of these last few weeks. He sees it in Father Tim's eyes when the man looks over at him with paternal pride. He sees it in the eyes of Father Tim's mother and father when the couple open the door wide to their house and their eyes flicker imperceptibly, recovering within a nanosecond, at the dusky colour of his skin. They force themselves to look right into his eyes and they see him, they see *him*. It takes only a beat for them to weigh his worth, to allow for his difference, to inform them of his passage to their land, to take him as a son along with their own and show him to a room the two of them will share with two narrow twin beds and a small colour TV perched on the edge of a childhood dresser.

Father Tim's mother beams as she shows them the improvements she has made to the room, the hand-stitched window coverings, the new rug, the heavy, down-filled pillows for weary travellers. She points to the framed photos of their ancestors on the wall, the faces fading, the edges browning, oxidizing. Father Tim smiles and nods his approval. Romulus can tell that Tim is a favoured son and feels no jealousy. He is grateful to be included. His heart swells in his chest. It feels so large that it hurts and he wonders if love can be the prelude to a shortage of blood-flow, an arrest of the heart, but it keeps on beating and he breathes, long slow breaths, the intake and outtake necessary for life.

He peers at one of the photos as Tim and his parents flow out of the room and he sees the woman from his nightmares and hallucinations. The woman of the green, green country.

"Who is this?" he asks, and Father Tim returns, looks over his shoulder, and says,

"Great Aunt Elsie. She went to the Americas a long time ago and was never seen again. To the islands, they say, to your land: Ayiti!" Father Tim grins. Then, grimly, "They say she lost her mind there. She was incarcerated at the end, there, behind bars, in an asylum… because she claimed she could see things."

"Things?"

"Yes. Like the future. Said she talked to spirits and things like that." Tim pauses. "I always wondered if she was some kind of mystic. Come before her time. They would have understood her here, I think, but she didn't want to stay. She left during the famine, you know, when everyone was leaving."

Romulus leans back into Tim and the men stand there, as one, braced, looking on at the photograph of a woman with a long, thin face, her eyes small and dark, her features fine, the cheekbones high, the oval head framed by long, black hair. A young woman in the prime of life. She is standing next to a chair wearing the clothes of a domestic worker.

"She kept house for a living," Tim continues, "until she left."

"What became of her? Did she marry?"

"They say she landed on the other side with child, but we're not sure after that except there was word of her being put away. A rumour really. I suppose they blended in, integrated, that kind of thing. She never came back. Elsie Maeve O'Connor."

Upon hearing the woman's full name, Romulus' mouth runs dry and he remembers the face floating on the wall in his prison cell. The woman whose voice he heard as Marc called to him from the streets alight with smoke and fire. The woman he never saw again after Ruth was struck down. They are braced against each other, like brothers, Father Tim and he, with one man thinking of the unseen land of his ancestor, and the other thinking of the blood on his hands.

At night, after a healthy meal of fresh, steamed haddock and greens with fried red tomatoes, they adjourn to the beach where they walk the length of its sharp grey stones to watch the tide break against the shore. To Romulus, each wave seems like a fish showing off its silvery scales and returning to its source. He has never felt so free and wonders if this feeling might be close to happiness, a word he's never considered before, and never thought he'd know after that fateful call from Brigitte, and the news of Christian's death.

They sleep in the twin beds side by side, Father Tim and he, like brothers. While Father Tim snores in the bed next to his, his head back on the pillow, his mouth wide open, Romulus thinks.

313

The whistling, wheezing sound doesn't disturb him. Rather, it wants to make him laugh. It tickles him with life. *This* is what it's like to have a brother, he thinks to himself, giddy with the normalcy of the moment, his bright eyes looking out into the dark of the room and the gnomish shapes of the furniture and knick-knacks suspended on the walls and sitting on shelves. *This* is life. Then he falls asleep curled like a baby on his side.

In the morning, showered and fresh for the day, they descend to the dining room. There are guests at the inn and the large space, a converted sitting room with a fireplace and bay window, is filled with tables, filled with bodies dressed in long pants and warm woollens, women and men and children, couples and families.

Tim's mother gestures them to a table for two in the middle of the room and they are served an Irish breakfast of toast and eggs, lean ham and stewed tomatoes. They pour milk in their tea in perfect unison and Romulus looks at their hands, white and brown, picking up the china teacups gently, as if they were to the manor born. His chest fills with mirth and his head swirls with the conversations going on all around them while they eat in silence.

Two women next to them are speaking conspiratorially, even though one speaks so loudly that the whole room can hear. *I didn't even recognize her*, she says of an old friend she'd come from England to visit after thirty years of silence. *She was round, I tell you, round and ruddy like a tomata. Is that you, I says to her, you know, when I see there aren't any other ladies with red sashes around their waist and her big, dimpled face breaks out into a smile and I'm thinkin' this can't be, she used to be such a skinny thing, my Suzie, and then this voice streams out of that wide face, a voice I recognize from our schooldays and I know it's her even though the package is altogether wrong and we talk for hours on a park bench. When I look at her, I can't believe it, I just can't accept that it's her, but when I shut my eyes and listen to her voice, I'm brought back thirty years and it's as if no time, I mean, no time, has passed at all.* The woman pauses as her companion munches thoughtfully on her toast. *Very strange indeed*, the woman continues.

As she falls silent, a group of four older women behind them pore over glossy brochures as they debate where their route will take them today. *To the Arans*, one of them says. *No, into the rough of the Burren*, says another, *to the Cliffs of Moher. No*, yet another says, *let's stay here in Galway and shop in the old square.* The glossy leaflets are passed around and around until the only one that survives is the flyer listing the hours of the ferry to Inishmore and Inishmaan. *Islands of islands.* Romulus smiles. Islands of islands.

Tim's father comes up and brings another chair to the table. He sits in it back to front with the curve of its high back against his chest and his arms folded across the rounded wooden frame.

"What will you lads be doing today?"

They shrug and smile conspiratorially. They haven't thought ahead.

"We should probably move on, Da," Father Tim says, the Irish creeping into the tonalities of his syllables.

"You only just got here!" Tim's father exclaims, then turns to Romulus with wide eyes, "You've go to show your friend here the lay of our land."

"You're right, quite right," Father Tim says like a chastised child, not having explained quite clearly that Romulus is his charge and completing his first rehab cycle by doing a work-release programme here in Ireland under his rightful name.

Romulus' eyes go back and forth between the men. He's aware that something has not been said. That Father Tim has spared him a humiliation that others might have lorded over him. He smiles. Tim's father smiles back and slaps his back.

"You need to see our islands, son! Let me take you there."

"Da'," Tim says, "that's all right. I can take him."

The father clasps the upper part of his son's arm in a gesture both firm and sweet and Romulus' heart lurches, again, at the thought of his lost Christian. Father Tim sees the quiver in his lips. Romulus looks away.

"Lad, your mother has been waiting months to see ya. Why don't you spend the day with her? That'll make her happy right enough."

"Sure, Da', sure," he says, realizing that even grown men sometimes need fathers. "Sure."

And they are off before the ladies behind them even have time to wipe their lips on the cream-coloured napkins and push away from their table littered with crumbs.

315

It's a short skip and a hop to the ferry. Or so Tim's father says as he drives speedily from street to street, the neatly appointed houses on both sides watching them go by. It's early and the town is sleepy. Still, the ferry is filled with tourists, the early risers set on seeing Dun Aenghus, the 2,000-year-old Celtic fort perched on a cliff above the rolling waters of the Atlantic. Yet when they set foot on the island, Tim's father leads them in the opposite direction from the crowd, down a furrowed road, past herded cattle and isolated brick and straw houses with clothes pinned to lines set out in the wind to dry. Tim's father leads them off the road and onto a path leading up a small mountain. The sea seems far away at their backs.

"You'll want to see this," he says, pointing to a small heap at the top of the mountain.

Romulus wonders what it might be.

It takes them at least a half hour to reach the spot. The closer they get to it, the larger the heap becomes. It's a small structure of hewn stone, an ancient church, so the salt-eaten plaque erected on its leeward side says, one of the first in Christendom.

"Look out there," Tim's father says, pointing into the distance, and Romulus turns. Below him is the rolling green, the green, green of his dreams and clusters of grazing, dappled cows on whom the scenery is lost. Beyond them, an indigo blue sea stretches out for miles. Romulus loses his balance and reaches out to the stone of the old walls, feeling their roughness against his palm.

"Sit, sit," the old man says, smiling still. "I knew you would like this."

How does he know? How does anyone know what will move another man to the core and make him fall to his knees in repentance? Romulus' head spins, the turns of his life beyond understanding. He feels Christian here, in the air, in the sweet sea-salt currents. He sits on the solid ground, the stone at his back, Tim's father looms at his side looking out onto the pastures and the cut of ocean beyond. They are quietly reverent.

As the spinning in his head recedes like waters at low tide and they ready to descend the mountain, return to the ferry, return to the house on the other side of the water, Romulus looks to the ground for a stone to carry, some small memento he might one day place on his son's grave.

He searches until he finds the perfect stone. It is the size of a small chicken egg but purple through and through. He finds it half-submerged in a small pool of water by an outside corner of the small church that no longer has a roof and is so small that Romulus wonders how it could have served congregants. He ventures that they must have been a small people, comfortable with tight spaces, with none of the modern revulsion at the everyday stench of working men and women. As he thinks this, he flips over the stone in his hand, warming it between his palms and when he looks at it, still wet and damp from the rainwater it had been sitting in, he notices a faint white marking in the rose-purple of the stone.

"This can't be," he says.

"What is it?" Tim's father ambles back towards him. He was already on his way down the hill.

Romulus hands him the stone.

"Well, Jesus, Mary and Joseph. I'll be damned."

And what they see rising out of the drying stone is the cloudy form of a faceless, winged angel blessing them with grace.

On wings of the wind, o'er the deep rolling sea
Angels are coming to watch over thee

And though the shadowy shape disappears slightly when the stone is completely dry, it is still there. They carry it down the mountain as if it is gold and take the ferry back to the mainland in silence, allowing the choppy waves of the sea and the chatter of the returning tourists to cocoon them in their solitary under-standing.

Tim's father sits next to Romulus, pensive, his eyes bright and sad, as if he too is a man who has lost men to all kinds of waters. Tim's father tells him of his great-great aunt, a woman who had crossed the waters and gone on to the islands of the Americas many many tens, no at least a hundred years ago. Elsie. Elsie Maeve O'Connor. Who had gone from Connemara and left them all behind, leaving her sister to fend for herself in Galway where the family had grown and stayed. As a child, Tim's father had dreamed of a place pungent with exotic spices, of anise, clove, nutmeg and bright red peppercorns to be cracked open with the back of a silver spoon, whose dust seemed to cling to the fibres of the old, mildewed letters his grandmother had kept from a ghost that had never returned to them in body. *Pregnant she became, on the journey over the sea. And later her child had a child and so on until they became one with the island people, brown like you and Irish too.* Tim's father tells Romulus the story as if he knows what Romulus had realized when he saw the face in the photograph framed in the room he shared with Father Tim, that nothing can be escaped, that the past is contained in the present as well as the future. The woman he'd seen in his dreams when he had been sleepwalking through the world was both Catherine's great-great grandmother and Father Tim's ancestor. He could not trace exactly how and when the genealogy of their ancestry overlapped, but he knew with certainty that the ghost of his hauntings and the woman in the photograph were one and the same.

Romulus sits next to Tim's father and wishes that he could cry the river of tears streaming from the back of his eyes down to his heart, squeezing the life out of him. He clasps the stone in his pocket instead. His son, Christian, suddenly feels both far and near.

That night, in the narrow bed next to Father Tim, Romulus tosses and turns. The pain is overwhelming. But he begins to fathom more profoundly the interlocking truth of joy and sadness, the impossibility of escaping completely from one into the other, the grave responsibility of acknowledging the entwined force of the dead and of the living as they co-inhabit space.

They had felt it at the same time, as they peered down at the angel in the stone. They had felt the same wind, unnatural and fierce, wash over them like a benediction. They had felt the same otherworldly force washing away their sins and their arrogance. Romulus could feel that Tim's father had gone through this ritual many times before. Today he'd had a witness. They'd both had a witness. As Tim's father's heavy hand clasped Romulus by the shoulder and guided him down the mountain, they were both aware that nature had seen them with uncovered eyes, seen their frailty, their shortcomings as fathers and husbands; that nature had conferred on them the great strength that made transformation possible, had whispered to them the simple secret to eternity, a simple truth that made them as vulnerable as newborn children, as exposed as the stone they trod upon: the exercise of compassion, the exercise of forgiveness. It was a secret that Tim's father already knew, a gift he had given to his own son. It was what Father Tim had known and drawn on when he'd seen Romulus return to the rectory, chastised and ready for a new start. It was a secret known to Christian, as he heard his father plead with him in guilt from the other side of life, a gift he now bestowed on Romulus in the form of a marking upon a stone, so that his father would remember the meaning of his christened name, given to him in a land in which one's true name, the one that contained, like a seed, the blueprint to one's destiny, was hidden in a string of names before the surname.

On this day, Romulus Pierre became known as Peter in an island strange and wondrous, the cradle of his second birth.

Angels are coming to watch over thee
So hark to the winds coming over the sea.

They set out for the youth centre the next morning, Father Tim and Romulus Pierre, now named Peter. They do not speak but watch the rough patches of land drifting past them on both sides of the little red Fiat. The land looks desolate: brown and red, outcroppings of wild growth and clumps of meadow flowers. The land is broken by small inlets of lakes and they watch as white swans crane their necks to see them chugging by. There are clusters of sheep and cattle, ancient stones marking the dawning of a spiritual age that Romulus feels has perhaps not yet seen its end. Father Tim tells him how long after the people were converted from the worship of the earth to a Christian God, they continued to believe in the spirit-dwellers of trees and dipping valleys, in the turbulent foaming of deceived souls beneath the dark peat they dug and cut to heat their dwellings.

In Romulus' eyes it is a ravaged land and a beautiful land. Romulus has never seen anything more beautiful. He sees in it the ground he has left behind, the burning city, the flooded

319

ground to the north of the capital, where the waters of the swollen river swept all living beings aside.

Then they emerge between high mountains cradled by clear lakes and the car sweeps around the edges of the green hillside like a ladybug on the lip of a leaf. They feel small and insignificant, but lucky. Father Tim does not know what is going on in the heart of a man who has spent the last twenty years of his life throwing life itself away, reneging on his contract to a higher power, who has only been awake for a few months. Even so, Father Tim can feel the energy emanating from his charge. It is this same energy that lifted Tim out of a life of petty crime, of sleeping in the doorjambs of big city life, and into a vocation that would have him save souls. They hum in silence into the crags of the mountains, as they head towards the awaiting youth with whom they will be working.

It is Romulus who sees it first, a small black stone erected at the side of the road. Father Tim has almost sped by it when he feels Romulus's hand on his arm, asking him to stop.

Tim's father had spoken of the marker and Tim remembered it too, a stone left to mark the passage of the dead during the Great Famine. He remembers that the South African clergyman, Desmond Tutu, had once come from far away to walk the walk with them, many years ago, when Tutu's own land had still been torn apart by strife and hatred. Tim recalls seeing scenes of apartheid South Africa on TV.

"Here. Stop. Here."

Father Tim brings the red Fiat to a halt by the side of the road and they step out into the dust and look about. There are a few older people about, walking along the stretch of the road, keeping themselves alive by walking to and from their neighbours' homes.

"How many did you say?" John become Romulus become Peter asks.

"Six hundred? Maybe seven. Four hundred or so died trying to get back home in the snows."

He can see it, as if it all happened yesterday, the hungry folk making their way to their master's house to beg for a crust of bread, some milk for the babies. They walked twelve miles and were turned away. Four hundred died on the trek back to shelter, vainly hoping that the heat of their bodies might keep them alive. Every year the walk is walked, remembered. Forgiveness, Peter understands, is not about forgetting, it is about taking responsibility for the dead.

The wind whips up around them, as it had up on the mountain in Inishmore. It winds and curls around their limbs as if tying them to a promise they'd both made *in utero*, as they were ushered from one world into another through the narrow passageway of a woman's flesh. The force of the wind makes Peter buckle to his knees in front of the marker no higher than a foot above the ground, and as his arms embrace it, the tears behind his eyes come forward in a great gush, like a dam broken and set to overflow.

Father Tim watches from a few feet away. This is what his life is for: to watch, to witness, to guide. This is what his life was saved for.

Some old folk on their way to their neighbour's home stop and stare. Two old men wonder what the man with skin of copper is doing among them. They remember vaguely the man the colour of dark oak who had been among them years ago, a man of the cloth with a purple sash tied around his waist, asking forgiveness of the ground and for the people rent in spirit in his faraway country.

"Do you think he's Irish?" one of the men asks of the other.

"Could be, the way all of them went away," the other responds, signalling with a limp hand swinging into the air those who had fled during the Great Famine, when work was scarce and the land yielded nothing but dead fruit.

"Could be," the first man repeats.

Then, an old woman walks by, aided by a cane. A small woman no more than four feet and four inches in height, the features of her youthful face hidden by a mask of wrinkles. Only the brightness of her sea-blue eyes, now blind, reveals the dreams of her younger days. She stops and leans over her cane, pressing its pointed end into the dusty earth. She stops and listens to the man as he sobs. She cannot see him, the colour of his skin, nor the way the slight frame of his body reveals the excesses of his lost years. She hears only the pain being poured out, the repentance, the rebirth embedded with every loosened cry.

"That's right," she says, "this is where the dead are buried."

After listening to the crying subside, she smiles at Father Tim, places a hand on his arm and says, "You always bring them back."

"I try," he says quietly.

Then, she turns back to the weeping man and says, "You cry, son. We're all Irish here."

Peter hears nothing, no trace of human thought, no murmur of man-made words, no disapproval from beyond. He hears only the cry of the dead and the song of the angels intermingling over the dust, rising up, granting him absolution.

ELSIE

Hear the wind blow, love, hear the wind blow
Lean your head over and hear the wind blow

Winter 1847, Connemara, Ireland

"Elsie!"

It was the sound of hearing her name called out from the main house that brought her out of her trance. Surprised by the cold rising from the spongy turf beneath her feet, and even more surprised by the layers of clothing binding her body, she stood bewildered for a moment and wondered where the warmth of the sun had gone. Perplexed, she tried to remember where she had found herself just a minute ago and what had brought her to this sodden ground. She remembered a blinding sun and a stench of burning – it had not been wood or the dried logs of peat the square-headed, vertical shovel she was holding against her body was used to make.

Someone kept calling out her name, a deep and steady voice she could not recall either to love or hate.

Wherever it was that her trance had taken her to, there had been chaos, dust sent flying into the air by running feet. She had followed one man in particular, still hoping against hope that he would be the one to realize the prophecy, the one she had seen at the reach of her hands, looking down one day while working the bog to see nothing but ocean all around her and her hands turned the colour of chestnuts from their usual chalk-white. It was then that she'd seen the vision that had driven her this far: a woman with knotted strands of stiff hair rising from the ocean like the Venus on her half-shell clam. But this one was no painter's fantasy, covering her private parts like she was some precious something with silken strands of red, straight hair, with fingers so thin the only thing they could be good for was spinning thread. No, not that kind of Venus. This woman was the sort that recalled matter more solid – salt or coal, or the peat bog sucking at her feet. Others might have been frightened to see it, but Elsie was not. It was the vision she'd been waiting for, the sign, even though she wasn't at all sure what it meant. It had something to do with that place of heat and that man she'd seen emerging from a barred bunker dug into a ground so red it could only make her think of blood. Perhaps she'd counted on the wrong man – she'd assumed only a man could understand but hadn't she, a woman, a woman cutting peat, been granted the gift of second sight? And this one was a gamble; he'd already frittered away more chances to redeem himself than were usually accorded. Elsie had found ways to reach him, over time, through time, when, somehow, she was able to find herself in worlds so different from her own. She was sure that one day she would leave the sodden, swampy earth of her birth, and flee to another ground.

This man, snivelling and weak as he was, was her charge. There were moments when it seemed to her that he was aware of her presence, that he seemed to listen, to be soothed by her voice. She spoke to him in Gaelic and, sometimes, in the tongue of the colonials. She could not quite make out the timbre of his words when he responded in languages that seemed so foreign to her world, nor was she sure that he could understand hers. Somehow, from time to time, he did seem to understand and progress would seem assured.

She had known him since his childhood. He had been sensitive as a child, susceptible, easy to reach, eager in his faith. Then, somehow, perhaps when she was muddling through her own troubles, something had gone wrong; he had become a different person or, simply, as the branches of trees are wont to do, grown in the direction of light in the way children bend towards whoever gives them the most attention, whether that attention is good or bad. At times, she despaired at the labour involved in finding a way into the crevices of his dreaming mind, befuddled with some noxious substance like ill-brewed poitín. At such times, he was simply intolerable. But, for one hundred and eighty-six days, the man had been in captivity – captive to her voice. It was going to be then or never, she had thought, as she witnessed the moment of his incarceration from far away, asking the sea goddess of her vision to guide her, to watch over them both.

She had chosen that time over giving into despair, over the difficulty of making her daily time-defying journeys, over having to wait for another long stretch of time, time that could span decades, even generations. She chose her moment and it had worked.

In prison, her chosen one had listened to her entreaties and finally recognized her face when his body cleared itself of the foreign substances that had been her bane. The drugs at last leaching from his system had turned his otherwise nimble mind (had he ever recognized his own intelligence?) into mush, like a septic tank full of images and half-processed memories. Elsie was convinced that, this time, he would cling to her as he had never done before, transforming her words in some alchemical way into a healing substance rather than into his songs for hire. Still, the problem with him had always been his love of the base, of the earthly, as if the humiliations of his childhood had somehow made him a believer in the worst humanity could offer rather than in the possibility of purity and innocence. These were qualities that human beings were prone to despise when they were embarked on some headlong fall from grace.

Quite often she believed she had made the wrong choice, a mistaken choice that the elders up above were too stubborn to undo. This hedonistic man did not seem up to the task they had set before him. But given her own place in the order of things between earth and sky, she had to persevere.

This was why she had followed her charge as he emerged from the dark cave of his cell. This was how she had found herself with him as he watched the chaos bubbling all around him. She had sensed his disarray and had pushed him to walk in the direction opposite the men dressed in fatigues, away from the jubilance of his half-clothed cellmates. She poured into him every ounce of thought she could summon, reminding him of all the work left undone through his drug-hazed years, pushing him to walk, then run, in the direction of his people.

She had run with him, becoming one with the tight knots in his calf muscles, breathing in the dusty, salty air, smelling the thick, acrid scent of smouldering tar and the bitterness of charring flesh.

"Romulus," she had heard a voice call out.

She had known before they turned that this was not a voice to be trusted or followed.

She had turned back towards the voice in unison with her chosen one, whose head had swivelled as if it were wood atop a mannequin's frame, legs going in one direction, the head pointing in the other, to the area he had just left behind.

She could feel now that *here* had been the crucial error. If she had only kept herself moving forward, her resolute force might have been enough to keep him pointed in the right direction. He would not have been so tempted. But he had gone so long without hearing his name called out, without a response to his longing.

This was his grand weakness. She had to acknowledge it. His Achilles heel: the need for the love of others beyond himself, even if what he received was not love but desire or adulation. He was a man so empty of love that he could no longer define the word or feel the emotion. He longed only to fill the void within him and life had taught him that what he lacked was not within but without.

She sighed. Her hands were growing cold holding the peat shovel. The water from the bog was seeping into her boots even though she had lined them with oilskins. She dreaded the end of day when she would have to work at sloughing off the dead layers of skin on the soles of her feet with hands numbed with rheumatism. The only thing to look forward to would be the heat of the water, the currents of stream rising to her face from the pail of water. She would have preferred to live in another time. She envied the woman from her vision, the woman she'd become as the vision came upon her, standing in the warm salt water, the waves all around caressing the taut muscles beneath the caramel-coloured skin. She envied her the breeze through the cords of hair stiff with sand and salt, as they trod water in unison, kicking at seaweed.

Sometimes, she wondered if the prophecy had been of the

future or of the past. All she knew for certain was that it was not of this place where she now stood and that time was like a circle defying chronology.

"Elsie!"

But the laws of the universe were such that she had to satisfy herself with the lot she had chosen. At least she was blessed with the ability to navigate the spaces between times. Without that gift, she would have been lost. She did not know how otherwise she would have survived the physical hardships of her existence in a place so cold and harsh it made her hold her breath against despair. The navigating allowed her moments of reprieve, moments in which she could breathe and feel connected to all of life.

"Elsie! Do you hear me? I'm calling you, Elsie!"

Such escapes did not make the present time any easier. It still had to be lived. It did not make having a living body made of flesh, blood and bone the most pleasant of things. But she knew enough about her life's path to understand that she had chosen it in some time before she had even become flesh. Even as she stood there in the muck of the bog, as the man she had spoken to through the years and fog of time had stood in the excrement of his cell, as she stood there doing work more suited to the male of the species, feeling the rub of the woollen trousers she had at least been able to conceal beneath her voluminous stiff muslin skirts, she knew she had chosen this of her own free will.

She had to be grateful for small mercies, however insignificant they seemed to others, the unawakened ones, like this one calling out to her, braying like a donkey, even though they both knew only *she* was the beast of burden.

"Com-ing!" she finally yelled out. Her mouth had worked the word until it pushed itself out in a small cloud of mist in the cool air about her, heavy with humidity. She wondered about a warmer climate, about how her body would feel elsewhere, as she began to move towards the voice calling out to her.

"Coming," she repeated once more. This time the word came out strangled, lifeless, just above a whisper.

She could see him hovering in the open door of what was called the Big House. This was her view of Ireland's serfdom. They had yet to be free in their own land and for the past several years had been dying upon it without a pence in their pockets as the landlords continued, somehow, to hold on to their power, even as the fields yielded rot and dark spuds not fit for eating, that they boiled up anyway because, well, what choice did they have?

She had worked in English homes and infertile, barren fields all her life. The lines of age etched in her face, along the rims of her eyes and the sharp, upturned edges of her mouth, told the story of harsh winds skimming across the surface of a landscape where the earth lay unprotected by the wide canopies of mature trees. Here, whatever growth there was clustered against the earth, clinging to the soil for dear life. Occasionally the odd bush struggled above the ground, flattened by the wind and grazed almost to death by the flocks of scrawny sheep. Miraculous, though, were the clumps of fuchsias, flushed purple and pink with their belled heads and sugared throats. When the babies were starving, they squeezed the plump base of the flowers to squeeze out the few sweet drops lodged there, but soon even these wilted away and there were not drops enough to soothe the raw throats that needed milk that the flocks no longer gave, starving too as they were.

She found herself distant from her people in Galway, on this barren ground not so much by will but by necessity. As she moved towards his voice, she wondered if there was any choice in it, whether she was so controlled by something larger than herself, in which she fervently believed, that it was impossible now to *make* a free choice. There were things beyond her understanding. This she knew. Freedom, she supposed, was a relative parcel of life. Hers had been sacrificed for a greater good, the greater opportunity for those who came after her to choose the outcome of their lives.

Elsie walked towards the house. He had left the front door open. She could see the red and orange glow from the peat fire burning within. For a Big House, she smiled caustically to herself, it was rather small. And the lord of the manor was better than most, though still a lord – English, of course, as if there could be anything other. And he was nothing like Elsie with her grey clothes and plain face.

Elsie no longer looked at herself in mirrors. She was afraid of

330

what she would see there. She had been called a beauty in her younger days but she knew the bloom of her youth had gone off. She was coldly practical. No need to observe what could not be changed. She was a realist despite her knowledge of other worlds, despite the fact that she had never set foot on the lands she had come to know so intimately from within. But now she yearned to be in movement, to escape the misery all about them. She had heard of the ships leaving from Cobh and was conspiring – the English Lord notwithstanding – to join the fleeing hordes.

Starvation and need had hit the land hard and the colonies offered food in return for labour. Elsie thought that she might fare better than her Irish counterparts in securing a place on one of the boats. For one thing, she was alone. For another, the lord of the house had been hinting at changing her lot, even appearing to be in love with her, so perhaps her womanhood might still be something to trade on in securing her passage. Elsie had never ventured to speak to him long enough to find out what his true feelings were. She did not think love was so transcendent that it could alight without communication and her lord and master had said nothing on that score, and for this reason she had countered his physical overtures with contempt and he'd sent her from the house to the boggy fields, as if time in the wetlands would temper her resolve and send her running back to his hearth. He did not know her. Out there in the fields, Elsie could get much more of her *Work* done even though it seemed to everyone else that she was daydreaming and shiftless, just another poor Irish girl trying to rob the English of their due.

Elsie was sure of this much: she had to get away from the peat bog, the Big House, the layers upon layers of clothing. She had to make her way to Cobh and cross the waters to America. She wanted to go to the islands. She knew something of slaves and sugar fields, hoped to trade the fairness of her skin for food and lodging in one of the British estate owner's homes in Jamaica or any of the islands. She'd heard the winds were warm there and the flowers sharp with colour. She knew in her bones it was the place of the rising and she was on her way to meet it.

She saw her master's shadow sweeping across the walls. She wished she knew something of his feelings so she did not have to wander into the field of her fear alone. Leaving had its costs too. And she had not been at the Big House long. Well, not as long as some of the others.

Elsie advanced towards the house, steadily, her shoes like suction cups against the wet earth, sure that it was the moment for her to give herself up to the lord in exchange for his patronage.

As she advanced, his shadow grew in proportion to the auburn light. For the moment, Elsie had forgotten Romulus and the goddess and the call of warm saltwater. They had all been replaced by an ache in her bones and an exhaustion too deep for words.

Spring 1848, Connemara, Ireland

> *Oh, winds of the night, may your fury be crossed*
> *May no one that's dear to our island be lost*
> *Blow the wind gently, calm be the foam*
> *Shine the light brightly to guide us back home*

"Elsie. Why should you be so stubborn?" he'd said. She was sure that was what he'd asked her, followed by, "Have you had so much better an offer?"

But it could have been some other utterance, something else he'd meant. She was beginning to show. It was a funny thing how a woman could be ripe surrounded by the signs of death and decay, as if fertility awoke as the sign of a species' waning. Or maybe it was just true that the English had better sperm than the Irish, hardier sperm. It wasn't hard to believe in the untruths these days as the Irish fell like flies and the English who had stayed to watch over their lands stayed merry, their pink cheeks flushed not by shame but by greed. She'd lost respect for William, her house's lord, as he had for her. They were struggling in a futile battle of wits, each wanting the other for something neither was willing to give, even though they'd been locked in fevered embraces every night through winter, as if that would be enough to keep the stench of death away from the door.

There was treachery in their mating and both knew it as they rocked with each other, their hungry, desperate copulation making Elsie think of the milking of cows, of the suckling of piglets or newborn babies as flesh cupped and slapped, body fluids slurped and they grunted and groaned. They had always looked alike to her, piglets and babies, and now she had one of her own on the way: a piglet baby, an English-Irish bastard. She was surprised at how bitter she felt.

Elsie could feel it when they conceived. Something came alive down there and she knew that her torment in the land of the dead was over. She was glad even though the baby had not been conceived out of love. She was just glad that there would be a way out. At the moment of conception, at the moment her heart swelled up in her chest from sheer gladness, Elsie also felt the disapprobation from up above. She could feel them all shaking their heads to and fro in pity and they evidently did not have enough faith in her to tell her what to do next.

No better than Romulus, she had opted for the weakness of the flesh. It was more expedient than blind faith but could they really want her to stay in this hell with the dead all around, the corpses bloating in the moist peat? How could they assume she'd have enough will to survive the blight outside the Lord's door? If they were down here with her, she thought ruefully, they'd be just like her, doing anything and everything just to get out. There weren't any Irish lads to marry. She was too old and, frankly, most of them were dead or dying and only if you married the oldest son was there any chance of getting land. And just now, it was only the land that mattered. No one had time to listen to the murmurs of the heart.

It wasn't a romantic age. She'd heard that some men were taking more than one wife, counter to the Catholic faith, in order to assure survival. Fat good it would do the women servicing these polygamous husbands if the men were dying from the fever on empty stomachs.

When she'd told her lord of the pregnancy, he assumed she wanted a ring for her finger, some declaration and show of love, but this was only because he wanted her for himself, the way he wanted everything, the way he owned the house and all the land around it and, by default, those who kept care of it for him.

Elsie was never entirely sure these days that what she heard was right. She was in between too many things, too many thoughts crowding her head. She was distracted.

"Elsie," he'd continued. "Are you listening to me? Such things are important to discuss."

She listened to his clipped English intonations. His manner of speaking was lordly even though he was a pauper by English standards, a pauper with land that made him rich in these parts, with the Irish looking at him with envy and hatred in their dark eyes.

Elsie was making soda bread in the kitchen, pulling the dough on the wooden board he'd installed for her when she'd come to be his temporary cook, then stayed on. She couldn't fathom how they had become so familiar except for the obvious fact that she was the only woman worth taking a look at for miles around, even though she was no longer sure who was considered marriageable and she felt too old to be the object of consideration. In this godforsaken place, though, age could be forgiven in return for childbearing. She still had a few years left for that and the men around had sniffed this out. It didn't amount to more than a stink of despair.

She told him about the baby on the way and of her plan to go down to Cobh and get on one of the ships leaving for the Americas. She told him she didn't want to go to America but to one of the islands cradled in the seas below it. She wanted another island, some familiarity. She proposed he come with them. How long did he think he might survive here? Most of the English were leaving and his supplies would run out sooner or later, wouldn't they? What did he have to lose?

"Are you daft, Elsie?" he said, his ears reddening in anger. "Those are coffin ships, all of them. So you'd rather die out there in some rotting wooden carcass than... than..." he hesitated, "with me."

He looked up at her with mild expectation as if she might suddenly reveal something more tender than what they'd exchanged without words in his frame bed the previous night.

Elsie knew William was a gentle man, despite his ardour between the sheets she had to take out to wash, out in the cold, in basins of steaming hot water, twice a week if she had the strength and time. It was one of the reasons she had chosen him, even though he thought he'd been the one doing the choosing. She'd chosen him because if getting with child by a man with means was the only way to leave the place, then she wanted it to be by a man who halfway cared and whose genes might give the baby half a chance of living on the other side of the ocean. She wasn't as daft as he was accusing her of being; she'd heard about the ships sinking and the people going down with them. She'd take her chances. What was the difference between staying or leaving? She could die staring at the bog or she could die with the waters of the sea enveloping her. Even if she died out there, at least she would have seen something other than grey death and maybe on the other side there would be green hills, like those of her youth and early childhood.

Her hands were dusty with flour. She wondered why he prattled on at her, though she knew she should have been listening more attentively because his words were no laughing matter. But he spoke to her as if he'd already won a bet, as if she were some kind of race horse he could put his money on, as if her answer was a foregone conclusion.

She could tell he knew she had made a decision. She'd felt the change in her body and knew he would be able to tell by the way she moved so purposefully around each of her stations in the house, the way she moved in the muck of the fields, determined, focused. However, he had guessed wrongly about the outcome of her deliberations. He would be disappointed, Elsie knew. She sighed and patted her hands against her apron, letting little clouds of white dust fly quietly at her sides.

She felt quite old. She was a spinster of twenty-eight years of age, though by Irish standards, since the onset of the blight, the age of marriage had steadily risen so that whereas she would have been past her prime in England, here she had possibility. She was within the scope of some man's desire, though this was something time had taught her not to think about too much. Life had kept her too busy to think about a husband and family, and though many little hands had clung to her skirts, none were of her own making. She'd had no time to chase after frivolities – she had become harsh with time. Time had become her taskmaster, she reflected, as she patted the two plump white mounds in front of her, then lifted them into two round baking pans with fluted edges that she normally used to make the summer's fruit pies filled with the berries she picked herself, when there were some. In winter, she'd liked to make apple and pear pies, with a touch of ginger and a couple of cloves buried beneath the mounds of sliced fruits.

Elsie had been at William's house for four years. The first three years had been a welcome change from her work as a child-minder and cook in one of Dublin's better-off boroughs. She had escaped the cramped servants' quarters and come back home just before the blight set on and found William in need of a house-keeper. It was her mother who had told her of the place and her father who'd taken her there with just a scarf full of things to call her own held on her knees.

Elsie slid the bread pans into the belly of the cast iron oven. The last year had been the most difficult as they had lost help on the land and the peat had grown heavy with water so that it took weeks upon weeks to dry the slabs out, only to find them in the end crumbling and useless. They'd lost hands to the sickness hidden in the pores of the land. The local physician had come round to warn them about the diseases locked in the bog, but the master of the house chose not to listen. He still sent Elsie out to work cutting the peat, despite the warnings.

If he hadn't come out to the bog himself, Elsie would have left earlier. But she needed the wages to save for her passage – and there was the food he could still import, the jams and pickled onions, the meat that miraculously arrived at their door after weeks of waiting. He was not one of the landowners who turned beggars away, but they were such a long way from the next houses that few of the hungry ever made it to their door. Some died trying, like the ones Elsie had heard of making pilgrimages from one English lord's to another's, expiring by the side of the roads, their bodies marking the way to hell for those who had turned them away. Children. Women. Men. Men who were otherwise strong, who had laboured for their keep, slowly losing their minds as they watched their women and little ones wretched with hunger.

She had found Duncan's body in the fields. Duncan who had

seen almost half the century go past, but had the body of an emaciated child. Duncan who had survived rickets and poverty, the loneliness of a life without wife and children. It was the peat that killed him, of this Elsie was certain, whatever *he* wanted to believe. She could smell the decay walking over the mossy earth. She could feel the earth whispering, lisping them all towards a cradled death in her dying arms. How could one imagine the life force of the ground being snuffed out? It was difficult to believe. The boats were leaving every day. Elsie had made up her mind to go. This was why she could not take his offer. In any case, he would be dead before winter. She could see it in his eyes, in his slow way of eating his meals at the end of the day.

"You must be jesting with me, Elsie," he continued, his voice soft with incredulity.

When she made no reply he realized she was serious. Either way he had to pay her passage. It was the only decent thing to do, but he himself would not leave this parched piece of land. It was the only thing, he thought, that made him a man.

How foolish men are, Elsie thought, to be so locked up by property and land. The living speck in her belly meant less to William than the ownership of dying land and he wasn't even Irish. She was only worth something if she stayed and the thought of adventure obviously terrified him. It would mean that he would lose status and title, and this was all he had to measure the weight and value of his life.

It wasn't as if Elsie didn't care for love, or hope for it. It wasn't as if she had never loved or allowed herself to be loved. It was simply that once she'd understood the nature of her *Work*, she found that there were few others who could understand the way her mind turned, the deep yearnings of her heart for something more than a home and a hearth with children who vaguely resembled herself, and a man with whom to live out her life.

It wasn't as if she hadn't tumbled in and out of a bed or two – and even on a haystack that matched the colour of their hair exactly – a warm, chestnut gold. That one had been with a boy who made her think of milk fresh from the cow's tit. The hollows of his palms seemed small for his long tapered fingers but they were just the right size to hold her small nubs of breasts. He had exclaimed at their softness when she'd first allowed him a touch, talked about their orange brown areolas, the freckles drawing a constellation between her small mounds. He'd taken each nipple into his mouth and suckled gently, and she'd wondered if the sensations would be the same with a newborn draining her of milk. He'd been gentle with her. Mesmerized. He'd hardly had a stitch of stubble on his chin and she hardly noticed when he entered her as softly as he suckled. Her thoughts were so focused on the pulsing below her navel she'd never experienced before that she hardly took note of the pain, there, between her legs, when he thrust. After all the Catholic school warnings, she'd never imagined a boy could be so harmless.

He was nothing like the others, so gentle, so poetic, like a girl with an extra appendage. It wasn't long before they were lost in each other, no longer able to tell each other's limbs apart. They both had legs covered with a blond down. The hay poked and itched but it seemed more than worth the heat and the pulsing and the sensations across her chest like the beating of butterfly wings when he cupped his small palms over her breasts as if they were some exotic fruit from a distant land.

David. It was with him that she had begun to talk of leaving for somewhere else, anywhere at all. But he had turned out to be just like the others, like her father, wanting her to stay put, to tend someone else's children in a rich household as if they were hothouse flowers, to be happy with being a chambermaid in the heat of a suffocating attic, in any city far from home. But she'd only got as far as Dublin.

David had dreamed of one day renting a farm, of making her his wife, but that was all. He had no instinct for gazing at the immensity of the stars above them, or thinking that in distant lands there were people so unlike themselves it would be worth the journey to discover them.

When Elsie repeated her desire to leave, he called her a traitor and other things she had since forgotten. Why would she want to set foot in the dark world of the English who told lies as they breathed and cheated the upstanding Irish of pence and crown? David called her a heretic and a fool. If he had only known the half of it.

She had made a mistake. But no one except her father knew about her visions, the night-time visitations, the dreams that came while she worked and entranced her into immobility. The *Work* had begun long ago and her father had taught her to keep it secret. After David, she'd tried a few times to find a love that could sustain her, but it soon became clear that she would have to keep herself. She used short-lived affairs to satisfy her desire and kept love entirely out of the picture.

"Elsie," William's voice came again from the front room. "What is it you have still to do?"

She wondered if he was reading *The Times* there, warmed by the peat fire, the peat from which, she was certain, emanated all forms of contagion. She went without it in her own room to escape the fumes and tried as much as possible to stay away from the front room. She never spent the nights in his room after they'd copulated for fear of the diseases that lurked there. She wanted to preserve herself.

She wondered how he was capable of standing her silence, of the way she let his questions fall to the ground like leaves.

His name was William but she never used it. She called him "Sir", or even "Lord", sometimes, often nothing at all. As soon as he'd promised her money for the passage, all she was thinking of was what she had to do next. That was all she'd wanted from him. She'd only invited him out of courtesy.

After the soda bread, after the boiling of the dry salt cod to bring it back to life, she daydreamed about David and wondered about her charge, Romulus, who had turned away from her and moved beyond the grasp of her vision. She watched the salt leach out from the white pieces of cod and turn the water opaque. When she broke her silence it was to ask which of the hands on his land they should call in for supper, ignoring the question he'd posed.

"Come now, Elsie," William replied, "how would it look to others if I let in every stray they refused?"

She heard the movement of the sheaves of paper as he continued to read, as if he could live with the death beyond his house, could live with the thought of beggars lying stiff as clay on the roads between Galway and Delphi. It would be days before news of the recently dead reached them. It amazed her that he would think that she would be interested in such a man as he, a man who could read so calmly of the Irish dead in his English paper and not jump to share his imported goods so that a few others could survive.

After preparing the cod, she peeled potatoes and dredged them with flour, then poured milk over them and added dabs of butter; the dish was now ready to cook in the stove already warmed from baking bread. That would be all there was tonight, but it was more than most around would get. Elsie did not know if she could bring herself to eat tonight or any other night. She would try to eat some of the potatoes but would forego the cod. He could choke on it and the two or three hands who hung around the house and fields could have her share.

Elsie wondered again if she had made the wrong choice in taking up the post with William. She had always been told that it was better to choose families with children. But she'd had enough of children, runny noses and temper tantrums. She'd chosen this out of the way estate for its promise of peace and quiet. She had not counted on William's and her desires for companionship. She'd thought her needs long extinguished. William was not unattractive for his age, for a man of his class and means. She could have done worse, but choosing him meant giving up on the *Work*, her calling, the visions and the premonitions. She needed these more than the grounding of marriage.

It was hours later, after she had taken her plate to her room to eat and returned to clean up after the men, when William had gone to bed after smoking a pipe, and the hired hands had left the house, when she was drying the stoneware dishes, that she saw where Romulus had wandered.

She saw, first, the blood streaking a floor decorated with a delicate floral pattern, long red lines like spilled watercolour paint. She saw men moving in and out of the shadows, looting drawers and alcoves for small treasures. She saw Romulus fallen to the floor in a dead sleep. She wondered if he was dead. She saw a woman with her stomach slit open, the blood emptying itself in a wide pool about her. *Oh, Romulus*, she thought, startled, her face close to his. She wanted to stroke his cheek, to coax him back to life. *Oh, Romulus,* she thought, saddened by the turn of events, *What have you done? What have you allowed?*

She had failed not once but many times. After the drugs, she should have let Romulus go and moved on to someone more promising. She had made the same error with another woman she had driven to madness long before. It was difficult to tell at times who could sustain the *Work* and who would fail. But Elsie also knew that the greater design of things was beyond her. She had only to find the right one, the true heir. Perhaps she had not yet lived long enough to recognize him or her. She had failed yet again or, perhaps, in failing, she had given fate a helping hand.

She put a hand to her belly, and knew from the seed within that the prophecy could be realized. She had only to shift all she knew to the one within. It would be the end of her double life and the beginning of a new dawn that she could pass down, as others had passed on the gift to her.

It was to his credit that William took her down to Cobh in his *calèche*, the hooves of the horses drumming against the hard ground in cacophonous syncopation. With every beat she felt the sounds of her future life calling her forward, even as William tried to call her back. But she had already gone. She listened to his words as one would the wind, as if a pleasant breeze had just tousled her hair. She kept her hands clasped around her belly as if to protect the seed growing there from his attempt to persuade her, as if to emphasise that her belly's contents were hers alone.

For Elsie, the parting in Cobh was without sentiment, even though William seemed on the verge of shedding tears.

"Was it all a ruse, Elsie?" he demanded, knowing full well the answer to the question.

She wished there was some sweetening she could offer, but there was nothing, nothing to say.

"I thank you," she said formally, as he clasped her hands in his.

"And shall I never see you again, nor the child?" he asked, when what he was thinking was that they would never survive the passage, even though he had found her a place in the strongest looking vessel, the one most likely to survive the choppy seas, one delivering goods to the New World, a world filled with heathens and savages of whom one heard stories fit to curdle the blood.

Elsie shook her head. She knew that it was William they would never see again. Not two months hence and he would be dead like all the others, his light-blue eyes staring vacantly up at the ceiling above the bed that had seen their amorous exchanges. She was sorry for him, though not sorry that this would be a journey she would face alone. The child would be hers to grow and tend. She'd never had such a luxury to call her own. There was a price to pay: she had to leave the *Work* to take up her role as a mother and let the new growth carry forward. She had forced the issue with the gods and taken her destiny into her own hands by dreaming of such faraway places. But surely they could not mean for the prophecy to die with her? Surely she meant more to them than that? For all she knew, Elsie rationalized, she was doing the bidding of the gods by following her own stubborn nature.

It was her stubbornness which, in the end, delivered her to new shores. She let herself be rocked and rocked by the careening of the boat and she told the growing child within her that it was only the wind coming by to bid it a hearty hello. Perhaps that was why, when the child grew up, it had a yearning to go to sea and no fear of storms.

Elsie grew a son who became a fisherman even though his pale skin could not withstand the heat and he went out to sea covered in shea butter and long-sleeved shirts, often using a shirt for a hat by tying together its flopping sleeves around his head. In this new land, she was not understood, a white woman who spoke to the gods, the *loas* of the land. They thought she was a sorceress. She walked into the ocean seeking the cradle of her visions. They thought she was hallucinating, wanting to drown herself at sea. Eventually, it was her grandchildren who, after the death of their father, had her put away in the asylum for the slow and the insane. Her son had understood his mother and would never had agreed,

Elsie's son looked like a younger William and he proved to be as passionate and as devoid of prejudice, taking a young African girl for his wife, though they never formally married. From these two came others of varied hues and strains of life, mostly girls, who, like their great-grandmother, had children that they alone

342

could call their own. They lived out their lives, generation upon generation, only a few streets removed from the port where Elsie had first set foot on the island she took as her own. A place known to its native-folk as, Ayiti, "land of the mountains", with peaks resplendent enough to cure her of homesickness, even as she looked out from behind the bars of her cell, towards the green, green hills of her own dying, and wretched land.

CODA: CATHERINE

March 18, 2004, in transit to Paris, France

This is all I know:
There are no answers.
Only: is and is.

Still, the questions haunt me like a dirge:

What strength had Canaan to withstand his father's curse? What witness of suffering caused Noah to betray? What nature of whim led forces of nature to conspire the oceans to overflow their beds, wiping out the believers, while the doubters watched on, untouched? What beasts of burden lurk beneath the earth's crust in wait as we go on denying visions and prophecies, the gifts of our forebears? What humility before the scarred world can the gods admit, to allow the angels, at last, in their loneliness, to sing?

Appendix

Irish Traditional: "Connemara Cradle Song"

(In the Public Domain: Adaptation by Delia Murphy)

The currachs are sailing way out on the blue
Laden with herring of silvery hue
Silver the herring and silver the sea
And soon they'll be silver for my love and me

CHORUS:

Hear the wind blow, love, hear the wind blow
Lean your head over and hear the wind blow

On wings of the wind, o'er the deep rolling sea
Angels are coming to watch over thee
Angels are coming to watch over thee
So hark to the winds coming over the sea

CHORUS

Oh, winds of the night, may your fury be crossed
May no one that's dear to our island be lost
Blow the wind gently, calm be the foam
Shine the light brightly to guide us back home

AUTHOR'S NOTE & ACKNOWLEDGEMENTS

The structure of this novel is loosely informed by the metaphor of the Christian labyrinth originating in Chartres Cathedral, France. During the writing (and revising) of this novel, I walked labyrinths in a number of locations, including southwest Ireland, Winnipeg, Vancouver, Baton Rouge and San Francisco. The experience of walking a labyrinth is a simulacrum of everyday encounters within the self and with others, known and unknown, past, present, and future. The objective is to follow a circuitous path to a central rose where one receives an insight into a problem, one's character, or life itself, and one is able to re-enter 'life', or the circuitry of the labyrinth, with this new knowledge in hand. As one walks out of the labyrinth, one is encouraged to meditate upon this epiphany. Whether or not the walker has the ability to act upon the results of the prayer or meditation is, perhaps, a question of will and predisposition, or even of circumstance. But this is speaking only of a solitary journey. The truth is that one is joined in the walking, and the interactions one has with others on the path (pleasant or unpleasant) reveal as much about the self as they do about the others. People walk the path, their life journeys, at different speeds, with different objectives, and in opposing directions, some yielding while others push their way through, each in their own world. Each walker brings with them a history, a past, a genetic code. Within this process, time and memory function in a non-linear fashion, interacting with each other non-chronologically in such a way as to inform lived experience both discretely and symbiotically.

Aside from the "text" of the labyrinth, and though the characters and situations in this novel are entirely fictional and not based on real people or circumstances, historical and spiritual details were gleaned from a number of sources, among which I am particularly indebted to Z'ev ben Shimon Halevi's *The Work of the Kabbalist*, Elizabeth McAlister's "'The Jew' in the Haitian Imagination", in Yvonne Chireau and Nathaniel Deutch, eds, *Black Zion: African American Religious Encounters with Judaism*; Ariel Scheib's "The Virtual Jewish History Tour/Haiti", www.jewishvirtuallibrary.org/source/vjw/haiti.html; Mark

350

Danner's "Postcards from History", www.markdanner.com/articles/show/79; Jeffrey Kallberg's *Chopin at the Boundaries: Sex, History and Musical Genre* and to studies of Chopin by various interpreters, chief among them Vladimir Ashkenazy.

I am also indebted to friends and colleagues who entertained tangential discussions on life, angels and mysticism over 2004-2005 in ways which have left their mark on this manuscript, in particular, Sally Lowder, Rachel Spence, and Laura Harris. Thank you to my cousin, Raphaella Nau, for her assitance with Kreyol phrases.

Excerpts from the novel appeared in *Small Axe*, #24, Winter 2007 and *Il Tolomeo* (Journal of the University of Venice, Italy), Winter 2006; I am indebted to editors David Scott and Franca Bernabei, respectively, for seeking out and printing the excerpts in their publications. As always, lastly but chiefly, I give thanks to all my ancestors and to the *loas*.

ABOUT THE AUTHOR

Myriam J. A. Chancy, Ph. D., is a Haitian-Canadian writer born in Port-au-Prince, Haiti. Her first novel, *Spirit of Haiti* (London: Mango Publications, 2003), was a finalist in the Best First Book Category, Canada/Caribbean region, of the Commonwealth Prize 2004. She is also the author of two books of literary criticism, *Framing Silence: Revolutionary Novels by Haitian Women* (Rutgers UP, 1997) and Searching for *Safe Spaces: Afro-Caribbean Women Writers in Exile* (Temple UP, 1997) as well as a second novel, *The Scorpion's Claw* (Peepal Tree Press, 2005). *Searching for Safe Spaces* was awarded an Outstanding Academic Book Award 1998 by *Choice*, the journal of the American Library Association while her work as the Editor-in-Chief of the Ford funded academic/arts journal, *Meridians: feminism, race, transnationalism* (2002-2004) was recognized with the Phoenix Award for Editorial Achievement by the CLEJ (2004). Her third academic book, *From Sugar to Revolution: Women's Visions of Haiti, Cuba and the Dominican Republic* is forthcoming from Wilfred Laurier UP. She has recently completed a collection of memoir essays entitled, *Fractured*, and is currently at work on a book length academic work entitled, *Floating Islands: Cosmopolitanism, Transnationalism and Racial Identity Formation*, as well as a young adult novel focusing on repressed Haiti-Louisiana ties, entitled *The Escape Artist*.

Dr. Chancy is Professor of English at Louisiana State University in Baton Rouge, Louisiana and Vice-President of the Association of Caribbean Women Writers & Scholars (2008-2010).

ALSO FROM PEEPAL TREE PRESS

The Scorpion's Claw
ISBN: 9781900715911; 2005; pp. 192; £8.99

Resistance, recovery and re-creation go to the heart of this novel, which tells the past and present of two generations of Haitians tied both by relations of blood and by the shedding of it. In the process, Myriam Chancy narrates the bloody history of the last six centuries of Haiti itself, from the violent years of colonialism and slavery, to the chaotic aftermath of the fall of the Baby Doc regime.

In a society in which men in blue "stick a gun to their hips and call it their life", and blood runs like rainwater through the streets, a family is flung apart, to the point of shattering. But it is Josèphe's act of remembrance, of bringing to voice her grandmother, cousins, friends, and herself, that brings down the barriers of place, time, even death, to bring the family together, and to relieve each of the weight of the past they have had to bear.

Review Comments

"somber and ethereal" — Colin Rickards, *SheCaribbean*.

"...readers can tell from the onset that the former professor has shed her scholarly cloak for a writer's mantle...[The] *Scorpion's Claw* is reminiscent of Arundhati Roy's *The God of Small Things*, in the emotions she evokes." — Malcollvie Jean-François, "Chancy Frees Voices in *Scorpion's Claw*," *Haitian Times, Sept. 2005*.

"Chancy may well become a grand dame of Haitian literature... luminous and realistic... [s]he captures her readers and never loses their attention... in evocative and illuminating prose... the story she tells of the plight of a Haitian family, serves as an important and worthy subtext for all the political and genocidal atrocities that haunt our television broadcasts on any given day." — Irene D'Souza, "Author releases Haitian people, landscapes", *Winnipeg Free Press*, June 19th, 2005.